What a Happy Family

Saumya Dave

Berkley
New York

BERKLEY
An imprint of Penguin Random House LLC
penguinrandomhouse.com

Library of Congress Cataloging-in-Publication Data

Names: Dave, Saumya, author.
Title: What a happy family / Saumya Dave.
Description: First edition. | New York: Berkley, 2021.
Identifiers: LCCN 2020055965 (print) | LCCN 2020055966 (ebook) |
ISBN 9781984806178 (trade paperback) | ISBN 9781984806185 (ebook)
Classification: LCC PS3604.A9424 W48 2021 (print) | LCC PS3604.A9424 (ebook) |
DDC 813/.6—dc23
LC record available at https://lccn.loc.gov/2020055965
LC ebook record available at https://lccn.loc.gov/2020055966

First Edition: June 2021

Printed in the United States of America
1st Printing

Book design by Nancy Resnick

What a
Happy Family

Also by Saumya Dave

Well-Behaved Indian Women

To my family:
Samir, Sahil, Akshay, Maansi, Dad, and Mom

To all families

One

Natasha

Any second now, Natasha's going to freak out in the exact way her therapist told her not to. She looks around the brunch table. Everyone's still in a good mood, a mood she'll definitely ruin after she makes her big announcement.

Maybe she should wait.

No, she's already put it off too long. And she should be able to handle everyone's reactions. Isn't that what being an adult is about—handling things?

Her boyfriend, Karan, is next to her, laughing at something his mom, Anita Auntie, just said. Anita Auntie tells another joke with a mixture of English and Gujarati words.

"And then," Anita Auntie says as she transitions from jokes to more general gossip, "instead of letting her parents look at her horoscope, she swiped left or right or in some God-knows-what direction on her phone. That's how they really met! The we-saw-each-other-on-the-beach-in-Jamaica-tale is just a cover story. Her mom told me at Patel Brothers."

Anita Auntie always uses a combination of charm and curiosity to learn everyone's business. In another life, she could have been a CIA agent. All Natasha's favorite aunties share an endearing and sometimes scary blend of ruthlessness and tenderness.

"She's smart, I tell you," Anita Auntie continues as Karan shakes his head in disbelief. "And so lucky to find someone when she's thirty-eight years old! Ever since I heard about how Meghan Markle started dating Prince Harry, I've told my kids that most people aren't that lucky, okay? Meghan may have gotten a fairy tale in her thirties, but everyone else, when they find someone good enough early on, they need to just seal the deal, like they say here. Otherwise, all the good ones get taken up and then you're left with nothing!"

"I should sew that onto a throw pillow." Natasha scoffs. "Attention, single people everywhere! Go after good enough . . . or else!"

"I'd get one for my dorm room." Her brother, Anuj, runs a hand through his thick, wavy hair, which he hasn't cut since he started his first year at Cornell. The combination of his hair and his boyish face reminds Natasha of Dev Patel.

"Cheers to that." Natasha raises her champagne glass in his direction. She can always count on him to back her up.

"Oh, Natasha!" Mom shakes her head. "Anita made a good point. You girls today don't have the same pressure we did, and sometimes it's important to make sure that, you know, you don't miss out on opportunities."

"Actually, we girls have a lot of pressure, from every possible direction, and don't need more," Natasha says.

Mom doesn't respond. She just purses her lips. Translation: This is not the moment for Natasha to dismantle the patriarchy. Plus, she's going to make Mom mad after she tells her everything. It's better to not rock the boat right now. Instead, she sips her mimosa and tries to ignore that odd mixture of panic and peace that overcomes her whenever she's about to be in trouble.

Her mind drifts to another lesson from her therapist: live in the present.

She can do that. She can be like those light and happy people in that yoga class she went to last weekend. She can smile and take deep breaths and go with the flow. That's how good Indian girls behave, and for the rest of this Sunday, she can at least try to act like one.

Mom hosts this joint family brunch at the Joshi house once a month. On the outside, it looks like a scene from one of those cozy Hallmark movies. Two families who have been best friends for decades. The parents, with their cups of chai and black hair flecked with gray. Their children, dating and working stable jobs that include health insurance. Bowls of green chutney and puffed rice are passed around. The scents of fried eggs and ginger permeate the air. A plate of jalapeño cheddar biscuits is at the center of the table. *I'm like Martha Stewart with cumin and chili powder*, Mom used to say.

Anita Auntie and Mom launch into another conversation, this one about how some random friend's daughter would be "the perfect match" for the local sari shop owner's son.

Karan squeezes Natasha's forearm. "Our moms are out of control."

"Seriously! And they both keep each other going," Natasha says. Anita Auntie always gets more talkative around Mom. "I get all the Atlanta news from family brunch."

Thank God nobody, not even Karan, knows her news yet. She tries to picture the way everyone will react and then how she'll feel just twenty-four hours from now. What if she hates living back at home? She always seems to regress to her middle school self when she's here. Maybe she's making a terrible mistake.

Her dad and sister, also therapists, would tell her she's catastrophizing again. Her dad and sister would be right.

"Karan, *beta*," Mom says. "Are you sure you're eating enough?"

Karan smiles and tilts his full plate toward her. "I took thirds!"

Mom beams, satisfied. Feeding people is her love language, but she takes it to another level with her precious Karan because she loves him and also because he's a sign that Natasha has her life together. To be fair, Mom's not the only one who feels this way. Everyone thinks that just because Natasha's in a long-term relationship, she must have some grand things figured out, when really, people in relationships can be just as messed up as people not in them.

Mom squeezes her hands together and says, *"Ketlo dayo chokro che."*

"Yes, we all know he is such a good boy," Natasha says.

"You're all great kids." Dad smiles.

Jiten Uncle, Karan's dad, nods. Mom and Anita Auntie exchange grins. What is with everyone today?

Natasha tries to motion to Anuj to ask him if he also thinks something's weird about the vibe. But Anuj doesn't shift his focus from the parents, who are all now laughing about the way Dad and Mom said "Francis Cut Key" when they were asked on the citizenship test who wrote "The Star-Spangled Banner." Apparently, one of their friends in Bombay had pronounced the name that way and it stuck. Dad's told this story a million times but still gets a kick out of it.

"Ah, we really had no idea what we were doing when we came to this country," Dad says, laughing. He and Anuj glance at their Apple watches. "Where are Suhani and Zack? Anuj, can you check on them?"

"I'll do it!" Natasha yelps before her brother has a chance to say anything. "I'm, uh, going to go grab some more stuff anyway."

By "stuff," Natasha means "alcohol." Once she's safely in the kitchen, she pours herself another mimosa the proper way, champagne with just a splash of orange juice. She takes a whiff of the fruity drink and wraps her sweaty palm around the cool, smooth glass. At least if everyone's in this great a mood, her news will be received better. She learned years ago that timing is everything when it comes to her family. Depending on the emotional temperature of their house, the same bad report card could result in either Mom yelling or everyone giving Natasha an endless lecture about her lack of trying.

She sends a quick text to her sister and brother-in-law: ETA?

SUHANI: Two minutes!

Suhani sends three smiley-face emojis. Suhani and Mom love using emojis and GIFs.

"Hey, where'd you go?" Karan comes into the kitchen and hands her a plate of fried potatoes. "I brought you some food."

"I don't deserve you." Natasha stabs four potato wedges with a fork.

Maybe it's because they're now in their early twenties, but she's starting to see how her boyfriend is perfect husband material. Conventionally handsome. Cultured. Caring.

And polite. Really polite. In every way, whether it's how he tucks in his Bonobos shirts, holds doors open, or says "please" before every question. Even his penis is polite, rising to the occasion (literally) only when Natasha's ready.

But then why has she been so off lately? Why has it taken more effort to be around him or around anyone?

It doesn't matter right now. All that matters is that she's taking the first big step to making a change in her life. She pictures herself two hours from now, after she's announced that she needs a break from everything. Of course, she won't say she got fired, gently fired—her boss gave her an it's-not-you-it's-us type of speech Natasha thought was only reserved for breakups on television. She'll tell everyone that she's done being an assistant at an ad agency, that she's taken the initiative and decided for herself that there will be nothing else besides focusing on her (not yet existent) comedy career. Like a charming talk show host, she'll make her point both clever and compelling. (In her mind, she says all of it in a British accent. Her imagined adult conversations are always in a British accent for some reason.) Her parents won't take it well, but Karan and her siblings will get it. And after the words are out, that'll be it. Just her and the sweet freedom of knowing she is officially going after her dreams. She is one step closer to being like those bold and brave women she's admired for so long.

Natasha and Karan go back to the dining room, where Dad is in the middle of one of his speeches.

"So, of course, he's fine now, but this really all goes back to social justice." Dad raises a fist into the air. He has a habit of turning even the most mundane anecdotes into dramatic monologues that somehow always conclude with a topic that riles everyone up. At Suhani's wedding, his toast ended with, "And here's to life! And better mental healthcare for all! And to never forgetting what's important to fight for!" A flurry of cheers and whistles erupted through the crowd and was repeated after Mom had finished with her part of the speech. A Deepak and Bina Joshi performance never ended quietly.

"Natasha." Mom motions to Natasha with a freshly manicured hand. "Come help me for a second."

Once they step into the hallway behind the dining room, Mom squints at her. "You didn't want to do your hair before brunch?"

"No."

"Or put on a little eyeliner?"

"No."

"Or stop biting your nails?"

"Again, no." Natasha pretends to ignore Mom's gaze scanning her from head to toe. "I'm going for the effortlessly chic look, emphasis on the effortless. You should try it. Once you wear athleisure and no makeup, there's really no going back."

The steely look in Mom's eyes makes Natasha think she's getting ready to run after her with tweezers or a mascara wand.

But Mom just sighs. "Fine. If you go to the laundry room, you'll see two gift bags by the sink. Can you go get them for me? They're saris for Anita Auntie."

"You got her saris just because?" Natasha asks.

Mom and Anita Auntie are always picking up little gifts for each other—lipsticks, novels with hot guys on the covers, spices from Patel Brothers—but saris are typically reserved for celebrations. When Natasha's sister, Suhani, got married, the upstairs linen closet was stuffed with yards of jewel-toned fabrics.

"I picked them up from that new boutique in Decatur a couple of weeks ago," Mom says. "Suhani wrapped them up nicely for me."

Of course she did, Natasha thinks. Her sister comes home every other week and somehow has no problem helping out with the most boring tasks. Natasha feels pangs of guilt and peace at the reminder of Suhani taking on the responsibility of always being there for their parents, even though she's married and works eighty hours a week.

"Okay, I'll go get them later," Natasha says.

"Get them now." Even though Mom is still smiling, there's an edge to her voice. "And then give them to Anita Auntie, okay?"

"Why did you get them for her?"

"Because she'll like them, that's why."

"Okay." Natasha drags out the latter syllable so it sounds like she's saying "Okaaaay."

She takes her time to walk to the other side of the first floor. The house hasn't changed in years. Mom found a way to infuse personality into each room through a combination of colorful wallpapers, framed family photos, and soft yellow lighting. Every shelf is adorned with a mixture of statues of Hindu goddesses and souvenirs from trips around the world.

Natasha returns with the saris and hands them to Anita Auntie.

"Thank you, *beta*." Anita Auntie leans forward to hug Natasha. "I can't wait to wear these."

She doesn't seem surprised at all to get two bags of saris.

Before Natasha can ask anything, Anita Auntie turns to Mom and says, "Ah, Bina, the house still looks so festive. I can't believe it's already been two months since Suhani and Zack got married!"

Natasha follows her gaze and takes in the perfect décor that was arranged for her perfect sister, who was, of course, a perfect bride. Jasmine garlands drape the windows. Giant brass pots are filled with floating candles and rose petals. Dyed rice is in the shape of a massive lotus flower by the front door.

"We love all of it." Mom nods in agreement. "I don't ever want to take the decorations away. Deepak's letting me indulge for another month. I can't even imagine the house without all this!"

Mom places a hand on her cheek as though she's delivering some sort of profound monologue. She may have quit acting decades ago, but her need for dramatic, grand statements will never disappear.

"Maybe you can just keep them up. You know, until you need

them again." Anita Auntie flashes a not-at-all-subtle smile toward Natasha and Karan.

"They do look good," Karan agrees. "How about le—"

"I think you should take them down," Natasha interjects. "They're quite intense."

"Oh c'mon, Natasha, your sister's wedding was beautiful. And brides are so much fun to see! All those gorgeous clothes, the youth," Anita Auntie says. "Didn't Suhani's wedding make you want . . ."

Anita Auntie makes a lot of her points by starting a comment and letting it trail off.

"Please," Mom says. "Natasha would never agree to a traditional wedding. She's already made that clear to us."

"But you'd look so nice!" Anita Auntie says as though she's made a groundbreaking scientific discovery. "Just like Priyanka Chopra!"

Natasha zones out as her boyfriend's mother gushes about every mundane detail of the celebrity wedding. Leave it to her to compare Natasha to a movie star when, in reality, Natasha was cast as LeFou, Gaston's sidekick, in her middle school's version of *Beauty and the Beast*.

"Yup, I'd look just like Priyanka, without the plump lips, thick hair, and toned body," Natasha says. "But Mom's right. I'm not interested in having a wedding like Suhani and Zack's."

Everyone laughs as if Natasha is a little girl saying a word for the first time.

"We know that's what you think, *beta*." Mom narrows her eyes. "Everyone knows. You can't keep your thoughts to yourself. Ever."

"And that's a problem?"

"Natasha, *beta*, you're so funny," Anita says in a feeble attempt to defuse the tension. "Remember when we all thought you'd be a comedian?"

"Uh-huh," Natasha says. "And that's actually what I still want to do."

She's giving you a window! Natasha thinks. *Just tell them all now.*

She had been reading about her favorite female comedians lately, how they were courageous enough to try to fail and create something of their own. She needs that now: courage.

"Who was that actress you wanted to be like?" Anita Auntie says. "You used to read her books and watch her shows. . . ."

"Mindy Kaling," Natasha and Karan say in unison.

"Oh, she's done thinking about all that," Mom says with a wave of her hand, as if Natasha's childhood dream is an unpleasant smell.

"Actually, she's not even just thinking about it anymore," Karan says. "In a couple of weeks, she'll be compet—"

"Karan, no." Natasha kicks his foot under the table.

Luckily, both of their moms are too distracted by Priyanka Chopra's Instagram feed to notice the conversation cutting off. Mom shows Priyanka's latest selfie to Anita Auntie as they both nod approvingly at her eye makeup.

There's no way they can know about Natasha's upcoming comedy competition. In just two weeks, she'll join twelve other aspiring stand-up comedians at the Midtown Comedy Center's Comedy Competition. The top four will be selected by a panel of judges and move on to the next round. The winner gets a standing open mic spot at Midtown Comedy Center. As if preparing a routine wasn't mind-wrecking enough, the venue also required each comedian to hand out fifty flyers in order to guarantee a slot. Natasha and Karan had spent three boring hours at Lenox Mall trying to get people to take a hot-pink paper that read COME TO STAND-UP COMEDY COMPETITION NIGHT! Only ten flyers were distributed and Natasha saw someone use theirs as a place to spit out their gum.

"What were we talking about? Oh right, Natasha is at a real job now, which is good." Mom darkens her phone screen and widens her large, almond-shaped eyes. "You know, we had to grow up so quickly, coming to America and all. So many things we weren't able to do or think about, so our kids would have a better life. And now they've realized they need to grow up, too."

Oh, Mom and the two rituals from India she refuses to part with: kohl eyeliner and guilt-tripping.

Suhani's high-pitched voice echoes through the house. "Hel-lo!"

Thank God, Natasha thinks. Suhani and Zack are here, which means Natasha has a chance to escape.

"They're here!" Dad says with an enthusiasm that's always been just for Suhani but has recently heightened now that they're both officially psychiatrists. She's his star now. In his field. She's even a third-year resident at his hospital.

Zack enters the dining room holding a bottle of Prosecco, which he hands straight to Natasha. His brown wavy hair is brushed to one side, which makes him look even more like Andy Samberg than usual. He isn't conventionally hot, but from the first time Suhani brought him home, Natasha could see how his easygoing attitude, sense of humor, and polished-but-not-trying-too-hard style gave him a level of sex appeal.

"Hey, you," he says as he gives Natasha a warm hug.

"Hey, I need a nap already," Natasha says.

Zack chuckles. "I'm not surprised. Just hang on for another hour or so. You'll be fine."

Natasha smiles. She got a brother-in-law who understands her. Everyone was worried how Mom and Dad would react when Suhani started dating a Jewish guy whose start-up was located at one of those cool coworking spaces and not some douchebag Indian doctor that they surely always envisioned for her. But it only took a few months for Dad to respect Zack's knowledge of finance and Mom to be charmed by Zack's charisma. The similarities between Jewish and Indian cultures also helped.

Well, all that plus the fact that Zack and Suhani have the perfect relationship. Unlike the other guys Suhani dated, Zack took pride in her ambition, in her need to constantly achieve and be more, do more, have more. He boasted about his "hot, go-getter wife" whenever anyone prompted him. Even when they fought, they found a way to speak to each other respectfully and come back together. And ever since they've been together, Suhani has been lighter and freer, a nice contrast to how intense and brooding she was growing up.

Natasha hears Suhani's soft, catlike footsteps getting louder. She always thought residents were supposed to look worn down and ragged, with unkempt hair and extra weight around their middles. But looking at Suhani only makes Natasha aware of her own frumpiness. She can't decide if being next to her sister makes her want to put on makeup or drown in tequila shots.

Suhani's red nails accentuate the three-carat princess-cut diamond on her left ring finger. She's wearing a sleeveless blush-pink knee-length dress. Despite the ninety-degree Atlanta summer heat, her hair is sleek and shiny without a hint of frizz. Just thinking about Suhani's morning routine of showering, blow-drying, toning, moisturizing, priming, and then applying makeup is exhausting. Women like Suhani are so fabulous that they remind you how not fabulous you are.

What would it be like to be her? Natasha wonders. To be beautiful, admired, accomplished, an Indian auntie's dream. Or really, everyone's dream. People are happily under her spell, as if she's some petite desi fairy who spreads magic wherever she goes. Babies always smile at her. Bartenders give her free drinks. Natasha's two best friends from college, Ifeoma and Payal, often refer to Suhani's Instagram for outfit inspiration.

"Nani," Suhani says as she wraps Natasha into a hug.

Nani means "small" in Gujarati and was what Suhani called Natasha the day she came home from the hospital in a white receiving blanket. Their parents love telling the story of how Suhani had begged them for "a baby sister I can take care of" every day for years before Natasha was born.

"Glad you made it." Natasha inhales a mixture of peony and jasmine flowers. She can feel her sister's shoulder blades jutting out through the thin fabric of her dress.

Everything about Suhani seems the same at first. Despite the fact that her makeup is all intact, the dullness in her eyes and the droop in her narrow shoulders give away that she's exhausted. Still, she's one of those women who always looks glamorous, even when tired, whereas Natasha throws on whatever clothing is closest /fits/ has been recently washed.

Suhani squints at Natasha. "What's wrong?"

Natasha considers smiling and saying she's fine, but that would be useless. She can't bullshit her sister. Throughout their lives, Suhani could take one look at Natasha and tell she was lying about anything. A shitty report card, a hidden container of weed, a regretful hookup.

Natasha rolls her eyes. "I'm just a little over brunch."

Suhani laughs. "Is it really that bad?"

"I don't know," Natasha says, and then, after seeing Suhani raise a skeptical eyebrow, adds, "It's not that bad. I just always feel like an outsider. Like everyone's waiting for me to screw up in some way." She regrets the words the second they come out. Suhani won't get it. Nobody will. Nobody understands that Natasha can be at her loneliest with the people she loves the most. Family, the place you're always supposed to belong, can be the same place that shows you you never really will.

"You know that's not true. You just have to get out of your head for a little bit, not overthink things," Suhani says as she reads Natasha's facial expressions. "Just have fun and be with all of us."

"You're right," Natasha says, and, seeing a chance for a quick escape, adds, "I'm going to grab something from upstairs."

She runs up the wooden staircase and breathes a sigh of relief once she's safely in her room. Posters of Jonathan Taylor Thomas and Shah Rukh Khan are plastered across the walls. The bottom row of her bookshelf is lined with Beverly Cleary's Ramona novels, Natasha's favorite series since she was in the third grade. She and Suhani still sometimes call each other Ramona and Beezus.

She falls onto her unmade bed. Her sheets smell like the lavender fabric softener Mom's used since she was in elementary school.

"Natasha! You've been upstairs forever!" Mom's voice jolts Natasha awake. She looks at her phone and realizes she fell asleep for almost half an hour. Shit.

"Sorry! Coming down!" Natasha yells.

She splashes cold water on her face. The first thing she notices when she leaves her bedroom is the absence of sound. Where did everyone go?

"Hello?" Her voice echoes off the high ceilings.

The wooden steps creak as she makes her way downstairs. Everyone left? Thank God.

But when she goes back into the dining room, Karan is standing with a bouquet of roses. His laptop is open on the dining table and there are pictures of them flashing on the screen. Right now, it's one of when they were eleven years old, in front of a roller coaster at Six Flags, strawberry Popsicles dripping in their hands.

"Hey, what are you do—"

"Natasha, I love you. I always have. I know things have been tough for you lately, but I'm here for you. . . ."

The rest of Karan's words blur into the background. They become one with the straw tablecloths from India and the Peruvian brass candlesticks. She picks up bits of him saying he wants to be with her, that he always has.

Her throat becomes dry and tight. She watches the entire moment as if she's suspended above it, somewhere near the spinning ceiling fan.

The words Karan is about to say linger over them. Panic seizes every inch of her chest. She takes a deep breath and tells herself to stay calm. Her nerves won't have to ruin the moment if she refuses to let them.

Karan reaches into his right pants pocket and kneels down. "Natasha, will you marry me?"

There it is. The question she's heard so many times in movies and shows. Even though she figured it would someday be asked of her, for some reason, she doesn't feel the way she thought she would. Instead of excitement, there's a pang of fear, and something else, something she can't quite recognize.

As Karan opens a slim velvet box, she sees that he even went to the effort to get a box that would be concealed in his pants. Her gaze shifts to the round sapphire on a platinum band. He knows she wouldn't like a diamond. Hot tears spring to her eyes. She doesn't deserve someone so thoughtful. She never did.

"I, um, I . . ." Natasha stammers.

Karan shifts his knee. For some reason, the hope on his face pushes Natasha to give him the only thing she can: honesty.

"No," she says, her voice clear. "I can't."

"Excuse me? What?" Karan shakes his head as though he's been woken up mid-dream and is now trying to process reality.

"I'm sorry," Natasha says. "I can't marry you. There's no way I'm ready for that now."

"Why are you saying this?" Karan's face falls, which is all it takes for her to hate herself. "You're kidding, right?"

"Me? I should ask if you're kidding! This is totally catching me off guard."

"That's sort of the point." Karan lowers his voice, a sure giveaway that he's mad.

"Yeah, but I mean, this is so random. I don't want to hurt your feelings, but shouldn't we at least talk about this? You really want to get married? *Married?*" Natasha asks, like she's learning the word for the first time. "And now? We're so young. . . ."

"Yeah, I guess we are." Karan frowns. "But I know this is what I want. I always have. We literally played together in our diapers. And I'm ready to start our lives together. Our real, adult lives. And you're the one who said I need to be more exciting and spontaneous."

"Yeah, I meant in little ways, like getting late-night McDonald's on a whim." Natasha shakes her head. "This is not McDonald's!"

A heaviness lingers over them like a cloud. She tries to see things from his perspective. Maybe he really is ready to start his adult life. He just got the job as senior accountant at Buckhead CPA and moved into a high-rise on Peachtree Street. They picked out furniture from IKEA and took some of her parents' hand-me-downs. Oh my God, was all that because she was supposed to move in there? How could she have missed the signs that he was planning this?

"I'm sorry, I really don't see myself as a wife right now, or even soon. I was going to tell everyone I'm moving back home today . . . to focus on my comedy full time." Natasha struggles to find words that seem good enough.

"You're moving back home? And making comedy your job?" Karan shakes his head. "Why?"

"Because. I want to. There are a lot of things I plan to do before I even think about getting married."

"But if you know you want to marry me someday, then what's the problem with doing it now?" Karan raises his eyebrows.

Natasha wants to tell him that employing his high school debate skills isn't going to get him far in this type of situation. But she stares at him and says, "Because I just don't want to. And I definitely don't think it would be right if I said yes just because I felt forced. C'mon, you're my best friend. We don't need to rush this."

More pictures flash on the laptop. Their families at Baskin-Robbins, Karan pushing Natasha on a tire swing, both of them sitting in the nearby laundromat next to a massive container of Tide. Karan has always been a part of her family. And he's right. This has always been the plan between them and, maybe even more so, between their families.

"You've seemed so out of it lately. And it's affected us," Karan adds. "I thought this would make you feel better."

"If you think things are off between us, then we need to work on it, not use a proposal as a Band-Aid for any issues. I'm sorry, but I can't say yes."

She considers walking toward him, holding his hand and telling him she loves him. She expects him to understand, like the rejected guys in her favorite southern romance movies. They always had the perfect I'll-be-fine attitude (and hair). She pictures Patrick Dempsey at the end of *Sweet Home Alabama* or James Marsden in *The Notebook*. Those guys must have had pretty decent lives after they were let down.

But Karan slams the laptop lid. "You know what? I'm done."

"Done? Done with this conversation?" Natasha says.

"No. I'm done with this." Karan gestures to the space between them. "It's always so complicated with you. I thought I got used to it but, man, you've always got something going on."

"Always? Really?" Natasha crosses her arms.

"Yeah. I can't ever get through to you. You know sometimes, you start crying and freaking out over things and then never let me help you. It's a lot with you, Natasha. It really is."

"I get that I'm a lot," Natasha whispers. She didn't need Karan to tell her that. She's known that for her entire life. And so has he. Since when was it an issue? "But can we at least talk about all this?"

Karan keeps staring at the hardwood floor. "I don't think there's anything to say."

"But if you cou—"

"Goodbye, Natasha." Karan slides the laptop under his arm and walks away.

"What's the problem here?" Mom interrupts as she steps into the room. "Just say yes!"

"*Mom!*" Natasha says. "What are you doing in here?!"

Three lines emerge on Mom's forehead. "We're all waiting back there for you to move things along already! Hurry up!"

"Don't tell me to hurry up!" Natasha says as the other eavesdroppers collect around Mom—Dad, Karan's parents, Suhani, Zack, and Anuj. Goddamn it, that's why they are all so excited today.

Karan's parents are standing on the side, quiet, their stunned faces turned toward the floor. What would it be like to have such placid parents? Would she have been more normal if she came from a family like his?

Anita Auntie clears her throat. "We should leave. Now."

"Anita, wait," Mom says.

Anita Auntie shakes her head. "I think we should be with our own families right now."

Our own families. Seemingly innocuous words but really, a message: our families are separate.

And just like that, brunch is over.

Two

Suhani

Can you believe the nerve of that girl? After *everything* she's put me through. Who does she think she is, doin—"

"Mom," Suhani interrupts. "Can you stop talking about Natasha? For just one minute?"

"How can I do that?" Mom asks, as if that's the most absurd suggestion in the world.

"Ugh, I don't even know why I try." Suhani shakes her head.

Mom and Natasha can never keep their emotions to themselves. Suhani, on the other hand, might be wounded—broken—on the inside, but even her husband won't always be able to tell.

Her husband. Husband. She's still getting used to the word. It's so adult. So real.

Five years ago, Suhani didn't know what a healthy relationship even looked like, and now she has a husband. On their first date, set up by mutual friends during her fourth year of med school, Suhani couldn't pinpoint why exactly she was attracted to Zack. He was the first white guy she'd ever been with, so a part of her was worried it had to do with his novelty. But over time, she saw that it all boiled down to the content, self-assured way he carried himself. How he smiled at strangers and made small talk with

Uber drivers. His dapper but relaxed style. His dad jokes and pride in not just calling himself a feminist but also acting like one.

And despite everyone's warnings about how marriage was hard work and the first year was the most difficult, theirs so far is like the rest of their relationship. Effortless. Fun. Tender. From the beginning, they split housework equally, which was so different from what Suhani saw with Mom and Dad. Zack made it clear that Suhani's career was as important as his own.

Whenever she's taking a break at work between writing patient notes or calling insurance companies, she finds herself daydreaming about the day-to-day details of their life more than she thought was possible. Everything about it seems special, even the mundane parts: the buzz of their electric toothbrushes, colorful stacks of Zack's boxer briefs and bow ties in their tiny dresser (their first non-IKEA piece of furniture), John Legend's latest album blasting through their speakers, Zack's natural, citrusy scent on their plush sheets.

Suhani's thoughts are interrupted by Mom's rambling. There's no point in trying to stop her.

She's on a roll, Suhani's best friend and co-resident, Vanessa, would say. Vanessa, an only child whose parents got divorced when she was ten years old, loves hearing about the never-ending Joshi family drama. *Tell me the latest thing your mom said*, she often asks Suhani during hospital rounds. *Give me the updates on Natasha's exciting life.*

"She's never going to learn." Mom shakes her head in disbelief. "I must have gone wrong somewhere. Really. I've always told you that and now I'm convinced of it."

"You've always been convinced of it. And it's never been true. Natasha is her own person and has the right to make her own decisions." Suhani ignores the cramping in her feet. Why is she wearing four-inch Louboutin heels tonight? Only chic television doctors can get away with shoes like that. They're way too painful for real life. She thought they'd be the ideal complement to her Huda Beauty smoky eye makeup and beaded black gown from Rent the Runway. The dress, shoes, and makeup were supposed to make her feel like a modern, sultry Princess Jasmine. Princess Jasmine if she was sleep deprived and had a histrionic mother.

"Okay, I think we need to change the topic," Suhani says five minutes later.

"What? Why?" Mom's eyes widen.

"Because, like I told you for the millionth time, we're at an event where I'm getting an award, you can mingle with Dad's coworkers, and everyone should take a break from the Natasha situation," Suhani says. "You know this is the first time Zack and I have been able to even come to this because I had to work in the emergency room during my first and second years of residency."

Suhani motions to the massive white banner that's hung across the stage: CELEBRATING OUR DOCTORS. Every July, Atlanta Memorial Hospital hosts a reception to welcome new interns, give out faculty awards, and share upcoming news about the hospital. For this one night, doctors change out of their scrubs and into tuxes and gowns, drink champagne, and pretend they don't have to be back at the hospital early the next morning. Dad and Mom have been coming to the event for the past fifteen years, since Dad started working at the Atlanta Memorial psychiatry clinic.

Mom gives a polite wave to one of Dad's coworkers, a bald old white man who always wears a single gold earring and walks with a sterling silver cane. Mom nicknamed him "Mr. Clean with a limp" years ago. She always provides the most vivid descriptions of people: "that brooding man who doesn't know how to shave" or "those sensuous women who men like getting massages from" or "that poor boy who always looks like he just licked a lemon."

Now Mom points to a group of doctors in the corner of the room. "That woman in the front there is going through a divorce. Her son is a med student who wants to go into orthopedic surgery, but nobody knows if he'll match. And that other woman behind her is a rheumatologist. Maybe you've seen her in some of my Instagram posts? She helps so many women at the temple with their arthritis. The man behind her just moved here from China. Someone in one of my WhatsApp groups told me he's single and apparently a very good cook, so if you know anyone available . . ."

Finally, Suhani says to herself. *She's calming down.*

"It's always so nice, being around all these doctors." Mom runs a hand over her brown silky hair, which she recently had trimmed to chin length. "So much purpose and satisfaction. Everyone should have that. I always told you that, remember?"

Of course she remembers. Mom first told Suhani that when Suhani was five years old. Mom was boiling chai on the stove for ten guests who were visiting from India that week. Something about her—her furrowed brows, the drop in her shoulders, a heaviness behind her eyes—told Suhani that she was stressed.

"What's wrong?" she had asked. "Do you need help with the tea?"

"Not at all. This is my job, *beta*." Mom shook her head.

"Then why do you look so sad?"

"I'm not sad. I'm just thinking." Mom kept her eyes on the pot.

"About what?" Suhani asked, oblivious about the far-off look on Mom's face until she'd revisit the memory years later.

"Just . . . life." Mom gripped the edge of the counter and turned to

Suhani. "If there's only one thing you ever remember me saying, please let it be to work hard and build a career for yourself, something nobody else can take away from you, so you're never dependent on anyone else. Anyone. And don't worry about that being too much for some man. It's not your job to make a man feel comfortable."

It took years for Suhani to realize how complicated women's relationships with ambition and money were. Whenever she told her friends about Mom's words, they'd often say, "Your mom told you that? Mine would never give that type of advice."

Just when Suhani thinks they're finally moving on from Natasha, Mom's nostrils flare. "I forgot to tell you that on top of all this, Natasha quit her job. Your sister thinks she's too good to work! Isn't that nice? To just wake up and decide you'd like to relax forever? Did she tell you?"

"Uh . . ." Suhani puts on her best I-had-no-idea face. Natasha told her she was fired two months ago. *I hated that boring job anyway*, she said. *And now I can work on my stand-up comedy.*

"I'm sure she plans to work again soon, maybe in a job that's more suitable for her," Suhani says, careful not to give away any details but still provide reassurance. No wonder she went into psychiatry. First-born daughters are live-in therapists for their entire families. "And she's going through a tough time. We should be supporting her."

"Please! She's fine."

"Karan said she's been crying and unhappy. What if something is really wrong?"

"Something's always wrong with Natasha," Mom says. "That's no reason to act like a child. She has to grow up and make decisions now—real, adult decisions—instead of just running away at the first hint of responsibility."

Even though Suhani wonders why Natasha wouldn't say yes to Karan, she won't say that out loud. There's an unspoken agreement between Suhani, Natasha, and Anuj that they'll never throw each other under the bus to their parents.

"She always has an excuse for everything," Mom adds.

Suhani shrugs. Mom does have a point. Natasha is always equipped with a reason for why something didn't go her way. The teacher didn't like her and gave her a bad grade. The landlord lost her check. Her alarm clock stopped working.

"What she needs is a reality check," Mom says. "She should go back to Karan, apologize, and make things right. She has no idea how many people she hurts with her rash decisions. How are we even going to explain this to anyone?"

"I don't think we should be focusing on anyone else's feelings besides hers. Maybe we should have her see a therapist," Suhani says, careful to not reveal that Natasha was seeing a therapist until she lost her health insurance.

"Talking to a stranger isn't going to change anything!" Mom says.

Despite her husband and daughter being psychiatrists, Mom still thinks of mental health issues in the same way so many people from India do: as something "you just get over" and "move on with." Dad used to say that the stigma toward mental illness in India was one of the reasons he went into psychiatry: *Everyone told me not to work with "crazy" people, and at some point, that stuck with me. I knew I had to fight for the people who are misunderstood and overlooked.*

Mom stares at her tiny cocktail plate. For a second, her face softens. "She has no idea what being depressed even means. She really doesn't. If only she knew how bad it could really be."

"What do you mean—"

"Hey!" Zack says as he slides his hands around Suhani's slim waist. The only benefit of wearing these painful heels is that she can kiss him without stretching her neck. At six-three, he's exactly a foot taller than her.

When Suhani pulls away from Zack, she catches some of the conservative, silver-haired attending physicians glancing in their direction with puzzled expressions. For a second, she considers pointing them all out to Zack. *See? They're surprised my husband isn't Indian.*

But it will only lead to yet another argument. It's taken a day for them to get over the most recent one, which started when she told Zack about a patient who needed a psychiatry consult. The patient refused to talk when he saw Suhani but, seconds later, was all words when the white male medical student came in the room. Zack insisted that while it might have been about Suhani's race, it also might not have been. *Not everything is sexist and racist, honey.* Suhani stormed out of their bedroom, which, now that she thinks about it, was a pretty anticlimactic move in their tiny apartment. She had to turn right back to grab her phone.

"What were you and Mom talking about?" Zack has a mixture of curiosity and anticipation in his eyes. He can gossip with Mom for hours if given the chance, something Dad and Anuj never do. Zack is the same way with his mom, Barbara, maybe because she and Mom share so many similarities: an emotional warmth that makes strangers want to tell them their darkest secrets, a need to make sure everyone is always fed, a tendency to know everyone's business in a way that's more curious than mean-spirited.

"Oh, you know, the usual." Suhani gives Zack a look that says, *Don't ask anymore.*

"I see." Zack senses Suhani's tension and hands her a skinny, spicy margarita, her favorite drink. "Sweetie, your colleagues are so fun. Shrinks are definitely the most interesting doctors around."

"I'm biased, but I have to agree," Suhani says. Only her husband can effortlessly mingle with a group of doctors who are obsessed with talking about their jobs. On their third date, Zack told Suhani he was always fascinated by doctors and believed this stemmed from his own dad, a family medicine physician who struggled with alcoholism and left Zack, Barbara, and Zack's sisters when Zack was in elementary school.

"I threw in some therapy terms and they were impressed," Zack says. "A little bit of 'she sounds like she has some real self-sabotaging behavior' and 'his pathological narcissism seems to cloud his judgment.' Pulled it off pretty well, if I say so myself."

Suhani laughs. "Of course you did."

She's reminded of how she ended up with a guy who is fun. Fun! During his undergrad years at Dartmouth, Zack Kaplan went to parties, did keg stands, and cheered at sports games, while Suhani spent most of her time at Emory in the library.

"So, what's going on? Are you getting excited about your award?"

"Eh, sure, not really." Suhani shrugs. "It's nice to have my work recognized but not a big deal."

"Ah, my beautiful and humble wife. She just doesn't know how to take credit for her accomplishments."

Taking credit isn't how Suhani got to this point in her career. Sheer hard work and discipline pull her out of bed every morning. This is how she has always been, obsessed with achieving the next thing, as if at any moment, it can all be taken away from her.

"Hey, I met some of the plastic surgeons and dermatologists.

They told me to let them know when I'm ready to make a Botox appointment, which I took as a hint." Zack points to the faint lines emerging on his forehead.

"I love your face. You don't need to get anything." She runs her manicured hand over his sexy two-day stubble and then across the pressed collar of his light gray suit jacket. Zack always knows how to look effortlessly polished.

He leans into her as Mom starts talking to Dad's former boss.

"I've gotta do whatever I need to do to keep up with you. You look so sexy in this dress." He moves his hand below her waist and gives her butt a quick covert squeeze. "I can't wait to take it off later."

"I know," Suhani says. "It's been way too long. I'm so worn out by the time I get home."

She recently read an article about the "normal" number of times newlyweds had sex. Are those people not working? Was nobody else in residency? Or simply exhausted? By the time she's done with twelve hours at the hospital and forty-five minutes at a Pure Barre class, she barely has enough energy to scarf down a boxed salad.

"Well, let's see what we can do about that," Zack whispers. "You're mine as soon as when we get into our apartment."

Suhani is about to tell him she's especially tired today but decides it's better not to. She has to be the woman Zack had just two months ago on their honeymoon in the Seychelles, when they couldn't keep their hands off each other for ten days. They spent every waking hour with their limbs intertwined on the plush king-size bed that overlooked the Indian Ocean. The entire trip was a blur of smells: cocoa butter lotion; champagne; sweat; and warm, salty air. Suhani wished she could bottle them all up, preserve them forever.

"Ha, I knew it!" Mom shoves her cell phone into Suhani's and

Zack's faces. There's a text message from Anuj: Natasha and I are going to a bar soon. We'll be back late so don't wait up.

"Knew what?" Zack asks.

"I knew Natasha would get Anuj to take her to a bar," Mom says with the satisfaction of a detective solving a crime. "She always pulls him into whatever fun she wants to have. I can't even remember the last time my sweet Anuj Babu went to a bar when he was at home. And within days of being with his sister, he's going out drinking."

"Who cares? He's in college. You know, around alcohol all the time. If he really wants to drink, he can," Suhani reminds her. "And they're both old enough to make their own decisions, right?"

"Your sister might be old enough in age, but that's where it ends." Mom scans the room and spots Dad. "I'm telling your dad we need to leave. Now. Before they go out."

"But they're starting the award ceremony in a few minutes. Can't you wait?"

Mom pauses as if to consider this but then glances at her phone again. "We are very proud of you, but we have to get home before your sister takes your brother to get drunk and do God knows what else. She might be fine screwing up her own life, but I'm not going to let her corrupt my innocent baby. You'll be fine, *beta*!"

Zack stifles a laugh. Anuj is far from innocent. The entire family knows that he and his roommate at Cornell experimented with all sorts of drugs, but, of course, Mom won't point that out.

"Okay, well, good luck." Suhani knows there's no point in arguing. Throughout her life, Mom and Dad have focused their attention on Natasha. When they were younger, they skipped Suhani's parent-teacher conferences to meet with Natasha's guidance counselors. Later, they would spend all of dinner asking Natasha about

what she wanted to major in in college or how she would apply for
jobs.

Suhani has a mixture of admiration and envy for her sister's
ability to always say, "Fuck this, I'm going to do what I want." It
would be so freeing to live that way. Growing up, aunties told Suhani to "take it easy like your sister" while they told Natasha to
"work harder like your sister." She wonders now how that constant
comparison shaped both of them.

"Just let them go," Zack whispers as he tilts his head in Mom's
direction. "If they stay, they'll be worrying the entire time. I'll send
them pictures of you getting your award."

He has the same don't-worry look in his eyes that he had on
their first date at Sotto Sotto and then again during their wedding
ceremony, when both of their moms tried to control every part of
their Jewish and Hindu fusion ceremony.

Suhani nods and ignores the tension building in her neck and
shoulders. Before she met Zack, this incident would have resulted
in her fuming for hours. Maybe she'd even have an imaginary argument with Mom in her head.

Twenty minutes later, Suhani's co-residents cheer when she gets
the award for Resident of the Year. Her program director, Dr. Wilson, discusses her "in-depth research and advocacy for women's
mental health," along with her "commitment to the field of psychiatry" and "hours mentoring junior doctors." She avoids the gaze
of hundreds of doctors and focuses on a spot in the back of the
room with the same concentration she gave Scantron tests in high
school. Every time Dr. Wilson mentions her accomplishments, the
first thought in her head is: *I don't deserve this. They must have made
a mistake.* She hears Mom's voice commanding her to sit up straight

and look gracious, then Zack's telling her she needs to not be afraid to take credit for her work.

"Way to win that and stick it to the man," Vanessa says when Suhani returns to their table. "We've got to stop the boys' club that is all of medicine."

"This is a middle finger to the patriarchy!" Suhani raises her plaque into the air.

"Yes, fuck the patriarchy!" Vanessa sticks both of her middle fingers into the air as a show of solidarity. The gesture is an endearing contrast to her ivory Sachin & Babi gown and delicate pearl drop earrings. Her dress has one of those plunging necklines that can only be pulled off by someone who can go braless.

Suhani and Vanessa met three summers ago during residency orientation. They shared the same dummy during CPR training, and within minutes, both of them commented on how none of the dummies were female, so nobody would be able to practice CPR on a chest with breasts. While Suhani kept this complaint to herself, Vanessa went to the instructor and demanded they teach another class with female dummies.

Over the years, they formed the type of raw, secure bond that can only come from late nights eating dinner from the vending machine, running group therapy with dementia patients, and bringing each other double-shot espressos before morning rounds. Vanessa took pride in being guided by principle. Unlike Suhani, she had no problems speaking up to authority, even if that made her less likable. Her brazenness reminded Suhani of Cristina Yang from *Grey's Anatomy*, if Cristina had also enjoyed Bravo shows and trying every new dating app.

"So, are you ready to finally take it easy now?" Vanessa asks.

"You got the award. Everyone knows you're a rock star. Now, chill."

"Please. She doesn't know how to chill," Zack says.

Vanessa gives him a look that says, *Cheers to that.* "Only Little Miss Type A could make a group of doctors in training look like slackers. I don't know how you do it. It's like you never stop."

"Trust me, I do," Suhani says, even though they all know that's not true.

"Yeah, right. You know, I've been wondering, where does it come from?" Vanessa asks. "Your need to keep going, going, going? People are rarely ever just born with that. And then you still seem to not be convinced that it's enough, that you can take a break."

"Oh, don't you dare analyze me! I'm a shrink, too, remember?" Suhani waves a finger in her friend's face, even though she's right. It's often a combination of things that makes someone this way, unable to be satisfied. And although people always jumped to Dad's career as the driving force behind Suhani's ambition, only those closest to her were aware that Mom played a bigger role, and nobody knew that what happened in med school also played a part. She would be damned if anything ever took her off track again.

The rest of dinner passes quickly. It's refreshing to take a break from talking about the side effects of Prozac or teaching breathing exercises for a panic attack or reading about family therapy. For the first time in a long time, Suhani can pause that frantic voice in her head: *Do your best. Work harder. Keep aiming higher.* She finds solace in the bubbles of the champagne tickling her throat and camaraderie with her co-residents.

By the time the waiters are serving coffee and chocolate-covered strawberries on white bone china plates, Suhani is ready to go home and change into her red lacy lingerie.

"Let's go," she tells Zack as she takes one last sip of her black coffee, her fourth cup today.

"The program is almost over." Zack motions for more dessert. "They just have to introduce the new faculty."

"And you want to stay for that?" While she's getting more tired every hour, Zack's only gaining steam. Usually, she's grateful Zack enjoys making small talk, but tonight she wishes he also needed time away from other people to recharge.

I get it, okay? You're always tired. The doorman knows you're tired, Zack said the other night during the argument about the psych consult. Within twenty minutes, he wrapped his arms around her and apologized. *I shouldn't have said that. I'm sorry. I love you.* They were back to themselves by bedtime.

Zack shrugs. "Might as well just wait it out. C'mon, all your co-residents are here. When do you ever get to relax with them? Or relax at all?"

"That's true," Suhani agrees, just as Vanessa says, "Yes! Stay!"

"We all know you're going to be chief resident next year," Vanessa adds. "But for once, can you just hang out and have fun?"

"Ha, I can try."

Dr. Townsend, the president of the hospital, walks onto the stage, taps the microphone, and clears his throat. His booming voice, Crest-commercial smile, and graying sideburns make him look more like a politician than a doctor. "Can we have everyone's attention, please? We would like to introduce some new faculty members to Atlanta Memorial Hospital. We are thrilled to have doctors join us from so many wonderful institutions."

Suhani glances at the stage, where six doctors are lined up. She's pleased to see four of them are women. They need more female physicians here. She's still called "sweetie," "honey," and "darling" more than she's ever called "doctor."

Dad sends Suhani articles about the variety of initiatives taking place to bring more women into medicine. The last one was titled, "Why We Need More Female Physicians." Dad put "Think there is hope!" in the subject line with a smiley face.

But after everything Suhani has been through, everything she saw Mom struggle with, and everything that almost ruined her in med school, she knew she wanted to be a female in power in health-care. She wanted to be part of why women would be treated more fairly as clinicians and patients. Maybe one of these new doctors onstage can be her mentor.

She scans the group again.

Her stomach drops.

At first, she assumes she must be hallucinating. Sleep deprivation must be taking a toll on her.

But then her heart rate increases as she takes in the large, bulbous nose that could only belong to one person. To him. From her periphery, she sees that new gray strands have emerged around his temples. Registering him floods her with a rush of dopamine and dread.

Fuck. Fuck. Fuck.

It's hard to understand why some parts about a person stick while others fade away over time. She spent years forgetting the contours of his face. His angular chin and distinct side profile. The intensity in his eyes, in everything about him. The way he whittled her self-worth into something that was barely there, whittled her into someone she didn't even recognize.

"Are you okay?" Zack faces her.

Suhani feels the color drain from her face. "Yeah. Fine. Just tired."

"Okay, okay, let's head out." Zack takes his suit jacket off the chair.

Suhani glances at the stage. It's definitely Roshan. He's descending the stairs, the stairs she was just on. How can he be here? After he graduated from UCLA med—two years before her—he said he was "never leaving the West Coast." They weren't supposed to cross paths ever again. That was one of the reasons she chose to come back home for residency. Not that anyone besides Natasha knows that.

She tells herself to look away.

But she's too late. They make eye contact.

Damn it.

The room becomes blurry. Suhani can no longer see the tables, covered with linen tablecloths and tea-light candles, the people bustling toward the bar, or her co-residents getting refills of red wine. All she can take in is him. The hair on his knuckles. His hands, dry from years of using harsh hospital soaps and not moisturizing despite how many times Suhani bought him tiny bottles of lotion for his white-coat pockets. The scuffed-up black Cole Haan shoes he's had forever. The future they both envisioned: two successful doctors, healing and achieving and growing together. That was before she discovered who he really was, what he was truly capable of.

He takes steady, smooth steps toward her. She ignores the voice in her head telling her to walk away. He'd take that as a sign of weakness. And weak is the last fucking thing she'll let him see her as.

"Suhani, hi," he says, as though he's running into any old friend and not someone he used to see naked every night. She forgot how deep his voice is. It was the first thing that attracted her to him when they started talking on the phone late at night, when they should have been studying. God, relationships could start for the dumbest reasons. They were supposed to be a place of safety, not anchored in something as trivial as how deep someone's voice is. She scolds her twenty-four-year-old self for not picking out any red flags back then. But was it all her fault? Are there always warning signs, clues about an inevitable ending, if you're willing to look hard enough?

"Hi." Suhani bites her bottom lip to prevent herself from having any facial expression. "I'm, um, I didn't realize you were going to be working here."

"Yeah, well, they offered me a great position in the neurology department." Roshan furrows his thick brows as he glances at her. "And I was ready for a change. There's a lot I've been wanting to do here. And figure out. You know, personally and profession-ally."

She nods as though it's perfectly normal to hear this from him, when really it makes no sense at all. Some covert Facebook re-search already taught her that he was an attending at UCLA, en-joyed living in a small house near the beach, and didn't seem to be in a relationship. It also taught her that his old roommate's girl-friend's nephew got a Pomeranian puppy, which is when Suhani realized she had gone way too far with her stalking.

She repeats his words in her mind. *Personally and professionally.* Could he have figured out what she did? No, that wasn't possible. She stops herself from indulging her paranoia. Years ago, she made sure that all her boxes were checked off, that there would be no trace of what happened. There's no reason for her to be scared of him anymore.

"They've pulled up our car. You ready to go?" Zack is behind her, his arms on her shoulders. She watches him scan Roshan from head to toe with a questioning glance.

Roshan's eyes shift as if he's unsure whether to stay or leave. Or maybe he's judging Zack, with his light gray suit, shiny Ferragamo shoes, polka-dotted navy-blue pocket square, and TAG Heuer watch. Roshan always took pride in being "above" dressing nicely and buying luxury things.

"Ready." She motions to Roshan and ignores the constriction in her throat. "This is Roshan. You know, from med school."

"Oh . . . hi." She watches Zack register the name. "Ah, so you're Roshan."

Zack extends his hand. Even when he's uncomfortable, he's still kind. Courteous.

"Yeah," Roshan says with a grunt.

"Nice to meet you," Zack says. "I, uh, didn't know you lived here."

"Same here. What a coincidence." Suhani hears a nervous laugh come out of her. She tells herself she's in control here. She won't regress to the woman she used to be. Someone quieter, more afraid. She studies both of them, side by side. Her husband next to the guy she once thought would be her husband.

At one point, she imagined running into Roshan at a conference, at a time when she'd be at her goal weight, full of purpose, hair and makeup in place. But when nothing happened for years, she realized she'd gotten lucky. She could take the most painful part of her life, the part that she could never face, and move on.

But now she's in a gown, an award in one hand, the other clutching her husband's. She's worked her ass off at the hospital. She's exercised and toned and strengthened every part of her body. She's perfected her posture and voice until they convey confidence. Nothing about her looks pathetic. Maybe she couldn't have seen

Roshan at a better time. Realizing this gives her a burst of courage. *My life is great now, even after you almost ruined me.*

"Well, I'm getting pretty tired," she says, making sure her voice has just enough nonchalance.

"We should head out." Zack wraps his arm around Suhani's shoulders, a gesture that's part territorial, part loving. To him, this is the guy she dated in med school and dumped one year before they met. He's irrelevant to their life now.

That's the story she told Zack. It's the same story she told herself for years until she believed it. She realized then that that was how people deceived themselves, by telling themselves something again and again, until the line between truth and lie eroded.

"Bye," Suhani says without making eye contact with Roshan.

Zack pats Roshan's shoulder. "See ya."

Roshan nods. He's still frowning.

Suhani feels the weight of something settling onto her chest. Shame and guilt. And something else, something scarier. She lets herself sink into Zack's embrace, and they step into the dark parking lot without looking back.

Three

Bina

"Bina!" Mira yells across the parking lot. "What is this playing on the speakers?"

"'Jolene,'" Bina yells. "My favorite Dolly Parton song."

Mira frowns as she takes quick, purposeful strides toward Bina's phone. The gold bangles on her wrist jingle as she scrolls through Spotify. "Can we put on something else?"

"Go ahead." Bina rolls her eyes. She should have known better than to think that everyone here would appreciate Dolly.

Mira puts on a Bollywood remix that's more appropriate for a wedding reception than a health fair. Bina considers asking her to put on something less let's-get-on-the-dance-floor and more we-are-volunteering-for-an-important-cause. But she has too many other things that require her attention. Years ago, her mother told her a woman's brain is always like that, bursting at the seams with everything there is to keep track of.

But right now, Bina has to focus. She has to put all her effort into getting through this event, and when Anita shows up, *if* Anita shows up, talk to her about announcing the idea they've been planning for weeks. They were supposed to do it after telling everyone about their children's engagement.

"You've done such an amazing job again. Everything looks great," Deepak says, interrupting her thoughts. "And it's going to be great."

Bina smiles with gratitude. She smooths her mint-green kurta top and cream linen pants. This is the third year in a row she's organized a health fair, and it's since grown to two hundred people congregating at the Atlanta Hindu Temple. She has to make sure everything is nutritious, so large containers of kale salad, roasted vegetables, lentil soup, nuts, and fresh fruit are arranged on the wooden table. Let the Indian attendees grumble about not having traditional food. At least everyone else will be satisfied.

Outside the temple, booths are set up across the vast parking lot for volunteer doctors, nurses, and physician assistants to take people's vital signs and blood samples and screen for different diseases. College students saunter through the booths to pass out flyers about local clinics.

"Have you seen Anita or Jiten?" Bina asks. Her stomach churns at the thought of seeing their closest friends for the first time since family brunch.

Deepak shakes his head. "Not yet."

"She and I were supposed to tell everyone about our kitty-party idea. I wanted to have the first meeting next week."

"Are you sure that's a good idea?" Deepak raises an eyebrow.

"Of course," Bina says. "Even with everything that just happened, it's still something we should do. And I really need this."

Years ago, after Bina accepted that she had to let go of the career she had built since she was a little girl, she told herself that she'd be fulfilled if she hit all the milestones expected of her. But despite getting married, moving to America, and raising children, she couldn't help but feel as though something was missing. On some mornings, as she chopped onions and the *Today* show droned in the background, Bina wondered, *Is this all it amounts to?*

Then when Devi, her closest friend from her acting days, planted the idea about a kitty party, Bina had an aha moment that would have made Oprah Winfrey proud. Something in her stirred for the first time in years as Devi told her about a student who put a kitty party in a script. What if you tried something like this with your married friends? Devi texted. Devi was always calling Bina's friends "your married friends." She got divorced ten years ago and spends her days teaching screenwriting in Los Angeles. Because of the time difference, Bina only gets to interact with her through a series of texts, WhatsApp memes, and a biweekly Zoom call.

Bina loved kitty parties when she lived in Bombay. Every month, women met at someone's house, ate, and talked. After Devi brought it up, Bina knew this was her chance. This was exactly what her life needed, something that brought women together, something that was truly her own and greater than her at the same time.

Bina explained the idea to Anita late last year and suggested they call it Chats Over Chai. (In her know-it-all voice, Suhani later claimed getting together to talk about people is just organized gossiping. But Bina is determined to make the group more than that, even though she thinks it's more than okay to take an interest in other people's lives. This country is so apathetic and detached. Real community means giving a damn about what others are up to!) And most of all, it's a chance for her to do something greater than herself, something that can also potentially give purpose to other women. Bina has heard too many women who came from India promise to do certain things once they were settled in America, once their children were grown up, once their parents were healthy. Year after year, she saw these promises become more distant and smaller.

"Maybe it's okay if you put it off for some time. You've already been so busy for the past two weeks organizing all this," Deepak says.

Bina counts the plates, bowls, and utensils. "You know busy is good for me, especially considering the situation."

Busy makes her forget that her daughter utterly humiliated her and her best friend. Busy lets everyone in Atlanta assume she's just another traditional housewife. Only Deepak and Devi know what can happen if Bina isn't just the right level of busy.

Deepak scans her face. "You're referring to Natasha?"

"Of course I am. I can't stop thinking about her!" Bina says. "Our daughter is out of control!"

The most frustrating part is that Bina was finally starting to accept that maybe she'd done a good job as a mother. She used to have the habit of combing through her regrets the same way she'd go through photo albums, lingering on some moments while moving past others. But over time, as the kids became more settled and she became more secure, that dwindled.

And then what happened with Natasha and Anita made her question everything she filled her days with. Every school lunch she packed, every dish she scrubbed, every countertop she wiped— all of it now seemed to mock her. She hates that her insecurity can be this flimsy, this malleable. Just when she thought it was small enough to be tucked away, something like this happens, and she feels it expanding, consuming all of her.

"There's nothing we can do," Deepak says. "You have to let this all go."

Natasha would be thrilled to hear her dad say this. She idolizes Deepak. All three of their kids do in different ways. They don't have to pick up his socks or cook him elaborate Gujarati meals. Deepak has a habit of making a grand announcement after doing one chore

and then disappearing into their library, where he spends hours buried in a psychiatry textbook. He is so brainy. He is so clueless.

"I can't just let it go," Bina says. "This is a big deal."

Deepak squeezes her shoulders. "I know. But you'll talk it out
with Anita on one of your morning walks and we will all move on."

Bina sighs. Deepak knows about her morning walks and every
other part of her day since he's been home more after scaling down
at work. She gets irritated, then feels guilty for being irritated, at the
nonstop questions. *Do you always drink that many cups of chai every
morning? Why do you chop okra on the cutting board and then carrots on
the counter? Are you still on the phone? What's that you're looking at on
Facebook?*

In those moments, she tells herself that it's just ordinary, run-of-
the-mill marital tension. It'll go away soon enough and make space
for other things. Marriage allows different emotions to run side by
side. Pride and annoyance. Gratitude and frustration.

Friendship does that, too, or at least, that's what she always
thought until now.

"I'm sure Anita hasn't told anyone about the proposal," Deepak
says, reading her face.

"She definitely hasn't. And I know she won't," Bina agrees.
"She's always run away from talking things out. She'd rather pretend they didn't happen at all."

Bina should just scamper across the parking lot and yell it to
everyone, the way the Bina of thirty years ago would have. *The
wedding I've been hyping up to all of you isn't going to happen! Thank you
and have a nice day!* She pictures the expressions on their faces, the
fusion of embarrassment and relief that will build up inside her
after the news is out.

"Anyway, I'm fine," Bina says.

"You're not and it's okay," Deepak says.

Deepak has been able to tell how she is really feeling since the day they met. He came to one of her plays in Bombay and stayed backstage just to speak with her. She immediately noticed his round glasses and the gentleness in his eyes, a combination that made him look inquisitive and curious, like the type of man who stared at a painting and wanted to discuss how it made him feel. His fingers were long and muscular. That night, she'd learn those fingers had helped him play the piano since he was five years old. Years later, Deepak would pass his artistic sensitivity to their son.

They talked until the theater closed and then went to Havmor Ice Cream, where he ordered two large scoops of butterscotch. She stood next to him and watched the way he made the cashier laugh. He carried himself with a sense of confidence that seemed rooted in ease, in being content with who he was, instead of ego like so many of the other slick, rich men who had tried to court her.

An hour later, they sat outside and watched motorcycles and rickshaws putter by as Bombay came alive for the evening. The smell of sugar and the summer air, damp from a recent monsoon, made Bina feel young and full of possibility. Street vendors shouted, "Fresh samosa! Cold soda!" In the high-rise apartments, televisions were turning to the evening news or latest Hindi soap opera. Families started their evening walks. Men wore white cotton tops with work slacks and the women were in jeans or flowing dresses.

Deepak leaned against a cool slab of stone and told Bina he knew she was scared while she performed. *I could see it on your face*, he said. This was years before her confidence would be taken from her, before she'd promise to make sure her future children never doubted themselves the way she did. Bina had been approached by many men by then (with five marriage proposals!), but none of them had the insight to point out her vulnerability or even care about it in the first place. She could be open with this man. She could be herself. She called her parents that night and told them she'd met her husband.

Ma was waiting for Bina when she got home. She was sitting at the dining table, next to a decorative plate with Queen Elizabeth's face on it. Both of Bina's parents loved collecting British royalty memorabilia. Ma's stern expression seemed to match the queen's. *You're making the biggest mistake of your life. That man won't be able to provide you with any of the things you're used to.*

Ma wasn't wrong about the latter part. One week later, Bina sneaked out of her parents' gated house in the middle of the night, to where Deepak waited on his motorcycle two streets away. They moved into the first floor of his college friend's house, where every time Bina had to use the bathroom, she took three flights of rickety stairs to the terrace and hoped that the common toilet was free. She channeled any doubt or frustration into her work, into every role she auditioned for. There were plenty of Bollywood parts where a woman left her family and defied the odds with her husband. A part of Bina relished this overlap between art and life.

But then it happened.

Bina's parents were sure Deepak would leave her after the first incident. But Deepak was at her bedside every single day. He brought her Havmor ice cream and met with the doctors. When she was discharged, he pushed her to act again, find a new project, a new group of people who wouldn't hold what had happened against her.

It happened again one week after Suhani was born. Bina had no idea that giving birth would turn her emotions into tiny tornados, ready to destroy everything in their path. By then, Deepak was in med school and too busy to give Bina the support she needed with the baby. She begged for her parents to take her back, just until she got into a good rhythm. And even though they agreed, it was clear within hours that things between them had permanently shifted.

During that first month postpartum, Bina stayed up every night in her hard, flat childhood bed while beads of milk or sweat trickled down her sore breasts and still-swollen stomach. Ma and Papa didn't have a full-length mirror so it would be weeks before Bina realized how unrecognizable her body was. Not that she had any mental space to focus on herself. She felt like she was underwater, constantly holding her breath. Every ten minutes, she pressed her hand against Suhani's tiny chest and made sure it was still rising and falling. When she told Deepak about her nonstop visions of something bad happening to Suhani, he took her to the doctor, who gave her a one-word diagnosis: hormones. There wasn't enough known about women's minds after giving birth to really say much else. The doctor wrote down a prescription and slid it toward them facedown, as if it was a secret. *Routine and stability are key to helping things get back to normal*, he said. *I don't think acting is in your future.* In a matter of months, Bina went from working next to the biggest movie stars in India to taking orders from Ma on how to just "get over it," "pray harder," and "be stronger."

On Suhani's first birthday, Deepak got a call from a classmate who had moved to Georgia and told him there might be a spot in the residency program the following year. They left the day after their visa was finalized. Deepak worked the overnight shift as a cashier at a gas station in Atlanta. It was the only job that gave him the flexibility to study for his boards and later apply for residency at Atlanta Memorial Hospital.

They lived in a family friend's windowless, mildewed basement during their first five years in Georgia. The adjustment wasn't difficult for Deepak, who was used to sleeping next to family members on the floor of the cramped bungalow he grew up in. Bina did her best to focus on their future. America was there to free them, give them the luxury to build a new life away from any judgment.

But after Deepak started residency and Suhani was enrolled in daycare, the endless days Bina spent alone suffocated her. A neighbor's son made fun of her accent the first time she tried to say hi. They couldn't afford cable or even the gasoline required to make a trip to the area's only Indian grocery store. Her hours went by in a blur of cleaning and cooking and folding and pleasing. She wondered if the problem was really her, if she wouldn't be accepted anywhere. Acting had been her way to slip into different identities, but here, there was no audience for her work, nobody who cared that she was once on her way to becoming someone. She had to face herself. Her raw, real self.

I'm going to lose it in this country, she told Deepak after one of his weekend call shifts. *We have to go back to India even if that means we failed and couldn't make it here.*

They looked up which tickets to Bombay they could afford and lugged their only giant suitcase out from under the bed. The next day, Deepak came home from the hospital and told Bina about Jiten, the only other South Asian doctor he'd met at Atlanta Memorial. They invited Jiten and Anita to their basement apartment, where the four of them ate sautéed chickpeas, rice with yogurt, and lentils. They bonded over their shared love and longing for Bombay as Suhani read her beloved *Corduroy* book.

Bina was sure that her excitement at being able to converse with someone besides Deepak came on too strong. But Anita showed up the next morning with a Tupperware container full of mamra. They shared the puffed rice and cups of chai on a rickety side table Deepak had found at Goodwill. Anita launched into a slew of complaints about their husbands' long hours, the lavish life she left behind in Bombay, and the racist landlord who scowled at her every time she got the mail.

Yes! This is the real her! Bina thought as she relished the catharsis that could only come from freely bitching with another woman.

After that morning, they saw each other every day. Their bond reminded Bina of the kind she'd had with girls when she was in school, rooted in circumstance but sustained by a natural, easy chemistry. Suddenly, all the mundane things that filled Bina's days had a purpose because someone else, someone she cared about, was doing them, too. They both made sure chai was on the table every morning and hot, cumin-spiced food was on the table every night. They both changed bedsheets and ironed dress shirts. They carpooled to the Indian grocery store to pick out the best okra, packages of spices that gleamed like jewels, and Cadbury chocolates. When their husbands worked thirty-six-hour shifts, they spent afternoons at each other's homes, sharing everything from Osh-Kosh B'gosh baby clothes to recipes for vegetarian dishes to childhood stories about Bombay. They piled tiny plates with stacks of Oreos, wrapped their babies in hand-block-printed shawls from Rajasthan, and watched *The Bold and the Beautiful*. They picked each other's families up from the airport. They learned the intricacies of a new country that seemed to oscillate between embracing and rejecting them. They co-planned birthday and anniversary parties with, first, Carvel cakes from the grocery store's frozen section and, later, tiered cakes from a hole-in-the-wall bakery. They learned to speak English without a Gujarati accent and then came to the realization that speaking with an accent didn't make them any less American.

Bina sees all that in a blur now, all those moments that created the scaffolding of their relationship. "I just keep wondering where we—I—went wrong. Natasha has taken us on a ride plenty of times, but it's as though she's committed to being self-destructive."

Deepak gives her the same sympathetic look she imagines he gives his patients when they're in the midst of a crisis. "We have to separate ourselves from what she does. Our kids are adults."

Of course, Bina accepted a long time ago that there are parts of her children she won't have access to. She's heard them lower their voices to whispers late at night, seen them minimize the windows on their laptop screens, and known they put the private settings on their social media accounts. But Suhani and Anuj always made sense to her. Natasha was always equal parts known and unknown, familiar and terrifying.

"You're always so easy on her," Bina says. "And look at where we are now!"

"So you're blaming me for all this?"

Bina sighs. "I didn't say that. It's just that obviously, at some point, we didn't do what she needed."

Mothers might have trouble admitting where they've gone wrong out loud, but they think about it all the time. Bina returns to a thought that she only visits in her lowest moments: *I deserve this.* Ma warned her she'd one day have a daughter who failed her, and only then would she know how it all felt. But until now, Bina never really believed disappointment would be their family heirloom.

"Or we did everything, and at the end of the day, she's her own person," Deepak says.

"That sounds nice, but you and I both know that everyone blames the mother when things go wrong with a kid." Bina purses her lips, which are painted with a new bright-pink shade Suhani bought her from Sephora.

"I'm going to give you some space. It'll be good for you to just not think about this for a little while, okay?" Deepak says in his calmest, most composed psychiatrist voice before he saunters into the parking lot.

I don't want space or solutions! Bina wants to say. *I just want to vent!*

As he walks away, she wonders if her irritation at his being home more is less about him and more about her. Maybe it reminds her that she didn't do enough with her own life.

"Bina! Are you okay?" Kavita, one of her and Anita's closest friends, approaches her.

Bina forces a smile. "Of course. How are you?" One of the best parts of her acting background is that she can always rearrange her face at a moment's notice to convey exactly what she needs. Devi once told Bina she could teach a class on just facial expressions.

"Great! Where can I put these?" Kavita motions to the giant tray of naan in her hands. Pockets of butter and garlic are collecting in the folds of the puffy bread.

Bina sees Mira behind Kavita, carrying a large bowlful of gulab jamun. As much as everyone loves the fried doughnuts, Bina wishes that her friends had listened to her when she said to bring healthy food.

"Ah, thank you for bringing this. I have a special table back here for you." Bina points to a corner away from the temple parking lot. The Indians will all congregate around here anyway. She's tried, again and again, to promote intermingling between her Indian and non-Indian friends, but it's useless. Kavita and Mira often switch to speaking in Gujarati so they can chatter without being understood.

Both Kavita's and Mira's husbands did their residency at Atlanta Memorial Hospital two years after Deepak and Jiten. Everything about them is entertaining, from the bright-colored saris they always wear to the way they oscillate between talking trash one second and seeming polite and well behaved the next.

"Push our dishes closer together," Kavita instructs Mira. "I want to put them both on my Instagram."

"A story or picture post?" Mira asks.

"Obviously, a story," Kavita says. "They aren't pretty enough for a permanent post!"

Bina leaves them as they're discussing the perfect filter. Her friends are obsessed with social media. They've mastered how to use filters and recently started incorporating GIFs into their text messages. Kavita is especially quick with sending ones with the perfect responses. Bina overused her favorite GIF, of Oprah cheering in a powerful red suit.

Bina rejoins Kavita and Mira as they're exchanging the latest complaints about their mothers-in-law. *She needs her chai right in front of her, three times a day, like some kind of high-powered executive. And every day is a different health complaint!*

"I've been meaning to talk to you both about an idea Anita and I have been working on. If you're both free next month . . ." Bina trails off as she notices Anita emerging from her periphery, as if she appeared on cue.

I miss you, Bina thinks as she takes in Anita's blue floral wrap dress, the one Bina picked out for her during their last trip to the outlet stores. A large bowl of mango ras is in her hands. Bina feels a stab of sadness as she inhales the aroma of the sweet dish. Anita knows it's Bina's favorite thing to have in the summer. It's no coincidence that she made it today.

To Bina's surprise, relief washes over her. Maybe Deepak was right. They'll talk everything out now and things will start to get back to the way they're supposed to be.

"How are you?" Bina reaches out to hug her best friend. There's safety and security from just knowing she's right here, next to her.

But Anita's entire body stiffens. "Fine. Just fine." There are prominent lines on her forehead. Her pointy chin is trembling. One of the best things about Anita is that her face always gives her away. From the moment they met, Bina felt that gave her a sense of sincerity.

"No, really," Bina presses. "Are you okay? We haven't talked in days."

Anita's face tightens. She hates confrontation, while Bina thrives on it, always has.

Before Bina can say anything else, Kavita interrupts them. "*Haaaaash*, have you seen Sonam's latest Facebook post?"

"What about it?" Bina asks, hoping Anita will jump in.

"She wrote this very long nonsense about how she believes men 'need to do more housework' and how she feels that her future husband better be ready to 'pull his weight.' And then she ends it with some research on 'emotional labor.' Can you believe that?!"

Mira and Anita nod in agreement with Kavita's disapproval of the post.

"So many of us have taken pride in just doing what's expected of us and not complaining. These young women are now finally speaking up! Isn't that good?" Bina asks.

"Good?" Kavita peers at Bina as though her eyes are adjusting to the light. "No wonder Sanjay hasn't proposed to her! I'd been giving him so much trouble for not asking, but now I realize why. The poor boy is scared."

Kavita hasn't been quiet about the fact that she's been waiting for Sonam's longtime boyfriend, Sanjay, to pop the question. She even bought herself designer saris and new diamond jewelry during her last trip to India. *I'll probably need all of it soon*, she'd said, beaming.

"I'm sure Sanjay already knows how she thinks," Bina says. "They've been together for a long time."

"These girls." Kavita shakes her head. "They think they can just mouth off and say whatever they want, do whatever they want. I thought it was an American thing and told Bipin that maybe we should have stayed in India. But apparently, the girls in the big cities there are just as outspoken."

"I don't think that's a bad thing," Bina says. They've all practiced so many types of parenting—attachment, tiger, helicopter—but none of them have helped them understand their kids more. Bina mentally records this as another thing they can discuss in their group.

"Ha, you wouldn't!" Kavita scoffs. "But even your Natasha knows when to stay quiet."

"I wouldn't be so sure about that," Bina says.

Mira turns toward her. "What do you mean?"

Anita widens her eyes and shoots Bina a look that says, *Don't say any more*. Bina can feel her friend's fear in a way that's only possible when you've been on the same wavelength with someone for years.

But despite that, Bina suddenly knows she can't stay quiet. Since when has that helped anything? Maybe if she had spoken up years ago, she would be living a completely different life.

She ignores the pressure of the words building inside her. "Karan proposed and Natasha said no."

"What?" Kavita asks, as though she didn't hear Bina.

Mira, for once, is speechless. They all turn to face Anita. The color has drained from her face. She gazes at Bina with a mixture of irritation and shock. "Y-yes. Karan asked."

"When?" Kavita asks.

"Two weeks ago," Bina says. "At our house."

"And Natasha said no?" Kavita asks. "Why?"

"Who knows?" Bina makes sure to sound blasé, like the type of evolved woman who can deliver shocking news without flinching. "But these kids—all our kids—have to decide what they want to do with their lives."

"But . . . but I was sure they'd be getting married next year." Mira frowns and is surely picturing the saris and intricate pearl jewelry sets she'd already planned to wear for Natasha and Karan's events. Before Suhani's wedding, Mira sent Bina dozens of pictures of her proposed outfits. It was as though her own daughter was the one getting married.

Anita stares at the concrete floor as if there's an answer there. Bina waits for her to chime in. When she doesn't, Bina adds, "Well, they're not. And that's that."

Finally, it's out. She feels lighter. Like a weight's been lifted, she thinks, understanding the phrase she's heard a million times.

This is what she had to do. She and Anita can move on now. And all of them can figure out a date for the first Chats Over Chai meeting.

She's about to say just that, but Anita starts walking away. "I have to get going."

"Wait," Bina urges at the same time Mira and Kavita murmur something along the same lines.

"No, no, no, I really should get going," Anita stammers.

And without another word, Bina watches her best friend run into the parking lot, get into her black Lexus, and drive away.

Four

Deepak

Anita and Bina will figure this out between themselves," Jiten says in the hospital cafeteria two days after the health fair. Jiten made statements like this often with a wave of his hand, statements that gave away that Anita handled all social ties for their family.

"They always do," Chand agrees. His tray has a bowl of black bean soup and foil-wrapped rotlis. "Mira worries so much about offending people. I always remind her we're all friends, right? We can all let these things go, not allow them to get in the way."

"Oh, I tell Kavita not to even get me involved in any of the ladies' drama." Bipin laughs.

Jiten and Chand nod in agreement. Deepak stays silent. He and Bina tell each other everything. They always have.

Or at least they did before the proposal. In the two weeks since Natasha rejected Karan, Bina spends her mornings locked in their bathroom and her nights on drives alone. Deepak tries to imagine where she goes but never asks. He learned years ago not to talk to her when she's in this state.

Bina hasn't taken drives like this since the kids were little. Every time he hears the slam of the door leading to the garage, the whoosh of her car's tires on their U-shaped driveway, he's taken back to those evenings when she'd shout, *I didn't sign up for this kind of life*, and then leave. He knew she didn't want him to come after her. He knew she always came back.

Throughout his thirty-five years practicing psychiatry, Deepak's seen that people will do a lot to avoid feeling discomfort: drinking, eating, drugs, burying memories, wrapping their identity around an entirely different life. But the discomfort always comes back unless it's processed.

And Bina never really processed what happened in Bombay. She hasn't accepted that in many ways, the life she didn't live has shaped their family as much as the one she has.

"Orthopedic surgery." Jiten snaps his fingers, making Deepak realize he missed a part of their conversation. "That's the field I would have gone into if I had the choice."

"Pediatric surgery," Chand says. "I could see myself bringing the kids candy and balloons. You know, being like Patch Adams."

Deepak laughs. He can see that, too. Both Chand and Mira are natural performers.

"Plastics for me," Bipin chimes in. "Although I do like GI more than I thought I would."

"I wouldn't change anything," Deepak says.

"You'd choose to work with the *gandos*? Why?" Bipin asks, echoing a sentiment Deepak heard again and again in India. Nobody's supposed to want to work with the "crazy" people. People often assume Deepak went into psychiatry because it wasn't as competitive as the other fields, which meant it was attainable for a foreign medical school graduate. But Deepak would have picked it even if he went to Harvard and graduated at the top of his class.

"Since I've stepped back and gotten closer to retiring, I've been missing work even more than I thought I would. This is the best field. And the one everyone needs exposure to," Deepak says. Even though his words are sincere, none of them knows the reason he picked psychiatry in the first place.

"Well, Anita always said you're the most pensive man she knows," Jiten says. "It makes sense that you enjoy thinking about people all day."

Deepak laughs. Bina and the kids always tell him he's lost in his own thoughts, unaware of what's going on in the world. But he notices a lot. He sees Suhani falling asleep while Zack tries to talk to her. He sees Natasha running to her room when she hears him and Bina downstairs. He sees Anuj keeping everything inside, for the sake of peace.

He wants to tell them it will all be okay eventually. They've been through much worse than this. But he knows they aren't ready to listen. Families break when everyone argues to win, not understand. So that's what he'll do.

He'll help them understand.

Five

Natasha

"I can't believe you've been working on this for months behind all our backs," Anuj says. He stretches and leans back in Natasha's black leather chair until his toes rest on her desk. He used to sit in her room like this all the time, alternating between doing calculus problems and talking to Natasha while she was busy thinking of more ways to procrastinate on her homework. Unlike Suhani, who always nagged Natasha—"if you'd try even a little, you could get better grades"—Anuj left her alone.

"I've had to," Natasha says. "And I can't believe it's actually happening in a few hours. I have to kick ass."

"Don't worry. You'll be fine." Anuj gives the same lackadaisical smile he's had since he was a toddler. He never seems to have a worry in the world. Must be nice. "And, hey, if you change your mind about telling anyone, you can always send them to your You-Tube channel!"

"Do *not* send that to anyone!" Natasha commands. Anuj is going to record her tonight so she finally has something to put on her still-nonexistent YouTube comedy channel. But nobody can see it.

"It's weird enough that I have to talk in public about how I lost my job. The last thing I need is for Mom or Dad or Suhani to be reminded of that," she says. "And anyway, if I make it to the next round, I have a chance to get a secure spot to perform every month at the comedy club. And maybe after that, maybe, we can tell them. I mean, a routine spot and Alexis's class should put me in a pretty good place."

Alexis Diaz, an Atlanta-based comedian, teaches an improv class multiple times a year. Natasha registered seconds after the link was active. She doesn't like improv (okay, it actually terrifies her) but she kept reading that learning how to think spontaneously helped a lot of comedians with their stand-up. Plus, Alexis Diaz is her idol. Natasha's been following her career for two years and waiting for the chance to meet her. The class sign-up was first come, first serve, and when Natasha got the confirmation e-mail, she took it as a sign that things were finally clicking into place. She was on the right path now. In months, she'll be performing and proving everyone wrong. Mom will be in the front row whistling and tapping the person next to her in excitement. *That's my daughter!*

Natasha's phone buzzes three times in a row. She's missed the first part of a conversation on an Instagram group thread with her two closest friends from college: Payal and Ifeoma. They met in the dorms after first-year orientation and instantly connected over a craving for Taco Bell. Payal, the only one with a car, drove them to the nearest one an hour later.

The plan was to pick up food and then get some sleep before the first day of classes. But Natasha convinced them to open the giant bottle of Prosecco she had taken from Suhani's apartment. The three of them sat on Natasha's hard, cold dorm floor, drank from red Solo cups, and drizzled hot sauce on a pile of bean burritos and chalupas. They made it halfway through the bottle when Ifeoma told them her mother was leaving her father and moving back to Nigeria.

Natasha wasn't sure if it was the jarring sense of freedom from no longer being under Mom and Dad's roof or the pangs of missing her siblings, but she found herself opening up to the girls about her family in a way she hadn't known was possible.

They kept talking in that hushed, free way that's only possible during conversations that happen in the middle of the night. When Payal noticed it was six a.m., they walked to the shared bathroom and stood at adjacent sinks as they washed their faces with Clean & Clear.

They lived together for the rest of their time at Georgia State. Every other month, Ifeoma and Payal went home with Natasha and spent the entire weekend in their pajamas, eating Cape Cod chips and watching *Sex and the City*.

The last message in the thread is from Payal, who sent a post from her favorite account, betches: One cannot drink cheap wine.

NATASHA: Since when do you drink cheap wine? Or cheap anything?

PAYAL: Good point. And there you are! We haven't heard from you in days.

NATASHA: Yea, sorry, been MIA because of working on stuff.

PAYAL: How are you? Did your mom come around?

NATASHA: No way. She's still freaking out and taking it personally like she always does.

Payal and her mom have one of those mother-daughter relationships Natasha thought was only part of fables. They share everything with each other, rarely argue, and even go on trips together.

Natasha's always been intrigued and jealous of their Rory and Lorelai Gilmore vibes.

IFEOMA: Any word from Karan?

NATASHA: Nah. Don't expect to hear from him, either. And my parents are still so pissed.

PAYAL: I bet. My mom told me to line up some dates after she heard about it. It's like she thinks what happened to you is contagious and we're all going to end up alone.

NATASHA: My mom is convinced I am. I'm sure she still has hope for the rest of you. At least you're on the apps and Ifeoma is already part of a power couple.

Ifeoma met her boyfriend, Jordan, during her first year of law school at Emory. They live together in Decatur.

IFEOMA: You knew it wasn't right for you. It's like when Carrie knew she couldn't end up with Aidan, so she wore his ring on her necklace and got all awkward and stuff.

NATASHA: True. Btw, do you realize how many shows work because none of the characters are children of immigrants? Carrie didn't have her mom calling her every five minutes asking her when the wedding planning could start and if she could invite all ten thousand of her actor friends from Bombay.

PAYAL: LOL, true! What does Suhani think of all this?

Payal always wants to know what Suhani thinks. She's a younger version of Suhani, pretty and premed.

NATASHA: She's keeping her opinions to herself for now. I'm sure she'll lecture me soon. Can't even blame her. I thought I was going to have babies with that guy, y'all. Like literally, a little version of him.

PAYAL: I get it. You have to distract yourself so you stop thinking about him. What are you doing today?

NATASHA: Not much . . . you?

She could tell them. She should. But something holds her back. Maybe it's a shift in perspective, a newfound awareness of how her life is in comparison to theirs. During her four years at Georgia State, Natasha couldn't wait to be a real adult. She pictured her future as a bright and shiny thing, full of possibility. That kind of blind optimism might have been sweet and even a bit badass in college. Now it just seems pathetic.

IFEOMA: You should practice some self-care. And do not look at Karan's Instagram. He hasn't updated it anyway, but it'll just make you feel shitty to see old pics.

NATASHA: I'll stay away. Promise.

"You're going to be great. You've always been the funniest person in the room," Anuj says as Natasha puts her phone facedown. Anuj has been wearing the same outfit since he got into Cornell's architecture program: a red Cornell sweatshirt and basketball shorts.

The knot of stress behind Natasha's sternum starts to loosen. Anuj always believes in her, and now, more than ever, she needs that: someone who sees her better than how she sees herself.

"Why not at least tell Suhani and Zack?" Anuj says.

Natasha frowns. "Why do you keep pushing me?"

"Because it might be nice?" Anuj fiddles with a stack of old CDs: TLC, Spice Girls, Backstreet Boys. When they were younger and had graduated from building forts out of blankets and pillows, she and Anuj would make teetering, Jenga-like towers out of Suhani's CDs.

"Nice? Nice?! You've got to be kidding me. It would suck. This is hard enough without any of them knowing about it. You know they'd find a way to make me feel even shittier about myself, especially after everything that happened with Karan. They think I'm the worst."

And sometimes I believe them, she thinks. She hates the way her self-esteem seems to shift every day, sometimes every hour. On some days she's ready to take on her new life, and on others she wakes up drenched in sweat, convinced she's fucked up yet another thing.

"Jeez, fine, I get it." Anuj shakes his head. He's grown his hair out past his ears so it's curling at the ends.

Natasha sighs. Why did she have to snap and go on a rant like that? Anuj was only asking.

She needs to get a grip. But without her job, she no longer has insurance. Her last therapy appointment was two weeks ago. The serotonin is probably bouncing around in her brain like Pop Rocks candy.

"What if I made a mistake? With the whole Karan situation?" Natasha asks.

Anuj puts the CDs down. "Is that what you really think?"

"I don't know. It's just so weird not even talking to him." Natasha sometimes feels as though she's lost a limb. And it isn't just the Karan of today she's had to let go of. It's the two-year-old Karan, who shared his sliced grapes with her, and then twenty-year-old Karan, who spooned with her on a twin bed in her dorm. Breaking up with someone means leaving all of their selves.

"I can't tell if walking away from something like that means I'm really brave or just really dumb. It's so weird how in a matter of days, my life looks totally different than what I thought it would. And obviously our parents also wanted it to work out."

"And since when do you let our parents tell you what to do? Or anyone?" Anuj smiles at her in that same knowing way he has since they were toddlers. In general, Anuj was a total do-gooder, but Natasha could always convince him to live a little.

"You're right," Natasha admits. "But sometimes I do wonder, even though people have told me it's good I speak my mind and do what I want, is that really what they want? Or deep down, does everyone hope that I just accommodate to fit some traditional mold?"

Natasha once saw a documentary about how girls and boys are encouraged to "dream big" when they're young but only girls are later judged if their ambitions get in the way of their becoming mothers and wives.

"*Natasha! Anuj! Dinner!*" Mom yells from downstairs.

Anuj opens Natasha's bedroom door. "*Be right there.*"

"I don't want another night of Indian food," Natasha says. "Let's head out for the show. We can pick something up on the way."

"Now?" Anuj looks up from his iPad. "I thought you didn't have to be there for two hours."

"I don't, but I can't stand being in this house. And I definitely can't sit across from Mom at the dinner table for another night."

Anuj shrugs. "It's not that bad."

But for Natasha, it really is. Everything seems to bother her these days: not having a job, the patriarchy, her unruly eyebrows. She can't even distract herself with social media scrolling because everyone else is thriving. Just an hour ago, she saw that Brian Wilkins, who left her in the middle of prom to hook up with the captain of the cheerleading squad, is now an Instagram influencer. Sure, she hasn't spoken to Brian since prom and should stop hate following him because he's no longer relevant to her life. But that's not the point. Because even aside from Brian, so many other people from her high school keep posting pictures of their glittering diamond rings or fancy jobs. And they all seem to be going on beautiful vacations, sipping jewel-toned cocktails, or looking out at some gaping body of water, while she's struggling and alone. This is not how things were supposed to be when she was twenty-three.

She forces herself to focus. Everyone else's perfect lives don't matter. What matters is that she has work to do. She has a life to start building.

From a rumpled stack of clothes in the corner of her closet, Natasha pulls out a pair of ripped jeans and one of Suhani's black shirts. One of the only perks of being home is that she can steal her sister's clothes the same way she used to when they were younger.

Mom's sitting at the dining table when Natasha and Anuj come downstairs. She's wearing her thick black reading glasses and flipping through an issue of *Vogue India: Bridal Edition*. An old episode of *Seinfeld* is on TV. Mom and Dad watched that show all the time when the kids were little. Once, on a family trip to New York City, Mom saw the actor who played George and ran across the street to tell him how much she loved him.

"We're going out to eat dinner," Natasha says. "Be back later."

"Natasha, so nice of you to finally come out of your room. You're going out again?" Mom looks up from her magazine. A giant photograph of a way-too-thin Indian model wearing a red wedding lehenga and heavy gold jewelry is on the page.

"Yeah, I've gotta see my friend in a show."

"How great that your friends are so important." Mom raises her eyebrows and mutters some Sanskrit mumbo jumbo about evil spirits and omens. It's the same stuff she lights incense and does hour-long prayer ceremonies for. "And what's so wrong with eating dinner with your parents?"

"Nothing's wrong with that," Natasha mutters, even though they both know that's the last thing she wants to do. She won't admit now (or maybe ever) that a lot of people would love to have dinner with Mom. But they got a different person. They got a funny, charismatic, lighthearted Indian auntie who listens to rap and seems so progressive in her thinking. Natasha's the only one who gets a critical, moody woman whose words are blades, ready to slice up any self-confidence Natasha has.

"Right," Mom says. "Just reminding you that this isn't a hotel, okay? Anyway, Chand called an hour ago and asked that you get in touch with him."

"For what?"

Chand Uncle, one of their close family friends, always brings his karaoke machine to parties and then belts way too loudly to Bollywood songs from the eighties.

"He might have a temp job in billing for you at his office."

"I don't need a job from him!"

"Why? Do you already have one in the works?" Mom asks. "And I mean a real job. Something that gives you money."

"Not yet. But I'm figuring it out." Natasha feels like such a loser when she says stuff like that out loud.

She and Mom frown at each other as Anuj clears his throat. She wishes Mom would just say, *Okay, I trust you. I understand you're doing the best you can.*

Instead, Mom mutters, "Of course, you always have it all figured out. Why do I even bother?"

"Thanks for the support," Natasha says.

"You don't think we are supporting you? You're staying here, aren't you? Do you even understand how lucky you are to have a place to live and eat and have everything taken care of for you?"

"Trust me, this is not ideal for me," Natasha says, raising her voice.

"Ah, not ideal for you. I'm so glad we uprooted our lives and moved to America so our children could go to bars and party with their friends." Mom says this as she faces the kitchen. She does this a lot: makes dramatic statements that seem directed to nobody on the surface but are really supposed to be a jab at Natasha. Maybe she got this habit from her career onstage.

"Wow, another guilt trip about how I'm not good enough!" Natasha says. "I'm so sorry you couldn't be an actress because you had to move here, but if we could go, like, a week without hearing about your sacrifices, that'd be great."

Mom looks at Anuj for support. "You're going, too?"

Anuj shrugs his shoulders and hesitates for a second. "Don't worry, Mom. We won't be too late."

Mom's nostrils flare. "So, anyway, ho—"

"We have to go. C'mon. Now," Natasha interrupts before Anuj can suggest they change the subject or, worse, talk things out.

Two hours later, Anuj is all set up in the front row to record Natasha's first ever performance.

Natasha rushes backstage, where she's directed to a cramped, dark waiting room that reeks of sweat and cheap beer. Her head is starting to pound from the four tequila shots she downed after she and Anuj ate at Bartaco. Ten other comedians are lingering in the hallway. A few seem as nervous as she feels, but some of the others have an aloof air about them that comes off as confidence in this type of situation. She's the only woman of color back here. Typical.

"Uh, I think you spilled something on your shirt," a thin brunette stage assistant says as she points to Natasha's chest.

"Shit." A streak of guacamole and salsa is across her left boob. "It's my sister's shirt. She's going to freak out."

The stage assistant nods and gives Natasha a sympathetic look as if she understands that Suhani is an uptight perfectionist.

Natasha hears the audience roaring with laughter at the current comedian. Great. Of course she's after someone amazing. She grabs a paper towel. The food comes off, but there's still a large wet circle outlining her boob.

"Perfect," she says. "I look like I'm breastfeeding. Why the fuck does it have to be my sister's shirt? And why doesn't she ever spill anything? It just makes the rest of us look bad."

"Ha," the assistant offers. "I have a sister with a shirt, too, if you know what I mean."

"Oh, I definitely know what you mean," Natasha says. "And I'm glad I'm not the only one."

She makes her way to the cracked, rusty mirror in the back of the room. She once saw Tina Fey pump herself up in front of a mirror during an episode of *30 Rock*, and since then, she does the same before anything that sends her anxiety into overdrive.

"You've got this," she tells her reflection. "Just get out there and do you. Don't think about your competition. This is your moment."

Granted, she didn't think her moment would be in a place that has crushed peanuts and crumpled wet beer-bottle labels on the floor, but it's still her first time to show what she can do, and that counts for something.

Natasha's phone lights up with a text from Suhani. It's a GIF of Amy Poehler doing a peace sign.

The assistant taps her shoulder. "Are you ready?"

"Yup." Natasha takes deep breaths and hopes they slow her heart down.

"Next, we have Natasha Joshi," a chubby thirtysomething guy says in a monotone voice.

Good, he got her name right. The Joshi children were used to people assuming their first name was "Josh." Every time Natasha was called to the principal's office, a hesitant voice on the intercom would say something along the lines of, "Uh, Josh Natasha, the principal needs to see you."

"Please remember to make as much noise as possible," Monotonous Guy continues. "This will help our judges pick the four contestants that will move to the next round. The contestants will be picked later this week, so make sure to follow us on Instagram and Twitter if you don't already. Now, without further ado, let's bring out Natasha Joshi."

There's a soft ripple of applause and then a murmur from the audience.

Natasha wipes her slick palms on the sides of her jeans and steps onto the stage. The light is so bright that she can see scuff marks and spots where the polish has worn away. Her stomach does somersaults. A blast of air-conditioning hits her face when she steps in front of the microphone. Luckily, it's at her height. Even though the room is dark, she can tell that it's a full house. Fuck. She scans the crowd for Anuj but can't distinguish him from the other silhouettes in the front row.

"Hi, everyone," she breathes into the microphone. "Wow, there sure are a lot of people here."

Silence.

Why did she start with that? She's supposed to get right into the story of how she got fired. This always happens to her. She thinks she's going to conquer something, and then, when the moment comes, she freezes. Her brain tries to pull up an image of her notes but comes up blank.

C'mon, c'mon, c'mon. Just say anything.

Seconds pass. There's just the sound of her breath on the microphone, her pulse in her ears. This is what she gets for procrastinating on rehearsing this routine. She deserves this.

"Say something!" someone hisses from the crowd. Another person cheers in agreement.

Natasha shifts onto the balls of her feet. "So, uh . . . yeah, stuff has changed in my life lately. And by that I mean it's been a shit week." *Shit.* "I, uh, was supposed to be engaged right now."

A snicker passes through the crowd.

Natasha sighs. "Yeah, me, the sloppy Indian chick with a breast-feeding stain on her shirt actually had a guy. A cute guy."

She focuses on a forty-year-old white guy in the front. His bushy eyebrows are raised.

"You don't believe me, do you?" She points to him and his entire table laughs. "Well, it's true. My cute boyfriend proposed and I said no. Why? Hm. Good question."

"Woo!" A group of women cheer from the back corner. Natasha makes out a tiara and sash. Ah, a bachelorette party. Perfect.

"I think I see a bride back there." Natasha shields her eyes with her hand.

Everyone turns to face the bachelorette. Some people clap.

"Yeah. You, the bride. Congratulations. I really mean that. You're exactly who my family wishes I was," Natasha says. "Oooh my family. My desi family. They've got a lot of opinions about me not being with this guy. But they really don't know what I was dealing with. We women, we really put up with a lot, am I right? And we do it with a fucking smile!"

And then, because of the alcohol, her nerves, and something else, something that feels bigger than her, Natasha goes into a rant about how sex with Karan had gotten boring, how it was true that guys who were cute weren't that great in bed, and how she couldn't see herself just being with this one guy forever.

Cheers pass through the entire crowd. One woman even whistles. Natasha sees two of the women in the bachelorette party stand up and raise their hands in agreement.

A rush of excitement and pure, adrenaline-driven thrill pass through her. *Is this how it's supposed to be?* She's never felt so alive, so connected to something greater than herself. It's a high that's bigger than anything she's experienced before. Every part of her feels like it's floating.

"I get that I'm the fucked up one here, okay?" Natasha grabs the microphone and paces up and down the stage. "I'm supposed to want this stuff. But it's complicated. And how do you explain to your boyfriend and your family that you're just not right in the head? Like, I always assume the worst is going to happen, okay? It comes from this little thing I struggle with called *anxiety*. Can any of you imagine telling your mom—your Indian, set-in-her-ways mom—that there's no way you can think about getting married? Because you think too much about everything? Your brain is so fried that even your vibrator isn't doing it for you? I mean, *hello*?"

A woman by the bar yells, *"Word!"* There's another round of cheers.

Natasha smiles. "And for all you married people, I'm happy for you, but fuck off."

The rest of Natasha's segment continues this way, addictive cycles of buildup and catharsis. She feels like she's watching herself from above the stage.

After all the comedians are done, she goes into the audience to find Anuj. Every few seconds, someone taps her shoulder and tells her she did a great job. Her face starts to hurt from beaming. For the first time in weeks, maybe years, she's on a high that's better than any drug she's ever tried. Maybe things can really turn around. Maybe she didn't ruin her life after all.

Six

Anuj

Anuj uploads Natasha's stand-up comedy video to her YouTube channel.

Perfect. He was able to lower the sound of cackling from one cluster of people in the audience, so Natasha's voice is clear and easy to follow. There's also a filter that gives Natasha a soft glow.

Ha! So much for those two guys in middle school who would push him into his locker and taunt him with questions like, "Yo, Mr. India, are you gonna fix my computer or what?"

If he could go back, he'd say, "Yes, I am, actually. And I'll fix your printer, too."

Of course, after Natasha spread a rumor that both of the guys had micropenises, they never bothered Anuj again. But still. How fun would it be to just give them a piece of his mind now?

He watches the video for the hundredth time. When Natasha's nerves don't paralyze her, she's hilarious—and in a universal way on top of that. He used to ask her why she felt the need to react to everything. Now he sees that quality is what makes her so funny. She gives a shit. She's moved by the world.

People often called her the "difficult" or "problem" child, but

Anuj wonders if that's just code for the child who feels the most in a family.

He gets out of bed and runs to her room. The sound of hip-hop music vibrates through her door, which still has a DO NOT ENTER sign Natasha got in middle school.

Anuj knocks on the white painted wood. "Natasha? Want to come down?"

They should go downstairs, open a tub of ice cream, and ask Mom and Dad to watch *Jeopardy!* with them. The ice cream and *Jeopardy!* combination was a tradition usually reserved for Dad's post-call days. It never failed to put their parents in a good mood. Or at least, a good enough one, which is a lot considering how often Mom and Natasha have been at each other's throats lately.

Anuj's phone buzzes with a text for the third time since they got home.

> KARAN: Hey, can we chat sometime? I know things are kind of weird right now but was just wondering if you're at all free . . .

Ah, the ellipsis. Classic. How is he supposed to respond? His gut tells him to ask Natasha first. But he should say something. Karan's been like a brother to him for years. He taught Anuj how to play *Mario Kart*, study for the SATs, pick the right beer. And now Anuj is supposed to act like he's a stranger?

> ANUJ: Hey man, I get that. It's a little hectic around here so let me keep you posted.

He puts his phone on silent and tucks it back into the pocket of his basketball shorts.

"Natasha? You there?" He knocks again.

"I'm not coming down. You go ahead. I'm going to go to bed," Natasha says a few seconds before she makes the music even louder.

They both know that's not true. Natasha never sleeps this early. But she's clearly in her leave-me-alone mode, as Suhani calls it. Funny enough, the first time Anuj heard about Natasha's leave-me-alone mode was when Suhani left for college and Natasha missed her so much that she locked herself in her room and cried. Mom and Dad told Anuj not to say anything about it but the thing was, he also wanted Suhani back home. He also wanted Mom and Dad to tell him she'd come visit soon. But there was just no space for his reactions when Natasha's were the focus.

"All right, good night," Anuj says now.

Mom and Dad are watching one of those black-and-white Bollywood movies. The sounds of sitar and tabla fill the first floor. Mom studies the movies for technique, while Dad usually cries, moved by the long-lost-lovers story lines.

The first time Anuj saw his parents watch a Bollywood movie was when he was in preschool. Mom had gone on one of her drives. Anuj, Natasha, and Suhani sat at the top of the staircase and waited for the headlights of Mom's car to illuminate the driveway. Hours later, Mom emerged through the door and apologized to Dad. They went into the living room and put on a Bollywood movie as though nothing happened.

Now, Anuj stops in the kitchen, which still smells like the roasted okra and rotli his parents had for dinner. He pops several Goldfish into his mouth, his favorite late-night snack, and then goes toward the living room. Every few seconds, he passes a painting from India of men and women in a circle. Mom bought several of them during a summer trip they took when Anuj was a toddler.

Ever since then, he feels like he sees these paintings in every Indian person's house, these scenes of nocturnal social gatherings, where the women showed a lot of cleavage.

Dad's voice is low, almost inaudible, as Anuj gets closer to the television. If only they could see how Natasha kicked ass tonight.

"You should tell her," Dad whispers.

"Absolutely not!" Mom says, not whispering back (Mom doesn't ever really whisper). "What makes you even think that would be helpful?"

"It could be a way for you to come closer together. Maybe she'll understand you better."

"Psh, she will not at all. Trust me, she's different with me than she is with you."

"I know, but if you maybe shared what it was like to be in the hospital and take that medication, she mi—"

"She might what?" Mom has an edge to her voice. "Not ever look at me the same way again?"

"Um, hey," Anuj says as he plays with the strings on his red hoodie. His eyes travel to the amorphous silhouette of his parents cuddling on the couch. It's moments like these that remind Anuj that Mom and Dad are the only ones in their friends' circle who did not have an arranged marriage. None of the other uncles and aunties ever cuddled, kissed, or even held hands.

"Anuj!" Mom immediately perks up. "I thought you were upstairs."

"I couldn't sleep," Anuj says. "What have you been up to?"

Two bowls of melted chocolate ice cream are on the coffee table in front of them. Ice cream soup, Anuj used to call it.

Dad yawns. "Just watching a movie. Before I forget to tell you,

Bipin Uncle is coming over tomorrow morning, you know, in case you want to talk to him about med school applications."

Bipin Uncle recently joined the admissions committee at Emory med school. The dude is everywhere, on the board of the hospital, involved with the national Gujarati newspaper, and now, with Emory med school. He's also scary as shit. Anuj always liked his wife, Kavita Auntie, but Bipin Uncle was the one parents brought up as the quintessential disciplinarian desi parent. *Oh, you think we're strict? Bipin Bhai sent his kids to boarding school in India when they behaved like this!*

"Dad, I don't need to talk to him. I'm in the architecture program." Anuj points to his sweatshirt, which just reads CORNELL in block letters. If only it read CORNELL ARCHITECTURE. Then this would be the perfect moment for a Friday-night family sitcom.

"I'm just suggesting you keep an open mind. You only completed one year of college and you can apply to med school with any major," Dad reminds Anuj for the fifteenth time this week.

Anuj sighs. Maybe he shouldn't have chosen a summer internship in Atlanta over staying in Ithaca. Dad could be so progressive: telling Anuj it was okay to cry and show his emotions, buying him poetry books from independent bookstores, encouraging him to watch foreign films.

Dad could be so old-fashioned: insisting Anuj be a doctor, believing it's always a man's role to court a woman (hence, he doesn't know Anuj is on Bumble), viewing America like some stern parent who has to be both respected and feared.

In therapy, the therapy only Natasha knows about, Anuj learned that the contradictory expectations and underlying message that no achievement is ever enough prevent him from fully opening up to his parents or even to his friends, no matter how supportive and easygoing they are. Despite everything Dad's said, Anuj still doesn't ever feel that he can truly be vulnerable with anyone outside of Natasha.

As if hearing his thoughts, Mom asks, "And how is your sister?"

Whenever she's mad at Natasha, she refers to her in relation to other people.

"She's fine. Going to bed," Anuj says. "What were you both talking about before I came in here?"

A flash of worry crosses Mom's face. But then she smiles. "*Kai nai.*"

"It didn't sound like nothing," Anuj says. "Everything okay?"

"Of course it is, *beta*. You should get some rest," Dad says.

He and Mom shift their focus back to the movie. Anuj lingers by the edge of the sofa to see if they'll retract their words or at least elaborate. When they stay silent, he turns around and heads to his room, telling himself he didn't hear a thing.

Seven

Suhani

"Our moms are going to kill us for eating out," Zack says as he thumbs through the large menu at Highland Bakery.

"Well, tomorrow we're eating out with yours, so she can't get mad at that," Suhani says, referring to the Sunday-evening tradition of going out for Chinese food, the same one Zack's family had growing up.

"Oh, she'll definitely get mad if she sees our fridge. Let's make sure to meet her in the lobby," Zack says.

One Indian mom plus one Jewish mom equals a fridge that's constantly full of food. Suhani feels a twinge of guilt as she pictures the untouched Pyrex containers full of paneer, chole, babka, and matzoh balls. She's in awe of how much patience both their moms must have to spend so many hours stirring and sautéing and seasoning. She gives herself a pat on the back for just cutting a pineapple. It takes so much more effort than she realized when she was a kid, just like a lot of things Mom did and Suhani didn't notice because she was too absorbed in her own life.

While both their moms cook to show love, Barbara's desire is also partially rooted in a survival instinct. Zack's dad, a family med doctor with alcoholism, used to come home and break things in a fit of rage.

He walked out on them when Zack was six, and since then, Barbara splits her time between working double shifts as an ER nurse and cooking for her children. *Ever since he left us, she's been obsessed with making sure we're never deprived*, Zack told Suhani on their first date. Barbara lives alone in East Cobb and splits her time between Atlanta, New York, and Portland, where Zack's three older sisters live.

When Suhani first met Barbara, she immediately liked her hot-pink scrubs, silver curls, and I-don't-give-a-crap attitude. Sure, she guilt trips Zack for not calling enough and gets aggressive about wanting a grandchild, but all in all she's a great mother-in-law. Everything she does is coated with a consuming and unwavering warmth. Though she has a lot in common with Mom, she also does things Mom would never do, like taking Suhani to dimly lit cocktail bars, sending someone to clean their apartment every month, and cheering Suhani when she kept her name as Suhani Joshi instead of changing it to Suhani Kaplan.

A waitress approaches their table. "Hi, I'm Meg. Can I take your drinks order?"

"I'll have a coffee and mimosa, thank you," Suhani says.

"Great." Meg scribbles the items on a thin notepad. She does a double take at Suhani and Zack. "How about, er, your, uh, how about you?"

"My husband will have a Bloody Mary." Suhani puts her sparkling engagement and wedding rings on full display. "Thank you so much."

When Meg walks away, Zack leans forward and rubs Suhani's hand. "I love how you said 'husband' like you were saying 'Mr. President.'"

"I had to. Don't tell me you didn't see the look on her face. She didn't think we could be together."

"You think everyone feels that way," Zack says.

"Because they do!" Suhani shakes her head. "We could have this conversation a million times and you still don't get it."

"I do get it. I really do." Zack lets out a loud sigh. "You just get so worked up."

They're interrupted by Meg, who puts down a mimosa, a large mug of coffee, a Bloody Mary, and two glasses of ice water. Zack keeps his hands over Suhani's and smiles as if to say, *See? I'm showing her!*

Of course it's easy for Zack to not notice how people look at them. He's a cute white guy. He's never had to feel like an outsider or wonder whether he belongs somewhere. And then when he's conscious about his privilege, he gets to be the considerate, cute white guy!

"So, are we going to talk about Thursday night?" Zack asks, referring to his work event at Canoe, where Zack's company reserved a table with a stunning view of the water.

"I think we have to," Suhani says. "I'm so sorry . . . again."

"I know you are, honey. And I'm really sorry for overreacting," Zack says as he cuts a cinnamon roll down the middle.

"You never overreact." Suhani scoffs. "That's really more my area of expertise."

Zack hates yelling because of how much his dad used to do it. Sometimes, when he and Suhani get into their most heated arguments, Zack shuts down, while she can keep going and going. Her mind drifts to a couples' therapy point she highlighted in one of her textbooks: "The person who marries you really sees the worst of you in a way nobody else does."

Confusion passes over Zack's clean-shaven face. "I still just don't understand how you could fall asleep while my boss was talking to us."

"I didn't want to!" Suhani says. "I was on call the night before and got to the hospital at six that morning so I could prepare for my presentation. And I didn't have time for a power nap, so I even chugged an espresso before having a cocktail. All I remember is that one second, I was laughing about everyone calling you the 'office dad' and the next, you were nudging me to wake up."

"I'm sorry you were so tired." Even though Zack's words are innocuous, his clenched jaw gives away that he's not over this.

Sure enough, he adds, "You're always exhausted and this is the only work event of mine you've made it to in months. I guess I was just surprised you couldn't be a little less tired for those few hours."

"You're still annoyed," Suhani says matter-of-factly as she prepares to apologize again. If she doesn't get her act together, she can picture Zack twenty years from now, sprawled across a psychiatrist's couch, some senior man who trained her at some point. *Yeah, everything started going to shit when my wife embarrassed me at a work dinner. . . .*

"I'm not," Zack says. But one glance at him tells her otherwise. Zack has one of those honest and open faces that make people in coffee shops ask him to watch their laptops when they go to the bathroom.

Suhani takes a sip of her mimosa. "You are and it's fine."

Sometimes they have the exact same fights over and over again. Suhani's lost count of the number of times her exhaustion has been a topic. She sees herself through her husband's eyes and feels a twinge of guilt, then frustration. It has to be difficult for him to come home to someone who is always so drained.

Don't let this job ruin what matters in life, Dad told Suhani the day she started as an intern at Atlanta Memorial Hospital. *It's too easy to take the people who love you for granted.*

"Hey, look, it's okay. I really am sorry for getting upset and I know things are hard for you. I want to be there for you." Zack wraps his hands over hers.

"I want to be there for you, too," Suhani says.

"You are," Zack says. "And your schedule will get better. I'll be so happy for you when you finally get a chance to just breathe."

Suhani doesn't tell Zack that as much as the long shifts drain her, she's also tired from the undercurrents of pressure and judgment that simmer below the surface of each day. The awareness that being in medicine means she's evaluated every second not only by her performance but also by her appearance. The having to smile whenever a patient asks her when the doctor is coming in. The mansplaining from male attendings. The fear that she can screw up and get criticized or, worse, lose it all at any given moment.

Sometimes Suhani wonders if she only exists in two extremes: either she's moving at max speed, able to accomplish everything, or she's stuck on the couch and can't even respond to text messages. The last time she remembers feeling free and fully absorbed in the present was during their honeymoon and, before that, when Natasha came to visit her once in med school. They packed a cooler with bottles of wine and spent an entire morning doing handstands on the beach. The day ended with dinner and cocktails with Devi Auntie, Mom's closest (and coolest) friend from Bombay, whom Suhani visited every few months when she was in med school.

"And within a matter of weeks"—Zack does a light drum roll on the edge of the table—"you'll be a chief resident! By the way, did you tell Dr. Wilson you're definitely running?"

"I'm sure he already knows. Everyone does." Suhani shrugs.

She can't imagine walking into her program director's office and announcing that she wants to be a chief. Despite getting a perfect GPA year after year throughout middle and high school, then excelling through four years at Emory, there's always a voice in her head telling her she got lucky.

"Even if he does know, he needs to hear it from you," Zack says. "I'm sure all the other residents who are running have already gone to kiss his ass. But none of them have made a partnership between the psych and OB departments or been the head of so many committees. You have to own all the work you've done."

She pictures Zack putting this all on a note and sticking it on their kitchen counter. Zack's a big note leaver. Sometimes, after a tough day, she'll find a yellow Post-it on the bathroom mirror: *I love my hot doctor! Congrats on finishing yet another hard call shift!*
DO NOT CLEAN THE APARTMENT! JUST RELAX!

"You make a good point, as always, Ben Wyatt," Suhani says. They nicknamed each other Ben and Leslie after noting the similarities between them and the *Parks and Recreation* couple.

Zack shakes his head and smiles. "You're so funny sometimes."

"What do you mean?" Suhani asks, even though she knows what he's going to say.

"You're so type A about everything except advocating for yourself. I really don't get it. If you were a guy, especially a white guy"— Zack winks—"you'd be puffing out your chest and bragging about all the work you've done."

"You know I'd love to walk around all day with that type of confidence. But you also know that I'd be punished for seeming too aggressive at work," Suhani reminds him.

The rules are always different for people like us, Mom told Suhani over and over again when she was younger. Mom was right. She always has to prove herself, let her work speak for itself, and not risk being seen as too greedy, too presumptuous, too anything.

"Oh, hello!" Zack exclaims. "Where are your parents?"

A chubby little girl, around three or four years old, is standing at their table. Her curly hair is held in place with a sparkly white butterfly clip. Zack waves at her and puffs out his cheeks. She erupts into a fit of laughter.

"My dress," she says as she points to her sky-blue dress.

"Like a princess!" Zack's voice says at a higher than normal pitch.

The girl smiles, pleased with his approval. Zack spots her parents in the back corner and walks her to their table.

"She's so cute," Suhani says when Zack comes back.

"Cute enough for you to change your mind about wanting one?" Even though Zack has a lighthearted smile, Suhani can see something on his face that looks a lot like hope.

"Why?" Suhani says. "Do you really want one?"

For most of her life, Suhani could see herself having kids as equally as she could see herself not having them. She waited for a flash of longing or the classic pang of baby fever so many of her friends had. But it never came. Instead, her future was a split screen, and she thought either side had its plusses and drawbacks. Accumulating scholarly or professional achievements never took away the gnawing sense that something about her was inadequate, not normal.

And then what happened in med school only further increased the divide between the two options. A psychoanalyst would have many theories about why. Despite how much she's accomplished, the one place where she constantly felt inadequate and unsure is when the topic of motherhood came up.

"If you do want one, we should talk about it." Suhani reaches across the table and brushes his hand. "Really."

"No, I mean, it crosses my mind sometimes, but it's not like I need to have one at this second," Zack says. "But I guess it would be good to revisit the idea sometime."

"We should," Suhani agrees. "Do you want to now?"

"No, no, definitcly not now," Zack says.

There are a few seconds of silence, which Zack breaks by saying, "So, moving on . . ."

Zack draws out "moving on" so it sounds like "mooooving on." It's one of his go-to phrases and the only thing he says with a southern drawl. His middle school health teacher, who also taught sex ed, said it whenever things got really awkward. Zack has used it ever since as a lighthearted way to change the subject.

"Have you seen Roshan around at work?"

The question is both so innocuous and so surprising that Suhani freezes. She pictures the unread text message on her phone. His number hasn't changed since med school and she hates that she has it memorized, lodged in her limbic system.

"I haven't seen him." Suhani pictures Roshan's bushy eyebrows, the earth-tone button-down shirts he always wears, his long face that's darker from hours spent outside, building things and hiking with his old Australian shepherd. He has the interests of Aidan Shaw from *Sex and the City* with the aloofness of Mr. Big. Not exactly the portrait of a dream boyfriend. How could she not have realized that years ago? It still takes her by surprise how one person can go from being a stranger to being the most important part of your life, then back to being a stranger.

"Why did you guys break up again?" Zacks runs his fingers through his cinnamon-colored hair and sweeps it across his forehead. "I mean, you told me that you drifted apart and felt disconnected and all that, but was that it?"

Early in their relationship, when she and Zack dissected their romantic pasts, she kept the details about Roshan vague. And even though her husband's tone is now curious, not accusatory or jealous, Suhani flinches at the question. "Pretty much. We weren't right for each other."

"Why not?" Zack asks.

"There were a lot of things that weren't compatible. That never were," she says. "But I was younger, more naïve and willing to put up with bullshit."

Zack digs into his cilantro corn pancakes. He's in his go-to weekend outfit of navy-blue T-shirt, gray pants, and charcoal Toms shoes. Being around him always makes her feel relaxed and rooted.

Maybe she should tell him what really happened with Roshan. He would understand.

Or maybe he wouldn't. Maybe he'd never look at her the same way again.

Ever since they got together, there were so many times the words lingered on the tip of her tongue and then she held back, convinced it was the wrong moment. But then the days passed, then the years, until it felt too late to tell him at all.

Zack frowns. "Yeah, I get that. I guess I could've sworn Natasha said some serious shit went down between you guys."

"Well, yeah, that's true. It was a tough relationship in a lot of ways. Too much drama," Suhani says as she remembers the times she clutched the phone in tears. Roshan made her one of those girls who had to overanalyze every single thing with her friends.

"I bet your parents were happy when they thought you'd end up with a doctor. A Brown doctor." Zack laughs.

"Trust me, it never would have worked for a lot of reasons," Suhani says as she remembers the dread that overcame her when she realized Roshan planned to propose. She'd found the round sapphire ring behind one of his anatomy textbooks.

Meg covertly slides the check onto their table and with a polite smile tells them it's "no rush."

"Let's go home and get back in bed," Suhani suggests.

They grab some pastries from the front of the restaurant for home, get into their silver Lexus, and drive the ten minutes back to their high-rise apartment in Midtown. Atlanta is still ninety degrees even though summer is almost over. Zack cracks the windows until the air-conditioning kicks in. Suhani puts a playlist on Spotify and pictures the rest of the relaxing afternoon unfolding in front of her.

When they're stopped at the intersection of Tenth Street and Northside Drive, she removes her phone from her black cross-body bag and scrolls to the text. The words are to the point, like the person who sent them.

I need to talk to you.

"Everything okay?" Zack glances at her as they stop at a red light.

"Yeah. Just work," Suhani blurts.

She feels a twinge of guilt as she processes that she just lied to her husband. And because of Roshan. What does he need to talk to her about, anyway? She made sure to cover her tracks. There's no way he could have found out about anything. She doesn't need to be scared anymore.

"Tell them you're busy spending the day with your needy husband and can't take care of anyone at the hospital." Zack smiles and then makes the music louder.

Just tell him, a voice in her head says. *He'll understand.*

You should be ashamed of yourself, another voice says, the one that's lingered in her head since she and Roshan broke up.

Zack parks the car and hums to the tune of a Lizzo song. Something about the relaxed smile stretched across his face and the whooshing of the car tires against the highway solidifies it for her. She'll tell him. Once they're inside their apartment, she'll let it all out.

They step into their building's lobby. The floor-to-ceiling windows fill the space with the buttery afternoon sun. Abstract art pieces line the hallways. Carlos, their doorman, waves at them as he gives a woman her Amazon packages. With a full mustache, rotund stomach, and large, happy eyes, he always reminds Suhani of a grown-up version of Mario or Luigi.

"Hel-lo to my favorite couple," he says with a tip of his black hat. "Looks like you've got a visitor."

He motions to the suede couch near the elevators. Suhani immediately recognizes the back of one of her floral-printed Rebecca Taylor dresses.

"Natasha?"

"Hey." Natasha turns around. A frayed yellow duffel bag is at her feet, which are in Rainbow sandals. Her toenails have chipped black polish. A smattering of acne is across her cheeks, which look rounder than usual.

"Nice dress. I've been looking for that one for weeks." Suhani ignores the urge to tell Natasha to wear some mascara or, better yet, toss those shoes into the nearby trash chute. "What are you doing here?"

"I, uh, need to crash with you guys for a little while." Natasha gives Suhani a guilty smile, the same one that's always helped her get away with things.

"What's going on?" Zack leans forward to give Natasha a hug.

"I just can't stay at home with Mom. She's always pissed at me or judging me or both. I can't work in that place."

"And?" Suhani taps her foot. Her jade-green heel makes a *clack, clack, clack* sound against the marble floor. What else is new? Mom and Natasha are constantly getting into fights. Dad and Anuj can listen to them and try to calm them down, but Suhani always finds herself getting riled up. It only occurs to her now that maybe this is why she's always friends with passionate women.

"It's worse than usual," Natasha says. "Like, way worse. She's really upset about the whole Karan thing and my job situation. She told me I'm wasting my life away."

"What did you think would happen when you moved back home and quit your job and had a breakup with her best friend's son?" Suhani checks her phone and is surprised to see that there aren't any missed calls or texts from Mom.

Zack gives Suhani a look that says, *Calm down.*

"I don't know. I thought they'd see that I'm trying to do something that really matters to me. Alexis Diaz lives at home with her parents."

"Does Alexis Diaz have a mother like ours? One who turns up the drama to full force if she thinks one of her kids has embarrassed her?" Suhani raises an eyebrow. "But I do see your point. It has to feel shitty to know Mom is judging you every second."

"Just stay with us," Zack says at the same time Suhani blurts, "You should talk to her."

"I can't talk to Mom! You know that." Natasha throws her hands into the air.

"Have you even tried? To calmly explain where you're coming from?" Suhani asks with an emphasis on the word "calmly."

"There's no point! She just wants to be dramatic all day," Natasha says.

"Then you'll feel much better at our place," Zack says as he puts his hand on her shoulder.

Suhani ignores the brief panic that overcomes her. Preparing for a Natasha visit is a process, and now she doesn't have time to hide the clothes that her sister will definitely "borrow" or put away the expensive wine that she'll "sample."

But then she sees the slump in her sister's back. Suhani feels a rush of protectiveness, the kind she used to have when Natasha would ask her questions like if it was scary to wear a tampon or how to kiss a boy. Questions Suhani had to learn the answers to alone, since Mom always told her that all that mattered was how she did in school.

The three of them step into the elevator.

Natasha rubs her eyes, which are red and splotchy. "I really needed this."

"And we're here for you." Suhani pulls her sister into a hug and doesn't say another word.

Eight

Bina

Everyone should be here any minute. Bina fluffs up the throw pillows in the formal living room, then double-checks the food: mini chutney-and-cucumber sandwiches, cashews spiced with chili powder and chaat masala, and spicy carrot chips. Next to the food, there's a turquoise teapot full of chai, a stack of gilded teacups, and bushels of mint leaves.

It feels like the first day of school, with that same blend of anticipation and excitement. She will soon be with her friends. Bina's always loved being around groups of women. During her highest and lowest points in life, they gave her comfort and a sense of belonging.

She glances at her reflection. Her outfit is chic but hopefully not trying too hard: a burnt-orange calf-length dress, thin gold bangles, and gold studs Ma gave her on her last trip to India. Per Suhani's recommendation, Bina filled in her eyebrows with one of those roll-up pencils and dusted blush on the apples of her cheeks. The makeup and outfit bring out the resemblance between her and her oldest child, something she often forgets about until people mention it.

She sends a text to Kavita and Mira—See you soon!—then scrolls through Facebook to pass the last few minutes. Mira's daughter,

Pooja, posted a series of stylish summer outfits. Bina knows that despite everything Mira says, deep down, she's proud of everything Pooja has built.

It's only after she's scrolled through Pooja's entire year of posts that she realizes how much time has passed. Maybe Deepak was right when he said her autopilot social media scrolling is taking up a lot of her time. (She responded to him by locking herself in their room and watching two dozen Instagram stories.)

Where are they? Bina wonders as she makes her way back to the formal living room.

Her phone buzzes with a text.

KAVITA: I'm so sorry. I won't be able to make it.

MIRA: Same. Can we do the meeting another time?

Something in Bina's chest drops. She starts to type. *Did something happen? Are you both okay?*

But she deletes it, then types: No problem. See you another time.

She stretches across the couch as dread washes over her. Something must have happened. It isn't like Kavita or Mira to cancel at the last minute. She had texted Anita about the meeting earlier in the week and never got a response. But a part of her held out hope that she would show up anyway, surprise her.

She scrolls to Devi's name in her phone.

"Hi!" Devi exclaims. On her end, Bina hears a man yelling, "Peaches! Blueberries!"

"Are you at the farmers' market? How LA!" Bina laughs.

"Ha! I'm in Napa, on a set that's supposed to be a farmers' market," Devi whispers. "Hold on, let me just step away."

Devi's work often takes her on exciting last-minute trips to a variety of places. The trips tend to end with big group dinners full of fine wine and even finer conversation. Bina always relishes her friend's freedom, the type that is only possible when you don't have anyone to answer to. She takes in her own surroundings: her big, empty house, the untouched food she spent the morning preparing, the earthy scent of the sandalwood candle lingering in the room. For a fleeting moment, she wishes she could also be untethered.

"So, what's going on?" Devi asks.

Bina gives Devi a quick run-through of the morning, starting with the food prep and ending with the texts.

"It's like I'm back in school," she says. "No, wait, this is actually worse than that."

"Because you were the queen bee back then?" Bina can hear Devi smiling.

"I wouldn't say that," Bina says.

"You don't have to. You're the only one who stood up to mean teachers. And everyone copied your style. Even when we were going for auditions, you had no problems telling certain problematic directors to watch their hands and not talk to you like a servant. So, yes, you were queen bee," Devi confirms. "And you still are, Bina. This is a new thing you're doing. There will be hiccups."

"Hiccups, sure. But the only two people flaking? That sounds like a dud." Bina stuffs a mini chutney-cucumber sandwich into her mouth.

"Did you hear back from Anita?" Devi asks, referring to Bina's text about the meeting earlier in the week.

"She never responded," Bina says. "I guess I was hoping she'd show up and surprise me."

"Two thoughts before I have to go," Devi says, putting her efficient professor hat on. Bina's always in awe of how Devi's brain is constantly so on. She's one of those people who makes Bina feel more inspired, more capable, after just one conversation.

"First thought. Why don't you expand Chats Over Chai to beyond your immediate circle? They're all nice, but at the end of the day, they're *dai chokri*."

"They are good girls," Bina agrees. "But they seemed interested when I told them more about it. I just don't know what happened. And Anita was so excited about this."

"That brings me to my second thought," Devi says. "Just figure this stuff out with her. It's obviously bothering you and needs to be faced and then put away."

"I agree." Bina pours herself a cup of chai. "But she doesn't even want to talk."

"Don't give her a choice!" Devi says. "And I'm adding a third thought. You have the house to yourself, right?"

"I do. Deepak's playing golf and Anuj is out with friends."

And Natasha moved out.

"Then enjoy it. I know you love hosting, but I also know you sometimes . . . well, don't," Devi says. "It causes all this stress and pressure and there's barely any space for enjoyment."

It's one of those direct statements that can only be made by a friend who isn't afraid to tell you the truth. Your truth. Bina tells herself she cherishes having people over, but, often, the second the guests leave, she's surprised to find herself both drained and relieved. Sometimes, she doesn't even know if she really loves things or if she's convinced herself to love them.

After she and Devi hang up, Bina removes onions and garlic from the fridge to get a head start on dinner. She chops the vegetables with a freshly sharpened knife, then RSVPs to three weddings they've been invited to, texts Deepak's aunt in a group thread to wish her happy birthday, calls Barbara to say hi, then makes a grocery list.

I never feel like I can just sit, she thinks as she focuses on all the things she should be doing, all the minutiae she does that ensure their lives run smoothly.

As she's scanning the pantry for things she needs to stock up on, Devi's advice to enjoy this free time crystallizes in her mind. She didn't know how to tell Devi that it's not as though Deepak or the kids even tell her to do all these things. It's all self-imposed. Somewhere along the way, she internalized the idea that if she wasn't struggling or tired or, better yet, struggling *and* tired, she wasn't doing her part.

But Devi had a point. Why doesn't Bina just take advantage of the unexpected free afternoon? Why does she rarely give herself the luxury to not be doing something for others?

Maybe because, outside of Devi, she doesn't see any woman give herself that. The world upholds selfless mothers, even if they're angry and exhausted. Bina still thinks of Ma drinking chai and eating Parle-G biscuits and saying, *This is just how it is. You'll get used to it.*

She pauses at a collage of family photos that she put together years ago, after she learned through Natasha's classmate's mom that this is the type of thing American mothers do. She found it sweet, especially since she could never imagine Ma sitting at a table, going through pictures, and cutting them into the exact sizes to fit. Bina went to Michaels and bought the biggest frame she could find. The project was done by the end of the week. They couldn't afford a nice camera back then, so all their frozen moments look slightly jaundiced. Bina studies the mosaic of birthday parties at skating rinks, Diwali celebrations, and graduations. Anita's in so many of them. Her hair is fluffier and there's an eagerness in her eyes that's dimmed over the years.

Devi was right, as always. She and Anita have to put an end to all this already. Anita is her family, her constant.

Ten minutes later, Bina is in her gray Audi. It's only when she pulls out of their driveway that she remembers she hasn't heard from the girls in days. She dials Suhani's number.

"Hey, Mom." Suhani's voice fills the car.

"Hi, *beta*. What are you up to today?"

"Not much. Just, you know, hanging out. Typical Sunday." Suhani's voice has a forced nonchalance.

"Natasha's sitting next to you, isn't she?" Bina asks.

"No! What makes you think that?"

"I can tell when you're trying to cover something up." Bina turns out of the neighborhood. She puts her hand on the Tupperware container of chutney sandwiches she packed for Anita.

"You can tell over the phone?" Suhani asks. "How?"

"Please." Bina scoffs. "You think I don't know when my daughters are lying to me? And covering for each other on top of that? How do you think I was able to figure out all those times you both were running off with those troublesome boys when you told me you were going to the movies?"

Bina is taken back to the slew of infuriating moments when she discovered Natasha and Suhani were dating behind her back. Despite how obedient Suhani was, the one way she continuously defied Bina was by having secret boyfriends. But the worst was when she and Natasha would lie for each other. Bina didn't realize how scared she'd be until both her daughters got their driver's licenses.

"That's all old news," Suhani says. "What are you up to? Wait, how was your meeting? That was today, right?"

Bina gives her a summary of the afternoon, a briefer and more filtered version of the one she gave Devi. "So, now I'm going to see if Anita Auntie wants to talk to me."

Bina turns into the neighborhood. Laurel Lakes. Such a placid name for the placid woman whose blue-shuttered house is on the last cul-de-sac. Bina passes the swimming pool and tennis courts. Hydrangea bushes line manicured front yards. A couple is walking with their golden retriever and baby. Ahead of them, there's a woman wearing sunglasses and shimmery sweatpants Bina knows are from Lululemon because Suhani has a similar pair.

The woman slows down and peers at her. "Bina?"

"Mona!" Bina rolls down the window and tells Suhani to hold on. "How are you?"

Mona is one of the five "Real Indian Housewives of Duluth," a nickname she gave her group of friends after she learned some of the actual Real Housewives of Atlanta lived in their neighborhood. The Real Indian Housewives of Duluth stand apart from other Gujarati wives for their extravagant taste in saris, elaborate parties, and modern grooming practices inspired by their neighbors or children: colored contacts, light brown highlights, tattooed makeup, intricate nail art. Anita, Mira, and Kavita preferred not to socialize with them too much, but Bina appreciates their openness and honesty, the conviction with which they navigate everything from their daily dramas to bigger decisions. She finds their lack of phoniness (and, sometimes, lack of politeness) refreshing. With the sheer number of South Asians in Atlanta, it's possible for people to break off into their select homogenous groups—the Gujaratis, Punjabis, Sikhs, Parsis—but Bina's always felt there should be more opportunities that bring them all together.

"Are you doing okay?" Mona leans on Bina's car. "I heard about Natasha and Karan."

"Eh, what can you do?" Bina shrugs. "I'm fine. I'm not sure if Anita is, though."

That's another thing Bina likes about Mona: she comes out and shares what she's thinking instead of dancing around it or pretending not to know.

"It's a hard situation, though. I've always gotten the sense Anita defines herself by what her kids do, you know?" Mona removes her sunglasses.

There are two types of women from their generation in India: the ones who were forced into tradition and the ones who naturally embraced it. Bina's only realizing now that she is in the former group while Anita is in the latter. While marriage and motherhood made Anita fold inward, Bina became less private, more willing to be seen. She always thought their differences made them complement each other. Obviously she was wrong. She was wrong about so many things.

"All our kids say things, do things, that upset us. It's not such a big deal! And I'm sure she isn't judging you in the midst of all this," Mona offers.

Oh, she definitely is, Bina thinks. Judging is one of Anita's favorite hobbies, as Devi observed during all her trips to Atlanta. *I'm that woman's worst nightmare*, she often says. Anita even judges Mona for being too "unconventional" and "making people uncomfortable," which are two of Bina's favorite things about Mona.

Bina and Mona talk for a few more minutes. Mona glances at her vintage silver watch and says, "Ah! I didn't realize how late it's getting. I have to get to the Bollywood Closet. They're holding an emerald-green sari for me."

"Have fun!" Bina waves.

Mona can shop all day and not get bored. When she travels to

India, she always takes a giant empty suitcase just to fill with the outfits she'll buy there.

Years ago, Bina heard that Mona once ordered Sabyasachi saris from a new online shop. She was convinced the retailer sent her fakes and mailed back the saris with a note that read, *You can shove these knock-offs up your butts!* Some people claim Mona's word of mouth is the sole reason that shop no longer exists.

Bina rolls up the window. "Suhani? Sorry, I'm back."

"No worries!" Suhani says, never one to complain about being left on hold.

A rush of anticipation passes through Bina as she gets closer to Anita's house, a house where Bina knows everything from the security code to where the fancy dishware is stored.

But her breath catches in her throat as she turns into the cul-de-sac.

"Oh my God."

"What is it?" Suhani asks. "What's wrong?"

Bina clutches the steering wheel with a white-knuckled grip. "Mira and Kavita are here."

"What do you mean? They're at Anita Auntie's house?"

"Those are their cars," Bina says, not sure if she's embarrassed, angry, or both. But then she feels the threat of tears. "Listen, I should go. I'll talk to y—"

"Mom!" Natasha chimes in. Ha! So she was right there! "Are you freaking kidding me?"

"What?" Bina asks as she feels a flash of triumph, then anger, at hearing Natasha's voice.

"You're getting upset over these women meeting without you? Go in there and confront them about lying! What they're doing is messed up!"

It *is* messed up, Bina agrees. Her daughters often know how to pinpoint what she's feeling even when she doesn't say much. As much as she loves talking to Anuj, she knows he'd never be able to do this.

"I can't go and confront them," Bina says. "There's obviously a reason they didn't want to come today or call me here. Anita isn't ready for us to reconnect."

"I think Natasha's right." Suhani's tone is gentle but firm. "You can't just let this go."

Natasha sighs. "Look, Mom, no offense, but when did you get so scared? You've always talked about how it's important to speak up. Didn't you get into fights with people because you talked too much when you were growing up?"

Bina leans back in her seat and absorbs Natasha's words. Maybe she's right. Maybe decades in America have made Bina a watered-down version of her younger self.

"Oh, so now both my daughters are pretending they're my mother?" Bina asks.

Suhani says "No" at the same time Natasha says "If that's what it takes."

"I understand what you're saying." Bina takes a deep breath. She refuses to let herself cry. "But now is not the time to confront anyone."

And then, before Natasha can convince her otherwise, Bina turns in the cul-de-sac and heads straight home.

Nine

Natasha

> **NATASHA:** Damn, he actually knew me. Really knew me.

> **IFEOMA:** Who? Karan?

> **PAYAL:** Why are you talking about him? Are you drinking?

> **NATASHA:** Only a little.

Natasha hides her wineglass as if her friends can see it. She also gets out of Karan's Instagram feed. He hasn't added anything new in weeks. He also hasn't deleted the pictures of the two of them.

She should have just said yes. Who cares if it felt too soon? Anything has to feel better than this, this never-ending pang of missing the one person she's spoken to every day since she was a baby. She considers telling her friends this. But this time she knows they won't get it.

> **PAYAL:** You better not be prepping for another comedy contest behind our backs.

IFEOMA: Agreed! And you don't need him. You have us. Sounds like you kicked ass the other night.

NATASHA: It felt like the audience loved it. The comedy club is supposed to call me any minute now to let me know if I made it to the next round.

IFEOMA: You obviously did. You're going to win the whole thing. Now it's just onward and upward.

Ifeoma sends a GIF of Michelle Obama pointing to the sky.

PAYAL: Agreed. Onward and upward.

IFEOMA: Maybe it's not the best idea for you to stay at your sister's place.

NATASHA: I'm good for now. Seriously.

IFEOMA: Come stay with us. Jordan won't care. We have an extra bedroom.

NATASHA: Y'all are studying all the time. Don't need a third wheel.

PAYAL: Do it! Also, I know Karan believed in you and all but tbh, I dunno if he could have really handled it. He's all proper and safe at the end of the day. Probably needs someone like his mom. Don't they all?

NATASHA: Maybe you have a point.

PAYAL: I know. Also, anyone down to go to Barcelona Wine Bar Friday? I'll be done with the freaking MCAT!!!!

NATASHA: Can't wait!

Natasha adds a thumbs-up emoji, then puts her phone facedown on the glass coffee table. It's been weeks since she became a full-time aspiring comedian. She's finally living the dream.

She waits to feel something. Something grand and purposeful. A sign that she's on the right track.

But all she can focus on is the steady hum of Atlanta traffic outside Suhani and Zack's curved living room windows and the occasional clank of the ice machine.

Did any of her role models ever mention that living the dream is kind of anticlimactic?

It's almost noon but she's still tired. She's so tired of being tired. Getting into bed early, like that WebMD article recommended, hasn't helped. Whenever her head hits the pillow, every thought possible comes to the forefront of her mind in an endless spiral.

From her duffel bag, she removes a pen that reads FLUOXETINE in bold blue letters. Dad used to get so many things from pharmaceutical companies—pens, tote bags, notepads—and he handed them out at home like Christmas gifts. A teacher once questioned Natasha when she showed up with a Xanax duffel bag and Natasha spent too long trying to convince her she wasn't selling drugs at school.

Anuj texts her. Just FYI, don't be too worried about the video I uploaded to your YouTube channel from the contest night.

NATASHA: Worried? Why would I be? Thought I was okay?

ANUJ: You were. Just haven't really gotten any views of the
video. It probably just takes awhile to get on people's radars.

Nobody cares to see her stand-up comedy? Even when she
thought she was pretty decent? Maybe she wasn't decent.

No, she can't think that way. Anuj is right; these things take
time. Any minute now, she should be getting a call from the Midtown Comedy Center telling her that her performance that night
was good enough to get to the next round.

And Alexis Diaz's improv class starts in a few weeks. A few
weeks! It'll be Natasha's chance to really connect with her role
model. She pictures Alexis stroking her chin and saying, *You're a
natural, Natasha!*

The reverie pushes Natasha to get out the black Moleskine she
uses for comedy notes. The first page reads ADOLESCENT INSPIRATION
and has a list of memories she wrote for potential jokes:

> *Sneaking behind Mom and Dad to log onto AOL Instant*
> > *Messenger and talk to boys*
> *The beautician's horror at my eyebrows the first*
> > *time I went to the threading salon*
> *Poking Karan's eyes with my nose during our first kiss*

She stares at the pages until they become blurry. Even though
those are her ideas and they once seemed like they had potential,
she now feels an odd sense of detachment from them.

This happens too often. She gets so excited and pumped up to do something, and then, when the moment comes and she finally has the time, something weighs on her and all of a sudden she can't act.

Just put something down, she tells herself, remembering the advice from one of the comedians she read about.

In the slanted handwriting that she was always told was too messy, she writes, *When the Only Place to Go Is Living with Your Uptight Sister.*

She glances around the apartment and scribbles, *My sister is beautiful. My sister is the reason I have low self-esteem. She's scary. Snobby. Judgmental. Always makes me look bad. Probably why I should go to therapy.*

Suhani and Zack will be at work for at least seven hours, so she has their entire place to herself. She stretches across their suede navy-blue sectional and pretends that this is her high-rise apartment, that these are her nice things, and that she has all her shit together. A tiny voice tells her to snap back to reality, but she ignores it. A little delusion never hurt anyone.

She gets up and walks around the apartment. Her gaze lingers on the large wedding photo in the front hallway. It's of Suhani and Zack laughing as they put rose garlands around each other. Grains of rice are suspended in the air around them. The picture is sweet, but Natasha didn't think it was special enough to be blown up and enclosed in a sterling silver Tiffany frame. Clearly she was wrong because the *Atlanta Journal-Constitution* thought it was special enough to feature it at the top of the Wedding section.

She moves back toward the living room and takes note of the modern artwork, designer shoe collection, and sleek Sonos surround-sound system.

I don't have any of this.

Before she can push the thought away, she feels it burrowing into the corner of her mind with a barnacle-like grip.

She opens her notebook again.

My sister's a shrink, which means she's intuitive about people. And she really is! She knows JUST when I'm starting to feel good about myself because that's the EXACT moment she shows up and makes sure I hate myself again! Isn't that something? I should give a shout-out to her great work ethic but she's been doing this since we were kids, so I think it's just one of her many natural talents!

Not bad. Maybe it's a little harsh, but she can tone it down later. It's the first time in so long that an idea has come to her that all she can focus on is the tiny victory of putting something down on paper, something she can hear herself performing.

She scrolls back to her text thread and pulls up Ifeoma's GIF.

Onward and upward.

She walks into the kitchen even though she already knows there won't be any good snacks. Suhani's weird about food. She once told Natasha that she thought cooking was a lot of work and taken for granted, something women did while the men sat in the adjacent room discussing big ideas and having fun. Maybe both of them ran away from becoming their mother in different ways.

Sure enough, the fridge is barren except for Tupperware and Pyrex containers full of Mom's and Zack's mom Barbara's food. Natasha drafts a grocery list on a sky-blue Post-it note. She can make a Publix run later this afternoon. She might be lazy, but she's no mooch.

The fridge side door has two chilled bottles of champagne.

Perfect.

Natasha opens the cabinets. One entire shelf has pairs of flutes, coupes, and tulips. Of course her sister has multiple types of champagne glasses. Natasha takes a coupe glass and pours a generous serving. If Karan was here, he'd shake his head and laugh with her. He's the only person who can appreciate how intense Suhani is.

In the moments Natasha has space to think, she realizes that's what she misses the most about him: the silent understanding that can only be shared with someone who often knows you better than you know yourself.

The bubbles tickle her throat as she goes back to her notebook. On the last page, there's something scribbled in her large, bubbly handwriting.

Self-compassion.

You need to practice being nice to yourself. You know, self-compassion, Dr. Jenkins, her therapist, told her during their last appointment.

Dr. Jenkins was in her forties and always wore fun shoes: turquoise pumps, glitter sneakers, flats lined with fringe. She spoke in a calm voice that was ideal for those mindfulness apps everyone loves. When she wore sleeveless blouses, Natasha took note of her toned and tanned biceps. She certainly was nice to herself, and Natasha found that inspiring.

But even though she liked her therapist, she felt like there were certain things Dr. Jenkins just couldn't understand, like the way Natasha had to always consider how her behavior impacted others or how her community saw going to therapy as a weakness or how, even though Dad is a psychiatrist, she never felt like she could tell her own parents about getting help.

She finishes her champagne and walks to the fridge for a refill. On the way back to the couch, she notices that Suhani and Zack's bedroom door is cracked. She steps inside and ignores Suhani's voice telling her not to even think about snooping.

The afternoon sun gives the entire room a soft glow. A sophisticated adult mixture of scents hangs in the air: perfume, spicy after-shave, eucalyptus oil. Their king-size bed is made, complete with hospital corners and a mountain of throw pillows. What's the point of having so many freaking pillows? It seems like so much work to remove them every night and put them back in the morning.

Suhani's dresser is covered with bottles of perfume that smell like different exotic flowers. At the edge, Natasha sees the hot-pink spine of a burn book. They both bought one after the first time they saw *Mean Girls*. There's a stacked makeup case with Suhani's latest splurges from Sephora. Suhani's tried (and failed) to get Natasha into everything from bronzer to fake eyelashes.

A pair of gold-and-white ankle bells from Suhani's kathak lessons are hung on the wall. Mom enrolled both of them in the North Indian classical dance class when they were in elementary school. The instructor, Kajal Auntie, had a habit of teaching steps by shouting dramatic commands: *You are a blooming lotus flower! Show me you are Goddess Saraswati! Twirl like a Bollywood actress!* Suhani used to practice for an hour before class while Natasha found reasons to get kicked out at least once a month.

At the corner of the dresser, there's a sepia-toned picture of the Joshi family during their first trip to Disney World. Mom and Dad are in the back in matching *Lion King* T-shirts while Suhani has her arms around Natasha and Anuj. Splash Mountain is behind them.

Natasha refills her champagne flute and then starts on the closet. It's an ad for the Container Store. Everything is labeled and folded and in its place. Someday, Natasha thinks as she sips her champagne and gazes around, she'll have enough money for nice things. Even if she isn't a girly girl like her sister, it would feel cool to have one kick-ass pair of shoes, like Dr. Jenkins, or a handbag that tells the world she's doing well. She scans Suhani's collection of satchels, clutches, and cross-body bags, then moves on to her wardrobe. Her hands graze dresses with vibrant animal prints, a blush-pink leather jacket, an impressive collection of hats. Some of it even reminds Natasha of Mindy Kaling's outfits that she posts on her Instagram account.

Zack texts her. Did Suhani seem mad this morning?

NATASHA: She's always mad. Don't worry about it.

ZACK: But something's been different about her.

NATASHA: Did she say something?

ZACK: No. Just a feeling.

Only a guy like Zack would be intuitive enough to pick up on something like that.

NATASHA: I'll see how she is when I talk to her. Will keep you posted.

She knows she should leave their room now. (Actually, she should have never gone in in the first place, but what's done is done.)

But something keeps her rooted there. She's not sure if it's the buzz from the champagne or boredom or just good old-fashioned little-sister nosiness, but she can't leave. On Suhani's white bedside table there's a candle from Anthropologie, a ring dish, a book titled *Freud and Beyond*, and, ah, the gold mine.

Suhani's journal.

Natasha looks around even though she knows nobody else is in the apartment. Excitement rushes through her, the same type that she used to get when she'd press her ear against Suhani's door and listen to her phone conversations.

She picks up the peony-covered notebook with the tips of her fingers, as if just one slip can result in it dissolving in her hands. The last page is dated earlier this week.

I'm worried Zack and I aren't having enough sex. I don't know what's wrong with me but I'm just not in the mood. Maybe I'm too tired or drained or something. I love living with him but sometimes I just come back from work and want my own space. All he wants to do is talk, talk, talk, and I feel like I hurt his feelings when I ask him to just give me a minute. And then when he does, his idea of giving me a minute is putting his mom on speakerphone! I know how selfish this is but sometimes I forget how we're supposed to just embrace each other's worlds in every single way.

Zack and Suhani are having issues like this? But everything between them always seems fine. Perfect.

Her thoughts are interrupted by her phone buzzing with a text. The comedy club!

When Natasha gets up to grab her phone, she realizes she's drunk. Very drunk.

MOM: I heard Karan is being set up with people!!!!! Call me now!!!

Her heart starts racing as she rereads the text. What does Mom mean, set up with people? Karan just proposed to her five minutes ago!

Mom has to be wrong. She's been wrong so many times with her intel. Mira Auntie probably just said something and it got blown up. Because there's no way Karan is being set up with anybody. He doesn't exactly have initiative in the romance department, aside from the terribly timed proposal. Natasha had to teach him how to kiss, then touch her boobs, then do everything else. She often felt like a strict health teacher pointing out a woman's anatomy.

She tells Mom she's working and will call later.

The champagne's starting to give her a headache. She sits on the corner of the bed. Maybe she should take a nap.

Her phone rings as she's about to doze off.

"Hello?" She clears her throat so it doesn't sound like she's been drinking.

"Is this Natasha Joshi?" a man's bored, low-pitched voice says back. He pronounces "Joshi" wrong, like most people, so it sounds like "Josh-eye" instead of "Joe-she."

"It is. May I know who's calling?"

"This is Ben. I'm calling from Midtown Comedy Center."

Natasha grips the bottom of the champagne glass. Her heartbeat quickens. This is it. The moment she's been waiting for is finally here. She pictures the looks on the girls' faces. And Zack's and Suhani's. And Mom! What will she say?

"Hi!" Natasha lowers her voice. "I mean, hel-lo. How are you?"

"So, you did not make it to the next round for our comedy competition," Ben says with the monotony of someone who works at the DMV.

Natasha checks the volume on her phone. "Excuse me? I think I didn't hear you. Can you repeat that?"

Ben sighs. "The judges did not select you to move on in our competition."

"Did not?" Natasha ignores the sense of dread that's pressing on her chest as she processes his words. Ben must be mistaken.

But he says, "Correct. You did not. Now, if you'd li—"

"Wait. I don't understand. I thought I did a good job. No, a great one. I mean, people were cracking up! A bachelorette invited me to do shots with her friends because of how much they loved my routine! If that's not the sign of a success, then what is?"

"The comedians this time were some of the best we have ever had . . ." Ben drones on as if he's reading his words from a script. A shitty script.

Natasha hangs up before she can hear any more.

Should she call one of her friends? They share everything with one another and she already knows how each one will respond. But then again, why be a burden? Someone they have to be worried about. She's already enough of one for her family.

This is what she gets after putting herself out there and pushing past her comfort zone. After everything she's been through, she's back at square one.

She returns to the living room. Her notebook is still open to the last page.

Self-compassion, my ass, she thinks. *Self-compassion is for people who actually deserve good things.*

She removes the champagne bottle from the fridge and places it against her lips. Without giving herself time to think, she throws her head back and chugs so quickly that she doesn't even taste the drink anymore. She should stop and take a break. But something pushes her to keep taking it all in, until there's nothing left.

Ten

Zack

"Hey, you okay?" Zack asks when he sees Natasha sprawled across their navy-blue sectional. This is how he finds her most days when he's back from work: buried under a faux fur blanket, wearing sweatpants, and nursing a glass of something that smells like it should probably be reserved for frat parties.

"Fine," Natasha grumbles. "Just some crap with my comedy."

"Do you want to talk about it?"

Natasha shakes her head and sinks deeper into the cushion. "My perform— I mean, some of my, uh, material got rejected and I wasn't expecting it because I thought it was good. Really good."

"I'm sorry. That's really frustrating," Zack says as he looks at the pink sky gaping over Midtown Atlanta. He loves that their view makes him feel small and part of the city at the same time.

"It's fine," Natasha mumbles in a way that indicates it isn't fine at all. "I didn't get any feedback, so I don't even know what wasn't good enough about it."

"Want me to take a look?" Zack asks. "I may not officially be a comedian, but Suhani does claim my dad jokes are the best."

"No!" Natasha freezes. "Sorry, I mean, you're busy and I should spare you that."

"Are you sure? I really wouldn't mind."

"I'm sure. But thanks." Natasha reaches for a Reese's peanut butter cup from the orange bag on the coffee table.

"Have you been eating candy all day again?" Zack asks, not meaning to come off like her parent. Then again, he can get away with asking Natasha questions that Suhani can't.

Natasha gives him a sheepish grin. "Maybe?"

Zack laughs. "I'm ordering us cauliflower rice bowls with roasted vegetables. Suhani and I get them from this place nearby and they're amazing."

"Sounds great. I should probably have a meal that makes me feel like I'm an Instagram fitness influencer instead of a kid who just went trick-or-treating."

Zack puts in a delivery order, removes two cans of sparkling water from the fridge, and sits next to Natasha on the couch.

Being constantly treated like a baby in his house made Zack want a younger sibling, someone he could provide guidance to and be there for. And to his initial surprise, he and Natasha have random things in common: an obsession with Reddit threads, overachiever older sisters, an ability to not take things too seriously.

Despite Suhani's occasional frustration, it's been nice having Natasha here. She's so thrilled to see him when he comes home. Excitement and interest light up her face as he tells her about work and they both wait for Suhani to join them.

He's about to tell her he's glad she's here, but when he looks up, Natasha's staring at the now empty Reese's wrapper in a daze.

"Hey, don't beat yourself up so much," Zack says. "Rejections are part of the process, right?"

"Yeah, that is what they say. I just didn't think they'd hurt so much."

"Of course."

"And I've been feeling so shitty lately. It's getting old. Heavy."

"Is it just the comedy or also because of the Karan stuff?" Zack asks, even though he's secretly happy it didn't work out with them. He always found Karan a little uptight and, frankly, kind of boring, like the guy you dread having to make small talk with at office parties. Of course, he never told anyone that. Part of being a good son-in-law was knowing when to keep your mouth shut.

Natasha shakes her head. "I don't think that's all of it. I'm just, I don't know, maybe a little lost."

"Well, you're figuring things out and that takes time," Zack says. "What do you think about getting out of the apartment more? I know that's not a big thing, but maybe you'll feel a little better if you're not cooped up here all day."

"I could do that. It's been harder to feel motivated to do anything, even take small steps like that."

Zack reaches for his own Reese's cup. "Have you considered talking to anyone in your family about how you're doing? Your dad and sister do specialize in feelings."

"There hasn't really been a chance for that," Natasha says.

"Don't your parents call you every day?"

"Um, technically, yes." Natasha flashes him a guilty smile. "But why ruin perfectly nice conversations, right?"

Zack snickers. He knows no one would consider Mom's judgment and Dad's softer questions about how Natasha's filling her days to qualify as perfectly nice conversations.

"Don't tell anyone, okay? I'm really fine and there's no need to bother them." Natasha gulps down her sparkling water.

It's a request she's given Zack many times. *Don't tell anyone, okay?* And he never does. He gets what it feels like to be an outsider in your own family. His mom and sisters often told him he was too sensitive, too reactive to things. They never understood how he was molded differently by his dad than they were.

Natasha throws the blanket off her. "Let me clean up these candy wrappers before Miss Queen of Order gets home."

"Good idea," Zack says.

"Has she seemed stressed to you?" Natasha asks as the wrappers make a crinkling sound in her hands. "Like, more than usual?"

"Let me think." Zack pretends to contemplate and then blurts, "*Yes*. A lot more!"

"She really is, right?" Natasha asks. "I'm glad I wasn't just imagining it."

"And she seems more closed off, too," Zack notes. Some people are like babies: you worry about them more when they're quiet. "I always try to talk to her, push her to open up, but that doesn't really work." To be fair, he knows that's something he should respect more, his wife's need for space when she's upset.

"Oh, nooooo," Natasha shakes her head. "You've gotta back off when she's pissed. We used to switch off who would wake her up in the mornings growing up because she was like a grumpy little tiger. She has to come to you."

They both laugh. Zack's filled with a rush of gratitude at being able to talk to someone who understands Suhani's emotional skeleton.

"We, uh, talked about kids for a split second," he says.

"And?"

"And I don't know. She didn't seem that into it. To be fair, when we were dating, both of us were undecided about it and could see ourselves with or without them. I guess I've just shifted a little since then," Zack says, wondering if, ironically, Suhani's encour-

agement that he learn more about his dad made Zack more open
to the idea of building a family of his own.

Their dinner arrives. Zack puts the brown paper delivery bag
on the coffee table, which is now candy-free. A receipt is stapled to
the outside and flutters under the air-conditioning.

"Has she always been like that?" he asks as he removes the cardboard bowls from the bag. "Not super into kids?"

"Kind of. I always assumed she saw too much as a kid herself."
Natasha mixes her vegetables. The smell of roasted Brussels sprouts
and sweet potato fills the living room.

"What do you mean?" Zack drizzles his cauliflower rice with
sriracha, something he only started doing after he and Suhani
moved in together. His mother-in-law made him a spicy-food lover.

"I guess she always had to be such a caretaker in different ways.
When she was really young, she taught my parents about the
American school system and translated random things for them
and later told them about stuff like visiting colleges. And then with
Anuj and me, she was left in charge sometimes." Natasha laughs. "I
swear, she was stricter than Mom. Now that I think of it, she's even
a caretaker in her job. She's just one of those perpetual fixer types.
And to be fair, she's good at telling people what to do."

"She is," Zack agrees as he pictures his wife sitting across from
one of her therapy patients, untangling their destructive thoughts
or teaching them how to notice patterns in their behavior, all while
another part of her brain is wondering how she can improve the
system at large. Zack always wanted someone ambitious but never
imagined he'd find a woman like Suhani, someone who is constantly thinking and working and expanding. When Suhani talks
about the changes she wants in medicine and mental healthcare,
she comes to life. Zack's sisters call her a "petite powerhouse."

"She's even gotten my mom to exercise more, live a little," he says. "She pushes me at work and buys me these books about parent abandonment so I can process what happened with my dad."

Natasha nods and then her eyes shift back and forth, as if she's sifting through something mentally. "I didn't think of this until you asked, but when she was in med school, we all wondered if something happened with her. She suddenly became so much more closed off and intense . . . until she met you."

"Really? What do you mean?" Zack says.

"I don't know. It was a vibe. I always wondered if Roshan had something to do with it. There was this weekend when I visited her and something just gave me a bad feeling. Then I told myself I was just thinking and worrying too much, like my mom. I asked Suhani about it a bunch of times and she always said she was just stressed."

"Hm," Zack says. His thoughts jump back to the Atlanta Memorial reception, where Roshan showed up out of nowhere, and the conversation at Highland Bakery, when Suhani made their relationship sound inconsequential.

"But she's always stressed, you know?" Natasha shrugs. "I've never understood how someone can be so confident when it comes to doing things for other people but then so unsure when it comes to herself."

"I say that to her all the time!" Zack exclaims. Sometimes, when he looks at his wife, he sees a scared little girl alongside a strong woman. He's intrigued by all the versions of her, all the contradictions that make her who she is. Even though his mom always envisioned that he'd end up with a nice Jewish girl, he was never nervous about introducing Suhani to her. He knew she'd fall in love with her. Everyone does.

"Maybe y'all just need a reset. You both work so much and it has to be easy to just slip into this inertia-driven daily routine. Maybe go do something different together."

"I think we need that," Zack agrees. Being chronically exhausted can bring out the worst in a person. On some mornings, when he's still buried in the emotional hangover of one of their fights, he'll wake up and realize the fight itself was so stupid and unnecessary. *Why did we even let it escalate to that point?* he'll wonder. Then later that day, he'll remind himself that fatigue and resentment can add fuel to even the most minor arguments.

"After the wedding and honeymoon, it was just straight into work and it's been nonstop for both of us. She's actually suggested we go out for drinks during the week instead of just coming home and planting ourselves on this sofa and staring at our screens for the night," Zack says.

They both stop talking when they hear the sound of the keys in the door. Two seconds later, Suhani's dropping her purse on the tiny table in the front hallway and saying, "Cauliflower bowls? Niiiice."

Zack pats the spot next to him. "Have some."

Suhani takes a bite and makes an *mmm* sound, conveying that she thinks it's delicious. "So, what were you guys talking about?"

Zack and Natasha exchange a glance. At the same time, they both say, "Nothing!"

Eleven

Suhani

H ey, you have a second?" Vanessa says as she opens Suhani's office door. She's in an outfit that they both have from a shopping trip to the outlets. Vanessa saw the bright-pink tweed dress on a mannequin and claimed it had Elle Woods vibes. She's paired it with blush pumps and fuchsia lipstick.

"Sure! I'm not doing anything except trying to see a dozen patients an hour." Suhani smiles and motions to her computer screen. "Haven't had a chance to eat or pee. My new intake patient wouldn't stop asking me where I'm from. I kept saying Atlanta and he still kept asking."

"Why didn't you tell him it's none of his business?" Vanessa asks.

"You know I'm never going to say anything like that," Suhani says. "And I honestly think he was trying to make conversation. At least he didn't ask where my grandparents were born."

To Vanessa's point, Suhani needs to get better at switching between different types of armors throughout the day: the polite armor, the assertive armor, the I-can-handle-every-task-and-never-need-a-break armor. Sometimes, she has brief images of another life: opening a margarita stand on a beach, working at an airy, sun-filled flower shop, becoming one of those fun ladies who lunch. She had looked up some of these alternative careers when she almost lost everything in med school.

Out of the corner of her eye, Suhani sees a text from Mom pop up on her phone.

> Have you had a chance to have a serious talk with Natasha?
> Dad and I still have no idea what she's even doing with her life.
> Maybe her friends know since they're the only people she cares about.

Suhani takes a deep breath. She really doesn't have the energy for a Natasha vent session right now.

> SUHANI: Don't worry. I'll talk to her.

Mom replies with a GIF of Priyanka Chopra blowing a kiss.

> SUHANI: Speaking of serious talks, we should have one about your GIF choices.

> MOM: People tell me they love mine!

Suhani puts her phone facedown on her desk.

"It's really been one of those shit weeks." Vanessa rolls her eyes and sits in one of the jade-green tufted chairs Suhani got for her patients.

They talk about the recent grand rounds lecture on antipsychotics, which hospital committees they've applied for, and how things are going with their therapy cases. Although one of the necessities of any job is having someone to vent with in an unfiltered, cathartic way, being able to do that with other psychiatrists is especially entertaining. Zack laughed the first time he realized how often Suhani and her co-residents casually threw in phrases like "that was such a covert narcissist move" and "he has sprinkles of obsessive-compulsive and dependent personality disorder."

"So," Vanessa says as she examines her oxblood-red gel-painted nails. "It's good you're meeting with Dr. Wilson soon. Did you hear that the Dans are now running for chief?"

"What? Both of them?" Suhani asks.

The Dans, Dan Fitzpatrick and Dan Marlin, are the quintessential southern gentlemen of Atlanta Memorial Hospital's psychiatry program. They've got a combination of good manners and Abercrombie & Fitch looks, which means every nurse is in love with them. Dan Fitzpatrick's dad is one of the top anesthesiologists at the hospital. Dan Marlin comes from Buckhead old money and is family friends with Dr. Wilson.

But they never expressed any interest in being chief. Why now?

"Crap. There's no way I'm beating them," Suhani says. "Dr. Wilson's apparently making every candidate have a list of reasons of why they think they deserve it. Even the thought of just saying it out loud makes me so uncomfortable."

"But it shouldn't," Vanessa says. "I can't believe someone who just won an award has to convince herself that she deserves something. Only women think they have to torture themselves this way. Men—fine, not all men, but many—go for more than they're qualified for. Seriously. I read about it this weekend."

"Of course you did," Suhani says. Vanessa's always reading about workplace psychology. She was "leaning in" before it became an official thing.

"And you've got this," Vanessa says. "I know we all have our own story about why we wanted to go to med school and how it's our calling and blah blah blah. But you actually live it. You do so much for your patients; you work harder than anyone and make psychiatry your life."

Suhani shrugs. "You give me way too much credit."

She always knew she wanted to be a psychiatrist. Not just because of Dad, but also because of things she learned from Mom: the fulfillment of learning someone's story, building long-term relationships, and being the person to be counted on. She even loves the parts that are supposed to be stressful, like calming down an agitated patient or mediating heated family arguments. And more than anything, psychiatry gives her the chance to make sure she can be there for people who hit rock bottom the way she once did.

"Well, I know I have to try," Suhani says. "Chief will be my first real chance to make a change in our system. Make sure residents feel supported, that we can get more female leaders in the field and, hopefully, see if there's a way to bring more attention to women's mental healthcare."

"You will," Vanessa says. Her equal parts tough and tender disposition always fill Suhani with confidence, with a steadfast faith that she really can do anything she puts her mind to. She starts mentally drafting her list of reasons for Dr. Wilson. Hardworking, cares for resident well-being, wants to make a big impact for people who really need mental healthcare. Check, check, check.

Their conversation jumps from topic to topic. After Vanessa shows Suhani the profile of her latest Bumble date, a Turkish plastic surgeon, she leans back in the chair. "How's Zack?"

"Fine." Suhani shrugs. "He brought up the idea of having kids."

"Wow, really?" Vanessa asks. "What did you say?"

"I didn't know what to say! I don't even know how I feel about them. No, wait, I do know the thought of having them anytime soon scares me. I mean, we've talked about how if we ever had them, we'd want them to know both of our cultures, and Zack's always said he would do everything possible to make sure my career isn't derailed. But it just totally threw me off guard when he brought it up."

She waits for Vanessa to nod in agreement or say something that confirms how Suhani feels is valid.

But Vanessa frowns and scrunches her lip, the same focused look she gets when they're having class discussions about complicated patients. "Um, Suhani, I understand what you mean about being scared of having kids. But do you think you're also really scared of having a marriage like your parents'?"

Suhani's breath catches in her throat. "Where did that come from?"

"It's something I've been wondering about for a while," Vanessa says. If she was talking about anyone else, this is when Suhani would laugh and say, *And this is what we therapists call confrontation!*

"You've told me so many times how your mom has all these regrets about leaving her acting career, how she left her entire life for love. And you've always felt so much pressure to make sure all her sacrifices weren't in vain." Vanessa clasps her hands together. "I know you and Zack are always good at the core. . . . I'm just curious about whether getting married brought things up in you about your parents' marriage."

Before Suhani says anything, Vanessa adds, "And, look, we've all got stuff we bring to a relationship. I mean, hell, my dad left my mom when I was five and I can't commit to a guy. It doesn't take someone from our profession to see the link. But with Zack's parents being divorced, too, I understand how getting married makes him want to build something of his own as a way to, you know, heal."

"I've analyzed all of this a million times and never once connected everything together like that." Suhani wishes she'd written down Vanessa's words. "Did anyone ever tell you you're a really good psychiatrist?"

Despite the lightheartedness of her words, Suhani knows that she'll spend the rest of the day dissecting everything Vanessa said. But even though she's right, Vanessa doesn't know the other reason, maybe the biggest reason, why Suhani can't even think about having kids.

She touches her phone as she pictures the text message from Roshan that she still hasn't answered: I need to talk to you.

There's a knock at her door by Marie, the front desk manager. "Dr. Joshi, I'm sorry to interrupt, but your patient is here. He's having a crisis and needs to see you early."

Marie's permed hair and teal-blue eye shadow always remind Suhani of the mom character in a feel-good family show from the eighties.

"I'll be right there." Suhani nods as Vanessa leaves her office. Her next appointment is with Dean, a forty-year-old software engineer who has weekly panic attacks. She reviews the breathing exercises that have helped him in the past and double-checks his most recent Lexapro dose. Before she meets him in the waiting room, she scrolls through her last texts with Zack.

SUHANI: Can we talk about some stuff tonight?

ZACK: Of course. What stuff?

Zack is always up for talking about feelings or, really, about anything. Every milestone of their relationship has been preceded by a long talk. Before Zack first met Mom and Dad, he and Suhani sat in a coffee shop for an entire afternoon and discussed why Dad might be skeptical about him and what they'd have to do to prove that they were in a serious relationship. A year later, Zack listened patiently when Suhani explained that it would be inappropriate for him to kiss her in front of the aunties, eat meat in front of her family, and wear shoes in the house.

SUHANI: Nothing important. Tell you more tonight at home.

ZACK: I'll be home late ☹. There's a CBD company that's taking us to drinks to try and convince us to partner with them.

SUHANI: Sounds fun!

Zack's a director at YourCare, a start-up that links people to doctors all around Atlanta through a single web portal. Although his hours are hectic, he's still able to do luxurious things like go to the bathroom whenever he needs to or eat unlimited fancy snacks in the company's kitchen.

ZACK: Remember to schedule your meeting with Dr. Wilson. And here's a Corgi going after a ball with all this determination. It's like you with everything.

Suhani clicks the video link and her screen fills up with an adorable puppy chasing a tennis ball. Its short legs and smile give her a quick breather from the day. For the first time in days, things between her and Zack finally feel the way they used to. Easy, tender, secure.

SUHANI: Ha! So cute!

A question tugs at her. When was the last time she surprised Zack with something? Her mind passes back over the conversation with Vanessa. Was she right about Suhani's being scared of having the same marriage as her parents? Were there things about her past that made her keep her guard up? She doesn't want it to be that way.

After her appointment with Dean, Suhani confirms a pickup order for chocolate chip cookies from Tiff's Treat's, Zack's favorite, and makes a silent promise to have them warmed and waiting on a plate when he gets home.

She scrolls back to Roshan's text. He needs to know there's no place for him in her life. She tells herself there's no reason to be scared. Not anymore.

Determination pulls her out of her chair. It only takes her twenty seconds to get out of her office and down one flight of stairs to the neurology department.

Roshan's office door is closed. Her heart rate increases as she sees his gold nameplate on the door. He's really here. In her hospital.

Suhani clears her throat and knocks on the door.

"Come in!" His baritone voice sends a shiver up her spine.

He's sitting at a large mahogany desk and scrolling through something on the computer. There's something about seeing him there, absorbed in his work, that makes her sadder than she expected to feel. She briefly sees him the way most people do, as a dedicated and caring doctor.

Roshan glances up with a look of surprise, then disdain. "Uh, hi."

His white coat is on a hook next to him. The walls of his office are barren, which could be either because he hasn't had time to put anything up or because he doesn't care to. Roshan was never into aesthetics. Even in med school, he had the bare minimum amount of furniture in his studio apartment.

"I got your text and figured it's better we talk in person. Because I have to talk to you, too." Suhani walks into his office and closes the door.

"About?" Roshan turns off the computer screen and raises his eyebrows. She wants to analyze his expression, know what he's thinking. But she tells herself it doesn't matter.

She has to project strength, the way she should have years ago. She has to get this conversation over with and return to her life. Her happy, full life. "You appear out of nowhere at my hospital. What the hell do you want?"

"Excuse me?"

"Excuse you." Suhani crosses her arms. "What are you doing here?"

"Work, if you couldn't tell." Roshan motions around his office.

God, that sarcasm. His straight lips and furrowed brows take her back to the night they met. She forgot how he looked at her as though he could see straight to her thoughts, in a way that made her feel raw and alive and vulnerable all at once. The qualities that made Roshan scary were the same ones that made him sensitive: the intensity to which he felt pain, the way he remembered details, how guided he was by his emotions.

"And that's it? Really?" She taps her foot on the scuffed floor. Just being around Roshan riles her up. She can't help but compare that to how she is around Zack. Content, easygoing Zack.

"Really," Roshan says. "I told you I always wanted to come back to Atlanta."

He did tell her that years ago. It was the first thing they ever connected on, being the only people from Atlanta at their med school.

"And you just happened to get a job where I work?" Suhani asks.

"The best hospital in the state? Yeah, I did take this job when they recruited me," Roshan says.

Her heart rate slows down. Maybe that's all this is, a dumb coincidence.

Roshan clears his throat. "I texted you because after I saw you the other night, I thought we should at least talk if we're going to be working in the same place. Then again, we could have talked years ago, if you hadn't just left and ignored me without any explanation."

"I didn't owe you an explanation," Suhani says as she recalls how she ghosted him before she even knew what ghosting meant.

He's holding a pen labeled ATLANTA MEMORIAL HOSPITAL. "It seems like you're happy now."

"I am," Suhani says, relishing that she means it.

"You know, I spoke to people from your class at UCLA. A couple of them mentioned you took some kind of official leave right after we broke up. You just dumped me and then left school for months. Clearly there's something you didn't tell me. I spent so long trying to understand why you'd do something like that."

"It doesn't matter now," Suhani says.

There's a tingling sensation in her limbs as she thinks back to how she filled out the paperwork for a medical leave, then spent days curled up in her bed. She wasn't sure if she'd ever feel happy again.

"It obviously mattered enough. I know it was something important, something I probably had the right to know about," Roshan says. "Otherwise you wouldn't have tried so hard to keep it from me."

"I don't think there's any point in getting into any of that." Suhani throws her hands up in the air and then tells herself to act as detached as possible. A bead of sweat rolls down her back. "I should have had better judgment from the beginning and known that you were never capable of being in a healthy relationship."

Roshan has the same intense stare he had at the end of their first date, when he told Suhani about how he'd always resented his mother for leaving their family. She should have seen that conversation as a red flag but instead, she told herself to give him credit for being vulnerable with her. They spent an entire Friday night on her creaky futon, sharing a bottle of Cabernet, discussing their family histories, then looking up potential residency programs for him. The night ended with the most exhilarating sex she'd ever had, sex that was both primal and tender, free of inhibitions. She later told herself that that was who they really were, that the moments he let his anger take over didn't define him, and with time, he'd change. It took her months to realize that she couldn't stay with someone just because of who they were at their best. Sooner or later, dating a man for his potential only took you so far.

"I never said the way I treated you was okay. And, yeah, it took me too long to realize I had a problem. A serious one." Roshan lowers his shoulders, and for the first time ever, he seems embarrassed. "But let's not pretend you did nothing wrong."

"I did plenty wrong," Suhani says. "I trusted you to be a decent guy. I wasted months putting up with you."

She savors the feel of each accusation leaving her mouth. He should have heard them years ago. But instead of ever calling him out, she kept all of it inside. This was their secret. To everyone at UCLA med school, they were the perfect couple. The perfect desi doctor couple.

The expression on his face hardens. "You know what? You show up here to what? Try and make some statement against me? Don't stand here and act like you aren't messed up, too. You stayed with me. You could have left earlier."

Suhani gulps. She used to feel the same way when she'd read

about women in her position. But she learned it was never that easy. Because Roshan brought her to such a low point that she often forgot she had a choice.

"Does everyone here think you're Miss Perfect?" Roshan asks. "Or does your program director know how you just left in the middle of a rotation and took a leave of absence?"

Suhani's voice is soft as she says, "He knows I went through something."

"Really? In detail?" Roshan raises his eyebrows.

"Are you trying to scare me, Roshan?" Suhani challenges.

"Not at all. All I'm saying is that maybe you should take a step back before using that holier-than-thou attitude. You've made plenty of mistakes, too."

What is he really doing here? Is she being paranoid? She's taken back to the woman she used to be with him, the kind who constantly doubted herself.

"I'm well aware of that. And I came here to tell you to leave me alone and stay out of my life." Suhani turns around and leaves.

This isn't the way it was supposed to go today. She felt powerful whenever she envisioned this conversation. She had planned to march into his office, give him a piece of her mind, and walk away with a smug sense of satisfaction.

But now she feels all her determination dissolving and making room for something else.

Something that feels a lot like losing control.

The apartment is pitch-black when Suhani gets home several hours later. She hangs her purse on a gold hook and drops her keys in a speckled turquoise Anthropologie bowl on the entrance table.

Since Zack isn't here, she can get away with having a large glass of wine, cheese, and crackers for dinner.

Out of the corner of her eye, she catches a blanketed mound rising and falling on the couch.

"Natasha?" Suhani turns on the light. "You're sleeping?"

Of course. This is how it's always been. Suhani works while Natasha sleeps or drinks or captivates people with her bold humor. Some people can get through all of life being their carefree selves, while others, like Suhani, have to hunker down and work, work, work.

Natasha stirs. She's wearing Suhani's maroon flannel pajamas, which she no doubt fished out from the bottom of Suhani and Zack's dresser. For a second, seeing Natasha that way makes Suhani nostalgic for high school, when in some ways life felt a little simpler.

But now she wonders if it really was simpler or if, with growing up and going through some shit, she's become more aware, or maybe just more cynical.

Suhani starts picking up crumpled tissues, Reese's peanut butter cup wrappers, and an empty Cheetos bag off her coffee table. A bowl of Cape Cod chips is dangerously close to the edge. The television is on the Netflix screen that reads ARE YOU STILL WATCHING?

Suhani feels a flash of irritation as she throws the trash away. "NATASHA, WAKE UP!"

Natasha jumps up as though she's been electrocuted. "Oh my God, you scared the crap out of me. Uh, hey."

Suhani opens the fridge door. "Did you seriously finish my champagne?"

"Oh, calm down," Natasha says. "I'll get you another bottle."

"Yeah, I'm sure," Suhani says, too tired to argue. "So what have you been doing all day?"

She removes a bottle of wine from the pantry. Outside, the Atlanta skyline glitters like jewelry.

Natasha scrolls through her phone. "Just, you know, working on stuff."

"Anything of note?" Suhani asks, torn between feeling sorry for her sister and feeling frustrated with her lack of initiative.

Natasha shakes her head.

Suhani avoids eye contact as she pours wine and arranges a slab of Brie, several crackers, grapes, and a tiny bowl of olives on a white marble cheese board. She pours another glass for Natasha and brings everything to the coffee table.

Natasha sits up and slathers Brie onto a cracker. "So, was work stressful?"

"Yeah." Suhani takes a big sip of wine. "You know, the usual."

"I wish it could get easier for you at some point. I feel like you're always working. Always tired."

"That's just how residency is. Every single thing I do counts. If I screw up, someone can really get hurt. And I'm then forever a bad doctor."

"You really need to let that worry go already," Natasha says. "You are never going to be that. Ever." She shakes her head on the word "ever." "Damn, don't you ever get exhausted just being so you?"

"What's that supposed to mean?" Suhani asks as she realizes it's a variation on what Zack's been telling her for the past couple of weeks.

"You're so on edge all the time that it makes me anxious," Natasha says. "Like, chill the fuck out already."

The statement lingers in the air between them. Natasha glances at Suhani, unsure of whether she's just said something too offensive. A couple of seconds pass. Natasha has a gleam in her eyes. Her gaze locks with Suhani's. They instantly break into a fit of laughter. Suhani feels some of her stress pour out of her in a way that's only possible when she's around her sister.

"Guess who I saw at work today?" Suhani says with a tone that reminds her of Mom excited to share gossip. She tells Natasha everything, ending with how she stormed out of Roshan's office.

"Whoa. Holy shit," Natasha says after Suhani's done. She launches into the questions that can only be asked with Zack not at home. "How did he look? Did you feel anything, even anything small, toward him? Are you going to talk to him again?"

"I don't plan to." Suhani takes a large sip of wine and pictures the lines around Roshan's eyes, the way his broad shoulders and palpable confidence flooded her with memories.

"Does Zack know about everything that happened with him?"

"What do you mean by 'everything'?" Suhani's stomach tightens. Natasha knows more than anyone else, but even she doesn't know everything.

"Like how serious you guys were? How intense it got? That that was the most formative relationship you were in before Zack? I mean, that guy got to you in a way I'd never seen before."

Suhani shakes her head as she thinks of the waves of rage and relief that only Roshan could send her on. "I don't think Zack wants any of those details."

"I think he would," Natasha says. "Wouldn't you if he had someone like that in his past who now works close to him?"

"I guess I would and wouldn't. Of course I checked out all of his exes when we first started dating. They were all white," Suhani says. "But I don't know if I needed every single detail of his relationships."

"I'd want to know," Natasha says, confirming that she and Su-hani have such different approaches to their pasts. Natasha doesn't believe in keeping anything to herself, even if it could spare some-one's feelings or stop her from getting into trouble.

"I did remember how intense things always were with Roshan. I knew it would all be easier with Zack. No guessing or mind games or any of that crap. All the really hard parts with him, espe-cially at the beginning, were about everyone else. Our parents not taking us seriously. Everyone judging us."

Natasha squints at her, a look of skepticism on her face. "Do you feel like you miss the drama? Or wish Zack was more passi-onate?"

"No, of course not," Suhani says, resenting herself for implying that there is anything wrong with Zack. "It's just that . . . no, never mind."

"What?" Natasha pushes.

Suhani sighs. "There were certain things Roshan and I never had to discuss, about our parents moving to America, being the oldest in a Gujarati family. With Zack, we had to make it a point to talk about all of that stuff, and sometimes he still doesn't get it."

She sips her wine and feels a wave of relief at being able to say all this and know Natasha won't judge her. Maybe Suhani should be kinder to her younger self every time she berates her for dating Roshan. Things weren't toxic in the beginning. He doted on her constantly. It took her months to realize that control could be dis-guised as love.

Natasha looks at Suhani as if she's examining her. "Is there ever a second when you wish you were with someone else? Or single? I feel like nobody ever talks about the bad parts of being married, like being trapped or wondering if you made a mistake."

"Never." Suhani shakes her head. "Even on our bad days, things with Zack are still good at the core. I've been so tired and stressed from work, but we both still try as hard as we can for each other. And he's always made me feel like I can do anything, be anyone I want."

Before Zack, Suhani didn't know that the way someone made her feel about herself was one of the most important parts of a relationship.

She wonders if she should tell Natasha about the last few times she and Zack have argued. It all feels so out of character for them, for the usual steadiness of their marriage. Natasha would know how to reassure her that it's just because of work stress and some miscommunication. Nothing to worry about.

"I get that," Natasha says. "Karan made me feel funny, for sure, but, like, I think he wanted a funny housewife. Not a comedian. Maybe I knew on some level that he thought I was fun-girlfriend material but not his type of wife material."

"I can see how it's easier to like the idea of someone more than the actual reality of being with them," Suhani says. "But don't you think Karan did really know you? He's been a part of our family forever. Maybe you both just need a little space."

Natasha frowns. "So you're saying I made a mistake?"

"I didn't say that at all. I just think you both know each other so well and maybe this is just a rough patch."

"Ugh." Natasha rolls her eyes. "I was just trying to talk to you about Zack, not get into why I screwed things up with Karan. Trust me, Mom has given me enough shit about it. And I'm sure his mom is thrilled I'm out of the picture."

Suhani catches a glimpse of her sister's eyes. There's anger in them, yes, but there's also a hint of something else. Sadness, maybe. Or could it be regret?

"So, how's your comedy going?" Suhani asks to change the subject. "Any thoughts on getting a day job?"

"Seriously?" Natasha asks. "You sound like Mom. She already tried to make me call that weird uncle for a job."

"Well, maybe we're trying to help. Because sometimes you shut down or block out your problems," Suhani says. "And you have to have an income."

"I don't shut down," Natasha says with a very distinct edge to her voice. "And I already applied for a job at Starbucks."

"As a barista?"

"Yes. I'm not beneath pouring coffee, okay? And just so you know, working on my comedy isn't all fun and games. It's actually really freaking hard and I could use some support." Natasha stands up. "I definitely don't need you to treat me like one of your therapy cases."

"I'm not!"

"Puh-lease. And I don't even expect you to totally understand," Natasha says. "You don't know what it's like to feel like a total failure. Like everyone's just judging you and waiting for you to screw up. You just don't get it."

Oh, I do get it, Suhani wants to say. *More than you know.*

"What don't I get? I want to be there for you, understand what you're going through. You didn't even tell me you were going to break up with Karan and I sti—"

"I wasn't going to! I was so caught off guard by the freaking proposal in front of our entire family!" Natasha interrupts. "I mean, he was my best friend and now I don't even know how he's doing."

Despite Natasha's firm, loud voice, Suhani detects an undercurrent of defeat.

Natasha wrings her hands. "Maybe I didn't realize how not

ready I was to get married until he got down on one knee! I mean, who the fuck proposes without discussing something like that with their girlfriend?! And when we're so young!"

"That's true," Suhani says. "I can't imagine how shocked you were."

"I really was," Natasha says. "I wish I just had the chance to tell him that I was happy with the way things were. And I always saw myself having a bigger and better life than this before I got married. There was stuff I thought I'd accomplish before I became a wife, if I ever became a wife. But it doesn't matter now. Everything's just gone to shit."

"It hasn't all gone to shit. Not at all," Suhani says. She knows it's not the right time to tell Natasha that until now, she's had an easier time than Suhani or Anuj in a lot of ways. Suhani had to dress up as an Indian princess for Halloween every year, but Natasha always found a way to convince Mom to buy her something new. Suhani and Anuj were both bullied throughout middle school, while Natasha's unapologetic confidence made her a consistent leader of the pack.

"Let's see what's on," Suhani suggests. She starts to feel the weight of her day. Suddenly, all she wants to do is take a hot shower and collapse into her king-size bed.

Natasha turns on an episode of *The Office*.

"This is one of the scenes Mindy wrote," Natasha says. "She was the only woman and person of color on the writing staff when she was hired. Can you believe that?"

Suhani shakes her head. "Sadly, I can. She's done so much for women, especially women of color."

"Totally," Natasha says. "If I ever make it with comedy, I'm going to make sure there's space for more women."

"I know you will," Suhani says. "And you're going to make it."

She stops herself from saying *If you put in the work*. Her sister has so much innate talent but often lacks the drive to follow through. But she won't offer that reminder right now, maybe because on some level, Suhani suspects, she already knows it.

Natasha leans over to Suhani's side of the couch and puts her head on her shoulder. Her curls brush against Suhani's cheek. For a second, Natasha's thirteen years old again, asking Suhani what a period is and how to wear a tampon.

"I'm sorry I freaked out. I know you're only looking out for me." Natasha chews on her bottom lip.

"It's fine." Suhani turns the volume up. "Let's just let it go."

Classic Natasha: pissing you off one second, melting your heart the next.

"I had to watch this show behind Mom's back and pretend I was studying," Natasha says. "But she always caught me. Remember how we'd wait to hear her breathing every time we talked to our friends on the landline? She was always listening from the downstairs phone."

"She was. She could have been a detective with the way she kept tabs on what we were doing. And she always denied it!" Suhani laughs. One time, Mom forgot to cover the mouthpiece and Suhani heard the telltale piano intro from her Hindi soap opera.

A few minutes later, Natasha pauses from staring at Jim and Pam and asks, "Do you ever think that we all put on an I'm-fine face for Mom and Dad? Because we know how much they struggled as immigrants?"

"I know we do," Suhani says. "I think we tell ourselves that they had it so much worse, having to leave their home, face discrimination, try to make ends meet . . . so there's no way our problems could ever compare."

She kept so many things from Mom and Dad throughout the years that by college, denial was just another reflex. No, she wasn't waxing her arms because someone at school called them hairy. No, she didn't sob in her car after getting a B on the calculus final. No, her ex-boyfriend never crushed her sense of self-worth and almost cost her her career. No, she doesn't feel insecure at work.

"Sometimes I get so sick of telling them I'm fine," Natasha says.

"I know you do." Suhani wraps her arm across Natasha's back.

They sit that way until the wine and cheese are finished. Natasha slumps onto Suhani's shoulder in the middle of the next episode. Suhani strokes her sister's wavy hair, which is crunchy from dry shampoo. They both drift into a dreamless sleep, with the television still on, as though they're kids again.

Twelve

Bina

"You decided to wear that?" Bina takes in her daughter's makeup-
and jewelry-free face, flip-flops, and wrinkled peach cotton sari
that's unevenly pleated around her waist. They're at one of the nic-
est hotels in Atlanta for a wedding reception and Natasha looks like
she rolled out of bed and wrapped a sari around her like a bath
towel. It's as though she was making it a point to stand out in the
sea of heavy saris and even heavier jewelry sets.

Still, Bina regrets her words the second they emerge. A part of
her wants to say she's only trying to help, but that'll only make
things worse.

Plus, Natasha's outfit did distract Bina from the dread she's had
all week over seeing her friends for the first time since the health
fair. Her stomach tightens as she thinks of the impending awkwardness. She hates how much of her identity is tied to being accepted by the people she loves. It reminds her of her first years in
America. Back then, Bina spent so much time wondering when
she'd finally feel like she belonged. Now, she wishes she could tell
her younger self to focus less on wanting to belong with others and
more on believing in herself.

She reaches into her gold sparkly clutch and wraps her hand around the folded place card that has her name and table number. The seating cards are at the entrance of the hall on a large round table with tea-light candles and a brass statue of Ganesha in the middle. Bina spots hers right away. Anita's is next to hers, with the same table number in the same elegant calligraphy. What's Bina supposed to do all night? Smile and act like everything's okay? She should have put Vaseline on her teeth, an old trick she used during her acting days to help her hold a grin for long periods of time.

"Mom. Seriously? Hi to you, too." Natasha groans as she sticks a toothpick into a cube of chili paneer, her favorite appetizer at Indian weddings.

Now that Bina has a second to notice, the entire cocktail-hour space smells like chili paneer, alcohol, and an array of perfumes. Bina could bottle up that combination and name it Desi Wedding.

Bina exchanges hellos and brief updates with people who pass by them. She knows people aren't supposed to like small talk, but she loves it, always has. It's always been one of her favorite parts of going to weddings.

"Dad," Natasha says, unaware or nonchalant to the fact that everyone can hear her. "Whenever Mom is done socializing with every single person here, can you tell her to back off with me? Who even cares what I look like here? We barely know these people. They only invited us because they invited everyone."

Natasha does have a point. But Bina doesn't tell her that. It's been three weeks since she moved out of the house. Three weeks of Bina wondering if Natasha is okay, what in the world she's filling her time with, and how fulfilled she can really be living on Suhani and Zack's couch. The second Bina saw her daughter walk into the

Whitley Hotel Atlanta Buckhead event hall, she couldn't decide if
she wanted to yell at her or tell her she missed her and wants her to
come home.

Deepak puts his arms around Natasha. "You look great, *beta*."

"Thank you." Natasha gulps her wine and gives Bina a see-I-
told-you type of smile. Looping Deepak into her woes has been her
daddy's-girl tactic since she was a toddler.

Deepak extends his arms and motions for Bina to come closer.
Bina's shoulders drop. Even if she and Natasha find a way to disagree on, well, everything, something about being in her presence
just feels so familiar, so comforting.

Natasha rests her head on Bina's shoulder. "So, Mom, on more
important topics, it looks like Chand Uncle is already revved up for
the dancing part of the night."

Bina, Natasha, and Deepak turn to the entrance of the cocktail-
hour space, where Mira's husband is at least three beers deep and
showing off his disco moves to a small audience of family friends
that includes Kavita, who is uploading a video of Chand's dancing to Instagram. Chand and Mira will be on many Instagram
accounts tonight. They both dominate dance floors at Atlanta wedding receptions and alternate from classic Bollywood moves to a
middle-aged version of swing dancing to even the tango.

"Hey, can we join in this group hug?" Zack asks as he and
Suhani approach them. They're both holding glasses of champagne
and, as always, are dressed better than the bride and groom. Zack's
in a custom-fitted light gray suit that's perfect for the balmy weather
and Suhani is in a bright-pink-and-gold Anita Dongre lehenga.
She's paired the shimmery skirt and top with a gold choker and
bulbous gold earrings. Bina notices a cluster of women gazing at
Suhani with equal parts awe and approval. Many of them know

and love Zack, but the ones who don't give him a double take, a common reaction to seeing a white guy so at home among a sea of Indian people. It's especially entertaining when they hear him speaking in Gujarati.

Out of the corner of Bina's eye, she sees Suhani reach for Zack's hand. Zack shifts to face her. His jaw is clenched. Suhani mouths, *I'm really sorry.* Zack shakes his head, then says *I'm sorry* back. He looks up and locks eyes with Bina, whose gaze is clearly fixed on them. Shit. Bina turns away quickly and pretends to be lost in the conversation between Deepak and Natasha. The last thing she needs is for Zack to think she's a nosy mother-in-law. She had a nosy mother-in-law whose meddling made Bina often want to punch a wall.

"Anuj! Get over here." Zack gives Bina a big grin as if to reassure her that everything is fine.

Anuj asks someone to hold his spot in the bar line and stands next to Bina. They have a collective group hug, the kind they haven't shared since Suhani and Zack's wedding.

My family, Bina thinks with a flash of pride. Her people are here. She'll be okay enough.

"How nice to see you all together!" Jiten's voice interrupts the moment. Deepak gives him a cheery "Good to see you," the kind that would make anyone observing them think that they're still best friends and that their wives still talk every day. Bina isn't sure whether to be annoyed or amused that men can have such simple and surface-level friendships, ones that rarely lead to conflict.

A knot of dread forms in her stomach as she sees Anita and Karan standing behind Jiten. Anita stares at the ground while Karan's gaze goes straight to Natasha. Bina feels the weight of sadness settle over her. It's unnatural to not run toward Anita and hug her, tell her how wonderful it is to see her.

"Hey," Natasha says to Karan.

Go, Natasha! Bina's proud of her daughter for not letting the sheer awkwardness push her into silence, the way it has for Bina.

"Hello," Karan says.

"How are you? What have you been up to?"

"Just the usual." Karan's curt in a way Bina has never seen in all the years she's known him. Why couldn't he and Natasha have worked things out? What was so bad that things had to end this way?

Bina forces herself to bury the questions as Natasha steps toward Karan.

"Just the usual? Are you really going to act like we don't know each other?" Natasha's eyes flash before she mutters, "That's really mature."

"Mature? *Mature?*" Karan asks. "You're telling me about being mature? That's rich!"

Everyone's necks turn to Karan, then Natasha, then Karan again. It's like they're all watching a painful tennis match. A few wedding guests, including their elderly neighbors, slow down to take in every detail. Bina gives them a look that she hopes indicates there's nothing to see here.

Natasha steps toward Karan again. "Maybe we can ta—"

"I'm going to grab a drink." Karan cuts her off and makes a straight dash to the bar.

Bina gives Anita a forced, awkward laugh. "It's good to see you."

"You, too." The sadness that was in Anita's eyes at the health fair is still there, but today it's submerged under a layer of regret. Her silver-streaked hair is pulled back in a low bun, and she's wearing a silk olive-green sari. The expression on her face and her outfit suddenly make her look older, like the type of woman who has had a difficult life. Bina wants to ask her if she's okay, if she's been sleeping and taking care of her self.

Talk to me, Bina wants to say. *I'm here for you.*

But Anita looks away as if she's distracted by something on the purple carpet. For the first time in a long time, maybe ever, Bina understands how a friend can break your heart in a way nobody else can.

Anita nods and puts on a tight smile as she calls for Kavita, who is dipping a samosa in chutney. Bina can't believe that in a matter of minutes, she, Anita, Kavita, and Mira will be sitting next to one another. For once she hopes the speeches and dance performances are long so she doesn't have to make too much small talk.

When Anita walks away, Natasha frowns. "You know what? Screw them! All of them! Who do they think they are, acting like we're strangers?"

"Natasha . . ." Deepak says in his strongest don't-say-more tone.

"I know. I know," Natasha says. "God forbid anyone here actually hears me telling it like it is, right?"

"*Beta,* maybe you should calm down," Bina says.

And maybe you shouldn't be drinking when you're this easily riled up.

"You know what, Mom?" Natasha's eyes are flashing. "I just don't think that's going to happen."

Natasha stops talking as they're approached by Pramila and Priya, twin sisters who married twin brothers and all live in a joint family household.

"Natasha, *beta!*" Pramila says. "We didn't realize you were here."

"We saw Karan over there," Priya adds. "Can you believe you two are going to have an event like this soon?"

Bina clenches her fists. *Natasha, don't say it. Don't say it. Don't say it.*

"Actually, we won't. Karan and I broke up."

"What?" Pramila places a hand over a pearl pendant that Ma would have called gaudy.

"Yup. So we're not getting married."

Bina wants to bury her face in her hands. Deepak shoots her a look that says, *Stay calm.*

Pramila frowns. "I see. I'm sorry about that."

"Thanks. But I'm good. I've accepted I'm probably not ever getting married."

"Oh, you're too funny," Priya says. "You always have been!"

Natasha raises her now-empty wineglass. "I really appreciate that because I am a full-time comedian now."

"A what?" Pramila cups her ear as if Natasha said *I am running away to join the circus.*

"I'm focusing on my real passion: comedy. Great, right?"

"Ah, well . . . of course it's . . . fun." Priya searches for the right word. "You are so cute."

"Cute? That's sweet. I'd hardly say I'm cute. I am, however, going to get more drunk. It was great to see you."

Bina freezes. The nerve of that girl! She takes a deep breath and commands herself to calm down as Natasha marches toward the bar, Anuj trailing behind her.

Pramila and Priya are pretending to be busy eating kathi rolls. But the shock in their eyes is clear.

A flush fills Bina's cheeks as she stammers, "What Natasha meant is, she's enjoying her time here."

"Of course." Pramila nods out of pure politeness.

When they leave, Zack hugs Bina and says, "Wooo! It's never boring with my family."

"That's one way to say it," Bina says. Waves of humiliation crash over her. Why would Natasha speak this way? She knows how embarrassing it is. Didn't Bina teach her better?

"Suhani, can you go reason with her, please?" Bina asks.

Suhani nods. "She's just upset. She needs some space."

"All we give her is space!" Bina lowers her voice in case any more random people happen to learn about the inner workings of their family.

"By space, I mean a little understanding," Suhani says. "Maybe we should let her be and, I don't know, you can go talk to Mira Auntie and Kavita Auntie?"

"I will be talking to them," Bina says. "We're at the same table, with Anita."

"Wait, Mom." A look of recognition passes over Suhani's face. "Did you not ever have your Chats Over Chai meeting?"

"No. I'm letting that go." Bina shakes her head. "It's not going to work out."

"Why not?"

"Because it just isn't." Bina sighs.

"So that's it? You're just giving up?" Suhani raises her eyebrows, sounding more like the mother questioning her daughter.

Bina nods. "It was silly anyway, to think of starting something new when I'm so old. That type of thing is for you youngsters. I don't even know why I got so carried away with it in the first place."

"I completely disagree," Suhani says as she drains her champagne. "You're in a way better position to start something like this compared to any of us."

"Why is that?"

"Because you've been through more. You have more perspective, more experience, more everything. I think you just need to see that about yourself, too."

"Oh, please." Bina waves her hand. "You make me seem so capable. I'm just a wife and mother. Nothing special."

Bina hopes that Suhani can't sense her dismay. She had waited for this period of her life, when her kids were grown up, and she could pursue other things. But that plan wasn't meant for her. And sooner or later, she needs to accept her life's limits. Disappointment is like any other chronic condition; after a point, you learn to live with it.

"That's not true at all," Suhani says. Bina waits for her to argue but Suhani gives her a quick hug and says, "Just think about what I said, okay? I'm going to go find Natasha."

A minute later, Bina sees Suhani and Natasha hunched over their phones, then laughing with Kavita's daughter, Sonam, and her boyfriend, Sanjay. Mira's daughter, Pooja, is behind them uploading a selfie. Anuj and Zack join them a few seconds later.

Bina's about to look away, but then she sees it again. Suhani reaching for Zack, but this time, Zack brushing her hand, then stepping away from her.

Just as she's about to text Suhani to ask if everything is okay, the deejay announces that cocktail hour is over and it's time for everyone to sit down. Anita, Kavita, and Mira are already at the table with their husbands. She can fake a happy smile when she sits next to them. She can fake so many things.

Mira is studying (translation: judging) the white hydrangea and orchid centerpieces. She turns to Chand and pretends to whisper, "I hate it when these young brides and grooms have their friends make so many speeches. We did it right in India. Food, dancing, social time. What these kids here don't realize is that none of us care if the bride likes cupcakes or the groom likes football! We just need to talk to each other."

Deepak squeezes Bina's hand and whispers, "It'll be fine." Bina braces herself for an evening of superficial, civil conversation.

But before she even reaches her chair, one on the opposite side of the table from Anita, Mira yells, "Bina! I can't wait for the next Chats Over Chai meeting!"

"What?" Bina asks, confused.

"Next weekend! I'm so sorry we couldn't make it to the first one."

Bina's not sure if it's boldness or exhaustion, but she blurts, "Because you were busy at Anita's?"

Mira's taken aback. She glances at Anita, who is busy talking to Jiten. "Yes, we were there. But because she was really having a hard time. Not because we don't care about you."

"You still could have told me," Bina says. "We've known each other for how long? We shouldn't have to lie to each other like that. I understand it's hard being caught between two of your friends, but there should still be room for honesty."

"You're right." Mira takes a deep breath. "We should have told you. I'm sorry."

Bina feels a weight lift. "It's okay." And to her surprise, it really does feel okay. Her daughters were right. Putting things out there in the open was much better than holding them inside herself.

"But this entire plan you have, to build a women's community, and do something just for us . . . it sounds amazing, Bina. I hope I can get off the waitlist!"

"Waitlist? What are you talking about?"

"The Instagram post all your kids just put up!" Mira holds up her phone. A black-and-white photo of Bina is on her screen. Anuj had taken the photo on his iPhone last year while Bina was cooking. The afternoon light is coating Bina's cheeks and chin as she's staring into the distance. A stack of rotlis and a wooden rolling pin are next to her hands.

"They what?" Bina grabs Mira's phone. There's a caption under her photo: *Our mom is a true inspiration. Many people know her for her warmth and ease with people, how she can become friends with anyone. Others know how she's always giving back to our community. But above all, our mom is a creator. And with her newest initiative, Chats Over Chai, she's creating a safe space for women to come together every month and connect on the various things going on in their lives. The first meeting is next weekend. DM if you'd like to be added to the waitlist!*

"I, uh, don't know what to say. . . ." Bina scrolls through the dozens of comments. Why would the kids do this without telling her?

"Say I'm off of the waitlist!" Mira yelps.

"Sure," Bina says. Mira motions to Kavita.

"What's going on?" Bipin, Kavita's husband, asks.

Everyone at their table faces Bina. "I've had this idea for us ladies to get together and talk about the things that are bothering us, really talk."

"Don't you all talk all the time anyway?" Bipin asks.

"Sure, we socialize. But I want us to dig deep into certain issues that are affecting all of us. We all have this need to make things look so polished and perfect on the surface. And I'm learning that it's really unhealthy. We have to start learning to be honest and open about the things we sweep under the rug."

"I don't know if we need to just air out our private lives for everyone," Anita says. Even though her lips are stretched into a smile, Bina notices a tightness in her friend's jaw.

"Actually, I think we sometimes do," Bina says.

"LET'S HEAR IT FOR THE FATHER OF THE BRIDE!" the deejay booms into the microphone. Everyone claps and cheers.

Before the next speech, Bina lowers her voice and says, "When I was growing up, all I knew was that I was supposed to sacrifice and take care of others, that that was my role. The first time Suhani told me about boundaries, I asked her, 'What do you mean by boundaries?' Nobody in India teaches girls about boundaries. And it occurred to me, as Deepak and I were driving here, that if we can talk to each other, all of us, we can learn. We can learn from our kids' lessons, their mistakes, and, you know, from each other. . . ."

She trails off as she sees Mira and Kavita nod with interest.

But Kavita's husband, Bipin, frowns. "There's no need for something like that."

"Well, it'd just be a women's group," Bina says. "And actually, Bipin, I was going to ask you if there's a way we can get a story about it in *Samachar in America*."

"I think it sounds great," Deepak chimes in.

Chand nods and takes a sip of wine. There's no doubt that he'll be cut off from any further drinking before the reception even starts.

"I understand what you're saying, but this really doesn't sound like the best use of everyone's time," Bipin says.

"What?" Bina keeps her voice firm. "Why not?"

She waits for Bipin to respond, but to her surprise, Anita says, "We have so many opportunities to meet and have fun together. I don't know if we need another one."

Bina knows she should just let it slide. She should smile and nod politely and move on. They are at a wedding reception, after all.

But something tells her not to back down. Maybe it's a combination of Deepak's faith in her, the residue of what happened with Anita, and something bigger, something with force.

"We do need another one," Bina says. "It's important for us to stop coming together just to talk about recipes and celebrity gossip. That's all fun and fine, but we need more. And why are we just there for each other for all those happy milestones—babies, weddings, anniversary parties?"

Bina hadn't actually thought of that point until now, but when the words leave her, she knows how true they are. "We need to also support each other through our embarrassments and frustrations, our victories."

"Bina, no." Anita drops her fork and knife onto her plate. The clink echoes through the hall.

Bina processes the moment as a blur, a hazy collection of sounds and colors, as her best friend's words sink in.

"Anita." She keeps her composure. "Do you think you should calm down?"

"You should," Anita says. "Maybe some of us don't want something like this! Did that ever occur to you? That maybe you should try to make things better instead of worse?"

"I'm not making anything worse!" Bina says. "I'm trying to help!"

It takes her a few seconds to realize that the deejay has stopped talking and is facing their table. Of course she spoke in the rare pause between the program items. Damn it.

Little by little, a hush spreads over the hall. Guests turn toward them. Someone even has an iPhone out. Great.

The hope pours out of Bina's body, unwanted, and is replaced by a suffocating humiliation. But she keeps a strong smile on her face. There are murmurs coming from the far end of the room, from people probably just now hearing that there's drama happening here.

She stands up, cups her hands around her mouth, and says, "Sorry for the interruption. Let's keep this party going!"

A man from the adjacent table whistles. Whether he does it because he's buying Bina's everything-is-good act or because he's too drunk to know any better is unclear. But his whistle leads to another one, then a stream of cheers from a table closer to the dance floor.

Bina walks toward her friend. But Anita shifts her chair so it's completely turned away from Bina, which is how she stays for the rest of the reception.

Thirteen

Natasha

"You're up!"

Natasha gulps. "Me? Already?"

"Yep. It's now or never. Go!" Alexis Diaz pumps her fists in a gesture of enthusiasm. "You've gotta help Chris move to the next thing!"

Nine eager students face Natasha, including Chris, whose burly six-foot-two frame is frozen in a running pose. It's up to Natasha to continue the skit. She prepares to give her best charming laugh but instead lets out a violent cough.

She was presumptuous to think she could just show up and know what to do in an improv class. Despite how impulsive she can be, something about having to think creatively in the moment makes her clam up.

But she has to try. She has to show Alexis Diaz she's capable. This class is all she has to show for her comedy right now. Well, the class and the ten views she has on her YouTube channel from the performance Anuj recorded. The performance that apparently wasn't good enough to get Natasha to the next round of the comedy competition. She can still hear the stupid, monotonous voice of the dude who called her and told her, more or less, that she isn't good enough.

She reminds herself that like she and Zack recently discussed, rejection is always part of the creative process. And she should be proud of herself. She got out of bed the first time her alarm went off, wore something other than sweatpants, ran a comb through her thick, curly hair, and made it here. She's excited. She's determined. She's . . . tired.

The thing is, she was supposed to be doing more by now. Dozens of people should be laughing at her jokes. Mom and Dad should be regretting telling her she made the wrong choice. Karan should be texting her that he knew she'd make it.

In the two weeks since the Midtown Comedy Center informed her that she did not make it into the competition, she doesn't know where her days go. The hours seem to be comprised of nothing productive, just oscillating bursts of panic and hope. Panic: none of the other Atlanta comedy clubs with open mic spots have availability. Hope: she's written a few more pages in her notebook that may actually be good. Panic: it's harder to stay awake throughout the day without anything tangible to hold on to. Hope: Alexis seems to like her already.

"Improv is about working with uncertainty and letting go of control. Don't think too much," Alexis says as the other students around her nod. Everyone nods whenever Alexis says anything. Within a couple of months of graduating from Georgia Tech, her YouTube comedy sketch series was endorsed by Tina Fey. She teaches a class for aspiring comedians every Saturday that's about how to use improv as a way to "master the craft of comedy." Of course, she's also attractive in a spunky and pretty Mila Kunis kind of way, so it's only a matter of time before she gets a gig on a hot TV show.

"I'm not thinking too much!" Natasha says. She's actually doing the opposite. It's always been a cruel irony for her that when she's nervous, her thoughts freeze while her heart races.

She glances at her scuffed black Keds and feels the weight of everyone's stares.

Jump, a tiny voice inside her says. *Just jump.*

Before she can think anymore, she listens. To her surprise, Chris starts jumping next to her and makes a hand motion as if he's holding a rope.

"That's it!" Alexis says. "You've taken Chris from running to jump rope! Keep going!"

Alexis seems energized by being able to tell people what to do. That type of bossy attitude reminds Natasha of her sister.

"Natasha, switch it up!" Alexis yells.

Natasha starts hopping on one foot, then the other. This is like a less embarrassing version of middle school PE class.

"You're playing outside! Hopscotch! Yes!" Alexis cheers.

Within a few seconds, another classmate joins. They enact a hopscotch game that then transforms into all of them making sidewalk art with chalk.

"Natasha, that was great," Alexis says. "You let yourself just be free."

Natasha smiles and then sits down on one of the black folding chairs that's at the perimeter of the otherwise bare room. Even though she's not really sure what she's accomplished, for the first time in weeks, Natasha feels something. Or rather, the absence of something, of darkness or urgency or maybe a force she couldn't quite pinpoint right now.

I can do this, she thinks. *I can really do this.*

She's late to meet the girls for brunch when class ends. She throws her phone and black Moleskine into her tote bag, the latest thing she's "borrowed" from Suhani's closet.

Alexis stops her just as she's about to leave. "Hey, can we talk for a second?"

"Sure," Natasha says as she waves bye to everyone else.

A flutter goes through her stomach. Someone mentioned that at the end of the seven-week block, Alexis picks a couple of students to be her interns. But today was just the first class. Is it possible that she already sees potential in Natasha?

The possibility sends Natasha on a wave of elation, the first one in way too long. All the crap she did mattered. Every comedy documentary she watched, every open mic night she tried to get into, all the hours she read and compiled notes on her role models. Someone sees in her what she's believed all along. And maybe someday not too far away, Natasha can do this for another woman who wants to be a comedian. She pictures herself as the perfect mentor. Someone who is as talented as Mindy Kaling, honest as Aparna Nancherla, sarcastic as Chelsea Handler.

Natasha can barely contain her excitement as Alexis guides her to the back of the auditorium. The chairs are now folded and pushed against the wall. Alexis grips the top of one. Her round eyes are framed with thick black eyeliner and a chocolate-brown eye shadow. "So, as you know, I do this a lot. I see so many people who want to make it in comedy. And I can pick up on things pretty early on."

"I bet," Natasha tries not to sound as giddy as she feels.

"This may sound weird, but is it possible you don't enjoy improv? Or even performing in front of people at all?" Alexis pauses as if allowing the questions to fill the space between them.

This isn't the way Natasha thought the conversation would start. Maybe it's some sort of test.

Natasha keeps her head held high. "Well, I mean, I don't know if anyone really enj—"

"No, there are plenty of people who actually do," Alexis says. She barely reaches Natasha's shoulder, but her proud posture and strong voice make her seem like she's more than six feet tall. "They thrive when they're in front of an audience. And I could be wrong, but I get the sense that this didn't make you happy."

Alexis squints as if she's looking right through Natasha, past any bullshit that can be thrown her way.

"I do get nervous in front of people," Natasha admits. "And maybe it does drain me sometimes. But I love comedy. I always have. This is what I'm meant to do."

She's taken back to a moment last year, when she and Karan were pressed against each other, their legs intertwined, on his twin bed in his dorm. He was in blue-checked boxers and his hair was damp from a recent shower. She felt cozy and delicate in his gray hoodie. They had come back from the Georgia State talent show, where she'd planned to perform a routine about being desi and premed. Natasha was so proud of what she had written and couldn't wait to share it. But then, when the moment arrived, the entire room just became a haze of sounds: her quick breath on the microphone, the thud of her pulse in her ears, the bored sighs of the seven people in the audience. She told herself to start, just start anywhere. But she couldn't speak or even hear herself think. All she could do was remain anchored under the dull spotlight, frozen with fear. The stage manager cut her off and announced the next person. Nobody booed as she made her way into the thin crowd. She wasn't even worth insulting. *You can try later*, Karan told her that night. *It isn't a big deal.*

But it was a big deal to her. She surprised herself when in the middle of the night, just hours after she'd tanked onstage, she woke up with an idea for another routine. She crept out of bed and started typing. When it was just her and the blue glow from her Mac, she could reach a state where words poured out of her and her mind was in a trance. It reminded her of the way people described meditating. She always liked the night for that reason. With everyone asleep and nobody around to judge her, she could regain a sense of control over her time. It was like she and the world were in on a juicy secret together.

"Being onstage isn't the only way to make it in comedy," Alexis says. "There are so many other routes you can take. And it's never a bad idea to take time to really reflect and learn and figure out the best fit for you."

"But I want this." Natasha realizes how childish she sounds as the words leave her mouth, like a second grader whining for more dessert. "I mean, not this as in improv, but I do want to be onstage. Stand-up is what I've been working toward! I don't need to take any time to learn or figure out anything. I want to do this now."

She remembers how Karan had once told Natasha to consider pursuing comedy when she's "older." *You know, after you're done with everything else you have to do. Working, kids, all that stuff.* Some aunties had said the same thing. Natasha always fought back. Why did women have to keep their passions as safe hobbies for most of their lives? Why did they have to make certain expected milestones the priority?

But now she wonders if they were all right. Maybe she's let her aspirations become larger than her potential.

"Look, I get what you're saying. But it's part of my job to push you to pick what's best for you," Alexis says. "Maybe it wouldn't be a bad idea to consider what your long-term vision for your career is and if you're investing your energy in the best places. All I'm saying is, this may not be the best fit for you."

Alexis does a there-there type of ginger pat on Natasha's shoulder. The worst part is that her face doesn't even have any disdain or meanness. Instead, she's gazing at Natasha with compassion. Natasha feels like she's being dumped. The excitement she had for the day shrivels up and disappears. But this can't be right. The first authority she's connected with in her dream field thinks she should try another way?

No, no, no, she wants to say. *You don't understand. This is everything to me and I don't have a choice but to kick ass.*

"Don't listen to her!" Ifeoma says an hour later, after she's ordered a round of margaritas at Superica, their favorite spot for their monthly brunch. "What the heck does she know?"

"Um, she knows a lot," Natasha says. "It's her job and area of expertise, remember?"

A waiter puts down two baskets of chips and tiny bowls of salsa. Natasha takes a handful of chips and dips them into the red and green sauces that are at the edge of the table. She gives a silent declaration of gratitude for being at a place that feeds her right away. Now she just has to make sure she doesn't fill up on the chips and actually has room for her entrée.

Within minutes, the tables around them are occupied. Every restaurant in Krog Street Market gets way too crowded on Saturdays.

An Indian couple sits next to them. They're both dressed in standard weekend casual wear: T-shirts, jeans, white sneakers, Warby Parker sunglasses on their heads. The guy comments on the industrial-chic décor and orders two margaritas. He slides his hands over the girl's and smiles when he glances at her ring finger. Three diamonds—one large round center stone, two smaller side ones—wink as they catch the light.

Of course you're newly engaged, Natasha thinks.

Why is she suddenly seeing engaged couples everywhere? It's as though in the last month, there was a public announcement made for all people who are engaged to show themselves.

She could have been one of them. Her weekends with Karan always flew by in a blur of food and friends and binge-watching a show. Why did she let that go? Were her parents right about her making self-destructive choices? And what if that really was the best she was ever going to get? She had heard of those stories of people who broke up with someone and then realized they fucked things up after it was way too late.

"Whatever, I don't care if that chick supposedly knows what she's talking about." Ifeoma waves her hand as if Alexis's qualifications are an unpleasant smell. "All I'm saying is that if I listened to every person who told me I couldn't do something, there's no way I'd be in law school right now."

"Yeah, but what if she's right?" Natasha scans the menu. She was going to try to be healthy today, but now she's craving comfort food. She asks for the hotcakes, complete with whipped butter and buttermilk syrup.

"She's not right!" Ifeoma takes a sip of her margarita and leaves an orange lipstick print on the rim of her glass. Her lip and nail colors are always bold. "You should show up to class next weekend and make it your mission to prove her wrong."

Ifeoma is always on the lookout for a mission. By their sophomore year at Georgia State, she had protested for equal pay for women, better legal representation for the underserved, and more recycling bins around campus.

"Are you going to tell your mom what Alexis said?" Payal asks. "I mean, she used to act. She probably knows what it feels like to get constructive criticism."

Ifeoma shakes her head and smiles. "I love your mom. That woman could stop a war with her food and charm. And I agree. She has to get what this is like."

"Does she, though?" Natasha says. "I feel like she's so far removed from that time in her life. She definitely doesn't behave like she understands anything I'm going through. And if she hears someone thinks I'm not cut out for it, it'll only validate everything she's already been telling me."

Mom's disappointment is palpable. It has a way of spilling over and submerging Natasha with its weight. She can picture Mom now, the skin tight around her mouth, her eyes narrowed as she laments how she could have raised such a failure of a daughter.

Natasha's phone buzzes.

DAD: Hope you are okay.

NATASHA: I'm fine. Sorry I missed the family phone call this week.

DAD: Don't worry. Suhani said you have been busy and we should give you space.

NATASHA: Didn't know she said that.

Ifeoma and Payal are staring at Natasha when she looks up from her phone.

"Sorry," she says. "Just my dad. I guess my sister had my back when my parents tried to do a group phone call the other day and I wasn't in the mood."

"You still haven't talked to them?" Payal asks.

Natasha shakes her head. "Suhani and I haven't really been getting along. She's been sending me job openings and judging my drinking and just always lecturing me about something."

She stops herself from saying more. It doesn't feel right to complain about Suhani. That's one of the most confusing things about her sister. Just when she's getting on Natasha's last nerve, Natasha's reminded of everything Suhani's done for her.

"Look, yeah, Suhani can be intense and I get you saying she should calm down sometimes," Ifeoma says. "But is it possible that she's right about some of the stuff she's telling you?"

"Like what? She has no idea what it's like to deal with the shit I do. And all she does is criticize me when I need some support." Natasha feels a prick of irritation as she pictures her pretty, smart, ambitious sister. Her untouchable sister.

"I don't know if that's all she does," Payal says.

"Seriously? You're taking her side?" Natasha asks, even though she shouldn't be surprised. Payal is the most Suhani-like of their group, but all Natasha's friends have revered her sister since they first met her. And while a part of her understands why, a bigger part wishes they'd see Suhani from her perspective for once.

"Of course not," Payal says at the same time Ifeoma blurts, "Yes."

"We have no idea what's going on with you," Ifeoma says. "You know we've always got your back. Always. But from my standpoint, you've broken up with your boyfriend, quit your job, and are crashing with your sister and brother-in-law so you can go after your comedy. I get why Suhani's worried. I have been, too."

"Worried? Why?" Natasha gives her best I'm-great smile. She's become skilled at appearing more fine than she really feels.

"You've been sort of MIA on our text thread and we haven't seen you in weeks." Payal smiles. "With all the stuff that's going on with you, we didn't know if something was happening . . . again."

"Again? You mean you thought I was going through one of those times?" Natasha asks, referring to the blurry, exhausting periods in college when she struggled to get out of bed for days. Karan was able to help her the first time but had to call the girls after that.

Payal shrugs and says, "I don't know. I guess so."

Natasha's friends exchange a questioning glance with each other. She looks at each of them, and the truth of why they were so eager to meet today comes into focus.

"Is this some kind of intervention?" she asks.

"I didn't think of it that way," Ifeoma says, "but I guess you could call it that."

"Oh, well, I appreciate you all caring, but I'm fine," Natasha says. "Really. There's nothing to worry about."

Suddenly, it's too warm in here. The light buzz from her margarita morphs into a pang of nausea. She wishes she could leave this conversation. This restaurant. It occurs to her that no matter where she goes these days, she doesn't fit in anywhere.

"Okay," Payal says with a nod. "We won't worry."

Natasha knows that isn't true and they'll keep worrying. She cuts a massive piece of hotcake, submerges it in syrup, and puts on her best cheerful voice. "I'm so tired of talking about me, especially when I don't know what's been going on with you two. I've been so behind!"

"Well . . ." Payal shifts her eyes, seeming unsure of whether to move on. "I wanted to tell y'all in person that I got my first med school interview! At Emory!"

"Oh my god!" Natasha shrieks as they clink their glasses together. "That's amazing! I'm not surprised at all."

Payal beams and adjusts the ruffles on her floral off-the-shoulder dress. "Thanks. I'm telling myself to stay calm because there's no guarantee, but still, it's a fucking interview at Emory!"

Hearing the word "fucking" come out of Payal's mouth is a giveaway that she's drunk. She orders another round of margaritas and updates them on her latest Bumble date (hot, boring) and her travels to Iowa for her temporary consulting job (monotonous, almost over). Ifeoma thinks Jordan plans to propose after their second year of law school.

Even though everything seems back to normal on the surface, Natasha can tell her friends are making sure to keep their updates upbeat and light. She takes it all in as though she's suspended above the table. One part of her wants to have fun, be rooted in the moment, and pretend everything is normal. But a bigger part is on the verge of panic, a panic that presses on her sternum and makes it hard to breathe. All her friends have their shit together. They're on paths that guarantee health insurance and a solid future, while all she has is a smothering sense of uncertainty. There should be a word for feeling happy for your friends while wondering when you'll be able to feel that same happiness for yourself. Usually, being around the girls makes Natasha feel free and understood. But today, it just reminds her of how lonely she really is. She doesn't truly belong anywhere.

They get the check, then walk around Krog Street Market for another hour. When they stop for chocolate croissants, Ifeoma notes,

"Another reason why Miranda is the best *Sex and the City* character. She actually eats food." The rest of them murmur in agreement.

After they eat, Natasha climbs into her used silver Camry and reclines the seat. Her car smells like weed no matter how many times she has it cleaned. Not that she can afford that now anyway. The money in her account dwindles by the day even though she isn't doing much. Maybe Zack can help her out. He's lent her money before and not told Suhani.

She turns on the air-conditioning and points the vents toward her eyes. The cold air jolts her awake. An old R & B song is on the radio and takes her back to college, the last time she remembers being close to happy. Will she ever feel that way again? That carefree and full of hope for the future? Why is it so hard for her to just be content?

The song ends and she's back in the present. It's funny how some parts of her life are measured more with soundtracks than with time.

Just as she's about to pull out of the parking lot, she sees a couple walk toward the entrance to Krog Street Market.

But on second glance, it isn't just any couple.

It's Karan with another girl.

Natasha slumps in her seat even though she knows they can't see her. She studies both of them. Karan, in a baby blue polo and gray shorts. His hair is shorter than usual but still thick and fluffy with a curl at the ends. Does he look tanner? Fitter? Both? He's almost the same height as the girl. Karan used to always complain about being five-six, but it was one of Natasha's favorite things about him. She didn't have to stretch her neck or stand on her tiptoes to kiss him.

The girl doesn't look familiar. She's in a sunflower-yellow dress and powder-blue heels. Large Chanel sunglasses cover her eyes. Her brunette highlighted hair is styled into big, bouncy curls. A black YSL bag with a gold chain hangs from her bony shoulder.

How is this possible?

Karan says something. The girl laughs. He looks relaxed, at ease.

Natasha considers getting out of the car and saying hi, as if it's a total coincidence that they're passing each other at the entrance to the market.

But something anchors her to the seat. She ignores the voice inside her demanding that she look away. No, she has to take in every single detail. She sees Karan the way that girl probably does: a cute, sweet, polite guy. Of course she'll hang on to him. Who wouldn't?

That's the type of person your mom would love, Natasha thinks, hating herself as soon as the insecure thought takes hold of her. Another follows, then another: *She's better than me. She's prettier. She looks less complicated. She dresses up for you.*

Her self-doubt always operates in this opportunistic way. It just takes one thought to give birth to another one, until she's lost in a web of her own making.

Karan and the girl start to join the crowd. Natasha watches them until they disappear.

Fourteen

Suhani

"You are one of our top candidates for chief," Dr. Wilson says as he taps a pen against his mahogany desk. "I'm sure you're not surprised to hear that."

"That's great news," Suhani says in a way she hopes is both confident and modest. Everything she's worked for since her intern year at Atlanta Memorial Hospital has led her to this moment: every agitated patient she helped soothe, every weekend she got here by seven a.m. instead of sleeping in and cuddling with Zack, every shift when she didn't have time to eat or pee.

She fiddles with her engagement ring and digs her nude heels into the carpet. Before she left the apartment this morning, she put on an extra layer of her plum Armani lipstick, aptly named Attitude. It's her go-to when she needs to look fiercer than she feels.

Part of her wants this meeting to hurry up so she can get it over with, while another part wishes she could freeze this moment, this feeling of getting recognized for all the work she's done.

"I know your father has already prepared you for a lot of what's ahead," Dr. Wilson says. "You've done a great job of building on

what he's taught you and also integrating your own clinical style
into your work."

The wall behind Dr. Wilson has framed diplomas from all the
places where he trained: Emory undergrad; Harvard Medical School;
Johns Hopkins psychiatry residency, where he was a chief resident; child psychiatry fellowship at Yale; geriatric psychiatry fellowship at Emory. A massive red textbook titled *Freud* is on his
desk. Underneath it, *Intimacy and Infidelity*. Sometimes being in Dr.
Wilson's office makes Suhani feel like she's in a *New Yorker* cartoon.
She's spent hours in here reviewing difficult patient cases, discussing
residency applicants, and receiving evaluations on her performance.
Hours establishing her career as a psychiatrist.

"Thank you," Suhani says. "His career has always inspired me, but
my mom's also a big part of why I went into medicine. She actually
gave me my first toy stethoscope when I was four."

Dr. Wilson leans back in his leather chair. He's wearing a black
designer suit, gray tie, shiny shoes, and thick, black-rimmed glasses
that Suhani once read were described as "geek chic."

"Really? I didn't know that." He takes a sip of black coffee from
a mug that reads PROGRAM DIRECTOR in red letters.

Of course he didn't know that. There was no space on the residency application to discuss Mom's steady mixture of criticism and
affection, the way it was given in the exact doses to ensure Suhani
would always be motivated to make something of herself.

"Yeah, she's the one who always checked my report cards for all
As and was concerned about me being well-rounded for college.
She was really upset when I took my first practice MCAT and got a
terrible score." Suhani cringes at the memory of Mom standing in
her doorway, covered with a contagious disappointment.

As she watches Dr. Wilson nod with understanding, she reminds herself to stay professional. He isn't her therapist. Suhani's always admired people like Vanessa, who can put their guard down at work, but she's never been able to be like them.

"And she also understands people in a way nobody else does. Why they do certain things, if they're hiding something, what they want—you know, all that insight about human nature that you can't really teach." Suhani smiles as she thinks of how much she's always enjoyed Mom's social commentary, whether it came from a place of curiosity or was straight-up gossip. "Anyway, if I do become chief, I want to start some initiatives that can have a big impact, maybe shift the way certain things have been done in the field."

"How so?" Dr. Wilson asks.

Suhani's heart rate increases as she tells herself to go for it. Make the pitch. Show Dr. Wilson that she's thought this through and is the best person for the job. "I've been looking into the barriers that hold women back from getting mental health treatment. One of the biggest hindrances is the lack of research around how different events, like menstruation or childbirth, play a role. I worked to create the partnership with the ob-gyn clinic because I realized some of those patients avoid psychiatrists when they really could be helped by one. And I'm glad residents are able to learn from a variety of cases, but I think we can take that partnership one step further."

"Meaning?" Dr. Wilson raises an eyebrow with interest.

"I think we should see if our residents can provide counseling to the ob-gyn patients who need it. There's a lack of interventions for the parts of women's mental health that are less understood, whether it's the emotional changes in the postpartum period or the psychological scars of abuse or the potential impacts of birth control. I'm worried we are missing the chance to see patients during their stressful times because what they're going through is just put in the category of 'women's issues.'"

She's taken back to that first meeting she had with her dean in med school. It was a struggle to just get out of bed, let alone dress up, and finally say what she had been ignoring for weeks. How did she not know then that something was wrong with her? She was nauseated the entire time she sat in that stiff, low chair, from where she could see the parking lot dotted with cherry blossoms and people—happy people—jogging. Even though her dean handed her a list with the names of therapists near campus, both of them knew Suhani wouldn't go.

"You know, that sounds like a great idea. And something we could definitely use in our program," Dr. Wilson says.

"Really?" Hope blossoms in her chest.

"Really." Dr. Wilson smiles. "I knew from the time I interviewed you that you'd do big things here."

On his desk, there's a picture of his wife—blond and big smiled, Miss America pretty—and twin sons outside the Fox Theatre. From Suhani's conversations with him and the gossip around the department, she's gathered that the Wilsons live a cosmopolitan life. Their high-rise apartment overlooks Midtown. Even though the kids are ten years old, they've never eaten at an Olive Garden, shopped at Macy's, or played at Chuck E. Cheese.

Without children, she and Zack can live an equally sophisticated life. He'll continue to thrive at his healthcare start-up while her days will be spent seeing patients, sitting on boards, and eventually becoming a program director herself one day. She can build a future that's the opposite of her mother's, one that's free of slathering peanut butter and jelly on slices of bread, finely chopping vegetables, and brewing endless cups of chai for guests.

"So, I'll be in touch soon," Dr. Wilson says. "We just have to finish speaking with the faculty members on our selection committee and get their perspectives on our top candidates. Due to some staffing changes, we've actually had to bring on some new faculty members to be part of the selection committee. You might remember a few of them from the gala night. Two of the internists and one of the neurologists were all part of the group that was introduced at the end of the reception."

Suhani makes sure to keep her expression even. Roshan was the only neurologist on that stage. This has to be some sick joke. Her ex has a say in whether she becomes a chief?

She considers asking Dr. Wilson for the names of the faculty members but decides that's weird. And Roshan wouldn't sabotage her, would he? That would be a new low and even he couldn't stoop there.

Dr. Wilson stands as a signal that the meeting is over. "I've got to head to the Brain and Behavior wing for a meeting."

Suhani nods and thanks Dr. Wilson for his time. She prepares to go back to her office but as she sees him go toward the elevator, she's compelled to join him.

"I'm actually heading there myself," she says.

During their brisk walk, she and Dr. Wilson discuss everything from new Atlanta restaurants to upcoming hospital events to his own journey to rising in hospital administration. Suhani's usually so on edge whenever she's with him, so eager to make a good impression. But now a rush of relief washes over her. Her hard work is finally paying off.

Atlanta Memorial's sterile gray hallways are bustling with white-coated residents conducting afternoon rounds and nurses typing orders into mobile computers. A physical therapist pushes an old man in a wheelchair. An overhead page for a call from Pharmacy booms through the intercom.

She texts Zack when Dr. Wilson stops to briefly talk to a colleague: I'm a top candidate for chief!

ZACK: Of course you are! Not surprised.

SUHANI: How's your day?

ZACK: Out of control. Still up for gimlets tonight at Little Spirit?

SUHANI: Can't wait.

And then, before she can think, she adds, I've missed us.

Zack texts back immediately. I've missed us, too.

After Dr. Wilson turns at a hallway marked CONFERENCE SUITES, Suhani steps into an empty patient room, savoring the quiet and the sunlight splashing the two stiff recliners that are pushed against the window for visitors. The rare moment of stillness infuses her with hope. Today is the day things will start turning around. She and her husband will be okay. Maybe everything from the past two months—all the misunderstandings, moments of irritation, arguments followed by grueling emotional hangovers—was simply run-of-the-mill marital adjustment. A standard rough patch, nothing more. And now they can finally move forward.

She just has to take care of one more thing.

In seconds, she's pacing down the hallway again. The pain from her heels is overridden by her impending closure, closure she's been craving for years.

Roshan is standing outside his office, slipping his arms into his starched, spotless white coat.

"Do you have a second?" Suhani says.

"I was just heading out." He adjusts his dark brown tie under the collar of his hunter-green button-down.

"Then I'll walk with you." A quick glance confirms that nobody else is around. Before they've even made it two feet, she turns to Roshan and says, "Are you going to get in the way of me being chief?"

"What?" Roshan frowns.

"You show up here and now you conveniently have a say in it. How are you even on the selection committee?"

Suhani ignores the warmth spreading through her limbs, one that feels way too much like fear. It's not Roshan's effect on her; that atrophied years ago. This is just a combination of her meeting with Dr. Wilson and her light lunch—an apple, chopped salad, and lemon Spindrift—making her dizzy and disoriented. Mom often called Suhani's meals "rabbit food" and remarked that it was "unacceptable for Indian people to eat like that."

"They've been needing an attending from neurology since the one who used to do it retired." Roshan pauses in the doorway of an empty boardroom that has a stack of black folders and gold ballpoint pens in the center of a large wooden table. A projection screen displays the teal-blue homepage of Atlanta Memorial Hospital. Suhani follows him into the room and pushes the door closed with her heel.

"So you're going to give your opinions on residents you don't even know?"

"They probably wouldn't take my input," Roshan says. "Unless I had something significant to say."

"What is that supposed to mean?" Suhani challenges. The jerk always knew exactly how to push her buttons. She wonders if everyone has a person like that from their past, a person who occupies most of their revenge fantasies. Sometimes she wonders why she never told anyone, not even Natasha or Anuj, about what really happened with her and Roshan. But then she turns back to the same answer: shame. Shame can shut a mouth in a way nothing else can.

Roshan looks unfazed, which only riles Suhani up more.

"If you think for one second you're going to get in the way of anything for me, you're fucking mistaken, okay?" she says.

They're interrupted by the low creak of the door opening. The first thing she sees is the black outline of Dr. Wilson's glasses. His wide eyes and slack jaw give away that he just heard everything or, at least, enough. But then he moves and she sees at least five other attendings standing behind him, all of whom are also shifting with discomfort.

"Hi!" Suhani plans to sound cool and professional, but the word comes out way too loudly, which makes her look even more suspicious.

Dr. Wilson clears his throat. "Hello."

"I should get going," she says.

Dr. Wilson nods. "We're late for our meeting."

"Right. You said you had a meeting."

"Yes." Dr. Wilson's eyes shift as if he's unsure whether to continue. "The meeting to discuss the candidates for chief."

Fuck.

Suhani lingers, unsure of whether to give a charming smile or make small talk. None of that feels right, so she just stands there. The silence fills the room with a thick, dreadful tension.

"I see," she says. "Well, uh, hope you have a great one. Take care!"

Again with the overly enthusiastic response. *Get it together, Suhani.*

The other attendings file in after Dr. Wilson. Suhani's only option is to get the hell out of there.

A few hours later, Suhani's perched on a barstool next to Zack. He's already ordered two cucumber-mint gimlets and is in a deep conversation with the hipster bartender.

If it were any other evening, Little Spirit would be able to remove her from the stress of the hospital. The dark wood panels on the ceiling, Prince soundtrack, and paintings of different musical icons on the walls transport her to a more relaxed headspace.

But now she feels a stab of dejection as she takes in her husband's head thrown back in a big laugh, the glint of light on his glasses. She has to tell him about Roshan and she has no idea where to start or how Zack will react.

"Cheers," Zack says.

"Cheers." Suhani takes a sip of her gimlet. The coupe cocktail glass makes her feel like she's in a movie from the twenties. If only she had a jeweled headband and beaded dress.

"I'm really glad we're doing this." Zack's knees graze her thighs. Suhani shifts her legs so that their ankles are crossed. It's her favorite way to sit with him when they're next to each other.

"Me, too," Suhani says, relishing the ease and familiarity of being in her husband's presence. In her daily autopilot mode, she often forgets to appreciate things like this. They need these moments that remind them of who they are at their core. Just hours ago, she was worried about the lack of quality time they've had lately, and now she's filled with faith that they will be okay. Like hearts, marriages can shift their shapes, contract, and relax.

"So, tell me everything. Were you able to tell Dr. Wilson about your plan for the women's mental health clinic? What did he think? How did you feel?" Zack taps his palms against the bar in the rhythm of a drum roll.

Suhani gives Zack a rundown of her meeting. They order another round of cocktails from the large chalkboard menu above the bar while Zack goes through a recap of his day. He explains some of the intricacies of advertising campaigns and funding rounds, stuff that's like a foreign language to Suhani. Zack doesn't ever say it, but one trip to his office told Suhani that his company is doing well, well enough to have a fancy coffee machine; fridge stocked with sparkling water, beer, and wine; catered lunch every Wednesday; and regular features on *Business Insider*'s site.

After the bartender brings them a bowl of chips, Zack turns to her and says, "So, I've been thinking about everything that's been going on between us."

Suhani nods. "I have, too."

He sighs. "I'm worried you're not happy, that I'm not making you happy."

"That's not true at all. Of course you make me happy." Suhani squeezes Zack's hands, his perfect, smooth hands, one of the first things she noticed about him when they met. His platinum wedding band is cool against her palm. "I'm so sorry I've been tired and stressed and just overwhelmed."

"I have, too," Zack says. "Both of our jobs are crazy. But you just seem, I don't know, somewhere else these days. Natasha said you were like this sometimes when y'all were growing up."

"You talked to Natasha about it?" Suhani asks.

Zack nods. "She understands. I mean, she knows you better than anyone. And she sees it, too, being at our place."

Suhani drifts to the past months. Despite her professional accomplishments, in many ways, residency has made her someone she isn't proud of. Someone rushed and frantic, someone who misses holidays and weddings and her husband's work events.

"Hey," Zack says, reading her face. "I really think it'll be better this year, with your schedule giving you some more space to just relax."

"Me, too. I've been waiting for that," Suhani says, telling herself that it is just a matter of time, that what she went through with Roshan doesn't have to have any impact on her and Zack.

"I know you have." Zack smiles. "Isn't it funny how the things we thought would be so hard for us weren't, but then other things were more challenging?"

"I was expecting so much drama for our wedding," Suhani says as she thinks back to how seamlessly the details fell into place. Zack and his friends were excited to wear kurtas, both their families were happy with a fusion Jewish-Hindu ceremony, and the guests got along. To her surprise, wedding planning showed her the benefit of being with someone from another cultural background. It forced them to proactively discuss their differences and preferences, which also gave them the freedom to build a relationship on their own terms and not take anything for granted.

"Our wedding, the holidays . . ." Zack says, referring to how they were both worried about celebrating Hindu and Jewish holidays but even that went more harmoniously than expected. Last year, when they were engaged, they went to Mom's prayers at the Hindu temple for Navratri, then met Barbara for Rosh Hashanah. Mom and Barbara even created joint rituals.

"Well, props to us for mastering those big relationship milestones, right?"

"Totally." Zack smiles and then says, "So, speaking of relationship milestones, something else happened at work today. We had a visit from this new male fertility start-up a couple of weeks ago. They have these take-home kits for guys to give sperm samples so they don't have to do it in those awkward rooms at doctors' offices, with the porn and little paper cups."

"Interesting." Suhani nibbles on the cucumber slice that came with her drink. "Are you guys partnering with them?"

Zack shrugs. "We haven't decided yet. But I did one of the kits."

"Excuse me, what? Why do you want your sperm tested?" Suhani tries to block out the visual of Zack in their bathroom, holding a cup in front of his penis.

Zack darts his gaze around them to make sure nobody heard her. Luckily for him, the only other people at the bar are a group of fifty-year-old blond women whose toned bodies and pastel shift dresses would make Mom peg them as being from Buckhead or East Cobb. They're toasting with glasses of Prosecco.

He looks embarrassed as he says, "You know, just out of curiosity. And it turns out that there's something—my motility or count or something—that might make it harder to have kids if we wait."

"If we wait?" Suhani asks. "I thought we decided that's not in our plans right now."

"We did. But then when I found out it might be harder for me to have them, I guess it made me wonder if we should revisit the idea sooner."

Suhani faces Zack as an avalanche of fear tumbles over her. "So you're saying that you want to try for kids now?"

"I think we should." Zack's full lips curl into a smile. "And I know you were worried about trying sooner rather than later because of work, but I promise you, I will do everything to make sure this doesn't affect your job."

"You can't really control that, honey," Suhani says. "That's something that can only change with better parental leave policies and less bias toward new mothers and—"

"I know the world is really behind when it comes to supporting mothers," Zack says. "But don't you think the idea of us having a family, our own little family, sounds so wonderful?"

People started dropping hints about her and Zack having kids weeks before their wedding. The aunties without tact warned Suhani that she was "only getting older," while the subtler ones lamented that they missed being around babies. (One even said, "Your wedding gave us joy, so next year, you'll give us a boy!") Barbara straight up asks when she can expect to play with an infant, even though all three of Zack's older sisters have kids.

Suhani finds all of it intrusive and disrespectful. It's nobody else's business and she resents that the world assumes all women in their thirties must be family planning.

"I'm sorry. I hear what you're saying," Suhani says. "But kids are a lot of work. And I love our life the way it is. Why would I want it to change right now?"

"They are a lot of work, sure, but don't you think they can also add a lot of fulfillment? And I love our life, too, but what if it just became greater? I mean, a baby would be the product of us. How could that not be amazing?"

The strong cocktails and their conversation are starting to make Suhani nauseated. She reaches for the first thing that comes to mind. "We haven't even discussed our thoughts on raising a child that's Hindu and Jewish."

Before Zack can say anything, she continues to rattle off one reason after another. The impact on their careers. Energy. Pressure to have a second child. Their sex life would plummet. They'd have to move out of their apartment. Time.

Zack has an answer for every single one. He's clearly thought all this through.

Suhani ignores the tightening in her throat. This isn't the way the conversation was supposed to go tonight.

The bartender gives them the check. She's grateful for the interruption. Before she can change the subject, Zack scribbles down a twenty-five percent tip, turns to her, and says, "Also, I promise I'd make it to all your prenatal appointments."

Hearing a word as clinical as "prenatal" from Zack is oddly endearing. He straightens in his chair and smiles. His face is confident, as though he's sure he's won his case.

Suhani admires her husband's strong jaw and the prominent dimple in his chin. Maybe she should change the subject and order another round of cocktails. Or maybe they can talk about this, move on, and have sex at home. Have a night that wouldn't be possible with a baby.

But the words she hasn't said build pressure on her tongue. She's not sure if it's her buzz or exhaustion. All she knows is that she can't keep this from Zack anymore, not for another second. The syllables spill out of her before she has a chance to filter them.

"I've been pregnant before."

Zack frowns. At first she thinks he didn't hear her properly, but then she sees the jerky movements of his hands, the line emerging between his eyebrows. Someone else, someone who doesn't know him, wouldn't even notice that he's different. But Suhani's stomach twists into a knot. She almost wants to say *Just kidding!* to break the moment.

"You have been pregnant before?" Zack asks. "What do you . . . What are you talking about?"

There's no going back now. Some fights in a marriage come out of nowhere, but others you can see coming. But she never worried, really worried, during any of theirs because, even when things were bad, they were still overall good. It was a concept she didn't know existed before meeting Zack, the idea that a relationship could have an impermeable layer of security that no disagreement could ever penetrate.

"I was pregnant in med school. And then I made sure I wasn't." There. She said it. And just in case it wasn't clear: "I had an abortion."

"So . . . Roshan, then?" Zack stares at her, his expression a mixture of confusion and shock. "But we've talked about this so many times and you never said anything."

He says this as though that line of reasoning can make her words untrue, as though she just got some facts wrong.

"It hasn't come up because I made sure it didn't."

"But I remember"—Zack's face shifts as he scans his mind—"us even discussing the idea of you being pregnant and you said you couldn't imagine what that would be like."

"I know." Suhani gulps. "I lied."

She says the words again in her mind. *I lied. I lied. I lied.*

"Wow . . ." Zack shifts in his chair. The defeated look on his face makes Suhani hate herself.

"Please tell me what you're thinking," Suhani says.

"I don't even know what I'm thinking." Zack shakes his head as though he just woke up from a bad dream. "I get why you wouldn't tell me about an abortion. That's your business. Of course I wish you felt like it was something you could tell me if it hurt you so much, but I get it."

Suhani bites her bottom lip. "I wanted to tell you, so many times. But there's a lot that went on in that relationship that I haven't been able to ever talk about, with anyone."

As much as she'd like to believe that she kept it a secret so she could move forward, a part of her knows that it was less about her resilience and more about wanting to believe she was a good girl. She never really let herself embrace her darkest parts, so how could she trust the man she loves to do so?

"But you didn't even think to mention how important your relationship with your ex was?" Zack says. "You made it seem like it wasn't even that serious. Why would you do that?"

"I don't know." Suhani's hands are shaking. "It was the hardest time in my life. I almost dropped out of med school. And I've spent years trying to put everything with Roshan behind me. And then when things got serious between you and me, I never figured out the right way to tell you. I guess I could always see my life with or without kids, but after I got pregnant, I didn't know if I ever wanted to be again."

"So you thought it was better to just not mention any of that? Even after we got married? I used to ask you, again and again, why talking about kids was so difficult for you. And it has to do with Roshan, of all people? The guy has an office just one floor below yours now!" Zack shakes his head as a look of recognition appears on his face.

"I know." Suhani stares into her glass, the mint-green cocktail now unappealing. "He never knew. He still doesn't. When I saw him today, I al—"

"Wait, what? You saw him?"

"After my meeting." Suhani's voice shakes. "I went to his office. He's one of the faculty members who has a vote in who becomes a chief."

"Funny you didn't mention that when I asked about your day," Zack says.

"I was going to. I promise. I've been wanting to since we first saw him," Suhani says. "I guess him coming back just brought up a lot of things I thought I had processed."

"Well, for the record, the guy sounds like a total jerk." Zack's voice softens as he looks at the ceiling, then back at Suhani. "In a weird way, I'm not even surprised you didn't tell me how serious you guys were. I've always felt like you keep this barrier that I can't cross. And, yeah, I get that when we first started dating, we had to make a lot of adjustments with us being from different cultures and all. But you've never really let me in."

"Of course I've let you in," Suhani says. "You're my husband."

Zack shakes his head. "Sure, I'm your husband, but you didn't tell me anything about the hardest part of your life. I can't believe you went through something so difficult, something that's still affecting you, and I haven't been able to be there for you."

Suhani hears Natasha's words from a few weeks ago: *You should be honest with Zack about everything.* She used to tell Natasha that she was sometimes too open. But now she wonders if her sister had a point.

"You are there for me." A tear slides down Suhani's cheek. "You have no idea how much being with you has helped me move on from that time in my life."

"You said there's a lot that went on with him that you haven't been able to talk about?" Zack asks. "What did you mean by that?"

Suhani grips the edge of the bar. Another tear dribbles to her chin.

"You know," Zack says. "You always say there's all this stuff I don't get about you, whether it's being a woman of color or things with your parents, but sometimes I almost wonder if you want to have some distance from me."

"Of course I don't want distance from you!" Suhani says. "It's just not that simple."

"Well, that's just great, Suhani." Zack shakes his head with disbelief. "You know what? Maybe I'm the one who needs distance right now." The legs of his chair make a scraping sound as he pushes away from the bar.

"Zack, don't do that."

Zack's never the one to react in the heat of emotion. She tries to put her hand over his, but Zack shoves his wallet into his back pocket, grabs his blazer, and leaves.

Fifteen

Bina

"You were right about Rajat Bhai's toupee!" Mira raises a triumphant fist into the air. "It almost fell off at the temple yesterday. I saw him catch it before it plopped into the moong dal."

"Ha! I told you!" Kavita says.

"I know someone else who has one," Mona chimes in. "You'll never gu—"

"HELLO!" Bina interrupts. "I think it's important for us to focus on why we're here today."

Everyone stops talking and turns toward her. There's a mixture of curiosity and hesitation on their faces. Bina's surprised to feel a tingling in her cheeks. Maybe this isn't a good idea. After all, she can't deny that she's also interested in the toupees. And what if Anita was right about this being a bad idea?

She considers bringing up Anita's name, asking if anyone has heard from her. Everyone here knows Anita and Bina apologized to each other for how things went at the wedding reception. Everyone also knows they haven't spoken since. Bina started and stopped three different texts to Anita over the past week. Last night, she scrolled through their shared photos on Facebook. Why does she resemble such a breakup cliché? This is not how things were supposed to be.

But there's no point in mentioning any of that now. Everyone has finally gotten over Natasha and Karan's disaster of a proposal. Mentioning Anita would only shift the attention back onto Bina's life and that's not why they're all here today.

"Right. You have been telling us to focus." Kavita smiles. Thanks to the recent Botox she thinks nobody knows about, the crow's-feet around her eyes are fainter today, as though someone ran an eraser over them.

"Yes, I have. Multiple times. And we keep getting off track," Bina says. Is this how her teachers felt all those years? How did they stay sane? She should send them a long overdue apology for every time she made it her mission to not pay attention. "Anyway, it's my fault for making this a potluck lunch and discussion. We should probably just stick to chai next time. Let's refill our cups and sit in the living room."

There's a buzz of agreement as all four of them collect around Bina's black marble island, which is covered with an assortment of plates.

"Bina, you always have the perfect spreads," Mira says as she admires the clearly-made-from-scratch pecan pie, avocado dosas, and spicy tandoori pasta. "We shouldn't have even brought food. I'll take a Pyrex full of your leftovers and give them to Chand for dinner. He'd rather eat anything you cook anyway!"

"Same with Bipin!" Kavita nods as she and Mira add extra teaspoons of sugar to their cups.

The mention of Bipin's name brings the conversation to an abrupt halt.

"Sorry," Kavita says as she pretends to focus on adding mint to her chai.

"I'm not sorry. I was wondering what was going on with your husband," Mona says in the same refreshing, unapologetic tone she had with Bina when she approached her at the end of the wedding reception.

Like every other Indian in Georgia, Mona also saw the Instagram post the kids put up. Bina told anyone who asked that Chats Over Chai was still a work in progress.

But Mona's blunt commentary on Anita's behavior, coupled with how she took Bina aside to a private hallway and told her to "screw everyone," compelled Bina to invite her today.

When she got here, Mira whispered, "I didn't know she was coming."

"I invited her," Bina said with her best you'll-get-over-it smile.

She's reminded of how right her decision was when now Mona adds, "Well, speaking of Bipin, are you okay from all that, Kavita? I bet that wasn't the most fun car ride home."

Kavita laughs. "Of course. You know him. He always has strong opinions."

"That he does."

"But he's sorry for how things happened that night," Kavita says.

"He said that?" Mona presses.

Mira shakes her head and waves her hands in a don't-ask type of signal.

"No." Kavita's face falls. "But I know he is sorry."

"Of course he is," Mira says.

What an egotistical asshole! Devi yelled on FaceTime the other day when Bina gave her a replay of the events. *You are going to have to put him in his place.*

Bina didn't know how to tell Devi that nobody puts Bipin in his place.

"Since we're discussing this anyway," Kavita says, "I would appreciate it if nobody told him I was here."

"Wait. Bipin doesn't know you're at my house?" Bina asks.

"He didn't think it would be a good idea for me to come. . . . I know he's just being cautious," Kavita says. "You know he's on all these boards and has these far-off dreams about running for office someday. He just wants to make sure our family has the best possible chance to succeed."

For him to succeed, Bina wants to say. From the looks on Mona's and Mira's faces, she can tell they're thinking something similar.

Bina pictures Bipin's face twisted into a scowl. Everything from his bushy eyebrows to his red, round nose make him seem like the type of man who is always on edge. She and Deepak have seen Bipin get upset plenty of times for plenty of reasons. Traffic. Cold dal. One of their kids not getting a good enough job offer. He snapped at waiters and flight attendants, something that always irritated Bina. It always struck her that Kavita seemed to be a direct contrast to him, with her bright eyes, wide smile, and tendency to laugh at everything. She always thought these differences made them an ideal pair, but now she wonders if there's a side to their marriage that's been kept behind closed doors.

"We won't say anything," Bina says. Mira and Mona nod in agreement.

Bina motions for them to move to the formal living room. They all settle on the gray leather couches. She's glad nobody's sitting in Anita's usual spot, the powder-blue armchair in the corner.

"So, who wants to start?" Bina asks.

Everyone stares at her in silence.

"Anyone?" Bina's lips twist into an awkward smile. Now she really feels like a teacher. Her friends are staring at their teacups, their laps, their phones. Anything to avoid eye contact with her. She glances at the clock. They only have fifteen minutes left. Where did the time go? She really needs to make sure to have a better plan for next time.

Kavita smiles at a large framed photo of the Joshi family after Suhani and Zack's wedding. All of them are wearing red, white, and gold, per Suhani's insistence. "You're really lucky you have a daughter like Suhani, who wanted to get married and gave you a son-in-law."

"Thank you. But let's focu—"

"A cute, white son-in-law! Now, they know how to keep their wives happy," Mira says before giving an apologetic look to Mona, who is stifling a laugh. It's no secret that Mira has a thing for white men. She once brought over the first *Magic Mike* DVD and passed it to Bina under the dining table as if it were an illegal drug.

"It must be nice to just sit here sometimes and look back on all these memories," Kavita notes as she gazes at the other happy, perfect photos of Bina's happy, perfect family.

"You really are blessed, Bina."

For a second, Bina sees the way they all view her, the way they've always viewed her. Maybe she should tell them she's less the so-fortunate type of blessed and more the bless-her-heart type of blessed, the latter being a common southern expression for delivering judgment or sass.

She takes a sip of chai and imagines sharing the thoughts unraveling in her mind: *Yes, I'm so blessed! I may have let go of my biggest dreams, filled my life with everything I thought I was supposed to do, and somehow still feel empty. But, yes, I am so very blessed!*

Instead, she smiles and says, "Kavita, your Sonam will have a wedding, too, when she's ready."

Mona nods. "She will. It's only a matter of time before you're getting sick of looking at centerpieces and lehengas and cocktail-hour menus."

"Only God knows when she'll get there." Kavita clasps her hands together as if she's about to pray. "Sonam doesn't even talk to me about any of that now. Says I'm putting too much pressure on her, but I think she doesn't want to commit and settle down like an adult. She and Sanjay have been together for almost ten years! And living together for three."

Mira frowns. "I thought you said they just got an apartment together last year."

Kavita shakes her head. "Oh, that was obviously a lie she told me to cover up that she's been shacking up with the man for a while. These girls all lie, I tell you. At least Natasha had the nerve to be up front and say no to getting married."

"Okay, then." Bina glances at the grandfather clock in the back corner of the room. "I can't believe I'm saying this but we've actually run out of time, so I guess our meeting is over."

Kavita and Mona collect their plates and cups. But Mira stays glued to the couch.

"Oh my God." Mira's eyes are wide as she scrolls through her phone.

"Is something wrong?" Bina asks.

"I, uh, don't know if I should say," Mira says.

Mira usually has no qualms about dispersing her social intel. She also knows how to do it in a way that makes people want to listen. (It's likely the same reason her daughter, Pooja, has become such a successful lifestyle influencer. They know how to keep people interested.) Bina once walked into Mira's house when she was on speakerphone with a customer service rep, who said, "Of course he went back to live with his mother! What a chump!"

"Now you have to tell us," Mona demands. "You can't start with that and just leave us hanging!"

"I know. I know. I shouldn't have said anything." Mira rubs her temples. "Bina, can we talk alone?"

"Sure. Why?" Bina asks. Is it about Bipin? Or Mira's daughter?

"Just trust me, okay?" Mira looks at Bina. Her heart thuds in her chest.

"Trust you about what?" Bina can't handle another second of this guessing nonsense. She grabs Mira's phone.

Her breath catches in her throat. Natasha's on the screen. Her Natasha. It looks like she's on a stage somewhere, somewhere dark and dirty. She's wearing one of Suhani's T-shirts that's in desperate need of a wash and iron.

"What is this?" Bina asks as a flash of warmth spreads throughout her body. "Where did you get it?"

"It's on YouTube apparently. Pooja sent it to me by accident. She told me not to watch it because she meant for it to go to one of her friends."

There's a PLAY button. Bina clicks it and watches her daughter pace back and forth. There are a few cheers but it's too dark for Bina to see if there's a big audience. When was this recorded? Where the heck is she?

Natasha's face has that flushed look that always tells Bina she's had too much to drink. She yells into the microphone, "Can any of you imagine telling your mom—your Indian, set-in-her-ways mom—that there's no way you can think about getting married?

Because you think too much about everything? Your brain is so fried that even your vibrator isn't doing it for you? I mean, *hello?*"

Bina gasps. Blood pounds in her ears. She turns off the video. Natasha talked about this in public? And now it's online?!

When she looks up, Mona, Kavita, and Mira are standing a few feet away from her. A strained silence falls over all of them. Even though Bina appreciates that they're doing their best to not react, their wringing hands and wide eyes give away how appalled they are.

"We should go," Mona says.

But Bina doesn't hear her or even notice them leaving a minute later. Rage flows through her, infiltrates all her organs. She picks up her own phone and considers hurling it across the room, letting it break. But she needs to watch the rest of the video. She needs to see how fully her daughter insisted on humiliating herself, all of them.

The front door creaks open. Bina doesn't even look up or ask who is there. She hears the fridge door open, then close. Deepak shouldn't be done with golf yet. Maybe Anuj is back from hanging out with his high school friends.

"Mom? Is your meeting over already?"

Bina's ears perk up. "Suhani? What are you doing here?"

Suhani steps into the formal living room. She's in a long blue-and-white tiered dress. Her eyes are red and sunken in, as though she hasn't slept all night. Everyone always commented on how Suhani was a younger version of Bina, with the same large, almond-shaped eyes, delicate chin, and pointy nose. But Bina's always thought of her daughter as more conventionally pretty, the type of pretty that people stop to admire. She also exercises and wears makeup, two things Bina rarely made time for even when she was in her thirties.

Bina is so thrown off by Suhani's presence that she temporarily forgets about what she just saw. It's only after Suhani moves closer to her that she sees the large black suitcase in the hallway.

"Why'd you bring that?"

"Oh, I'm going to stay here for a little bit," Suhani says. "You know, Zack's traveling for work and it gets boring being in the apartment by myself and all."

"Isn't your sister there?" Bina asks as she takes in a whiff of jasmine and tuberose from Suhani's perfume.

"Yeah. She is." For a second, Suhani seems to lose her composure. But then she stands up straighter. "I just needed a change of scenery."

"*Beta*, are you okay?" Bina grips Suhani's bony shoulder. "Is something wrong with you and Zack?"

"What?" Suhani asks. "No! Of course not."

"Are you sure?" Bina presses.

Even though Suhani looks okay, Bina has to make sure. Whereas Natasha puts her wounds on display, Suhani keeps them folded inside herself.

Bina first learned this when she went to Suhani's fifth-grade parent-teacher conference. Suhani's teacher, Mrs. Lane, told Bina that Suhani struggled to finish reading assignments and kept to herself during recess. Bina was shocked. Suhani always told her school was "so much fun." When she told Mrs. Lane this, the old, frizzy-haired woman shrugged and whispered in the most condescending tone, "Not all kids are meant to succeed. Sometimes it's hard for parents to accept that." Bina later cried in the parking lot and hated herself for not scolding the woman when she had the chance.

"Seriously, don't worry." Suhani smiles. "I should be asking you if you're okay. Were you crying?"

"Ha! I should be." Bina opens the link from Mira and tosses her phone toward Suhani. "You should see what Mira just sent me . . . and what everyone else is no doubt already watching in their cars."

Suhani frowns with confusion. But then she starts the video. First she says, "What the heck . . ." then, "Oh my God," then, "She said what?"

Bina can't tell if Suhani is shocked, amused, or both.

"Can you believe her?" Bina asks. "The nerve? She puts me in her performance or whatever it is and then doesn't even tell me? And I have to find out about it from Mira!"

"I really don't even know what to say, Mom. But I guess at least she's putting herself out there, right? This entire time, we were worried she wasn't doing anything."

"Putting herself out there? Is that what this garbage is called?!" Bina snatches her phone out of Suhani's hand. She clicks on the tiny link at the top of the page. It takes her to another site. "Oh my God. There are more!"

"More? Really?" Suhani scoots next to her on the couch.

The next video is of Natasha on a windowsill. Atlanta's skyline is behind her.

"That's my apartment!" Suhani scrolls to the middle of the video.

"My sister's a shrink, which means she's intuitive about people." Natasha strokes her chin in a forced contemplating pose that Suhani usually finds funny. "And she really is! She knows *just* when I'm starting to feel good about myself because that's the *exact* moment she shows up and makes sure I hate myself again! It's okay, it's okay. I just remind myself about how uptight she is and how at the end of the day, I may not be as accomplished as her, but at least

I don't have to pull a stick out of my ass! You've gotta count the wins, people! Count. The. Wins!"

"Oh my God." Suhani falls back on the couch. "How could she say that? Why would she?"

"Because we let her get away with too much nonsense, that's why," Bina says as she clicks on another video, this one also taken against Suhani and Zack's window.

"So, my family's technically Hindu," Natasha says. "I say 'technically' because I don't really practice anything myself. But I can get on board with the reincarnation idea. And if I can choose who to come back as, I'd love to come back as God. But a God who can do some drugs, daydream, and still be worshipped. In other words, I want to come back as my brother."

"Drugs? Anuj has tried drugs?!" Bina feels as though someone delivered a swift punch to her stomach. She wraps her hands around the phone until her nails make tiny half-moons in her palms.

"I don't think that's what's most important right now," Suhani says.

Bina wants to scream. But to her surprise, her voice is soft and low as she turns to Suhani. "Call her. Now."

"Are you su—"

"NOW!" Bina says. "She's been ignoring my calls for days and I know she'll pick up if it's you. And if she doesn't, I'll go to your apartment myself. But she will be hearing from me!"

Suhani nods and calls Natasha, who picks up in two rings.

"Hi!" Natasha says, oblivious. On her end, a man's voice yells, "Jim! Tall Americano! Daryl! Grande cappuccino with extra foam."

"Are you performing at a coffee shop?" Suhani asks.

"What? No. I'm, uh, well, I'm actually at Starbucks for my training."

Bina starts to ask what training Natasha's talking about, but Suhani holds up her hand as a gesture to stay quiet.

"Training?" Suhani asks.

"Yeah. I was going to tell you and Zack later tonight that I got a job at Starbucks. Since I'll finally be making money again, I can afford to get my own place somewhere else. Probably somewhere shitty, but whatever." Natasha pauses then adds, "I'm trying. I really am. It's been hard to get so many rejections and not have anything to show for what I'm doing, but I do want to stand on my own."

"By serving coffee?" Bina jumps in. "Is that what you consider a valuable use of your time?" Natasha has to be kidding. First the videos and now this? Is this what she and Deepak came to America for?

"Mom," Natasha stretches out the word so it sounds like "Moooooom." "Where did you even come from? And, no, I don't think any job is beneath me, but of course I should have expected you to have an opinion about it."

Bina feels a flash of worry, followed by anger. "I think as your mother, I have the right to weigh in on your choices. My mother wouldn't have let me out of the ho—"

"UGH, you just don't get it!" Natasha yells. "I don't want to be like you, Mom. I want to do big things with my life, okay? How come you're so okay pushing Suhani to work and work and Anuj to take his time to figure out what he wants, but with me, all you do is put me down?"

"Oh, I see," Bina says. "You can talk about me putting you down while you talk about all of us on videos? *Public* videos?"

Natasha's silent. If it wasn't for the whir of the coffee machine and staccato of people's footsteps, Bina would think they got disconnected.

"What are you talking about?"

Suhani whispers, "Let's stay calm so she hears us," but Bina ignores her. "Mira showed me your recordings or whatever they're called. You think this is comedy? Making fun of your family? What is wrong with you? What are you even doing with your life?"

"Mira Auntie showed you that? How?" Natasha's voice is softer than before.

"Does it matter?" Bina challenges. "You humiliated all of us. How dare you?!"

"I wasn't trying to humiliate anyone! I was creating material for my comedy. Obviously it's exaggerated and embellished. But it's helped me process things . . . about my life. About us."

"Wait," Bina says. "You think this is somehow helping you? Are you being serious, Natasha?"

Before Bina can say anything else, she hears the telltale click indicating that Natasha has hung up.

Sixteen

Natasha

F*uck.*
 The word replays in Natasha's head until it doesn't even sound like a word anymore.

Fuck. Fuck. Fuck. Fuck.

Mom's words on the phone come back to her. *You humiliated all of us. How dare you?!*

Maybe Mom has a point. How dare she? But comedians use their lives as inspiration all the time. Natasha couldn't have crossed the line when she only did what countless other artists have done, right?

Or maybe she did.

She sends a text to the thread she has with Anuj, Suhani, and Zack.

I'm really sorry for hurting y'all with my videos. Love you all so much.

The conviction she had just seconds ago is replaced by a sharp regret. How could she have said those things? Why didn't she even consider what would happen, how they'd feel, if they saw? The thought of them, all of them, hearing all that makes her nauseated. She sees herself the way they see her. The troublemaker. The disappointment. The hassle.

But right now, she has to focus on the next hour. She has to get it together, or at least appear to get it together, before she has the conversation she's been anticipating for days.

She takes one more deep breath and glances in the mirror. She tries to conjure an inspirational quote from the multiple ones she read on Instagram this morning. But her mind draws a blank.

Never mind, she doesn't need Instagram therapy to get through this. All she needs is the faith that today, she's going to start taking control of her life.

The Starbucks bathroom is poorly lit but she can still make out her full cheeks, round eyes, and the new layer of fat on her chin, all such contrasts to Suhani's and Mom's angular faces. It's as though the Joshi DNA decided to soften before it got to her.

She crouches under the hand dryer in an attempt to get rid of the wetness that pooled under her arms during Mom's phone call. She should have taken one of Suhani's perfume samples. And some of her makeup.

She sees Karan just when she opens the bathroom door, at a round table near the entrance, wearing a salmon-colored Lacoste polo that has to be new. It's surreal that he's just sitting here and scrolling on his phone, as if he's anyone else and not the person she grew up with and thought she'd be with forever. This is the longest they've gone without seeing each other and she's reminded of the things that define him, the ones that became blurry in her memories, like his widow's peak and the scar above his left eyebrow from a fall on the ski slopes during one of their joint family trips. Depending on who you asked, Karan could be either "adorable cute" or "hot cute." Ifeoma and Payal always thought he was too short. But Natasha would take Karan's compact, huggable build over height any day.

He sees her from his periphery. "Hi."

"Hey. Thanks for meeting me. It's really good to see you." Natasha feels her facial muscles twist into the most awkward smile. It's the first time in too long she's felt anything close to anticipation. She considers grabbing his face and kissing him, the way she first did in middle school when they snuck outside during a Diwali party.

"You, too."

I've missed you so much, she thinks as she takes in all of him.

Karan doesn't seem mad at her. In fact, the gleam in his eyes gives away that he's missed her, too. She's overcome with a mixture of excitement and relief.

"How's it going?" Karan's chair screeches against the floor when he shifts toward her for a hug. Natasha means to sink into his broad shoulders but at the last second bumps into his chest like a frat bro at a football game. So much for a graceful reunion. Nobody here would ever think that two months ago, Karan was bending down on one knee and asking Natasha to marry him.

"Oh, you know, just livin' the dream." Natasha motions to her green apron and name tag. Even though she had so much conviction when Mom questioned her about the Starbucks job, now she suddenly feels stupid.

Karan chuckles. "Yeah, look at you all dressed up for work. It suits you, actually."

"Oh really? A green apron suits me? How kind of you!" Natasha smiles.

"I'm just saying, I'd like to get a coffee from you." Karan gives her a knowing smile. Is he flirting with her?

Natasha moves the free chair at the table so that it's directly across from him. "It's so weird being here with you like this. But I'm glad we're doing this."

"I am, too. So, what's going on? How's your comedy?" Karan takes a sip of his drink. Natasha doesn't even have to ask to know it's a pumpkin spice latte. Karan always craved the seasonal drinks at Starbucks, even after they were deemed "basic." Now that she thinks of it, he embraces a lot of things that are dismissed as being commonplace, like dinner at the Cheesecake Factory or a Taylor Swift concert or those giant fingers people wear at Braves games.

"Eh, it's fine," Natasha says. "A lot of ups and downs."

It takes all her self-resolve to not tell him everything that just happened with Mom and Suhani. More than ever, she craves someone who understands her and her family in a way that can only come from history.

But then she remembers that she can't tell him because he's a part of the videos and not in the most flattering way. Damn it, why did she have to go and do this? Why couldn't she have just kept her mouth shut, the way so many teachers over the years had advised her to?

Karan raises his eyebrows.

Natasha tells herself to stay strong and put on a brave face.

But as she and Karan lock eyes, she feels herself crumbling, unable to keep it all in anymore. "Okay, so maybe more downs than ups."

She gives him a summary of how Alexis's class was harder than she thought it'd be and how she froze last night during an open mic segment at the Punchline. Someone in the audience even shouted "Get off the stage, already!"

"And there are other ways to pursue comedy, I know," she says. "I've applied for internships at some of the comedy clubs I've tried to go to for open mics. But they don't really pay much, if anything, and that's if I'm lucky enough to get a spot. Nobody will even interview me because of my lack of experience. What a catch-22, right? I can't get experience unless someone will give me a chance but nobody will give me a chance without experience. So, here I am, your favorite neighborhood barista."

She gives a big I'm-fine smile. And for this moment, she is a little closer to fine than she has been in weeks. It's cathartic to purge her mind, to tell the person who was her best friend everything that she's been keeping locked inside.

"I see," Karan says as he stares at his latte. "Wow. That really is a lot."

"I know. Sorry I just unloaded on you. I haven't been able to really talk about any of this with anyone," Natasha says. Why did she let go of the one person she used to talk to all the time?

"What about the girls? And Suhani?"

Natasha shrugs. "I know they all care, but they've got their own things going on. Things that are really different from anything I'm doing. They try but they don't fully get it. And I don't blame them. Even I don't always fully get why I'm doing all this."

Karan's eyes are heavy with concern. "Natasha, don't take this the wrong way, but are you okay?"

"Yeah, totally. I'm fine," Natasha says, then adds, "Fine enough. I mean, sure, things have been tougher than I thought they'd be, but I'll get through it."

Tears line the corners of her eyes. But she can't cry. Karan shouldn't see her like this. "It's just hard to stay motivated and keep going after I'm rejected over and over again. Then I tell myself to keep creating more ideas but my brain is running so fast sometimes that I can't even produce anything."

She doesn't say that within minutes of talking to him, she already feels more at ease. It was always so easy to talk to him. With his nonjudgmental questions and occasional nods, he's what Suhani calls an "active listener."

"But I didn't want to get into all this today. More than anything, I wanted to tell you I'm sorry for everything," Natasha says. "I know the way I reacted to the proposal was hurtful. And instead of getting so freaked out by you asking, I should have just told you I'm nowhere near ready to get married. But that doesn't mean I don't want to be with you."

Natasha fidgets with the cardboard sleeve on Karan's cup, which reads *Karen* in black Sharpie. When they were in elementary school, Karan would get so annoyed that people thought his name was Karen, but by ninth grade, he tried to find the humor in it. *It's my white-person name*, he'd say.

"You never reached out to me after that." Karan presses his lips together, which enhances the dimple in his chin.

"I know. I've wanted to but I needed to think," Natasha says. "And then, when I thought about calling, it felt unfair to bother you when you were clearly so upset. I thought a little space would help."

"Help what? Help me forget that you rejected me?" Even though Karan's cheeks are flushed, his voice is still soft. He would never get visibly pissed in a Starbucks. He and Anita Auntie are alike that way, careful to maintain public decorum no matter what, while Natasha's gotten mad at Mom in all types of places.

"No, I'm not saying that." She starts tearing the cardboard and relishes the feel of each piece in her hands. Then, because she's feeling bold, impatient, or both, she blurts, "I want to get back together."

"What?" Karan clutches the table. "Are you serious?"

"Of course I'm serious."

"Are you asking this just so there's something stable in your life?"

"What? No, of course not! I've known you since I was a baby." Her legs start to shake as she says, "And I've always seen us growing up together. You're my family."

For a second, Karan's face looks brighter. Happier. But then he shifts his hand away from hers. "I don't think that's going to work."

"What? Why not?"

"Because," Karan says.

"Because what?" She almost expects him to say *Because I said so,* the way he did when they were younger and she'd ask for explanations for the random facts he'd tell her.

"It's just not a good idea."

"Why? Because you went on a date with someone else?"

His eyes widen with surprise.

"I saw you at the market weeks ago, when I was getting ready to leave brunch. She seemed nice, you know, if you like those pretty, skinny, stylish, happy types." Natasha smiles.

"Oh," Karan says. "You mean Anisha."

She waits for him to tell her that Anisha's a long-lost cousin Natasha somehow never met.

But Karan's lips are downturned as he stares at the floor and mumbles, "She's my girlfriend."

"Your what?"

"My gi—"

"How do you already have a girlfriend? It's been, like, twenty seconds since we broke up." Her mind is flooded with the image of them from that day. Karan's large, easy smile. Anisha in her dress and heels. Of course Karan likes a girl like her. A Suhani-type girl, as put together on the inside as she is on the outside. There's no way Anisha snoozes her alarm too much or takes forever to respond to texts for no legitimate reason or oscillates between being angry at everyone and then not caring at all.

"It's been weeks since you said no to marrying me," Karan whispers as he looks around. Natasha wants to tell him nobody can hear him, and even if they can, nobody cares.

They've been together for years—*years*—and he can just be with someone else within weeks? What's worse is that he didn't even really replace her; he upgraded. If you randomly polled anyone—an auntie, a twenty-year-old, or a high schooler—all of them would agree that Anisha is a catch.

"So that means you just got another girlfriend?" she asks, suddenly feeling nauseated. "But when I asked you to meet, you seemed excited. Like you really wanted to see me."

And you're the only person I have left, she wants to say. *Nobody else gets what's going on.*

"I did want to see you," Karan says. "I wanted to make sure you're okay since my mom had heard from some of the aunties that things have been tough for you."

"You got your intel about me from your mom and the aunties. Shocker," she says.

Anita Auntie could have gotten her Natasha updates from Kavita Auntie or Mira Auntie. Both are equally likely. Mira Auntie likes sharing everyone's business as much as possible, but Kavita Auntie, even though she seems quieter, is actually the one who gets the information in the first place. Suhani's always thought that people tell Kavita Auntie more since she puts on a pretty convincing I-don't-care-about-gossip act.

"Yeah, and I mean, at that wedding a couple of weeks ago, you got into that argument with your Mom during cocktail hour. So, I dunno, it seemed like you weren't in a good place."

"Well, thanks for caring." Natasha scoffs. "But I'm fine and I definitely don't need your support."

She expects him to be irritated or maybe even mad. But when she looks up, what she sees in his eyes is way worse: pity. Stark, straightforward pity, the kind that stings more than anger would.

When Natasha and Karan were dating, he'd often note that he couldn't believe he was with someone so fun. He assumed he was too dorky, too serious, for her. But now it's clear that Karan has won. It turns out that in the game of life, being the funny, outspoken one doesn't get you very far.

"If I can ask, how did you meet Anisha?" While a part of her wants to play it cool, a bigger part is way too curious to not know more details.

"We met on Dil Mil." Karan shifts in his chair. "She's nice. Not complicated or all over the place."

"You mean, like me." Natasha clenches her fist. Of course she's now Karan's crazy ex-girlfriend. A part of her isn't even surprised.

She thinks back to the episode of *Sex and the City* when Carrie realizes she's too complicated for Big, confronts him after his engagement party at the Plaza, and walks away without looking back. If only Natasha had the strength for that type of badass gesture now.

"That's not what I said." Karan puffs out his cheeks. "I meant Anisha and I want the same things. A simple life. Stability. Family."

"Oh wow. I'm sure your mom is thrilled," Natasha says, hating that her words are weighed down with bitterness. Damn that desi dating app. Natasha can picture Anita Auntie entering in all the preferences on Karan's behalf: *Sweet, polite, perfect boy seeks girl who is as opposite of Natasha Joshi as possible.*

"I think we should stop talking about this."

"I think you're right." Natasha crosses her arms, feeling like a five-year-old who just got told she can't have dessert.

Karan glances at his phone. "I should get going."

"Good idea. I have to get back to work anyway," Natasha lies.

The weight of the entire day settles on her shoulders. She's a disappointment to everyone: her family, her friends, her ex-boyfriend, herself. Why did she ever think she could be anything else? She never fit in, and now she understands that she never will.

After she watches Karan pull out of the parking lot, she grabs her tote bag and gets in her car. She's gotten a few responses in the group thread.

SUHANI: That was really messed up. Please don't call me. I have enough going on in my life and don't need anymore stress.

ANUJ: Agreed. Didn't even know you made one about me. I helped you with YouTube and then you do that? Seriously?

ZACK: Think we should all take some time to process.

Zack also texted her separately. It'll blow over soon. Don't worry.

Ah, sweet Zack. If only he accepted that nothing in their family ever blows over soon. They're all master grudge holders.

Even though there's no traffic on I-75, she finds herself taking another route. A longer one. Cruising down the Atlanta back roads always takes her back to that exciting burst of freedom she got the first time she got in a car and drove by herself. She could take herself to her friends' houses, Chili's, or the mall, and her parents wouldn't know.

She slows down on West Paces Ferry Road, which is lined with mansions and sprawling green lawns. When they were all younger, Mom and Dad would take them on drives here. Inside all those houses, Natasha always pictured well-dressed, happy families, families with parents who didn't have a chip on their shoulders because they were poor when they moved to America, families where everyone was accepted for who they were instead of who they should be. Who knew she'd miss those car rides when she, Suhani, and Anuj were squeezed into the back seat, Dad drove, and Mom sang along with her latest favorite hip-hop song, "Welcome to Atlanta."

She feels an unexpected twinge of longing that's so intense that she's compelled to turn onto the highway and drive home. But then she remembers the texts. For the first time ever, she knows that nobody in her family wants to see her.

She ends up outside Fado, her favorite Irish pub. Only two other cars are in the parking lot. Nothing makes you feel like a loser quite like getting to a bar before the evening crowd.

The inside of Fado is dark and drafty as usual. The wooden beams on the ceiling and mahogany bar always make Natasha feel like she's in Europe. She perches on a barstool. Behind her, a group of guys a little older than her are watching a football game.

"What can I get you?" A bartender puts a coaster in front of her. His shaggy red hair and kind eyes remind Natasha of Ed Sheeran.

"Corona," Natasha says.

She finishes it in a few gulps. There's a tingling in her body as the bitter liquid goes down her throat. But instead of feeling relaxed, Natasha has a thought: *I am so goddamned alone.*

"Can I get another one of these?" Natasha asks. "And a shot of tequila?"

Ed Sheeran gives her a questioning glance but still puts the drinks on two coasters in front of her.

She downs the shot and then grips the sweating beer bottle, determined to make it last. The word "alone" keeps echoing in her mind. *Alone, alone, alone.* Maybe Karan was right and the only reason she wanted to get back together was to have some stability. Maybe some people have loneliness woven into their bone marrow.

Ed Sheeran slides her the check and a heavy gold pen before Natasha even asks for it. She has trouble scribbling her name on the receipt. When she gets off her barstool, she feels buoyant. Damn it, she shouldn't have had that last shot. There's no way she can drive to Suhani's place in this condition. She fumbles with her phone and somehow manages to call an Uber.

A black SUV pulls up a few minutes later. Natasha watches the driver study her face and then nod with recognition. Once she's in the car, he asks her what part of India she's from and tells her about his daughter, who has to be Natasha's age.

"My daughter's going to be a doctor." He smiles in the rearview mirror.

"That's nice." Natasha's words come out slower than she intends, thanks to her drunkenness. Individually wrapped mints and water bottles are in the cup holder next to her. She takes one of each.

"And what type of work do you do?" he asks. He switches the music to Bollywood songs. Indian Uber drivers often do this to Natasha. She's never sure if they feel more comfortable listening to it for themselves or if they're doing it for her.

"I, uh, you know, I'm figuring it out. Taking it one day at a time." Natasha intends to flash a confident smile but ends up feeling like she's having a facial spasm. She leans back in the leather seat and closes her eyes.

"Make sure you know soon." He points his index finger into the air as if he's about to impart some groundbreaking wisdom. "Before you know it, it'll be time for you to get married, have babies. You don't want to be too old."

"You know what?" Natasha asks. "I think I'll just listen to some music now."

She catches his judgmental stare and can practically hear him thinking, *There's another one of those girls who has been corrupted by America.* Thankfully, they reach Suhani's apartment quickly. Or at least she thinks it's quickly but is really too drunk to be sure.

She stumbles through the revolving doors and into the lobby. Carlos tips his hat and says, "Good to see you again, Natasha."

Carlos looks so kind and easy to talk to. It must be the mustache and potbelly. That's always been one of Natasha's favorite combos on an older man (she blames Santa Claus for this). For a second, Natasha wonders if she should just stay in the lobby and tell him everything that's happened today.

But then she snaps back to reality. There is no need to burden this sweet doorman with her issues.

"Good to see you, too, Carlos." She gives a quick nod and then heads to the elevator.

Nobody answers when she rings the doorbell. Wait, what if they're having sex? She presses her ear against the heavy wooden door. Nothing. She rings the doorbell again.

After pacing the hallway for a solid two minutes, she removes the key that she never returned and lets herself in.

The apartment is pitch-black. Atlanta's skyline glimmers in the floor-to-ceiling living room window. A pair of gym socks and gray sweat pants are on the shag rug in their bedroom. Their bed is unmade.

Natasha breathes a sigh of relief, her first one all day, at having the place to herself. She thumbs through Suhani and Zack's wine collection and pours herself a generous serving of Cabernet Sauvignon. The word loops and loops in her mind like an annoying song on repeat. *Alone. Alone. Alone.*

Her head starts pounding and she's not sure if it's from the alcohol or the pressure of too many thoughts. She sits on the cool, smooth kitchen floor and runs her bare feet over the ridges between the tiles. The wine is smoother, gentler, than the beer from earlier.

For years, Natasha assumed happiness would come after she achieved the right milestones. But after she was in a decent relationship, graduated college, and got her first job, she realized that that's not how it works. Some people are meant to live in a state of perpetual dissatisfaction. It's as simple as that. She's always had a gaping rift between who she is and who she wants to be.

Her future reveals itself in snippets, like a drab PowerPoint presentation. She sees herself waiting for a dark, drafty club to call her back, someone to give her a chance.

Maybe she can't get herself to write any decent jokes because she actually isn't a good comedian. Maybe things don't work out because something is inherently wrong with her. Even when she was a little girl, she was always so much more reactive than Suhani or Anuj. How many times did Mom and Dad say they had to be extra careful with their words around Natasha? How many times did she know they were all more relaxed when she wasn't there?

It's only a matter of time before her siblings and friends get wrapped up in their real, fulfilling lives and won't have space for her. Suhani's schedule will only be more packed when she's an attending. Anuj will be consumed with his classes and friends at Cornell. He won't have the time to deal with Natasha's daily dramas. And her friends are all moving on, becoming legitimate adults with lives she's so proud of but knows won't have space for her.

Zack's the only one who might have the patience to keep putting up with her. But soon enough, his compassion will wear out.

She pours another glass of wine. With each sip, the truth becomes clearer. She's a burden to the people she loves. There isn't a single place she belongs. And no matter how she tries to spin it, she's a failure in every role of her life.

I can't take this anymore, she thinks.

The room starts to spin as she pulls herself off the floor. She stumbles to the bathroom. It smells like a mixture of Zack's minty aftershave and Suhani's floral perfume. Natasha leans over the white toilet and waits to throw up. Nothing.

The medicine cabinet above the sink is full of luxurious toiletries and every possible over-the-counter item someone could need. Pepto Bismol, Advil, Tylenol, Tums, Q-tips, safety pins, bobby pins, tweezers, Band-Aids, an assortment of Drunk Elephant skincare products, serums for the morning and evening, clay face masks.

Her head pounds as she shuffles through all of it. She removes a bottle of extra-strength Tylenol. She takes one and then, before she has a chance to think, she takes another. Each pill is smooth and easy. There's a brief second of satisfaction from just doing something, anything, besides sitting here and waiting for her mind to quiet down.

She takes another Tylenol. At some point, she starts existing outside herself. She has to get rid of this pain, to stop feeling anything, to escape.

As everything becomes hazy, she rolls multiple pills in her chapped palm and tosses them into her mouth. *Fuck it. Just fuck everything.*

In moments of emotional chaos, she's always caught a brief glimpse of clarity. It hits her now. She's so tired of caring. She's just so fucking tired.

She crawls out of the bathroom and back into the living room. There's a sharp pinch in her gut. Maybe she should call Suhani or even Dad. One of them would know what to do right now.

But she can't pick up her phone. She can't bring them into this. Just before her eyes close, she enters her passcode and lies on the floor as everything starts to feel numb.

Seventeen

Suhani

It takes Suhani a few seconds to process the summer evening sounds of the suburbs: cars slowly gliding over pavement, the occasional barking dog, the hum of voices and clink of glasses on the neighbor's back deck.

How did she fall asleep at this hour? The last thing she remembers is watching Natasha's videos again and again, until she had the words memorized, and then texting Vanessa the link to Natasha's YouTube channel with the message I can't even.

She sits up and runs her hands over her pink rose-printed sheets. Mom has been using the same floral, frilly bedding since Suhani was in high school.

She checks her texts. None from Zack. I hope you're doing okay, she types to him. Before sending, she adds, I miss you.

There are messages from Vanessa and Natasha.

> VANESSA: WOW. I have a LOT of thoughts on this. Call me when free.

> NATASHA: Don't be mad.

The three simple words are a time capsule, transporting Suhani back to all the moments over the years when Natasha was well aware Suhani was furious with her but made the request anyway. *Don't be mad.*

Suhani types, "What did you expect?" But something hinders her from sending the message. Buried underneath her embarrassment and anger, she feels something else emerge: pride. Pride for her sister's innate talent. The videos take away Natasha's usual stage fright, leaving space for who she is underneath the nerves. And she is funny. The type of funny people would want to pay for and hear more of. And even if she hit below the belt, a lot of what made her videos so biting was the truth woven into her words.

Suhani shifts to her e-mail. Dr. Wilson hasn't responded yet about whether she's still in the running for chief. His last message to her ended with *I'm sure you understand the committee members still have various factors to consider before making our final decisions for chief.*

Even though he didn't write it, she knows that by "various factors," he's referring to the conversation with Roshan. How could she have been stupid enough to lose her cool like that? Now everyone knows something happened between her and a faculty member and that'll be it. She will have lost the one thing she's been working for for three years.

From downstairs, she can hear Mom, Dad, and Anuj, busy with their post-dinner ritual of cleaning the kitchen and watching *Jeopardy!* She doesn't have the energy to see them right now. They can read her better than anyone else, so it'll be a matter of seconds before they know she's lying about why she came home. As much as she takes pride in being a real, respectable adult, she regresses into an eager-to-please sixteen-year-old whenever she's here.

The tall white bookshelf next to her bed is as unchanged as

other parts of her room. Old issues of *Glamour* magazine and year-books from fifth grade to senior year line the bottom shelf. There are framed photos of her with friends from high school, many of whom she's no longer in touch with outside the occasional like or comment on social media. Stray safety pins are in the corners of the shelves, which are no doubt from the itchy, confining saris she pulled off over the years. Growing up, Suhani's favorite ritual after weddings or pujas was to come home, rip off her Indian clothes, change into flannel pajamas, and watch Disney Channel shows with Natasha and Anuj.

She's usually too rushed and exhausted on her visits home to go through any of the stuff in her room. But today, her eyes pause on the gold spine of her seventh-grade yearbook. She flips to her picture. Nobody who knows her now would believe that's actually her. The baby fat, braces, frizzy hair, thick glasses, and forced smile make her look like another person. A sadder, softer person.

She's taken back to the musty gray locker rooms where she was too self-conscious about her weight and hairy legs to change in front of the other girls. One day, Blair, the school's queen bee, asked why Suhani always ran into the bathroom stalls after PE. Suhani tried to ignore Blair (in her fantasy, she told Blair off, but really, she awkwardly laughed, then ran away). Blair then appointed the rest of the popular girls to start chanting "Suhani is a dark and hairy man!" every day after class. For the rest of middle school, Suhani gave up on getting out of Blair's way. Instead, she cried on the bus ride home every afternoon, and when she walked through the door she focused on the two things she could control: getting perfect grades and pretending she was fine. It was too easy to tell Mom and Dad everything was great as she asked them to sign below her row of straight As. The only time she felt anything close to relief was over the summers, when she'd sit in the back-yard alone with a dripping grape Popsicle and a Baby-Sitters Club book in her hands.

Two years later, in an attempt to be less of a target at school, she mastered the art of being likable and polite. She learned to keep controversial opinions to herself, nod even when she disagreed with someone, and brush off insults. She also discovered waxing, contact lenses, calorie counting, and makeup tips from the *Glamour* magazines she still has. Beauty was supposed to shield her, but sometimes she forgot whether she was growing up or giving in and just becoming who the world wanted her to be.

And while the bullying stopped, the more subtly corrosive dis-crimination continued. She got called "exotic." Minutes after she was voted "Most Likely to Succeed," a teacher asked if her parents were setting her up to have an arranged marriage. Once, when she picked up tampons from CVS, a customer told her to "go back to India." During her lowest moments, she had fleeting thoughts about what it would be like to end it all, and then she'd snap back to reality.

She never told Mom and Dad about any of it. There was no need. They had already been through bigger, tougher things. She was supposed to be the one who made them proud and set an ex-ample for her sister and brother. When Mom used to go on her solitary, late-night drives, Suhani gave Natasha and Anuj bubble baths, packed their lunches for the next day, and taught them how to properly eat rotli and shaak, by ripping off a piece of rotli and using it to scoop up the vegetables. When Suhani scored below average on her PSAT, Mom shook her head with disappointment and said, "Suhani, this is unacceptable. You have to focus if you really want to make something of yourself." Mom then muttered something about the importance of "making enough of your own money one day" and "doing everything to be taken as seriously as a man" and "never forgetting we have to prove we belong in this country."

Suhani only realizes now that she never told Zack about any of this, either. She scrolls back to the last text he sent her two days ago:

> You always have the right to your privacy. It just feels like there's constantly been stuff you don't tell me, whether it's big or not.
> You don't trust me to be able to be there for you.

Maybe he's right. Is it possible that she used to keep things from her parents for the sake of self-sufficiency, and now she doesn't even know how to be vulnerable with her husband?

When she opens her room door, she can't hear anyone. Her parents and brother have retreated to their own corners of the house. She puts the yearbook back in its spot, grabs her phone, and tiptoes down the stairs.

To her surprise, Mom's whispering on the phone. "Now, you remember what I said: tell his mother you won't take her nonsense anymore! Yes, it was nice to meet you, too! Maybe I'll see you next time I'm in line at Target."

Suhani suppresses a laugh. Mom makes friends wherever she goes. Both she and Natasha do. People turn to them whenever they enter a room. People love them. People rarely ever have to deal with their difficult parts.

"I was wondering where you were, *beta*." Mom's fingertips are covered in flour. She dips them into a glass container that's stuffed with a massive ball of dough.

No matter how old Suhani is, whenever she thinks of Mom, this exact image comes to mind: Mom shaping a piece of dough into a sphere and using the wooden rolling pin to flatten it into a perfectly round rotli.

"Why are you cooking this late? I thought you'd be getting ready for bed by now."

"There's no way I can sleep right now after everything," Mom says. "I can't stop thinking about it. I've been trying to distract myself with phone calls and TV, but none of it's really helping."

"I know what you mean," Suhani says.

"You must be hungry." Mom raises a recently threaded eyebrow. "Were you asleep?"

Suhani forgot that in the midst of replaying Natasha's videos, she had changed out of her maxi dress and into teal-blue Athleta pants and a faded gray Pleasant Hill High T-shirt. Her nails are chipped for the first time in months. Zack always joked that he could tell how Suhani was doing based on the state of her nails.

"Uh, no. I was just sitting in my room." Suhani takes two Oreos from a box on the counter. With her outfit, glasses, messy bun, and now the cookies, she almost looks identical to her seventh-grade yearbook picture. "Why are you cooking again?"

"Just in case Dad wants one as a midnight snack," Mom says, and Suhani can almost hear her adding the word "duh."

"Can't he figure something else out because he's an adult?"

"You know I can't just do that to him," Mom says, as if leaving Dad to eat a bowl of cornflakes or pick up late-night Taco Bell would be some sort of crime. Suhani doesn't even know what Zack eats most of the time. She couldn't handle one week with a dynamic like Mom and Dad's.

"I think it could be good for both of you if he fends for himself once in a while," Suhani says.

"I'm fine. We're all fine," Mom says with an edge to her voice. "Whenever you come here, you think it's your job to dictate the way the house runs. Even when people were visiting a few months ago, you got so upset."

"Somebody has to say something about this throwback to the 1950s!" Suhani says as she thinks back to the extended family members who visited Mom and Dad over the summer. Of course Mom could never suggest they stay in a hotel. Instead, she made them chai multiple times a day, cooked them fresh meals, did their laundry, took them to Stone Mountain and the Coca-Cola museum, and sent them home with a combination of gifts and some of Anuj's old video games for their own kids.

But it's not just about that visit. It's about Suhani always seeing her mother put herself last. It's about how politeness and accommodating others were a part of her language, like the syllables of Gujarati mixed with English. And now that it's just her and Dad at home, she should cook less and tell him to do his own laundry. Why does she accept this for herself? Why doesn't she demand more? She can't believe this woman in front of her—the one concerned with when Patel Brothers will restock ginger or if she's slacking by buying ready-made dosa batter—once recited lines onstage in front of hundreds of people.

"Trust me, I made peace with all this years ago. It's not worth it for you to get so worked up. And I'm glad this isn't your life, *beta*." Mom gazes at Suhani with a look that takes her back to countless afternoons when Suhani studied at the dining table while Mom cut fruit. The rush of nostalgia and wistful expression on Mom's face

make Suhani wonder if she should just tell her everything going on
with Zack and work and Roshan. Maybe she won't judge her.
Maybe, since Suhani is now an adult who has proven herself, Mom
will listen and provide support.

But then Mom's phone rings with a WhatsApp notification. She
rushes to pick it up with an urgency Suhani thought was reserved
for doctors responding to codes. She watches Mom scroll through
the message and knows her moment to tell her anything has disappeared. Throughout Suhani's life, there have been narrow windows of time when it felt right to confide in her mother. Once they
were interrupted—by a phone call, something bubbling over
on the stove, one of her siblings needing something—it was as
though the air between her and Mom had shifted, and it no longer
made sense to bother her with anything.

Mom tucks her phone into the side pocket of her nightgown.
"I'm going to bed."

"Already?" Dad walks into the kitchen. He's wearing an outfit
that's a confused cross between loungewear and nineties soccer
player: a buttery yellow shirt that reads KEEP TALKING; I'M DIAGNOSING
YOU and a pair of black Umbro shorts that he definitely took from
Anuj's room.

"Yes, I'm going to watch that new Bollywood series on Netflix
until my eyes close." Bina gives Deepak a hug, then pecks Suhani
on her cheek.

"Now, why are you awake?" Suhani asks Dad after Mom is gone.

"I was hungry. Ah, my favorite!" Dad picks up a warm rotli, adds
chickpea curry, and rolls it all up like a burrito. He's been eating his
Gujarati food like that since residency. Now the ensemble has been
named a "kathi roll" and is sold at Indian restaurants everywhere.

"So . . . I was telling Mom you should be able to cook for yourself and finish other chores that she's been doing forever. Now that it's just both of you at home, things should be split more equally."

She waits for Dad to argue or explain why this setup has always worked.

But to her surprise, Dad puts down his food and says, "I agree."

"You do?" Suhani asks.

"Of course. Why do you think I encouraged her to start these meetings? I know she should be spending her time doing different things. And the events she's always planned were great, but even with those, she became the go-to cook and coordinator. She needs something that challenges her, helps her connect with people the way she was always meant to and make a bigger impact. I want that for her. I've always wanted that for her."

"Does she know that? Have you told her?" Suhani asks as she realizes that sometimes it's the words people don't say that can shape a relationship, a life.

"I always assumed she knew but clearly, I was wrong." He takes a glass and fills it with ice and water from the fridge, which is covered in magnets that have different drug names: Prozac, Xanax, Lexapro. "I was convinced I'd be different—the Indian husband who actually made sure his wife had as big of an identity outside the home as he did. But then we had more kids and I got so wrapped up in my own work and we were surrounded by people who divided things in a more traditional way. I guess at some point both she and I surrendered to that."

He turns to her, his eyes heavy with something Suhani can't pinpoint. Regret? Sadness? "Your mom had to sacrifice a lot for me, for all of us. She couldn't go back to the life she had planned for herself. And I think that eventually, managing all this"—he points to the house—"became her way to prove herself."

Suhani always thought of Mom's endless daily tasks as a function of the patriarchy. But maybe by keeping their house in order, Mom could ensure her regrets were organized and manageable. Still, she can't decide if this is a healthy coping mechanism or a sign that underneath the cleaning and folding and pleasing, her mother is depressed.

And she always assumed Dad was content being absentminded about anything that happened at home. Instead of seeing her parents clearly, she wonders if it's her default to view them through a lens that's clouded with her own bias. Maybe with family, the past is always too intertwined with the present.

"Isn't it funny how we get used to things so easily?" Dad says. "I forget sometimes that I went to medical school for her and, of course, for our future children."

"I forget you went to med school for Mom, too," Suhani admits. "For all of us."

She absorbs a truth that she usually pushes to the far corners of her mind: her parents shifted their entire lives and never looked back, all so that she and her siblings could do things they never had the chance to. She pictures Dad at her age, standing behind a cash register at a gas station in the middle of the night, masking his anger while customers mocked his accent, not being able to afford any phone calls to the family he left in India, and playing with the three of them whenever he was home, regardless of how exhausted he was.

Unlike Mom, he's always kept his emotions to himself. But maybe he doesn't do that because he wants to. Maybe it's because he always thought he had to.

He nods with understanding, then looks away from her. "You know I'm not the only one, right? No, never mind."

"Never mind what?"

"I shouldn't have said anything," Dad says, lowering his voice.

"About what?"

Dad sighs. "Did you know Zack was willing to do the same thing?"

"What? What are you talking about?"

"You apparently told him the story of how I was determined to win over Mom's parents, even if that meant changing my career path." Dad has the peaceful look that he gets whenever he talks about a happy patient story. "And when Zack thought we or our community wouldn't accept him, he called me and told me he'd go to medical school if that's what it took."

"Zack said that to you? He never told me. . . ." Suhani tries to picture her husband in a white coat or hunched over fat textbooks for hours. After his dad left, Zack thought it was his responsibility to do what he could to help his mom. He started with working at a movie theater in high school and, eventually, at McKinsey after he graduated from Dartmouth. And even though he's always been interested in Suhani's work, he's maintained that he could never study for so many tests or be in school for years.

"He didn't want you to know," Dad says before he tells her about how Zack asked him to coffee and then said he'd do whatever it took to prove he was serious about Suhani. "And, ironically, this was the same week that something else happened. And I always wondered if the universe was sending us a message."

"A message? About what?" Suhani sits on the island.

"Ah, so Natasha never told you." Dad raises his chin into the air, a look of recognition on his face.

"Told me that Zack was willing to be a doctor?"

Dad shakes his head. "No, that we ran into the boy you used to

be with at Lenox Mall. Rohit? Roshan? It was only a few days before
Zack asked me to meet. Anyway, Mom and I were window-shopping
and stopped to get California Pizza Kitchen. He came up to us while
we were eating. He introduced himself, asked if we remembered
him."

"And?"

"And"—Dad shifts his gaze to the floor—"he told us you meant
a lot to him, that he was going to reach out to you about settling
back in Atlanta."

"How are you only telling me this now?" Suhani's thoughts go
back to that time in her life when she was fully wrapped up in her
relationship with Zack. She remembers that one night when she
realized it had been months since she'd thought of Roshan. It felt
like a true accomplishment to finally be that detached from someone she thought would haunt her forever.

"We debated about whether we would ever tell you," Dad says.
"But at that time, we were confused. And wrong. You have to
understand that Zack wasn't who we pictured for you."

He wasn't who Suhani had pictured for herself, either. Then
again, her younger self's idea of the perfect husband came from a
mix of Bollywood and Disney movies. Not the most reliable mash-up
for a real future.

"We worried about how your different backgrounds would
affect your future together. We didn't understand why you would
purposefully make your life harder when marriage is already
hard enough," Dad says. "When we came home from the mall we
told Natasha everything. She really let us have it." He shakes his
head and chuckles, confirming one of Mom's long-standing complaints about Dad: he always lets Natasha get away with everything.

"She actually sat us down and said we were being closed-minded and stupid. And she reminded us that we went against our parents to marry each other, and here we were, doing the same thing to you. Isn't she clever?" Dad smiles. "We didn't think about things the right way. Yes, we weren't perfect as parents, and I think in a lot of ways, Mom and I always worried about you the most. Because when something was bothering you, you kept it inside. When you were a lot younger, it showed in how you were in school. We were shocked when you didn't get into the gifted program, but after we met with that terrible teacher who put you down, we realized you were showing your frustration with her by not trying in school. After that, we felt you needed more consistent encouragement to make sure you really lived up to your potential, regardless of how other people may or may not treat you."

If anyone else heard what Dad had just said, they'd probably assume he was referring to Natasha, who, to everyone's surprise, got into the gifted program right away.

"That racist fifth-grade teacher was the worst," Suhani says. "And I can't believe we all forget that Natasha is the one who used to do well in school, without even trying that hard."

Suhani always took pride in her ambition and steadfast work ethic. But is it possible that Natasha was more equipped to achieve while Suhani had the potential to take more risks? She thinks back to the times Natasha told her she wanted to be different from Suhani, have her own things going for her. Did both of them become who they are just because that's how they were shaped by their worlds? And were they both pushed to become the opposite of each other? Were they like a photograph and its negative, their complementary parts exposed and darkened?

"Natasha's never needed anyone to push her when she decides she wants to do something," Dad says. "And that day, she wanted to make sure we knew we were making a mistake by even considering Roshan could be a better fit for you. And she reminded us of how much happier and, really, bolder you became once Zack came into your life."

Suhani taps her fingers on the marble island in the center of the kitchen. Each tap is a tidbit for what Dad told her. *Tap.* Zack was willing to go to med school. *Tap.* Her parents ran into her ex-boyfriend, who wanted her back. *Tap.* Natasha defended Zack. *Tap.* Suhani wasn't meant to succeed.

"Wow, this is all a lot." Suhani feels a sting of impending tears as she runs through all of it again. She has a sudden pang of longing for her sister. For years, she assumed Natasha either didn't understand her or, worse, resented her. But now she sees that her sister gives her a type of safety nobody else can.

"Of course, it took a lot for us to realize we needed to change," Dad says, echoing the words he used during his speech at Suhani and Zack's engagement party. She'll never forget how Dad raised his champagne glass, looked at her with a soft smile, and in front of all their family and friends said, *"Beta,* this is exactly why we came here, so you could choose the life *you* wanted." As the St. Regis ballroom filled with applause and a wave of "aws," Suhani realized how much she had underestimated her parents. And because they accepted Zack, all the uncles and aunties did, too.

Natasha was right. Zack did make her different. Someone more willing to take risks, to not be so afraid.

She unlocks her phone, opens her e-mail, and types a response to Dr. Wilson:

Hi, Dr. Wilson,

I think it's important that we meet to discuss the situation. After
all the hard work I've done, I don't think it would be fair for a
past relationship to hold back my being considered for chief.

Before she can think anymore, she hits SEND. A wave of panic
rises in her. She's never sent an e-mail that direct before.

"Sorry," she says to Dad. "I was just sending an e-mail to my
program director."

"When do you find out about chief?"

"Soon, I guess." Suhani chews on her lips. "You know how these
things go."

Dad nods. "I was so shocked when I found out I was chief."

Suhani's heard this story a million times but she says, "Really?"

"I thought there was no way they'd pick the Indian resident for
chief, especially back then. But my program director's assistant—she
really liked me—told me that she vouched for me in the meetings. It
was a stressful job, making everyone's schedules, accommodating
requests, and doing my regular job, but I learned so much that year
about administration and managing people. And I felt that I made
some real changes."

Usually, Suhani enjoys hearing about Dad's experiences at work,
the way he defied the odds to even get a residency spot in Atlanta,
then graduated as a chief.

But today, her thoughts keep shifting to Zack.

A few minutes later, in typical Dad fashion, he ends his story with a
series of grand statements. "So it really came down to the value of lead-
ership. And fixing our broken mental health system from the inside."

Dad glances at his Apple watch. "Oh! It really is late! Let's both try to get some rest."

As soon as she hears the click of Mom and Dad's bedroom door shutting, her phone vibrates with a text message alert.

Zack!

 I'm outside your parents' door. Are you awake?

Suhani runs to the foyer. *My husband*, she thinks. *My husband is here.*

Through the beveled-glass door, she makes out brown wavy hair and glasses. She opens the door. Her husband is just standing there, as if it's totally normal for him to show up here late at night, when they haven't been talking.

"I can't believe you're really here. I've missed you," Suhani says as she jumps into his arms and inhales the mint and rosemary of his Jack Black body wash. She didn't realize until now how much she's missed his smell.

Zack's posture is stiff. "Sorry, I didn't come here because of us."

"Oh." Suhani feels a drop in her chest.

"Is Anuj home?"

"He's still out with friends," Suhani says. "Why?"

"We have to go. And don't say anything to your mom and dad yet."

"What's going on? You're scaring me." Suhani's throat tightens as she takes in Zack's red eyes, the urgency on his face.

"Natasha's in the emergency room."

Eighteen

Bina

She can't sleep.

To be fair, Bina was always a bad sleeper. Ma said that even when she was a baby, she'd just stare at the ceiling as if she was lost in thought.

She goes through a breathing exercise that's Suhani approved. (She told Suhani she found the exercise through *Psychology Today* when really she found it on WhatsApp, her main source of information. Suhani got irritated every time Bina started a sentence with "I found the best remedy on WhatsApp. . . .")

Deepak's on his side, snoring. His white undershirt is bunched around his waist. He can fall asleep anywhere: on the recliner while they're watching *Jeopardy!*, during the short drive home from Anita and Jiten's house, in the middle of monotonous speeches at weddings. He said it was because of residency-training sleep deprivation, but Bina's always thought it had to do with his mind being at ease. Meanwhile, she just saw a post online that read "a woman's brain is like an internet browser with dozens of tabs open" and she's never related to something more.

She pushes the cloudlike duvet cover off her legs. The blue-gray morning light peeks in through the blinds. When she's stretched out on the recliner in the living room, she pulls up Natasha's videos for the tenth time since Mira showed them to her. Maybe if she watches them enough, she'll be able to view them more like a spectator than a mother.

But as she takes in her daughter's vulnerable but strong voice, the glint in her eyes, she knows that'll never be true. She can't decide if she's in awe of Natasha's courage, appalled by her audacity, or both.

Bina pauses at one section of the video that she hasn't been able to stop thinking about.

"Some of you may be wondering why I'm here if I'm feeling so shitty," Natasha says. "And I get that. I really do. But here's the thing. I'm trying to get out of my head. And telling all of you how shitty I'm feeling helps me because now all that crap that was brewing around in there is out there with you. What I'm trying to say is, thank you all for coming here and being my therapists."

Bina presses the PAUSE button. The only sound is the faint chirping of birds outside the living room window.

I know why that part is getting to me, she texts Devi. It's what I said about acting. I used to tell my parents I wanted to get out of my own head. I stopped telling them that because they just didn't get it.

DEVI: She's your daughter. In every way.

BINA: Awake?!

DEVI: Jaya visiting, remember? Went to In-N-Out and watched that new Ryan Gosling movie.

Devi and her daughter, Jaya, have one of those mother-daughter relationships Bina thought only exist in urban myths. They rarely ever argue and are best friends, doing everything from sharing clothes to trying new restaurants to going on road trips. Devi claims their relationship got much better after her divorce because she was less stressed.

DEVI: Your girl has nerve. Like someone else I know.

She adds the winking face emoji.

BINA: That's a nice way to put it.

DEVI: It takes nerve to say no to getting married to someone you've been with for so many years. She could have strung it all along.

BINA: True.

Bina's hit with a pang of longing for Natasha. Even though her strong will gave Bina a lot of stress throughout the years, she knows deep down that she wouldn't want her daughter to be any different. She wishes she could call Natasha and tell her she knows she's just trying her best. They both are.

"Mom? What are you doing?" Anuj walks into the living room. His red Cornell sweatshirt is in need of a wash. Despite his six-two build and ample facial hair, his round eyes and relaxed smile give him a perpetual boyish look.

"Nothing! Just couldn't sleep and was texting with Devi," Bina says. She didn't realize she had eaten an entire sleeve of Parle-G biscuits. A pile of biscuit dust has collected on her lap.

"Yeah. I can't stop watching the Natasha videos, either." Anuj

settles on the recliner next to her and covers himself with a bur-
gundy throw Bina and Deepak got on a trip to Morocco.

A trip, she thinks. *Maybe we need a family trip.*

"I know, *beta*," Bina says, appreciating how Anuj comments on
things so matter-of-factly.

My sweet, sensitive boy, Bina thinks. She feels relieved, then guilty
for being relieved, at being able to sit here with her son, who won't
jump into problem-solving mode like Suhani or defensive mode
like Natasha.

"Are you still really mad?" Anuj asks.

"I'm not sure what I am, to be honest. You?" Bina sighs, appreciating this type of moment with him. She can't remember the last
time they talked, really talked, about things that weren't logistics.

Anuj's curls sway as he shakes his head. "I was pissed."

"Yeah?" Bina asks. She rarely ever hears a statement like this
from him: *I was pissed.*

"Totally," Anuj says. "There's stuff about her, about everyone,
that pisses me off all the time."

"I didn't know that." Bina sighs.

Sometimes she thinks she knows her son so well. Sometimes
she thinks she doesn't know him at all.

"Well, I'm fine now," Anuj says. "Or at least, better. I get annoyed with Natasha sometimes, especially in the past weeks. And
then I'll take a second and remember that she may seem tough but
she really is fragile in lots of ways."

It occurs to Bina that everyone in their family has this with each
other: moments of frustration followed by moments of forgiveness.
Maybe that daily push and pull is what sustains a family over time.

"Yes. She is," Bina agrees. "You know, I was just feeling bad because I was glad you're the one I'm able to discuss this with. If Na-

tasha was home right now, she'd get so defensive that she wouldn't even hear anything I was trying to tell her."

"Yeah, but, Mom, do you think that's all her fault?" Anuj's tone is gentle as he shifts to face her.

"What do you mean?"

"We're all really hard on her sometimes, harder than we are on anyone else," he says. "I kind of get why she doesn't always feel accepted with us."

"So you're saying this is our doing?" Bina asks.

"I'm saying it's complicated," Anuj says. "I mean, c'mon, Mom. If you really ask yourself honestly, can you say that you parented all three of us the same?"

As a toddler, Anuj would ask things that could have gone into an episode of Oprah's *Super Soul Sunday*: *Why are we on the planet? Why do you care about how you look? Can't everyone just be nice to each other?*

Bina slumps in the recliner as she considers his questions. She's always focused so much on how different her children are. But is it possible that she gave all her children different proportions of her regrets, resentments, and reliefs?

The three-toned chime of the doorbell fills the house.

"Who could that be right now?" Bina asks Anuj, who shrugs in response and says, "I'll go check."

A second later, he yells, "Mom!" from the foyer.

Before Bina can fold her blanket and throw away the empty biscuit sleeve, Mira, Kavita, and Mona walk into the living room. Mira's holding a steel thermos. Kavita is balancing a cake dish in her hands.

"What are you all doing here so early?" Bina asks.

"We were all awake and wanted to make sure you're okay after yesterday," Mira says. "I'm sorry I showed you Natasha's video. I shouldn't have. It couldn't have been easy to see that."

Anuj gives a quick hi and bye to the aunties, then goes to his room.

"Don't apologize." Bina puts her hand up. "It was already out there. Not your fault she went and did that."

"Look, we've all been through shit with our kids, right?" Mona glances at Mira and Kavita. When they stay silent, she says, "Fine. I'll start. When Arjun was in high school, he was caught for under-age drinking and I had to pick him up from the police station. *The police station.*"

Mira inhales as if she's preparing to perform a monologue on stage. "Pooja struggled a lot in graduate school. She almost failed out. We were so worried, and it turned out it didn't even matter because she's not working in business anyway."

Mona and Mira turn toward Kavita. If they were all decades younger, this would turn into one of those drinking games their kids pretend not to play, where everyone shares something and takes a sip of some cheap alcohol.

"I know Sonam doesn't want to get married because she's scared about having the same type of marriage Bipin and I do." Kavita's voice is soft. "And I don't blame her."

"I'm so sorry," Bina says, turning toward her. Every time Kavita mentioned Sonam not getting married, she never told them she knew exactly why. Bina wonders how much they've all kept tucked inside themselves.

Kavita shakes her head, indicating she doesn't want to discuss it further. Bina clutches her shoulder. She wants to tell Kavita she understands. When Zack proposed to Suhani, Bina was relieved.

Her daughter wouldn't have to make herself smaller for the sake of others the way Bina had to.

Bina feels the discomfort of vulnerability dissolve and create space for something else. Is it possible that she was so scared of being judged that she never gave any of these women a chance to be there for her? Did she let shame push her into the folds of loneliness?

Then she has another thought. It's better Anita isn't here. This discussion would make her so uncomfortable. Maybe they've always been less compatible than she let herself believe.

She realizes that this is actually the first Chats Over Chai discussion. This is what she had been hoping for when they met previously.

"There. So we've all been in denial about our kids in some way. It's all out," Mona says, proud of herself for starting this. "Now, I'm getting some plates and cups. We brought banana bread and chai."

"You shouldn't have come here, so early, and with all of this food." Bina is taken aback by their sheer thoughtfulness, the power and comfort that only women can give one another.

"Don't cry," Mira says.

"No, no, they're happy tears," Bina says. "For once."

"Your idea for us to get together and honestly talk is what we all need," Kavita says. "We should have started something like this years ago."

The doorbell rings again. What is going on today? It's the most eventful morning Bina's had in years.

"I'll get it," Mira offers.

A few seconds later, Bina hears Mira's voice and then a forceful "NO!" It's hard to tell whether it's angry or funny.

"Mira!" Bina shouts. "Is everything okay?"

She hears the thump of quick footsteps on wood, then tile.

"STOP!" Mira yells.

"Bina?" Deepak asks from the master bedroom, his voice muffled with sleep. "Is everything okay?" Anuj steps out of his room upstairs. "Mom?"

"Let me go check what's going on." Bina jumps up and briskly walks to the hallway. She sees the chin-length bob and petite frame before she gets to the front door.

Anita.

Anita shifts to the side of the foyer when she hears Bina's voice.

That's when Bina sees Bipin.

Shit.

"Bipin!" Bina exclaims. "What are you doing here?"

Bipin's nostrils flare. He doesn't even bother to say hi. "Where is Kavita?"

"She's with us." Bina points toward the living room.

Bipin walks past her without taking off his shoes.

Bina steps in front of him. "Is there a problem?"

"She needs to come with me." Bipin raises his voice and adds, "Now."

"We're just talking." Fear lodges in Bina's chest as she takes in Bipin's flushed cheeks. But she can't just stand here. "What's going on?"

"Bina." Bipin holds up a palm in front of her.

Maybe she should stop. After all, Bipin and Kavita should discuss this between themselves.

But something about Bipin's clenched jaw and hunched shoulders scares her and also pushes her to keep going. She glances at Anita, who is still standing by the front door with her arms crossed.

"What did you do?" Bina asks.

"Bipin called me and asked if I knew what Kavita was doing. She had texted me last night and asked if I wanted to come here with her. . . . I thought it was for another meeting, so when he asked, I told him . . . ," Anita says, her face heavy with regret.

"Well, I hope you're happy," Bina says. "And just because you aren't ready to talk to me doesn't mean you had to do this to Kavita."

Bina imagines how all this would play out if they were on one of those volatile talk shows she used to watch when the kids were at school. She would sit next to Natasha on one side of the stage. Karan and Anita would be on another. Anita would point to Natasha and yell, *She ruined everything!* Karan would then point to Natasha and add, *She said I was boring in bed! In public!* The audience would erupt in a loud *Boooooo!* A bald security guard would stand between them and hold out his muscular tattooed arms as buffers.

Sometimes, while Bina is washing dishes or scrolling through texts, she remembers flashes of their friendship. Sharing rides to parties. Jiten opening the door in the middle of the night, five minutes after he texted her that Anita's father passed away in India. Anita, sweeping up shards of glass after Bina dropped a stack of dinner plates out of sheer exhaustion. How they stopped keeping track of Pyrex containers because they'd go back and forth between their houses anyway. A joint family trip to France where Anita and Bina spent every afternoon sitting in cafés, drinking cappuccinos and people watching.

She wonders if this is real loss: a tangled mix of anger, betrayal, humiliation, and longing.

Bina scampers to Bipin. When she's behind him, she stretches to her tiptoes and taps him on his shoulder. "Bipin Bhai, I'll ask this clearly so there's no room for misinterpretation. Do you have a problem with us meeting to talk?"

Bipin stops and turns to face her. Goose bumps erupt on Bina's arms. How could she have missed seeing this part of him throughout the years? Sure, she always knew he was stern and even intimidating, but right now, for the first time, he's terrifying her. She's not sure if she's overreacting or if she's finally seeing him clearly.

"I don't want Kavita here," Bipin says, his low voice more jarring than his yelling from before. "And that's that."

When they get to the living room, Kavita is already waiting with her powder-blue satchel around her wrist.

Her head is lowered as she walks toward Bipin. "I'm sorry."

Don't apologize! Bina wants to yell. *You didn't do anything wrong.*

"Let's just go," Bipin grunts. "Bina, I told you how I felt about these meetings. Now you've given me no choice."

"No choice for what?" Bina asks. A dormant kernel of confidence, one she thought disappeared years ago, sprouts in her. How dare he speak to her this way.

Bina's phone rings. She darts to the coffee table and silences it.

Bipin wipes a bead of sweat off his forehead. "You'll be hearing from me. Soon."

Bina tells herself to look more assured than she feels, something she used to do before she went onstage. She puts her hands on her hips and takes deep, heavy breaths.

"Great," she says. "I look forward to it."

Everyone else pretends to be busy wiping away crumbs and taking plates to the sink. Mira doesn't even bother to be subtle about staring at Kavita and Bipin walking away.

"Should we go after her?" Bina asks.

Mira shrugs. "I don't know what to do."

Bina's phone rings again. She takes a quick peek at the screen and sees five missed calls and a voicemail from Suhani.

That can't be right. She clicks on the voicemail.

The blood starts to drain from her face the second she starts listening. From the first syllable, she knows something is off.

"Mom, call me the second you get this. Natasha's in the hospital. My hospital. You have to come here now."

Nineteen

Natasha

Natasha feels another wave of nausea as she watches three stretchers being pulled into the emergency room.

Fuck. How could she have done something so stupid? What was she thinking?

When she closes her eyes, the answer comes to her. She was both thinking too much and not thinking at all. Her mind kept telling her she wasn't good enough, again and again, until it became like a steady background noise, one she just wanted to finally shut off for good.

But it was all a mistake. Taking the Tylenol was a mistake. Calling 911 was a mistake.

She rubs her temples in an attempt to stop her throbbing headache. But it's no use. It's as though someone is stabbing her head from the inside.

Wailing sirens collect outside the emergency room. Natasha watches a cluster of doctors take fast, purposeful strides to an area marked TRAUMA BAY. All of them are wearing scrubs. None of them look anything like the ones in her favorite medical dramas.

. . .

Her breathing gets faster as she hears high-pitched screams from a nearby patient's bed.

The rancid smell of vomit lingers in front of her. It takes her a second to realize that the smell is coming from her. In the ambulance, she had vomited until there was nothing left. The green-yellow bile collected in the folds of a plastic bag that was held by a woman in a black EMS uniform.

"Let it out, sweetheart," the EMS worker had said as she rubbed Natasha's back. Her dark eyeliner and uneven haircut reminded Natasha of Janis Ian, her favorite character in *Mean Girls*. In the daze of her fatigue, she remembers being comforted by that thought. She may have even called the woman Janis.

She has to get out of here. She has to see a doctor, explain that she didn't want to die; she just wanted to stop feeling so shitty.

She swings her legs over the side of the stiff hospital bed. The beige sheet just barely covers the squeaky blue mattress. On the wall next to her, there's a blood pressure cuff, one of those constantly beeping monitors, boxes of purple latex gloves in small, medium, and large sizes, and a tub of antiseptic wipes. Now that she thinks of it, the entire place reeks of those antiseptic wipes. Antiseptic wipes and sickness.

The teal curtain that's supposed to separate her bed from the person's next to her rustles and a second later gets pushed aside. It makes a jingling sound that reminds Natasha of her shower curtain at home.

Home. She needs to go home.

"Um, are you okay?" Dr. Goldstein, the psychiatry intern who saw her when she got here, asks as he steps closer. "Your, uh, sister is on the way."

Jeez. This guy's anxiety is so palpable that Natasha has to stop herself from comforting him.

"My sister? What about my brother-in-law? I thought I gave you Zack's number."

"I think he, uh, told Dr. Joshi. I mean, er, your sister," Dr. Goldstein stammers.

"Great. Just great." Natasha kicks the thin white blanket off her.

"Yep. So just sit tight, okay?"

"But I'm fine now," Natasha says as she looks at Dr. Goldstein. She keeps her head held high (she once read that conveys confidence and figures shrinks must always read body language). "I know I made a mistake and I think I just need a referral for a therapist. Someone I can talk to."

"Do you, er, want to tell me what's . . . what's wrong?" Dr. I'm-Anxious-as-Fuck asks.

"You know what? I think I'm good. Thanks." She flashes the best smile she can muster.

He nods and looks relieved that she doesn't want to confide in him. Damn it, why is this guy a psychiatrist?

"Can I leave after my sister gets here?" Natasha stares at her chipped and chewed-down nails. "You know her. She'll tell you I don't need to be here."

"Well, uh, I don't know. You were, uh, quite upset. We usually let people go if it's just a, uh, panic attack or something, but you, you know, swallowed pills."

"But I threw them up . . ." Natasha mutters as her face becomes warm with humiliation.

Someone in a bed down the hall asks a nurse for more pain meds. Two policemen bring in a guy in handcuffs. She can't handle being here for another minute.

Dr. Goldstein nods. "I hear you, but, uh, I'll have to discuss this with my senior resident and get back to you. You have to wait here until then."

He walks away before Natasha has a chance to protest.

She should make a run for it. The exit is all the way on the other side, but maybe if she sprints . . .

Yes, Natasha, that'll definitely show everyone that you've got your shit together.

The senior resident comes in after what feels like hours.

"Natasha. I'm Dr. Chan." She extends her hand and her gold-studded wedding band winks in the fluorescent light. A Cartier Love bracelet dangles from her wrist. Natasha only recognizes it because Zack's sent a link of it to her before as a potential gift for Suhani.

Zack and Suhani. Where the hell are they? Didn't the intern say they were on their way awhile ago?

"Nice to meet you," Natasha says. "I don't know if Dr. Goldstein told you but I'm all better now and really ready to leave."

Dr. Chan has a badge clipped to one of her belt loops. Underneath where it reads KONNY CHAN in bold blue letters, there's a picture where her eyes are brighter, her hair shinier. It had to be taken years ago, maybe even before she was bogged down by the drudgery of residency, because now her skin has the dullness of being indoors and awake for too many years. Still, she's elegant in a black turtleneck and tiny pearl studs.

"I'm happy to hear that you're feeling better now." Dr. Chan smiles and Natasha can tell she means it. She comes off as kind and no-nonsense. One of those women who's comfortable in her skin. Natasha bets she always wears minimal makeup—even on special occasions—and enjoys fine wine and classical music.

Natasha cringes as Dr. Chan does a quick once-over of her scuffed

Keds, faded T-shirt, and ripped jeans. Surely the doctor isn't judging her outfit. She hears Mom's voice: *See? It's always important to look presentable.*

And for once, Natasha wishes she did look more put together. It would at least motivate Dr. Chan to discharge her as soon as possible. She glances at the clock above Dr. Chan's head. Based on her knowledge of the emergency room from Dad, Suhani, and the one time she came here with Ifeoma when she had appendicitis, Natasha estimates that she can get out of here in an hour if she plays it cool. Suhani will root for her once she gets here, too.

"Thanks," Natasha says. "I've never done anything like this before. Or even really thought about hurting myself. I was just freaking out."

"Well, it sounds like things were really bad. Can you tell me what's been going on?"

"Just a lot of quarter-life-crisis stuff," Natasha mumbles. "Nothing that's really that bad."

"Has anything changed recently?" Dr. Chan props her hand under her chin. "Or been more stressful?"

A slew of doctors and nurses run to the other end of the ER. A deep, overhead voice yells, "CODE BLUE IN ED BED FOUR," on the intercom. Dr. Chan's not fazed at all by the chaos, while Natasha just wants to scream at the top of her lungs. She could really use a weed brownie right now.

"Yeah. A lot has changed," Natasha says. "I broke up with my boyfriend—my best friend since I was a baby—right after he proposed. And I thought we could get back together. I mean, just because I don't want to get married doesn't mean I don't want to be with him. But he's already moved on with some chick who's better for him. Or at least, better than me, that's for sure."

Natasha pictures Karan's face when he sat across from her at Starbucks. He had some stubble on his chin and she stopped herself from rubbing it. It's jarring that a best friend can turn into a stranger in a matter of months.

"Oh, and before that, I was fired from my job, but I was okay with that at first because I've always wanted to be a comedian," Natasha says. "But it turns out I kind of suck at talking to audiences, unless I'm totally wasted. I totally freeze, even when I think the stuff I wrote is pretty good. So my only real job right now with any kind of promise is being a barista. And I hate it. I keep thinking about how much comedy I could be writing if I wasn't busy smiling while people bitched at me for not frothing their milk enough."

Even though this is a really dumb place to start with telling the doctor what's changed, letting it all out for the first time in months, maybe ever, feels surprisingly cathartic.

"I've had all these role models in comedy," Natasha continues. "It started with Mindy Kaling and then I started reading about Aparna Nancherla and Lilly Singh, and anyway, I thought I had all this stuff in common with them, being women of color and misunderstood sometimes and all that. But they're really on another level, one I won't ever get to. I guess I'm finally getting the realization that just because people think I'm funny and I can write good jokes doesn't mean I have what it takes to really make it in the one thing I've dreamed about for my entire life, you know?"

It should be more humiliating to ramble about all this to a woman who so clearly has her shit together. But to her surprise, Dr. Chan looks like she empathizes with what Natasha is going through.

"That must be really difficult," Dr. Chan says. "Do you have any support? Family? Friends?"

"I do. . . ." Natasha says.

"But?" Dr. Chan scribbles something Natasha can't make out onto her spiral yellow notepad.

"But they don't get it. They've never really gotten me. Ever. Yeah, I'm the one who cracks them up, but honestly, most of the time, I'm the burden. It's basically an accepted joke that I'm the black sheep of my family, and now my friends are moving on, living real adult lives."

Natasha pictures the girls depositing their paychecks and having a slot in their wallets for insurance cards and signing leases and drinking fancy, colorful cocktails on dates.

"So you don't feel as though you can really talk to any of them about what's going on?"

"I really don't want to bring my friends down with my shit. Sorry—stuff." Natasha shakes her head. "And my family just won't understand. My dad's always known something's wrong with me. He's tried to be nice about it and said I have 'trouble coping' or 'feel things more than most people,' but that's all code for 'messed up.' My mom just calls me dramatic. If they wanted to be honest, my parents would straight up admit they wish I was like my sister, who's basically perfect. I'm sure you already know that by her work here. And my brother doesn't ruffle any feathers, so that just leaves me as the one to freak out about. I've always known I was messed up. Always."

Saying all this makes Natasha wish she could just jump out of her skin and turn herself inside out. Self-loathing feels like wearing an itchy sweater she can never take off.

"Have you ever tried telling your family how you feel?"

"I used to try. I really did. But after a certain point, I didn't want to be this constant problem for my parents after they've already struggled so much," Natasha says as her eyes fill with tears. "They've sacrificed so much for me. They were really poor when they came to America and their families weren't supportive of their marriage at all. And when they had a little financial stability, they moved to the neighborhood we've always lived in because of the good schools, even though it meant my dad commuted for an extra hour in traffic every day. They never even took vacations alone so we could all experience whatever they could. I can't ever think about everything they've been through without feeling so shitty."

"Having just one of those things weighing on you would be so difficult," Dr. Chan says. "But all of that together must be so over-whelming. I'm so sorry to hear that's how it's been for you. Have you ever wanted to hurt yourself before?"

Natasha shakes her head. It's better to lie. If they know she's thought about it in the past, they'll be more likely to keep her here. She knows this much from the way Dad and Suhani have discussed cases at the dinner table. And even if she has wanted to hurt herself, she's never actually tried to before. She came close in college once, while she was high, but Anuj called her right then. She never told him what she was about to do.

"Look, I know what I did was wrong. But I feel better now," Natasha says. "I'm not even sad anymore. I just feel numb some-times. And on some level, I know I'll always feel this way. It's like there's always been this cloud or something hanging over me."

"Hm." Dr. Chan scribbles something else down in big cursive loops. "Why do you say that?"

"Because I don't want to live the same life everyone else does, especially everyone in my family. They want to go to school, work a stable job, get married. And for a really long time, I told everyone that's what I wanted, too. I even told myself that. But I think I did that, and a lot of other things, to avoid really focusing on how I was pretending to just be normal, when I'm not."

When Natasha looks back, she did a lot to ignore her feelings. In elementary and middle school, she learned how to forge her parents' signatures so she wouldn't have to face the fact that she wasn't trying. And then throughout college, the partying, smoking, drinking, and maybe even the making everyone laugh were all there to distract her from how she really felt, who she really was.

"I see," Dr. Chan says. "Natasha, when you called 911, you said that you didn't see a point to anything anymore. Is that true?"

How exactly is Natasha supposed to respond to a question like that? How is she supposed to tell the doctor that everyone else seems to get through life so easily, while everything's a struggle for her? They can change their last names, careers, minds. They can float in and out of accomplishments, while at her best, all she does is remind people of an Indian female Ferris Bueller.

Natasha shrugs. "Sure. I don't really see the point of getting out of bed a lot these days but I'm just sort of stuck. And really, I feel so much better than before, so if I can just get the therapist refe—"

"You have to understand that what you did was very serious. Yes, you threw up the Tylenol, so I'm hoping that your labs show no liver damage, but we can't downplay the fact that you could have really hurt yourself. My guess is that you've been in a lot of pain for a while." Dr. Chan furrows her brows. "It must be exhausting to keep pretending you're okay."

Natasha's heart starts pounding. Suddenly, the room is too warm. "Is my brother-in-law here yet? He'll tell you that I'm fine to go home. So will my sister, Suhani Joshi. I'm sure you've worked with her before?"

"I don't know if your family is here yet," Dr. Chan says. "And yes, I have worked with your sister, but we—the people who have seen you tonight—have to make our own assessment and do what's best for you."

There's a frantic voice on the other side of the curtain. "Natasha?"

"That's my sister!" Natasha jumps up. "She's here!"

The anger Natasha has been holding on to is replaced by an all-consuming longing. Over the past few weeks, every time Natasha has scrolled to Suhani's name in her phone, the same jumble of questions stops her from calling:

What if we talk and you make me feel even worse about myself?

Are you annoyed with me?

Why haven't you called?

Are you okay?

Dr. Chan stands up and says, "I'll give you both a minute." Outside the curtain, Natasha hears the low rumble of Dr. Chan's voice, followed by Suhani whispering, "Thank you so much."

"Oh my God," Suhani says as she slowly pushes the curtain aside. "We've been waiting to see you for hours. They wanted to make sure you spoke to the intern and senior resident first. I'm so sorry. . . ."

Hot tears trickle down Natasha's face the second she registers Suhani's petite frame. Suhani's large, almond-shaped eyes are wide with a mixture of shock and sadness.

"It's okay, let it out." In one swift gesture, Suhani grabs Natasha. "It's going to be okay."

"I'm so glad you're here." Natasha presses her face against Suhani's T-shirt and feels a wave of relief as she inhales Suhani's jasmine shampoo. It's surreal seeing her here, in this place she comes to every day to make people—people like Natasha—feel better.

Suhani's eyes are wet when she pulls away from their hug. "Can you tell me what happened?"

Natasha takes Suhani's hand and says, "I'm really sorry for all the stuff I put about you in my comedy sketch. It was shitty of me to do that."

Suhani waves her hand. "Don't even think about that. Let's just focus on what we can do for you right now, okay?"

"But I made you so mad."

"I've made you pretty mad, too. And maybe seeing everything riled me up because it was true," Suhani says. "I know I can be judgmental. And bossy."

"It's always been part of your charm. Your aspirational image," Natasha says in a British accent. They both laugh. It's nice to have a moment that feels somewhat normal. "But speaking of your image, what were you doing today? You look ready to climb the rope in middle school gym class."

"Oh!" Suhani's eyes dart down like she's only now noticing her large glasses, frizzy bun, teal-blue pants, and high school T-shirt. "I was just relaxing at home and found some old clothes."

"You were at home just because?"

"Yeah." Suhani shrugs.

"Are you okay?" Natasha asks.

"Of course!" Suhani's voice has a forced reassurance to it.

Natasha nods but inside feels a tiny kernel of worry.

Suhani's voice is soft as she says, "I'm glad you could turn to Zack when you were having a crisis."

"I, well, you know how he's so calming in these situations . . ."

"Yeah, I get that." Suhani nods as if she understands, but her pursed lips and downturned eyes give away that she's hurt. Really hurt. And Natasha can't blame her. She's the psychiatrist and her older sister. How could she not be the one Natasha called?

"Wait, where is Zack?" Natasha asks.

"He's in the waiting area. Mom, Dad, and Anuj are on the way," Suhani says.

"WHAT?!" Natasha pulls away from her. "I don't want them here! He shouldn't have told them!"

"He didn't. I did."

Natasha clenches her fists. "Why would you do that?"

"Because we all love you," Suhani says in a gentle voice. "And we're here for you."

Natasha feels a rush of anger alongside relief. She always has so many contradictory emotions rising in her these days.

"I'll text Zack to keep them occupied, say they can't be in the ER yet," Suhani offers. "But they will want to see you. And I can't blame them for that."

"Yeah, I can't, either." Natasha tries to ignore the heavy guilt that's spreading throughout her body. She also feels shards of something else poking at her insides, something she can't quite pinpoint.

Despite what she just told Suhani, all she wants now is to be in the fetal position in her four-poster bed at home. She wants Mom to bring her a large mug of chai and Dad to sit at the foot of her bed, reassuring her the way he did when she got in trouble in high school. She wants to hear the hiss of the pressure cooker and the creak of wooden floorboards as her parents go to the living room and turn on a black-and-white Bollywood movie. She wants the smell of roasted mustard seeds and chilies to waft up to her room.

She had a similar feeling when she got to her dorm room years ago. The entire summer before college, she couldn't wait to get out of her parents' house. But seconds after she unpacked her last box of Easy Mac, she wanted to go back. The dorm suddenly felt like a dungeon. She cried in bed and hours later called Mom and Dad to tell them she was having the time of her life.

"Food services!" A woman wearing a shirt that reads HOSPITAL DINING comes in and asks if Natasha wants some water and peanut butter crackers. Natasha shakes her head. The woman looks at Suhani, then says, "Dr. Joshi? Is that you?"

"Nancy!" Suhani grins. "How's it going?"

"I didn't even recognize you!" Nancy smiles. "Thank God it's almost shift-change time. I'm exhausted."

"Oh, I bet! I'm glad you're almost done and can be with your beautiful family," Suhani says.

Nancy beams, then pulls up a picture on her phone of an adorable chubby baby boy with golden curls and large blue eyes.

Over the next few minutes, other hospital staff members come in and out. Almost all of them perk up when they recognize Suhani. Natasha feels herself swelling with pride during each interaction. *This is my badass sister at work.* Seeing her sister so easily slip into this other identity is jarring in the way it was when Natasha was five years old and learned her teacher didn't live at school.

Once there's finally a lull between people coming in and out, Suhani hands Natasha a slim box of tissues and says, "Can you tell me exactly what happened?"

"A big mistake happened. That's what all this is." Natasha's voice squeaks.

"Just take a deep breath. I promise you it's going to be okay," Suhani says in a voice that's both gentle and calm. She's shifting from big-sister mode to assertive-but-caring-doctor mode. Natasha takes another tissue and Suhani rubs her back. Is this how she is with patients? No wonder everyone at work loves her.

"I don't even know where to start."

"Start from wherever you want." Suhani rests Natasha's head on her shoulder, ready to listen.

Twenty

Suhani

Natasha starts with the hours before she called 911. How she saw Karan and found out he has a girlfriend (how does he already have a girlfriend?!), her solo trip to Fado (why does she always drink alone?), the overwhelming dread that engulfed her when she was at Suhani and Zack's apartment (why did Natasha ever leave their place?).

I'm supposed to be there for you, Suhani thinks over and over again as she listens to every detail. *Even if we're mad at each other, I'm always here for you. You should never feel that alone.*

How could she have missed this? She's a freaking psychiatrist, for God's sake, and Natasha was staying at their place for weeks. And no matter what she and Natasha are going through, she always thought she'd be aware if Natasha was really struggling.

Her mind jumps to an array of moments: showing Natasha how to pick out the right jewelry for lehengas, marking up her math homework with a red Sharpie, getting annoyed when Natasha took her clothes, analyzing her fights with Karan, mediating drama between her and Mom and Dad. Is it possible that despite everything they've been through together, there are parts of Natasha she's never known?

"I'm so sorry you got to that place and I wasn't there for you," Suhani says. "I'll never let that happen again."

"I'm the one who's sorry for this entire mess." Natasha taps her heels against the edge of the bed. *Tap, tap, tap, tap.* "How soon can we get out of here? This place is the worst. I don't know how you work here."

Medical school and residency desensitized Suhani to the jarring parts of the hospital. She gazes around her and tries to see the surroundings the way Natasha would. A drunk man curses as he's brought in on a stretcher. In one of the neighboring beds, a petite doctor frantically presses on an old woman's chest as a team surrounds her. Nurses scurry from computers to patient beds and back to computers.

"I know it's not easy to be here." Suhani is careful to weigh each word. "But I'm not sure we can leave soon."

Natasha's eyes are bloodshot. "Why not?"

"You've obviously been struggling for a long time, longer than any of us realized. Because you did something really serious." Suhani tries to block out the image of Natasha taking pill after pill. If she'd swallowed even a few more or hadn't thrown up, they wouldn't be having this conversation. The thought lodges in the corners of her mind and threatens to launch her into an all-consuming panic. She almost lost her sister. Forever.

But she can't focus on that now. All her energy has to go toward making sure Natasha is okay. She takes deep breaths until the panic lifts and leaves behind a tangled knot of protectiveness, sadness, and regret. What she'd give to wave a magic wand over the situation and make it all better.

"Yeah, but I can meet with someone and talk all that out. Go to weekly therapy. I'll even go twice a week if you want!" Natasha pleads. "Isn't that what you and Dad recommend to the people who are really messed up like me?"

She says the last part with a half smile, an attempt to make light of the situation.

"You're not really messed up," Suhani says. "We just all have to do what's best for you. What's safest for you."

Suhani's had this conversation with patients dozens of times. This should be easy. An attending once told her that everything's different when your own family member is the patient, and now she understands how true that is. All her years of training feel irrelevant.

She clutches Natasha's hands and keeps thinking, *We could never lose you.* "Look, it's one thing to have thoughts about wanting to hurt yourself, which is already so tough, but taking that step to put pills in your mouth, multiple pills . . . that takes things to another level."

She waits for a flicker of understanding on her sister's face.

"But I'm fine now. Really," Natasha insists.

My sister tried to kill herself. My sister tried to kill herself. My sister tried to kill herself.

The words repeat in Suhani's mind and it takes all her strength to quiet them. She tries to see the situation the way she would as a doctor and not as a sister. The drained wine bottles at her apartment, Natasha living in her pajamas, her dread of seeing her friends.

Suddenly, everything becomes clear. And there is no easy way to say it.

"You need more help than just therapy," she says. "This was really serious and you could have died. Do you understand that?"

She watches Natasha's face shift from shock to defensiveness. Every part of Suhani wants to agree with her and say, *Yes, of course you'll be fine. Let's just go home.* But she can't do that.

"I get it, bu—"

"I don't think you do," Suhani interrupts. "This isn't one of those times like the others where we can all laugh off what you've done, not let you deal with the consequences. This is your life."

Before Natasha can say anything, Zack walks in. "Uh, hey."

Suhani refrains from jumping up and wrapping her arms around him. At the house, she didn't have a chance to soak in Zack's presence. But seeing him bathed in the fluorescent hospital light plunges her deeper into the emotional hangover she's been buried under for the past week. A part of her still can't fully process that that's her husband, his tired eyes and slim, long-limbed body. That's the man whose socks are folded in the drawer below hers. That's the man she shares a DoorDash account and her nakedness and countless glasses of wine with. That's home. She's overcome with comfort and, to her surprise, raw desire, a longing to push him into bed and rip off his clothes.

"I was wondering when I'd see you," Natasha says.

"Sorry it took me awhile." Zack slings his hands into the back pockets of his slim-fit olive chinos. "Anuj and your parents are here so I was trying to buffer."

"Ugh, thanks. I really can't handle them right now. And I'm trying to get the fuck outta here, anyway." On the word "here," Natasha does a big, circular motion above her head to indicate the whole hospital.

"I'm glad she called you." Suhani faces her husband.

I love you, she stops herself from saying. *And I'm so sorry for everything.*

Seeing Zack solidifies what she's known since this morning: they need to be home together. They need to be back in the corner of Atlanta that's just theirs.

The night they moved into their apartment, Zack undressed Suhani in the middle of the bare living room. Goose bumps erupted on her spine as he licked her earlobe and the curve of her neck. She clutched his shoulder with one hand and with the other took sips from a chilled bottle of Moët & Chandon. The only light was from the Atlanta skyline. She needs to take their marriage back to that moment, so ripe with hope and excitement and promise.

"I'm glad she called me, too." Zack faces the floor. "Natasha and I have been talking about how she's been feeling."

"Talking? When?"

A shadow of guilt crosses his unshaven face. "In the evenings, when you've been busy with work."

Natasha and Zack exchange a knowing glance. If they were at the casting for that *Indian Matchmaking* show on Netflix, they'd be up for the roles of "funny, free-spirited woman" and "even-tempered white guy," while Suhani would be the "uptight, know-it-all bitch" they've both been mad at.

A nurse, Shelly, comes in to check Natasha's vital signs. She pauses when she sees Suhani. "Oh, Dr. Joshi! How nice to see you, darlin'."

Shelly is one of the best ER nurses at Atlanta Memorial Hospital. Her gray hair, thick glasses, and southern accent give her the vibe of a loving grandmother with an edge, someone who regularly bakes cookies and also shares stories of her wild youth.

Suhani nods. "You, too, Shelly. We should be wrapping up here soon."

Shelly understands to not ask any more questions and gives a singsong, "Lovely."

"Lovely" is the last word Suhani would use to describe the moment, but she does appreciate Shelly's ability to inject some cheer into even the bleakest situations.

"We'll give you some space to take her vitals." Suhani pushes aside the curtain and motions for Zack to follow her.

Anticipation fills her, one similar to the kind she had when they first got together and she'd get all dressed up for their dates, waiting for Zack to pick her up, wondering where the night would lead.

"You look tired," she says once they're standing in an empty corner of the emergency room.

Zack gives a weak laugh. "Thanks."

"No, sorry, I don't mean bad," Suhani says. "I can just tell you haven't gotten much sleep. I know it sounds strange, but I like seeing you this way."

"I always liked seeing you when you were tired, too," Zack says, his usually enthusiastic voice flattened today.

"I'm so glad you're here. Not *here* here, but you know what I mean," Suhani says as she reaches to cup his face the way she's wanted to for hours. She loves his face, plain and simple. She loves his full lips and the dimple in his chin. She loves the way his smile stretches all the way up to his deep-set eyes, which are framed by black square glasses.

But Zack steps back as if he's dodging a punch. The move is so jarring, so unlike him, that Suhani first thinks she must have misread it. But then she sees the firmness of his posture, his navy-blue All Birds shoes glued to the floor.

"What are you . . . ?" Suhani trails off, confused. "What's wrong?"

"We're not in the best place, remember?"

The words bring her back to reality, their reality. Her stomach churns as she thinks about how she packed her suitcase and left the apartment, how she texted him after she was in her childhood bedroom.

"Obviously, I remember," she says. "But I've missed you."

"I've missed you, too." Zack sighs. Despite his words, a gnawing dread forms in the pit of Suhani's stomach.

"My dad told me about how you were willing to go to med school," she says, needing him to know how much she appreciates everything he's done for them. "You did so much to make sure we would work. You always have."

Zack sighs and tilts toward her. "You've done things for us, too. I know you have."

"We both have. Remember what we said at Little Spirit about how we made it through so many big things that should have been stressful?" she asks.

But as the words leave her, a truth materializes in her mind. Even though marriages are often defined by the big events, it's the smaller, day-to-day moments that really form their tapestries.

Zack stares at the floor, which is covered in scuff marks and a speckled pattern that always makes it look a little dirty. His silence pushes her to keep going.

"Maybe we can go home and talk," she says. "And just be together."

She waits for him to say *Yes, of course* or *There's nothing I want more* or maybe even his go-to *Moooovin' right along!*

But when he looks up, his hazel eyes are coated with a heavy sadness. "I think I need some more time apart."

"What? Time apart from us?"

Zack bites his bottom lip. "Yeah. From us."

Instead of comforting her, the calmness in his voice is like a fist around her windpipe. Because Zack doesn't make big, empty statements. No, that's a trademark of the Joshi women, to say things in a fit of heightened emotion and then take them back later.

And in the four years they've been together, Zack has never

been the one to want space. Even after their most heated fights, he pushes them to talk it out and not go to sleep angry, while Suhani always needs to cool off.

"But we should talk, and there's no way we can do that with more space," Suhani says.

"I know we need to talk. I just have a lot to think about before we do."

An overhead page calls for a neurology consult and then a stroke code. The metallic smell of blood wafts over from the trauma bay and in seconds is masked by the sting of antibacterial cleaning solution. Suhani makes fleeting eye contact with one of the junior psych residents on call. She knows she shouldn't be embarrassed, but for some reason, she doesn't want anyone from work to know about what's going on with her sister. But it's just a matter of time. On Monday morning, Natasha will meet several of the junior residents and two of the attendings on the main ward.

She shifts her focus back to Zack. "What do you have to think about?"

Zack glances around them and runs his hand through his wavy brown hair. "This isn't really the best place or time to get into it."

"Roshan?" she asks, not even wanting to say his name.

Zack nods. "That is one of the things, yes."

"What are the other things?" Suhani asks. "Work and kids? I know we can get through those. I really believe that."

"It's not that simple." Zack wrings his hands and she stops herself from grabbing them. "I guess I realized that we're not as close as I thought we were if you can keep certain things from me. I don't make you comfortable enough to be open with me."

"Of course you do," Suhani says. "There's way more to all this than you know, than I even realized until I really had time to think about it. Being at home and then talking to my dad made me see that, yes, I have kept my guard up with you. And I know I should have been more open. But I picked you, we picked each other, because of who we are together."

I didn't think I deserved to be happy, she thinks. For years, she heard Roshan's voice in her head, telling her she wasn't good enough. It was the adult version of the girls in middle school, always reminding her that she was defective in some way or another. No matter what she accomplished or who she became on the outside, she'd always be broken.

"I don't know." Zack shakes his head. "All I do know is that we've had some distance for a while and I just need to figure out what's best for us."

No, no, no, no, Suhani thinks as she hears the certainty in Zack's voice, a certainty that fills her with fear. Is what they're going through just a rough patch that comes with the first year of marriage or a deeper sign that they don't fit? She refuses to dwell on the latter.

Natasha would know how to talk through this with her. She'd give the most essential mixture of reassurance and analysis.

"I just need a break." Zack shoves his hands into his pockets.

"A break from our marriage? Really?" The question doesn't even sound real. How is he saying this? "You can't just do that!" she says. "You're my husband."

You're my world, she thinks. She wants to pull him into her, inhale the mixture of his natural, citrusy scent and Jack Black body wash. She wants to rub the back of his neck, tuck her chin into the groove of his slim shoulder, feel the edge of his glasses press into her cheekbone.

But something about Zack's stiff posture and the hard expression in his eyes keeps Suhani rooted in place. For the first time ever in their relationship, she's hesitant to touch him.

Another request for a neurology consult, this one more urgent, echoes from the overhead speakers. Brian, one of the phlebotomists, waves and wheels past them with his cart full of needles, tubes, and syringes. Suhani's grateful for the brief interruptions even if she and Zack shouldn't be having this conversation here.

Zack sighs.

Please argue with me, she wants to say. She knows from her own training that as unhealthy as it is to bicker nonstop, it's much more dangerous when a couple stops fighting, when there just isn't much left to say. Silence only leads to hopelessness, and after that, there really isn't anywhere else to go.

"SUHANI!" Mom's booming voice travels from the other side of the ER. No wonder she used to act. The woman's voice is powerful.

"Mom. Try to calm down," Anuj says.

"How?!" Mom points to the rows of curtains. "Which one is she in? They won't tell us anything! Since Dad's only been seeing a few patients in the clinic, he doesn't know the doctors working in the emergency room now. He's talking to the charge nurse to ask where she is."

"I know the doctors here and she's in great hands." Suhani points down the hallway. "She's in a bed over there and doing okay. Don't worry."

"I'll go check on her," Zack says before he gives Mom a hug. "She'll be fine. I promise."

Suhani watches Zack leave and ignores the compulsion to run after him.

"But what's going to happen to her?!" Mom's eyes are wide with alarm. It's as if she doesn't know whether to scream or cry.

"Let's step away from here." Suhani motions for Mom and Anuj to follow her to the waiting area. Stiff puke-green chairs line the room. A triage nurse sits behind a tiny wooden desk. The wall behind her has a stethoscope, blood pressure cuff, and crate full of alcohol swabs and Band-Aids.

Anuj squeezes Mom's shoulder and says, "It'll all be okay. She'll be okay."

Mom instantly relaxes. "Thank you, *beta*. I really needed to hear that."

Suhani stops herself from saying that she just gave Mom a similar message seconds ago and it only riled her up more. She's reminded of how, even during the same moment, all three of them get a different version of Mom. It's been that way for their entire lives. Suhani got a hopeful, struggling mother, which fueled her ambition. Natasha got a strict and scared mother, which instigated her rebellion. Anuj got a softer, more secure mother, which gave him comfort.

"How could we have missed this?" Mom asks Suhani. Her maroon paisley-print kurta top, dusty-rose cardigan, and black leggings make her look out of place in this drab environment.

"Okay, listen." Suhani tries to act calm in the hope that it rubs off on Mom. "I'm going to walk you through what's probably going to happen."

"But wha—"

"Mom, you have to pay attention and keep it together," Suhani says.

Suhani gives Mom a breakdown of what to expect over the next twenty-four hours. To her surprise, Mom doesn't interrupt or even cry. She just nods slowly the entire time, as if she already knew what Suhani was going to say.

"I just wish I had realized something was wrong sooner." Mom shakes her head. "I can't believe I let her get to this place. What kind of a mother doesn't even know her child is suffering like this?"

What kind of a sister doesn't know? Suhani wonders. But she grabs Mom's soft, wrinkled hands and says, "It's not your fault. And we can't spend this time blaming ourselves. We just have to figure out the best way to be there for her."

"I need to see her," Mom says.

"Let's go see her together," Dad says as he approaches them wearing one of Anuj's old T-shirts.

Dad places his hand on Mom's lower back. He and Mom sink into each other, covered in their own silence amid the chaos swirling around them. Normally, Suhani wouldn't have even registered any of this, but today, with everything going on with Zack, there's a dull weight in the pit of her stomach as she takes in the brief series of gestures that shows how in sync her parents always are. Despite all the sacrifices they had to make, all the regrets Mom carries, she and Dad always have an unshakable understanding between them.

Suhani used to notice this all the time when she was little. Maybe she was more observant then because she was alone so often. During their early years in America, it was just Suhani, Mom, and Dad living in a family friend's basement while Dad made minimum wage in residency and Mom's job applications were rejected by Office Depot, Kmart, and Kroger. Suhani was always the last kid picked up from daycare and the perpetual odd one out during gatherings with their friends who didn't have kids yet. But she never minded. She filled her time with books and her own thoughts.

And when the three of them were finally together, she always felt loved. Every evening, they sat on the floor, spread out a tablecloth, and ate khichdi. Even now, the turmeric rice, lentils, and yogurt give her more comfort than any other type of food.

If her parents can make it through so much, why is it so hard for her and Zack? Is all this a test of their relationship, a way to see what they're capable of overcoming? Or is it a sign that they're not as compatible as she once thought? She refuses to dwell on the latter possibility.

As Mom takes quick, purposeful steps toward Natasha's bed, Dad turns to Suhani and says, "You know they're going to keep her here."

"They have to," Suhani says. "I know she wants to go, but it would be unsafe to discharge her. I just can't believe this is happening."

"I know, *beta*." Dad wraps her in a hug. "But let's hope this is all for the greater good. Her greater good. She will be monitored, put on the right medication, have the support she needs."

Suhani nods, knowing he's right. *How different we are at the same job*, she thinks. *He's so calm and collected, while I'm constantly on edge.* Maybe she's more like Mom than she realized.

"Suhani!"

At first, she thinks that her eyes are playing tricks on her. But a second glance confirms who called her name.

Roshan.

"Oh. Hi," Suhani says. "I can't really talk."

Her gut tells her to walk away. But then she'll look like she cares about his presence, taking up all the space in front of her.

"Is everything okay?" Roshan frowns. He looks right at home

here. A brief look of recognition passes over his face before he says, "Hi, Uncle."

"Hello." Dad clears his throat in an attempt to mask his surprise. "How are you?"

"The usual, just working," Roshan says. "I'm on call tonight and there was a stroke code, so I had to come in."

"Right, I heard that before. I hope your patient's okay," Suhani says. "Sounds like it's going to be a busy night."

Roshan clutches the bell of his stethoscope, which is looped around his neck. Suhani tries to ignore the tightness in her chest as Dad's eyes dart back and forth between her and Roshan. This guy could have been in their family. For a second, she imagines the three of them meeting at Atlanta Memorial, running through their days, then going home together for a big family dinner. Mom would tell jokes in Gujarati. Anita Auntie would stop by and say she hoped Karan grew up to be like Roshan.

Dad, clearly noting it's a good time to exit the conversation, says, "Okay, then. Good to see you. I'm going to find the attending psychiatrist on call."

"Look, I have to go," Suhani says.

"What's wrong?" Roshan asks.

Suhani plans to answer with a curt *Nothing* or *Don't worry about it* but because of the sheer emotional weight of the day finds herself saying, "My sister's going to be admitted to psych."

"What? Natasha?" Roshan's eyes widen. "I'm so sorry. I hope she's okay. If there's anything I can do . . ."

Suhani had forgotten that Roshan always had a soft spot for Natasha. Both of them identified as misunderstood middle children, could get easily riled up, were able to shift from being charming one second to angry the next, and had a tendency to hit below the belt during fights.

As her gaze locks with his, she realizes that they never truly let each other go, at least, not in the way they should have. Maybe he had a point that day in his office. She ran away and never told him why. And maybe that made them hold on to their relationship far longer than they ever should have.

"There isn't." Suhani shakes her head. "But thanks."

She can hear Mom and Natasha fighting before she even reaches Natasha's bed.

"What's going on here?" Suhani asks as she shifts the curtain toward the wall. Dad is shaking his head, his go-to move when he's frustrated with their arguing. Zack is drawing an imaginary figure eight with his sneakers. Anuj is staring off into space.

"Mom freaking said that my comedy is the reason I'm here! Can you believe that?"

"I didn't say that." Mom raises her palms into the air. "I was just saying that maybe such an unstable career path isn't the best thing right now."

"You know what, Mom?" Natasha challenges. "Just because you didn't make it as an actress doesn't mean you have to ruin things for me."

"Whoa, whoa, whoa," Suhani says. "Look, there are a lot of heated emotions right now, but let's all just take a second, okay? Natasha, Mom isn't blaming your comedy for what happened. Mom, maybe you should think about how your words can be a little harsh and maybe it's better to say nothing right now."

"You girls," Mom mutters. "You have no idea what harsh even is. If you only knew the way my mother spoke to me, then you'd realize a thing or two. And we clearly have a problem here. Look at where we are!"

"You never un—" Natasha starts, but Suhani cuts her off.

"Yes, we are here. But we have to figure out a way to move forward."

"I should have known something was wrong the day of Karan's proposal." Mom squints. "You never told me you were having doubts about him. You never tell me anything!"

"ARE YOU KIDDING ME?" Natasha yells. "What is wrong with you? All you care about is whether I get married!"

"Yeah, the Karan situation is not relevant right now," Suhani says.

"Don't you start with me. I know *you* also don't tell me plenty of things." Mom points to Suhani. "Both of you keep me out of the loop."

"When have I kept you out of the loop?"

"Where do I even start?" Mom furrows her brows. "How about with that going-nowhere-in-life guy you were with at Emory? The dull one who played that stupid game with beer and Ping-Pong tables?"

"My college boyfriend?" Suhani asks. "What does he have to do with anything?"

"Oh yeah, that guy." Natasha smirks for the first time since Suhani's seen her.

"Is that funny to you? And I'm sorry, how did this become about me?" Suhani asks. "I'm just trying to help both of you calm down, as usual."

Dad clears his throat.

"Yes?" Mom holds out her palms.

Dad scrunches his eyebrows and says, "I'm wondering if you're all arguing because it makes this situation a little less painful."

Zack nods and stays quiet, well aware that it's better to not get involved in any arguments with the Joshi women. Suhani's relieved her husband knows how to keep his cool regardless of whatever chaos might be swirling around him.

Anuj smirks.

"Is something funny?" Suhani asks.

"Dad has a point with his shrink talk." Anuj smiles. "And it's kinda nice seeing you guys just being you."

"I'm going to second that," Zack chimes in.

"Actually, now that you guys say it," Natasha says, sighing, "this is the first time I've felt like myself since getting to this place."

"Hello! Everything okay in here?" Dr. Chan's bright, strong voice fills the space on the other side of the curtain.

Translation: *I just heard you all yelling at each other.*

"Of course," Suhani says.

"Everything is good!" Mom says, her acting skills coming into full force.

Suhani returns Dr. Chan's polite smile, wondering if things will ever really be good again.

Twenty-One

Bina

"I'm so sorry, my *betu*." Bina rushes back to Natasha after Dr. Chan leaves. "I don't know how to handle this situation and I said things I shouldn't have."

Deepak's words, followed by Dr. Chan's brief visit, made everything come into sharp focus. Nothing Bina and Natasha have ever argued about matters now. All that matters is that Bina's baby is in pain and she needs to take it away.

"No, I'm so sorry. I'm such a screwup." Natasha starts sobbing. Rings of mascara—Suhani's mascara, no doubt—have smeared under her bloodshot eyes. Natasha's unraveled hair and tear-streaked cheeks make her look the way she did as a little girl. She always cried so easily. *My emotional little girl*, Bina used to say. *You feel everything too much, like I do.*

"Shh, just take a deep breath." Bina runs her fingers through Natasha's tangled hair. Why did she have to bring up Natasha's comedy or Karan? Why is she so obsessed with her children being married? Why can't she ever keep her mouth shut, even when it can bring peace?

She feels the weight of Suhani's arms around her and Natasha. "It'll be okay."

Bina's phone rings with a call from Mira. A quick glance at her screen shows that she's received more than a dozen WhatsApp messages in just the last hour. She puts her phone on silent and buries it at the bottom of her large plum leather handbag, last year's Mother's Day gift from the kids.

Deepak, Zack, and Anuj are unfazed as Bina and her daughters hug. Everyone knows this is the reliable pattern of all their arguments: bursts of anger followed by a steady rush of sadness and regret.

Bina clutches Natasha and makes the same *hush, hush* noises she had made when Natasha was a baby. Nothing else put Natasha to sleep during her first months in the world. After a certain point, Bina wondered if she was doing the rocking and soothing more for herself than for her daughter. She was so worried Natasha's trouble sleeping would lead to the same overwhelming fears she had after Suhani's birth, or even something worse. But to her surprise, her thoughts didn't spiral out of control. And while childbirth broke some parts of her, others were slowly stitched together with a new sliver of hope. Maybe before, she wasn't just being dramatic and difficult. Maybe it wasn't all in her head. Maybe her parents were wrong and she wasn't damaged.

Of course you're damaged, her mother's voice challenges in her head. *After everything you've done, look at where your own child ended up.*

It's true. Natasha did end up here. Bina takes in the sea of faces coming in and out, the pamphlet on depression Dr. Chan left on the table, the smell of sickness lingering everywhere. She'll be damned if Natasha thinks she's going through this alone. That's the worst part of reaching a place so low—the corrosive sense of isolation—and there's no way she'll allow Natasha to be submerged in that.

"Are you sure you're not mad at me?" Natasha hiccups and gazes at Bina.

"Mad? I'm not mad at all, *betu*. All we"—she points to the rest of the family—"want is for you to be okay."

"And I want to go home." Natasha faces Suhani. "Can you get them to hurry up and discharge me?"

"*Beta*, we should talk to you about that." Bina keeps Natasha in her firm grip. She's exhausted and wired at the same time.

"About what?" Natasha asks.

Silence stretches across them. Suhani gives Bina a look that says, *I'm going to tell her now*. Bina is compelled to stop her. They can tell Natasha later. Or maybe they can find a way to get her home.

But she takes another look at Natasha's sunken eyes. This has to happen even if the thought of Natasha being on a psychiatric ward terrifies Bina to her core. She has to push that aside and keep Natasha safe. Sometimes the best thing you can do for your child is protect them from your own fears.

"You're going to have to stay here," Suhani says. "For multiple days."

"What? Why?!" Natasha's eyes widen. "I don't want to be here!"

"I know. We don't want that for you, either. But it's what you need," Suhani says. Deepak nods in agreement behind her.

"So you're keeping me here against my will? Even though I could go home with two doctors? Two psychiatrists?"

"I'm sorry but this is what's best for you. And, yes, if you're not going to go willingly, it's technically an involuntary admission." Suhani squeezes her eyes shut and takes a deep breath, as if to force herself to stay calm. Underneath her sadness, Bina senses a new-found pride for Suhani being able to deliver such emotionally charged news with compassion. Her daughter has grown up to be an empathetic doctor and sister.

"NO!" Natasha jumps off the bed. "YOU ARE NOT LOCKING ME UP!"

Two security guards rush in.

Deepak holds up his hands. "We're fine in here. Thank you."

"Wait, what's going on?" Bina asks. "Why are they here?"

"If Natasha refuses to go, they might have to medicate her." Deepak is composed as he explains the horrifying protocol the hospital has for patients who resist admission.

How are you saying this so calmly? Bina thinks.

Suhani once told Bina that Zack and Deepak are similar in that way, both of them able to maintain a sense of tranquility no matter how charged the situation. This is one of the best things about them. This is one of the most irritating things about them.

"They can't do that!" Bina says.

Deepak clasps his palms together as if he's about to give an important lecture. "Maybe everyone should step out so Natasha and I can talk."

Bina hesitates. It feels wrong to leave Natasha's side at all. But Deepak's firm expression tells her it's what she has to do. Suhani grabs Bina's hand while Zack puts his arms around her.

"It'll be okay, Mom," Anuj says once they're back in the waiting room.

"He's right," Suhani agrees. "And I'll check on her throughout the day when I'm at work. I can make sure the resident taking care of her is on top of everything. Trust me."

Suhani hands Bina a printout that has the main psychiatric ward's visiting hours, rules of the ward (Bina can't bring anything with cords or sharp edges), and names of the head psychiatrists.

"I don't understand how Natasha can be depressed," Bina says. "We've given her everything. We've given all you kids everything. All Dad and I wanted was to make sure you didn't struggle the way we did."

"Mom, depression is a lot more complicated than that. There are a lot of reasons someone can have it. Sometimes people have a chemical imbalance, and that's not their fault or anyone else's," Suhani says. "And just because she didn't go through what you did doesn't mean everything's been easy for her. All of us have had to figure out how to fit in here and worry about honoring everything you and Dad sacrificed. You had things pushing you, motivating you, to make it here. We didn't. I think Natasha always felt like she wasn't good enough, like she wasn't making you proud or happy by being herself. And that's a lot to carry."

Bina pulls her cardigan around her. A thought settles into her mind. She tells herself to keep it there, but it emerges as she absorbs the truth of her daughter's words.

"I've been a bad mother." Bina stares off into the distance. "I really have."

"Don't say that!" Suhani says as Anuj gives Bina a side hug. "That's not true at all. We've all had misunderstandings, and now we just need to be there for her."

Bina's stomach grumbles. She clutches it and laughs.

"Let me grab you something from the cafeteria. You'll need your strength," Zack says. He turns to Suhani. "Do you want anything?"

"No, but I'll go with you," Suhani offers.

"It's okay." Zack starts walking away. "I'm good."

"*Beta*, is everything okay with you and Zack?" Bina asks.

"Of course." Suhani flashes a tight smile. "I think we're all just worried because of this situation."

To anyone else, this explanation would be enough. But Bina takes note of the high pitch in Suhani's voice, the tension in her shoulders. Suhani may be better at lying than Natasha, but there's always a brief moment that exposes her.

"Are you sure?" Bina presses. "Because it seems—"

"That's weird," Suhani interrupts as she pulls out her phone. "I have texts from Mira Auntie asking if you're free. She says she's been trying to reach you."

"Oh! Right." Bina digs through her handbag, which is packed with way too many snacks. Her phone now has fifty WhatsApp messages.

"What the heck is going on?" she mutters as she scrolls through the endless threads with her friends. Usually they're filled with sassy memes or recipes or fun videos or Ayurvedic remedies. But today there's just a flurry of words. First, a slew from Mira:

3:00 p.m.: Have you heard from Kavita?

4:24 p.m.: She's not picking up her phone.

7:30 p.m.: It's been three hours and still no answer.

8:55 p.m.: Bina, any luck? I'm getting very worried.

9:30 p.m.: YOU HAVE TO SEE THIS!

The last message is followed by a link to *Samachar in America*, the online Gujarati newspaper Bina, Deepak, and all their friends have been reading for years. Bina clicks the link. She gasps when the article fills her screen.

Local Women's Group Threatens Cultural Integrity

A women's group started in Atlanta by Bina Joshi, wife of Dr. Deepak Joshi, is spreading dangerous ideas that threaten the integrity of South Asian culture. Joshi named the group Chats Over Chai in an attempt to make it seem innocuous. However, Dr. Bipin Patel has stated that this group is spreading unhelpful messages within their community.

"I'm very concerned," Dr. Patel said in an exclusive interview. Patel's wife, Kavita, was a former participant in the group.

Bina stops reading. A flash of rage swallows her whole. She scrolls through her contacts and calls the only person who will know what to do.

Twenty-Two

Natasha

"I really don't need this. I can walk." Natasha leans back in her wheelchair.

Shelly, the same nurse who took Natasha's vitals in the ER, pats Natasha's shoulders. "It's protocol, sweetheart. I know it's not fun."

Shelly's sparkling Minnie Mouse brooch and round glasses make Natasha want to give her a big hug. Well, those and the fact that Shelly is clearly giving Natasha special treatment since she's Suhani's sister. She took Natasha on the "extra-scenic" route through Atlanta Memorial Hospital by wheeling her past the nursery with all the adorable babies and the new cafeteria that has freshly baked chocolate chip cookies. It's similar to how teachers used to get excited when they'd learn Natasha was related to Suhani, until they realized that she was exactly the opposite as a student.

Shelly removes a brass key and opens the two doors leading to the Psychiatric Unit. They really need two doors? A sign on the second door answers her question: STAFF, KEEP DOOR LOCKED BEHIND YOU TO PREVENT PATIENTS FROM LEAVING.

Natasha isn't sure whether to scream or cry. There are dozens of people walking up and down the unit in skid-free socks and gray scrubs, the same types of scrubs she was forced to change into in the emergency room. She had to put her clothes, phone, ID, ChapStick, and hair clip into a plastic bag that was given to a security guard. The only way she'll be able to use her phone while she's here is by filling out a request to have it for fifteen minutes a day under supervision.

Some of the other patients make direct eye contact with Natasha, while others, the ones who worry her more, stare at the vinyl floor in a daze. Shelly wheels her past a room that's empty except for an old piano and a stack of dusty gym mats. The one next to it has large wooden tables with benches that remind her of summer camp cafeterias. A stale smell, like old bread and mildew, permeates the entire place.

Shelly helps Natasha out of the wheelchair and gives her a brief run-through of the unit. Natasha can only process it in snippets. Visiting hours are strictly enforced. Only certain items can be brought by visitors for patients. There are multiple therapy groups throughout the day.

Natasha goes to her assigned room after she gets a folder, notebook, pencil, and printout of the rules. It's freezing and sterile, and there's one flickering fluorescent light that makes Natasha think of every creepy psych-ward movie she's ever seen. Two twin beds are bolted to the floor. Suhani once told her that some patients tried to end their lives by having the beds collapse on them, and ever since then, all beds were fixed to the floor. A sink and mirror are at the back of the room. There are no handles for water, just buttons, so there's no risk of anyone using the metal parts to hurt themselves. Natasha's roommate is fast asleep and facing the stone wall.

"Try to get some rest," Shelly said before she left the unit.

Take me with you! Natasha almost screamed. *Please! I'm not like these other people!*

She lies in bed and stares at the tiled ceiling. *So this is what it's like to be committed to a psych ward.* This is where she really is. She feels like she's suspended above her body, watching herself in this stiff, cold bed.

Without her phone, Netflix, or music, all she can do is think. *Maybe I can somehow use this in a stand-up routine.* She used to reassure herself this way whenever anything shitty happened. *At least it's material.* Dad always claimed Natasha had a knack for making the most concerning situations entertaining in retrospect, whether it was how she negotiated getting a D raised to a C or the way she talked back to misogynistic family members in India. *You refuse to play by any rules,* Dad would say with a mixture of amusement and disbelief.

To Natasha's surprise, she feels a sharp, aching pang for her family. Mom's probably gazing up at her own ceiling, her thoughts spinning like the fan as Dad snores next to her. Suhani's sitting up in bed, her face stained from the blue light of her laptop as she makes an action plan to ensure Natasha has the best possible hospital stay. Maybe she's even on the phone with Anuj. Zack is next to her. He and Suhani will be okay. They have to be. They're her ideal couple. If they can't make it, there sure as hell isn't any hope for anyone else.

Her thoughts are interrupted by her roommate murmuring, "What time is it?"

"I dunno," Natasha says without peeling her eyes from the ceiling. "Super late."

"Natasha?"

Natasha's head snaps up. How does her roommate know her name? She slowly turns and registers the features one at a time. Thick, dark hair that's matted from hours spent against a pillow. Petite and perfect-postured frame. Rings of eyeliner.

Holy shit.

Alexis Diaz.

Her role model, Alexis Diaz!

The Alexis Diaz is her roommate on the Atlanta Memorial Inpatient Psychiatry Ward. How?!

"Wha . . . what are you doing here?" Natasha clutches her sheets. If she was a character in an old Disney Channel movie, Alexis would be a fun and friendly figment of her imagination.

But she's real. And here. The woman whose videos Natasha's memorized, whose Wikipedia page she turns to for motivation, that woman is in her own uncomfortable bed right next to Natasha.

"Wow, what a coincidence, right?" Alexis smiles and scoots to the edge of her bed.

"That is one way to say it." Natasha isn't sure why she laughs. Is it because of sheer surprise? Nerves? "You're literally the last person I ever expected to see here."

Alexis nods. "I checked myself in a couple of days ago because I knew I was getting to a bad place."

"You're here voluntarily?" Natasha raises her eyebrows. "Seriously?"

"Seriously. I have bipolar disorder. Got diagnosed a few years ago after I was running around naked on Peachtree Street and screaming I'd be a queen someday. They had to restrain me and stick a needle in my ass and put me in my own room here. It traumatized me so much that I'll do anything to make sure I don't go through that again."

"Oh my God. I'm so sorry you went through that," Natasha says. Hearing her role model discuss her mental illness so matter-of-factly gives Natasha an unexpected sense of comfort. Maybe she isn't defective. Maybe it's okay to be struggling.

"It's okay. I'm in a better place now . . . well, not now, but in general," Alexis says. "I know myself better than I did back then. I know when to warn the people in my life that I'm not doing well."

"Are your parents supportive about everything you're dealing with?" Natasha asks, careful to not give away just how much she's researched Alexis's life. From Alexis's references to them in her YouTube comedy sketches and the pictures on social media, they don't strike Natasha as the let's-discuss-our-mental-health types.

"It took awhile and there are still days they don't get it. Which I expected, them being conservative and Mexican and believing you just deal with whatever happens to you," Alexis says. "But every month gets easier. My dad was super depressed after my parents came to America. He never got any help for it, but I think he and my mom now realize how much it affected their marriage, my childhood, our entire lives, really. But they've also always lived in neighborhoods with people who understood them and spoke the same language and ate the same food. I didn't have that."

"Yeah, I totally get that," Natasha says, finding comfort in relating to Alexis even more than she realized was possible.

"So what happened with you?" Alexis asks.

Natasha gives Alexis a summary of the past day. It's a smoother version of the one she provided for the nurses and Dr. Chan. Telling the story gets easier each time.

"Jeez." Alexis shakes her head. "That really sucks. All of it."

Natasha shrugs. Something about sharing the Karan part makes her feel especially pathetic. She's supposed to be working to be a serious comedian, a woman she's proud of.

"When are you going to leave?" Natasha asks.

"I'll let the team decide that," Alexis says. Her voice is coated with nonchalance, as though she's simply deciding what to order at a restaurant, not considering how long she'll stay locked up on a psych ward.

"They just decide when you're ready?" Natasha asks in disbelief. How is a group of people supposed to know when she can go home?

"Basically." Alexis nods. "Just so you're aware, they are going to make you go through every detail all over again, but, like, to an audience. Nurses, a social worker, some residents, an occupational therapist. And then they'll recommend something, probably a medicine, and tell you to go to as many groups as possible. The groups are going to seem cheesy and sometimes they kind of are, but they help. They really help. So does getting a therapist."

"I actually had a therapist before," Natasha says before she gives Alexis a brief run-through of her sessions with Dr. Jenkins.

"Girl, no." Alexis puts her hand up. "Look, that woman sounds nice and all, but you need a therapist who gets it. Really gets it."

"Gets what?"

"Everything. Being a woman of color. A child of immigrants. Having parents who went through some real shit." Alexis holds up one, two, then three fingers with each point she makes. "All that stuff white people haven't experienced but, you know, makes us who we are. Tell the team that's what you want. Trust me on this."

"I don't know how my parents will feel about me going to therapy," Natasha says. "My sister's the only one who knows I saw Dr. Jenkins. And that sounds weird, especially since my dad's a psychiatrist. But he and my mom don't always get what I'm going through."

"Of course they don't," Alexis says, unfazed. "But that's sort of the point. You can show them another way. My therapist told me that going to therapy is to learn and unlearn. I'm supposed to learn about myself and also unlearn some of the toxic and unhelpful messages that my parents and our culture put in my head. Honestly, you should consider some family therapy."

Natasha scoffs. "And you should meet my mom and then try to suggest that."

Natasha pictures Mom scaring the poor therapist out of the

room by using a combination of criticism and blatant scolding. Or even more likely, Dad and Suhani sharing their elite mental health knowledge and that scaring the therapist out of the room. Every scenario possible leads to the therapist getting scared and needing to leave the room. The world needs good therapists, and for the sake of them everywhere, Natasha just can't suggest family therapy.

"I'm serious! Having a professional outsider to moderate can be a total game changer. I bet the team will recommend it for you. And you know," Alexis continues, "getting a better grasp over all my shit has really helped my comedy."

"Really? I thought comedians were supposed to be depressed and anxious. I've been telling myself that my anger's a part of my comedic charm," Natasha says, half-joking, half-serious.

"Ha, I used to think that, too. One of the biggest mistakes I made was justifying how bad I felt because so many of my idols struggled. But trust me. You can create better when you don't have so much weighing you down." Alexis folds her hands and reminds Natasha of the monks in India that Mom used to pray to. "And, speaking of creating, do you wanna tell me why you stopped my class? Yes, I noticed."

A weight settles in Natasha's stomach. "Um, do you not remember squashing my biggest dream? Telling me I didn't seem like a comedian?"

"I didn't say that!" Alexis's loud voice takes away any residual fatigue that's been lingering in Natasha's body.

"Yeah, you did," Natasha says as she remembers how Alexis's words looped in her head for weeks.

"I said I didn't see you as a stand-up comedian yet," Alexis says.

"Same thing!"

"It's not at all. Natasha, can you tell me what you even like about stand-up?"

"Of course," Natasha says with a burst of confidence. "I like writing things and then, um, expressing them with the power of the microphone and feeling the greater purpose and fulfillment of the bright spotlight. . . ."

Alexis looks at Natasha with an expression that says, *Do you even hear yourself?*

"Fine, so I hate being onstage, but who cares? It's something I have to work on," Natasha says.

"Maybe. Maybe with some time, work, and the stuff you can accomplish here, it'll feel more natural," Alexis agrees.

"But I love writing things that make m—"

"Exactly!" Alexis interrupts. "You love writing. And I remembered your writing from when you applied for my class. It was good. Really good. I think you've got something a lot of people would want to see. Doing stand-up comedy is writing and performing. I know that if you work on your writing first and then move to performing, you have the potential to someday be the type of comedian you want."

"But I have been working on it," Natasha says.

"I mean really working in a way that reshapes you." Alexis makes a fist. "Not giving up when you get feedback. Not playing it safe. If you're committing to this life, you're committing to rejections and instability and travel and going against a world where women are told they have to be pretty and agreeable, not hilarious and aggressive."

"So you're saying I need to get out of my comfort zone and try harder?" Natasha asks. She could have gotten that advice from a collection of Instagram quotes.

"Yes!" Alexis says. "And work your ass off for you, not to prove something to your family, the guy you almost married, or even the world."

Natasha lets Alexis's words settle over her like a cozy blanket. Just one conversation with her makes Natasha feel like a different person, one full of possibility and promise. Mom always told her that there was nothing more empowering than being around a woman who let you emotionally expose yourself. Devi Auntie does that for Mom. Natasha used to think Anita Auntie did, too.

"I never thought I was trying to prove anything. But maybe on some level I was. I tried to get to this place where I wasn't the weirdo anymore and where I had everything," Natasha admits. "My best friend becomes my husband. My family proud of me. My friends understanding everything I'm going through." Natasha's voice becomes softer as she pictures her hypothetical life. Sunday brunches with her and Karan's families. Being a bridesmaid in Ifeoma's wedding. Suhani, Zack, and Anuj cheering for her at a comedy club.

Is it possible that despite all the times she's rebelled, a big part of her was still convinced that if she wasn't following a conventional life, she was a failure?

"I know this is easier said than done, but if you really wanna live on your own terms, you've got to be okay with disappointing people, even the ones you love," Alexis says. "Maybe especially them."

They're interrupted by a nurse asking Natasha if she's ready to meet the treatment team. The next hour is exactly how Alexis described. Natasha goes to a big room where a dozen staff members are sitting around a table with coffee and clipboards. Thankfully, Dr. Chan is sitting in the center and encourages Natasha to take her time going back through the events that led her to calling 911.

At first, Natasha feels like a zoo animal, trapped behind glass, solely there to be observed and gawked at. But something about Dr. Chan's confident and warm voice makes Natasha's breathing slow down.

"If at any point any of this becomes too much, let me know and

we'll take a break," Dr. Chan says. The residents on either side of
her are taking frantic notes. One of them is looking through a
pocket textbook that reads *Synopsis of Psychiatry.* Is this who Natasha
is to them? Someone who can just be looked up and referenced?

Like an idiot, she only now remembers that these people work
with her sister. And they're going to know the most humiliating
thing she's ever done!

But everyone's faces are unfazed as she gives them a recap. It's
obvious that they've heard it all. As traumatic as the last twenty-
four hours have been, a part of her is relieved that nobody looks
shocked or disgusted.

The interview ends with Dr. Chan recommending therapy and
a low dose of Prozac. (Spot on, Alexis!) Natasha heads back to her
room. All she wants to do is sleep.

"Natasha!" Jean, the unit security guard, stops her. "You've got
a visitor waiting for you in the dining room."

"Already? I thought they weren't allowed on the first day," Natasha says.

The hospital nonslip socks are way too tight around her ankles.
She'll ask for a bigger size after she sees whoever is here. If it's Suhani,
she'll make sure Natasha knows all the patient perks. Or maybe it's
the girls. She can see Anuj or Zack telling them to check on her here.

But when she gets to the dining room, there's only one person
inside. An Indian dude in a white coat.

Shit.

It's not just any Indian dude. It's Roshan. Suhani's Roshan.

"Um, hey?" Natasha says. "What are you doing here?"

She's instantly transported back to that weekend she visited Suhani in medical school. Roshan was stuck to Suhani the first night.
Depending on who was judging him, Roshan's furrowed brows

and deep voice could be considered sexy in a Heathcliff, brooding kind of way. Yes, Heathcliff! Natasha had called him brown Heathcliff after she met him.

"I had to see a patient here for a neurology consult and thought I'd say hi," Roshan says. "And let you know I'm here if you need anything."

"Why?" Natasha tries to register his presence. It's so weird that this is who Suhani was with before Zack. Chill and content Zack. Talk about not having a type at all.

"Because I know Suhani's worried about you," Roshan says.

"And how do you know that?" Natasha asks.

She knows she can push someone like him because in some ways, she is someone like him. He's also got the same dark, Scorpio energy she does, and in another life, they would maybe even be good friends. She pictures them meeting at a bar, drinking whiskey, and bitching about people who are simpletons.

"Uh . . ." Roshan frowns. "I'm not sure what you mean by that."

"I mean, how do you know what Suhani's worried about?"

"Is that some sort of trick question?" His frown deepens. "She's your sister. You're here. Obviously she's worried."

Damn, he wants my sister, she thinks. Natasha has always been able to tell when a guy liked Suhani. There was a certain tenderness in their voices, an eagerness on their faces when they spoke to Natasha. It was as if they were trying to win her over.

But then she has a sinking feeling in her stomach. It's the same one she had when she visited Suhani in med school and saw her and Roshan together. Something was just off. Maybe it was sisterly intuition or just his vibe, but Natasha thinks back to Suhani seeming stressed, Zack's worries about her being more closed off, and it all becomes clear. Roshan has something to do with it. She's not sure what but she knows it's something. And even though he's expressing concern about Natasha now, she senses something else under his words. Power? Dominance? Whatever it is, it doesn't seem right.

"Are you okay?" Roshan asks.

"No, I'm not," Natasha says. "Look, I know some major shit went down between you and my sister. But you need to leave her alone."

"Whoa, Natasha, I'm not trying to bother her, okay?" Roshan says.

"But that's the thing. You just being around isn't helpful for her. You think I don't know all about you? You think she and I didn't talk about you guys?" Natasha tries to rearrange her face into its best I'm-ready-to-intimidate-you expression. She always wished she had a solid resting bitch face. Instead, her undereye circles and puffy cheeks give her more of a girl-who-needs-rest face.

Natasha furrows her badly-in-need-of-threading eyebrows. "I'm sure you're coming from a good place but whatever you guys went through is in the past. And it needs to stay there."

Roshan looks surprised, then hurt. Maybe Natasha is being a little too bitchy. After all, the guy is trying to check on her.

But when she sees his clenched fists, she knows she hit a nerve. Because everything she told him is true. And if for nothing else, she has to do this much for her sister and brother-in-law.

"All right, then." Roshan stands up. The wooden chair screeches against the floor as he pushes it with his heel. "Good to see you. Take care of yourself."

Relief washes over her as Roshan walks away.

Go, she thinks. *Leave her alone. Forever.*

Now if she can only just get her own shit together. She shuffles down the hallway, ready to get back in bed.

Twenty-Three

Suhani

Three days.

Zack's slept on the couch for three days. And she's barely even seen him there. He's been leaving early for work and returning after Suhani's asleep.

She scrolls to the text he sent her yesterday.

ZACK: I still need time.

She pictures him driving on I-75, the air-conditioning blasting, listening to his favorite business podcast. She should call him and ask how they could have possibly gotten to a place so low. Or maybe she can drive to his office right now and surprise him. Be the spontaneous Suhani who once existed sometimes with Zack. Only with Zack. She pictures herself wearing black stilettos, a trench coat, and nothing else. They can play hooky, get a hotel room, order champagne and room service.

But he doesn't want that. And she has to respect his desire for space.

Suhani studies her reflection in their bathroom mirror, still foggy from her long morning shower. The sole perk of being unable to sleep now is that she has plenty of time to do a hair mask, exfoliate, and shave her legs. Zack's razor is on the counter.

After her shower, it only takes her ten minutes to apply primer, foundation, powder, blush, eyeliner, and eye shadow. She puts on a crisp white shirtdress and slings gold Mejuri hoops through her ears. Her look is complete with one coat of red lipstick. A quick glance in the mirror confirms that she looks ready to take on the day, even if all she wants to do is curl into the fetal position on the floor.

Her gaze lingers on her platinum wedding band and three-carat engagement ring. The creepy stillness of the apartment makes her feel as though she's suspended in a dream. Outside, the roads swell with morning rush-hour traffic. People are clutching iced coffees and crossing streets and putting in AirPods.

Work. She has to get to work. Natasha can take a terrible situation and inject humor into it. Take lemons and make a margarita. Mom can do that, too. But Suhani's only way of coping is to put her head down and get shit done.

An hour later, she's sitting across from Dr. Wilson. "Thank you for meeting with me."

"Of course."

"Look, I understand what you saw between Dr. Shah and me," Suhani says. "We did know each other in medical school, but there's nothing to be concerned about now. And it won't have any impact on how I would be as a chief."

If I still even have a chance, she considers adding but then decides not to.

"Suhani, I appreciate you sharing that, but we've already made our decisions." Dr. Wilson twirls a Montblanc pen like it's a mini baton. Suhani has an impulse to grab the pen out of his hand and yell, *Tell me already!* She needs to process the news and move on. Rip off the Band-Aid.

"All right, then," Suhani prepares to leave. "That's gr—"

"You are going to be one of our chiefs."

"Wait, what?" Suhani asks. "I am?"

But what about what he and the other committee members saw? What about the e-mail?

"Of course you are. To be honest, I'm dismayed that you had so much doubt."

"I guess I thought after everything that I was out of the running." The truth hits her in waves. She's going to be chief! Everything she worked for mattered!

Zack. She has to call Zack.

But will he even want to hear from her? She thinks back to the text. I still need time.

"Because you have a personal life?" Dr. Wilson raises an eyebrow. "Once I realized there was some history with you and Dr. Shah, I made sure he would not have any input on our decision."

"You did?" Suhani asks. Did she really let her anxiety push her to assume the worst?

"Of course. It's my job to look out for you," Dr. Wilson says. "And you deserved this position. May I ask where all of this self-doubt is coming from? I ask this as a program director, not a psychiatrist."

"Ha." Suhani feels the tension in her shoulders melt. "It's complicated."

"Can you try to explain it to me? However much feels comfortable?" Dr. Wilson leans forward and folds his hands on the desk. Regardless of what he just said, everyone knows this is his classic therapist pose, focused and ready to listen.

Her mind jumps back to the moment her baby left her, the odd mix of regret and relief that devoured her body. Even though she told herself she did what was best for everyone, a part of her was always convinced she did something wrong and that someday she would pay the price. Shame was tricky in that way. It distorted how she saw her past and what she thought she deserved in her future.

But maybe she needed something that poked holes in the pristine self-image that she spent years constructing. Maybe the constant pressure she put on herself would have boiled over at one point or another and forced her to reevaluate what really mattered, who she really was underneath the achievements.

She sees everything in a blur: pushing herself to live the way her mother never could, making sure all her parents' sacrifices weren't in vain, setting the perfect example for her sister and brother, excelling in everything she pursued. Even her relationship with Roshan was like that, another accomplishment that checked off all the right boxes on the outside.

All of it made her unable to deal with anything that couldn't be controlled.

"I guess in medical training there's so much evaluation, and it all matters," Suhani says. "We're taught that a single negative comment can derail an entire career. It's made me have this fear that I'm always just one mistake away from losing it all, that I have to be perfect and overdo everything to make sure none of this is taken away.

"It just adds up after a while. There are the evaluations from one side and then from the other, people doubting your title or making constant remarks about your appearance. All those things, even if they may seem small, can have a really massive impact. And I think in my case, it's made me defensive and on edge."

Dr. Wilson's eyes shift as he thinks about what Suhani's just said.

"We are seeing this a lot. Too much. Qualified women are not going after certain things because they think they don't deserve to. The more I'm learning about this as a program director, the more I'm seeing that we have an institutional problem with making female physicians feel that they can advocate for themselves."

"I didn't know this was something you were seeing across the board," Suhani says.

"I wish that wasn't the case," Dr. Wilson says. "One of the things I'm hoping you can do as chief is think of ways we can improve this at Atlanta Memorial."

"I really can't wait." She feels a flutter of excitement. After everything she's been through, she can be a part of change so other women don't have to endure the same.

She leaves the meeting and thanks Dr. Wilson for everything. For the first time at work, her thoughts aren't racing. She's in the moment.

In the empty gray stairwell, she leans against the railing as she feels something in her release. Roshan didn't ruin her. No matter how much he tries to intimidate her or show he still has control over her, she can shut him out entirely. That part of her life truly is over.

When she checks her phone, she sees Mom has sent three texts in the last hour.

MOM: How is Natasha?

MOM: Tell us if we can bring her anything.

MOM: Hope she is doing okay. When are you going to be able to check on her?

SUHANI: I'll see her in a couple of hours.

Then, before she has a chance to hesitate, she sends Zack a message.

I understand you still need time. Just wanted you to be the first person to know I'm officially going to be chief. Please know that I'm so grateful for everything you did to help me get here. And again, I'm sorry.

She waits to see if the typing-in-progress bubbles appear. But the screen remains unchanged for a couple of minutes. His Instagram and Twitter also don't show any recent activity, but that might not mean anything. Zack's more of a lurker on social media.

Her finger lingers over the CALL button. But before she can press it, there's an incoming call. The first digits give away that it's from within the hospital.

"It's Dr. Joshi." Suhani keeps her voice low as she walks back to her office.

"Hi, it's Konny Chan," says the calm, confident voice on the other end.

"Hi! How's Natasha doing?" Suhani says, relieved her sister has one of the strongest residents on her case.

"Fine. It's still early so I'm hoping we see progress every day. She sleeps a lot," Konny says. "I know the Prozac will take time to kick in, but if I can encourage her to go to some therapy groups and at least stay out of bed more, she'll start to feel better. She's already really close to her roommate, which is good. And we've had a few good one-on-one talks. I think long-term individual therapy will be very helpful for her."

"That sounds great," Suhani says. "I'll stop by this afternoon to check on her."

"There's also one more thing you should be aware of," Konny says. "We recommended family therapy. And Natasha didn't seem too keen on it but we really believe it could be helpful."

"For our family?" Suhani asks, even though there's obviously no other family Konny would be referring to. The thought of all of them, especially Mom, sitting in a room and being guided by a therapist, is unimaginable. Even though her husband and daughter are psychiatrists, Mom thinks Americans focus "too much" on therapy and "telling strangers their business." She'd make that poor therapist wish they went into another career.

"I hear what you're saying," Suhani says. "But do you think that would be productive? Or even good for her?"

"I do. Natasha has brought up a lot pertaining to your family's dynamics. And it seems as though many of the ideas she has about herself are shaped by her role in your family. We really do feel even a few sessions would be useful for her," Konny says, then adds, "for everyone."

Suhani thinks back to how often she and Natasha were compared to each other throughout their lives. Relatives, aunties, and friends would say things like, *Look at how talkative your sister is!* Then they'd turn to Natasha and remark, *You should dress more like your sister!* Suhani assumed both of them got used to this nonstop commentary. But now she wonders how much damage things like this caused over the years.

Is it possible that all of them played a part in making Natasha feel inadequate? Unaccepted? How would her parents even process those possibilities? Suhani can't imagine them taking it well. She tries to picture Mom smiling and saying, *Oh! Natasha's depression partially stems from my parenting? Thank you so much for that insight! I'm enlightened!*

Konny's voice brings Suhani back to reality. "I know it's especially tough in Asian American families to discuss these types of things. I've actually been looking into it for my residency research project. There are so many barriers to treatment, but so far, the data I've found shows that many Asian Americans don't go to therapy because of the stigma."

"Oh, definitely," Suhani agrees. "But I guess with both my Dad and me, we thought we were doing a better job."

The moment the words come out, she's compelled to take them back. She should be professional. Pretty soon, she'll be Konny's chief. She should be guiding her, not sharing something so personal.

No, it's fine to be open and real, she tells herself.

Every time she's vulnerable at work, something in her mind tells her to dial it back, make sure that she's not doing anything that could risk her being taken seriously.

"I'm sure your family has been doing a lot," Konny says. "Really. My parents won't even tell people I'm a psychiatrist because they're so embarrassed. Some of my aunts still beg me to consider becoming a 'real' doctor."

"Ugh, I've heard that before," Suhani says. "I know my dad did all the time in India and here."

"Gotta love that immigrant mentality, right?" Konny laughs. On her end, Suhani hears residents typing and talking. "We still have so much work to do as a community when it comes to openly discussing these types of things."

"We really do," Suhani says. "I think there's so much of this idea that having to see a mental health professional means parents have failed in some way. And that really isn't the case."

Suhani thanks Konny for everything. After they hang up, she checks her text messages, then her e-mail.

Still no response from Zack.

A few hours later, in between her therapy cases, she goes to visit Natasha. Even as she's using her key to get into the ward, a part of her still can't process that her own sister is in one of these rooms, rooms that she's been in dozens of times.

Natasha's room is at the end of the hallway.

It's going to be strange seeing Natasha in the gray scrubs and nonslip socks Suhani's seen on patients for years. She braces herself for all of it and commands herself to stay calm.

But when she peeks inside Natasha's room, the first thing she sees is her sister asleep under the thin covers, her chest rising and falling.

My Nani. Suhani clenches her fists and presses her tongue against the roof of her mouth, her go-to moves to ensure she doesn't cry. The truth fills her like water in her lungs. Despite everything she and Natasha have been through, Suhani wasn't able to stop her from getting to a place this low.

That can't really be her sister right here, in the psych ward where she works. No, it has to be someone else who happens to have the same unruly hair and chipped nails. Her sister belongs in her apartment. Suhani would give anything to find Natasha on her couch, wearing her clothes, drinking her wine. It's funny how when things fall apart, all you want back are the parts of someone that used to annoy you.

As Suhani leaves the ward, Shelly calls out to her from the nursing station. "Dr. Joshi! You doin' okay?"

Suhani shrugs. "Taking it one day at a time. I'm so grateful Natasha has you as her nurse."

"Oh, she's just wonderful!" Shelly smiles. "And popular! She's already had people drop in to visit. Your parents, brother, her friends called and asked when they can come and oh! That new neurologist, the Indian one, I forget his name . . . he stopped by to see her, too."

Suhani freezes. There must be some mistake. But then she knows there's not. This is exactly the type of thing Roshan would do.

"Dr. Shah?" She asks, thankful Shelly is oblivious to her reaction. "He saw Natasha *here*?"

"Ah, yes!" Shelly nods. "Dr. Shah. He had a consult here and said he wanted to check on her."

Before Shelly can say anything else, Suhani says she has to go. She takes quick steps out of the ward and lingers in the quiet hallway. She presses her palms against the wall as a knot of panic forms behind her sternum. Her hands start to shake. Deep breaths. She has to take deep breaths. There's an ice machine at the end of the hallway and she's reminded of a grounding exercise she's suggested to patients but never tried before. She presses the green button on the machine. Once the frozen pebbles fall into her hands, she closes her eyes and focuses on the cold feeling taking over her. The temperature and tactility of the act pull her back to the present.

Before she can talk herself out of it, she types the text to Roshan that she should have years ago.

I know we went through a lot. But none of that matters anymore. I've moved on and you need to do the same. That means staying away from me and anyone I care about. I wish you all the best.

When she sends the message, she's surprised that instead of anger, she feels a surge of stillness. She always thought avoidance would eventually give her a sense of closure. But all along, she needed to face what they went through and give herself the space to heal.

Her pager emits the loud *beep, beep, beep* of an urgent message.

Doctor, Natasha is awake and asking for you. Shelly

Suhani goes back to the ward, ready to see her sister.

Twenty-Four

Bina

"I should have canceled the meeting today."

"No way!" Devi yells through the phone. "Everyone's there. And you can't let all of the work Deepak, Suhani, and Anuj did go to waste!"

"They did do a lot of work," Bina agrees as she opens the Chats Over Chai Instagram page Anuj set up. She already has more than one thousand followers. Over the past weeks, Deepak and Suhani have been teaching her about group therapy and helped her make an agenda for the meetings so they're more structured.

"Exactly," Devi says. "Plus, you can't visit Natasha for another few hours, anyway."

Bina breathes a sigh of relief at hearing Devi's voice. She had offered to take the next flight from Los Angeles when she heard Natasha was admitted to the psych ward. But Bina insisted there was no need. When she told Devi about today's Chats Over Chai meeting, Devi said she'd be there on FaceTime.

"She must be so scared, all alone in that place." Bina shakes her head. "I hate that they only allow visitors once a day there. Even Deepak and Suhani told me that was better for her but it doesn't feel right."

"I know it's hard not to worry. But she'll be okay. The girl is tough, like her mother," Devi says with a wink. Devi can get away with things like winks and curse words in ways other people can't. She looks the same as always in a bright-yellow dress and black biker jacket with gold trim. Her hair has streaks of dark red from her routine henna-dying treatments.

"Well, according to this, her mother is leading a cult." Bina picks up this morning's edition of *Samachar in America*. "Bipin strikes again! How am I even supposed to face these women after this?"

Ma was right all along when she said a reputation is like glass, transparent and easily shattered. Maybe Bina never should have done this.

She waits for Devi to tell her that she understands how humiliating this must be and not to worry, everyone will get over it and move on.

But Devi crosses her arms and stares at Bina like a disappointed teacher. Two frown lines are between her eyebrows. "Bina, you're kidding me, right?"

She doesn't have a trace of the Indian accent that coated her monologues when she and Bina used to perform together.

"Excuse me?" Bina asks.

"Excuse you, is right," Devi says as she adjusts the gold pendant on her necklace. "You're still so scared about what people will think."

"No, I'm not!"

Devi tilts her head and gives Bina a look that says, *Don't bullshit me.* "The Bina I knew was obsessed with her husband and didn't give a rat's ass about what anybody would say when she decided to run away with him and ruin her relationship with her parents."

"That's not entirely true," Bina interjects. "I did care."

"Of course you cared about your parents' feelings. But you still did what you had to do. And you were unapologetic about it. Now you're getting upset over some patriarchal bullshit and worried what a group of women in your living room are going to think about it. A group of women who are here because they value you and what you have to say!"

"It just feels wrong to be doing something like this"—Bina motions to the living room, where everyone has been waiting to start the meeting—"when my child is suffering. It feels as though I've done so much wrong for things to end up this way."

"We've all made mistakes as parents. Sure, Natasha has struggled. But let me tell you something about her." Devi's voice is gentle but firm. "She's a fighter. Why do you think she wants to figure things out in her own way? Does that remind you of anyone? Someone who, I don't know, told several rich, arrogant guys to screw themselves because she was going to marry this sensitive sweetheart?"

Bina nods, but inside, she looks back at her younger self and wonders, *Did I really do that? Was I really that bold and full of hope?*

"Your kids are loving, empathetic, strong kids," Devi says. "And there's a reason you're going to go in there and get this done. You needed fulfillment from someplace other than your family. You always did. And as much as you tried to ignore it or convince yourself that you'd find enough by being everything to everyone at home, it wasn't enough for you. And that's okay."

Bina's stomach seesaws. "Then why doesn't it feel okay?"

"The guilt," Devi says. "You've been carrying around so much guilt ever since you had to let go of acting. It's as though you think you have to suffer in some way. But you don't, Bina. You really don't."

Devi's words hang in the air. She stares at Bina with an intense focus. Bina can't help but compare the chemistry she has with Devi, one that almost seems rooted in magic, to what she has with Anita, something that's made more of circumstance and convenience. Both are valid in their own right. And both bring out different things in her. She wonders what would happen if Anita were to ever move away. Would they be able to pick up right where they left off on yearly visits and weekly phone calls, or would they get absorbed into their new lives?

"I'm telling you this because I love you," Devi says. "And I don't want you to do the same thing your mom did to you. I don't want you to pass down bitterness and guilt and some fixation on how you're 'supposed' to be."

Bina feels the sting of sadness. Devi is totally right. She has internalized her own mother's disapproval and unforgiving standards. And she's given them to her kids in different ways.

"This group you're hosting is about being honest and vulnerable, right?" Devi asks. "What about putting that into practice with Natasha? Telling her about what happened in India?"

"What? I can't do that! It's not relevant to my, our, life at all anymore. . . ." Bina's voice becomes soft. "And I don't even know how she'd handle it."

Bina drifts back to when she emptied the bottle of pills into the toilet. She cried with relief as the tornado of water swirled and swallowed them all. She was going to be okay. She could put this part of her life behind her and never deal with it again.

"At least think about it. And in the meantime, maybe you can take up my offer to send her here. She'll love it." Devi points her phone toward the beach. Waves tumble onto the shoreline. A group of teenagers are playing volleyball.

"Maybe I need to send myself there." Bina laughs.

"Come with her. But I'm telling you, this internship is a real op-portunity," Devi says, referring to a position that opened up on one of the late-night shows.

"But it barely pays!"

Devi scoffs. "It's not about the money at first in these industries, Bina. This is a chance for Natasha to learn and really get to know people in her field. At least tell her when you go see her."

Bina nods, even though she's unsure how she feels about letting Natasha move across the country to pursue a career that's so risky, so full of rejection.

"I guess we should start this meeting." Bina picks up her phone. "I'm sure everyone's already had a chance to get their food and mingle a little."

"Yes! Take me in there with you and let me be a part of the type of meeting only you, Bina Joshi, can lead."

Bina pours chai into her favorite teacup, bone china adorned with a giant pink rose and a gilded rim. Queen Elizabeth's face is on the inside. The tea set is the only thing Bina took from Ma's house after she passed away.

"I just heard about the *Samachar in America* piece! We have to put a stop to this. Bipin Bhai is out of control!" Mira comes march-ing into the kitchen as though she's preparing to go to war. "Who does he think he is?"

"He's a very respected person in our community. And on the board of the biggest newspaper for South Asians in America," Bina says. "Remember all that?"

"He still needs to be put in his place." Mira raises a clenched fist in the air. Her giant emerald ring catches a glint of light.

"I agree with you," Bina says. "But let's have our meeting first and then we can figure out Bipin's takedown."

"Okay, fine." Mira nods as if Bina suggested Mira grab some more crackers, not plot a friend's demise. Mira shoves her hands into the pockets of her cashmere leopard-print cardigan, something she definitely bought after it was featured on Pooja's Instagram page. She can complain all she wants about Pooja's posts, but it's obvious to everyone that she's obsessed with everything Pooja puts out there.

They go back into the living room. Thirty women are sitting on the couches and floor. Thirty! Maybe Bipin inadvertently helped her spread the word about this. Oh, the irony! Even though Bina had told Mira and Mona it was fine to bring anyone interested in attending the meeting, she didn't realize there would be this many women here today. She barely made enough food and makes a mental note to stick to her rule about only serving chai. A woman Bina doesn't even recognize has two plates stacked with spicy paneer tacos and pesto, mozzarella, and artichoke naan pizzas.

The naan pizzas make Bina ache for the kids. Whenever Deepak had weekend calls, Bina made those for dinner. It was the only meal she allowed them to eat while watching a movie. Natasha usually got upset that she didn't pick the movie, Anuj sulked with his pizza, and Suhani told them both to get over it. Bina would scarf down her own pizza and then mediate the kids' fights for a solid hour. She used to fantasize about the moment she'd finally have weekends to herself, but now she'd give anything for one of those rambunctious nights.

What should she have done differently back then? Could one

conversation or compassionate statement have made the difference? If Bina was more patient, happier with the life she got, and not constantly wondering about the one she could have had, would Natasha not be on a psychiatric ward right now? Would Suhani be more at peace? And would she know Anuj better?

"Sheesh." Mona shakes her head as she picks up the latest issue of *Samachar in America*. "You're certainly making waves in Atlanta, aren't you, Bina?"

The rest of the women laugh, some with nervousness, others with amusement. It only now occurs to Bina that that may be why some of them are here: to see the scandalous woman with their own eyes.

"She did always want to make an impact on a big scale," Devi says. "Remember our Bina here walked away from a career in Bollywood."

Mira stares at Devi on the screen as if she's some exotic installation at the High Museum. Bina almost wants to shake her and say, *Yes, she's divorced AND teaches screenwriting AND goes on dates with men she sometimes invites back home! Would you like to interview her about any of those things?*

"Cultlike!" Mona shakes her head in disbelief as she reads the article on her phone. "I still can't believe this is how they're describing you!"

The word echoes in Bina's mind. *Cult. Cult. Cult.*

But as she watches the women read the story, she knows they're right to be upset. Is this what she gets for trying to organize something that makes a small difference? Is this how she's going to get treated after years—years!—of putting on community events, bringing people together, finding ways to give back?

Bina received a slew of Facebook messages after the first *Samachar in America* piece.

They fell into one of two categories:

1. Those who agreed with Bipin and thought Bina was a culture killer and a danger to South Asian women everywhere
2. Those who thought Bina was doing exactly what she needed to "teach these chauvinistic jerks a lesson" or "show the men who's boss" or, her personal favorite, "tell them to stick it where the sun don't shine"

(Who even thought of that phrase? It's quite clever. At first, with the sun reference and all, it seems innocent, but then when you put it together it actually—)

"Bina!" Mona's voice snaps her back to reality. "You were saying that we need to focus on why we are meeting here today."

"Right. Our topics for today are invisible labor and boundaries," Bina says. "And as a reminder, we are here to have meaningful group discussions about things that interest us and may usually be hard to talk about. As much as I'd love to discuss the article, we are not going to use our precious time together to start some riot against Bipin Bhai or anyone else who doesn't support what we're doing here."

Bina watches women put their phones facedown in front of them or tuck them into their purses. Within a few minutes, everyone is quiet and facing her.

She's ready to start.

Twenty-Five

Natasha

G roup therapy is sort of cheesy but, overall, not that bad. Natasha has been going every day for the past week. Today there are eight patients, including Natasha, sitting around a wooden table. Dr. Chan and another psychiatry resident, Dr. Murphy, moderate the group.

"Just reminding everyone that anything we share in here is confidential," Dr. Chan says.

Brooke, a blond girl whose spunk and petite build remind Natasha of Kristen Bell, raises her hand. She has a habit of ending all her sentences with a high pitch, so they sound like questions. "Does anyone else think it's hard to see your family when you're in this place? It's like, I get bored and lonely and stuff, but then it's weird to be with my mom and get reminded of how she doesn't get it."

"I totally feel the same way," Natasha says. "It doesn't matter how much progress I think I'm making . . . all it takes is one conversation with my mom and I'm back to feeling like crap again. I know she and my dad have dealt with a lot, coming to America and having no money and all. But it's almost like I have no right to feel bad because what they went through was obviously worse."

Brooke nods as if she agrees, even though Natasha knows from a previous session that Brooke comes from three generations of WASPs. Then again, maybe every family is messed up in some way.

"What about other members of our family?" Dr. Chan suggests. "Does anyone feel this way with people they're related to outside their parents?"

Natasha raises her hand. "My sister and brother are great. They really are. But they make me feel crappy, too. My sister is perfect. Literally. And she doesn't understand that not everyone can get whatever they want. She works hard for what she has, yes, but it's like she doesn't know any other way. She puts so much pressure on herself and then does the same for anyone else in her orbit. And my brother tries to get it. But he's almost the opposite of her. He's so chill that nobody would ever have an issue with him. He's at home all summer and I know my parents find it relaxing to have him around . . . but when I was at home for even a couple of weeks, it was a total hassle."

Maybe she shouldn't have said anything. These two doctors know Suhani. They probably idolize her. She considers taking her words back.

But Drs. Chan and Murphy just nod, almost in sync, as Natasha continues to talk. She wonders if this type of thoughtful nod is something they were taught to do in their training.

"Siblings do define us more than we may realize. And it can be tough to reconcile our role within our families," Dr. Chan says. "But I wonder, what's your influence been like on them?"

"Meaning?" Natasha asks.

"You've talked about how they've affected you and your sense of self. How do you think you've impacted your sister and brother?"

"I'm not really sure." Natasha bites her bottom lip. She doesn't really ever think she's affected Suhani or Anuj.

"Does anyone else have something they'd like to add to that? Thoughts on your impact on your family members?" Dr. Murphy looks around the room.

Chris, a sophomore at Emory who was admitted for a manic episode, clears his throat. At first glance he looks like he's straight out of a cologne commercial: buff and broad-shouldered with a chiseled jaw. If Ifeoma or Payal saw Chris at a bar, they'd definitely think he was super hot. Chris told Natasha earlier that he'll probably have to take a leave of absence from school since he's in and out of the hospital so much. During this most recent episode, he tried to cut up his entire left arm with a butcher knife. His wounds are covered with gauze that he tends to pick at during group therapy.

"I feel like my family does the best they can," he says. "It took me awhile to realize that. But the older I get, the more I see that they're trying to figure things out, too."

Geraldine, a woman around Suhani's age who was diagnosed with schizophrenia two years ago, nods in agreement. Everything from her Barbadian accent to her sparkling eyes to her flawless skin reminds Natasha of Rihanna.

"My entire family was overwhelmed when I first got sick," Geraldine says. "Some of them have cut off talking to me altogether. But some have stuck around . . . so I guess that's better than nothing. I think a few of my family members think I'm cursed or what I have is contagious or something."

Natasha feels a stab of guilt as she imagines how tough that must be for Geraldine. She knows that no matter what, her family would never cut off talking to her. She thinks back to how she got into an explosive fight with Mom at Anuj's graduation party during Dad's speech, how she got too wasted at Suhani and Zack's wedding and threw up on the dance floor at the reception.

Tears pool in her eyes as she remembers the arguments that ensued after each of those events. Despite how angry everyone was, within days, they were hugging her and telling her it was okay. She's put her family through a lot and they still stick by her.

She pictures Dad, giving Mom and Anuj information on depression and medications. She pictures Suhani and Zack, figuring out what to do next. Maybe they're all on the phone together. Mom has to be calling and texting Suhani nonstop. They must be so worried about her. She hates that she's doing this to them.

Her mind drifts to something Dr. Chan brought up yesterday, when they were meeting one-on-one. As much as Natasha thinks Mom and Suhani are tough on her, is it possible that she's also pretty critical of them? Does she hold them to a higher bar and pick apart their behavior more than she does for Dad or Anuj or even Zack? Does she see more of them in herself than she wants to admit?

The next morning, Natasha is awake before the call for breakfast. She sits up and gazes around the dark room. She's immediately taken aback by it. Or rather, the absence of it. There's no weight or haziness in her head.

She brushes her teeth, takes a long shower, and changes into a clean pair of scrubs.

It often boils down to just taking one step at a time, Dr. Chan said the other day. Getting out of bed. Making yourself get dressed. Sometimes you have to act first and the motivation will follow.

The giant clock above the doorway confirms that it's seven a.m.

"I think I just slept—really slept—for the first time in months," Natasha tells Alexis, who is reading *Dear Girls* by Ali Wong.

"That's a sign you're getting better!" Alexis grins. Yesterday she told Natasha she will be getting ready to leave soon. "You should tell Dr. Chan. Once they know you're sleeping better and you say you don't want to hurt yourself, they'll start making a plan to let you go."

"Let me go . . . but where?" Natasha's excitement slips away and she feels a familiar sense of dread. She'll go back to Suhani and Zack's apartment with no plan, no job, no open mic spots. Then again, the confinement of the unit has made her realize how much she misses little things about her life. If she leaves soon, at least she can eat what she wants and use her phone. Be outside.

"Most likely to your parents' house. That's always their preferred discharge plan. You know, be around family, where you're always watched, can get help coming to therapy appointments. Blah blah blah."

"Ugh, I don't know if being around my mom is the best idea right after I'm out of a place like this."

"If it's any consolation," Alexis says, "the days after I'm out of the hospital are some of the best ones I have with my family. I know it sounds strange, but it's true. We all sit together for dinner, watch a movie, talk . . . it's actually really nice."

Natasha leans back on the thin pillow and is suddenly overcome with a longing for Mom, her scent of sandalwood and vanilla, the reliable sound of her laugh whenever Natasha puts on an old comedy, including movies like *The Hangover*, which she appreciates more than any other Indian auntie ever would. There's a lot that's fun about Mom.

"Since you're feeling a little better," Alexis adds, "maybe now is a good time to think more about your YouTube videos?"

Natasha freezes. "You've seen my YouTube videos?"

"Yep. Weeks ago." When Alexis sees the confusion on Natasha's face, she adds, "I always check to see if my students are creating content. Anyway, your stuff is pretty good. I think the whole family angle is working."

"Well, it was inspired by you," Natasha admits. "My favorite parts of your YouTube sketches were always the ones where you talked about your family."

Before she can hesitate, she asks, "Did it ever cause issues with you and them?"

"Of course it did." Alexis laughs. "But they got over it eventually. And now it barely fazes them. I realized most things worth doing are always hard at first. It's about whether you're willing to push through that hard part that determines if you'll really make some good art."

"So you never regretted it? Putting your family into your work, even when it wasn't, er, flattering?" Natasha asks, wishing she had a Post-it note so she could write down Alexis's wisdom, return to it later.

Alexis shakes her head. "Never. I think what I love most about comedy is how it lets me take the hardest parts of my life, share them with people, and make them funny. It almost takes away some of the power from the shit that haunts me. Performing gives you a high, yeah, but it's a temporary high. After it's over, you have to deal with yourself. You have to embrace who you really are when you're alone."

Natasha pictures Alexis's words floating above them in a bubble as if they're in a comic strip. *Embrace who you really are when you're alone.* Natasha's spent so long being ashamed for who she is, she never took the time to reflect on the parts of herself she appreciates.

"Plus," Alexis adds, "when I make stuff nobody else can make, there's a good chance it's going to help someone."

That thought fills Natasha with a warm hope. If she can even help one person in pain, one person who also feels unworthy and not good enough, she will have succeeded. For years, she assumed she was drawn to comedy because she was funny and it seemed like the right fit. Now she realizes that there's a greater purpose to it for her. She wants to use her potential to make sure people feel less alone.

"Natasha Joshi!" a nurse's voice booms from the intercom. "You have visitors!"

"Hm, I wasn't expecting anyone," Natasha tells Alexis before she shuffles out of her room.

The ward is already in full frenzy. Two new patients, both at least ten years older than her, are brought in in wheelchairs. Nurses are administering morning medications to patients who are organized in a single-file line.

Natasha goes to the dining room, which for two hours a day is also the visitors' area.

Ifeoma and Payal are at a wooden table in the back corner. It's odd seeing them just sitting there in their summer dresses and sneakers, surrounded by patients in scrubs.

"Oh my God!" Natasha shrieks. "What are you doing here?"

Payal bursts into tears. "You're okay! Thank God you're okay. Anuj called us."

Ifeoma nods. "We couldn't wait to see you. How are you feeling?"

"Better," Natasha says, relieved that she means it.

When she's done filling them in on the past week, Ifeoma grabs her hand and says, "I just wish we could have been there for you."

"It's not your fault. I pretty much isolated myself. I've learned here that depression can make you do that," Natasha says as she thinks back to the countless hours she spent on Suhani and Zack's couch, ignoring texts and phone calls, drinking and staring at the television screen until her vision blurred.

But now she sees she could have trusted her friends. They've always been there for her.

"It's obviously been an intense week, so any chance y'all are up for talking about something other than psych wards?" Natasha asks.

"Are you sure?" Payal says.

"Yes! Please," Natasha says. "I've had nonstop group therapy and individual therapy. I need to hear about the outside world. You know, kind of like how after finals week, I'd read a bunch of celebrity tabloids."

They catch her up on their lives. Ifeoma and Jordan looked at engagement rings and they're going to Nigeria next month to meet her extended family. Payal got three more med school interviews.

"Damn, well, aren't you both just kicking ass?" Natasha says as she beams with pride. Her friends are making their biggest dreams happen.

"Yeah, things are falling into place," Ifeoma says. "But you're the one out of all of us really taking the risks."

"Me? The one sleeping on her sister's couch? Yup, I'm really thriving." Natasha smiles, actually enjoying the self-deprecating view of herself.

"No, you don't understand. We were talking about this on the way here. All of us were so full of hope and promise in college. We had these big goals. I wanted to travel and start an environmental advocacy organization, remember? And Payal was going to live in France for a year. But then we graduated and got disillusioned with the real world and all caught up with prestige. You're the only one of us who stuck to her true passion instead of what she 'should' do."

"Look, for me, a job is just a job. If it pays my bills and makes me happy enough, I'm good," Payal says. "But you have something you're really passionate about. That changes everything."

Natasha never saw it that way. She always assumed, on some level, her friends saw her as struggling. It occurs to her now that she's spent years projecting her biggest fears onto the people she loves the most.

"That means a lot," Natasha says, moved by seeing herself the way they do, as someone bold and capable, someone putting herself out there.

"It's true," Payal says. "I bet Suhani feels the same way, even if she hasn't told you."

"She has, actually," Natasha says. "But I've never believed her. And in thinking about what I 'should' do, I've realized that's where Karan fit in. I thought I was supposed to end up with a guy who checked off all the boxes for my family. And it was way scarier to face the unknown than to be with someone who was good enough."

Ifeoma and Payal exchange an uneasy look.

"What? What is it?" Natasha presses.

"Do you feel ready for some gossip?" Ifeoma asks.

"Hell yeah, I do," Natasha says. "The only gossip I know around here is that one of the nurses is having a fling with an intern. It scratches my *Grey's Anatomy* itch but I need more!"

Payal hesitates, then asks, "Even if it's about Karan?"

"What about him?" Natasha asks with a more removed tone than she expected. Maybe this is what moving on means, wondering about an ex with just a low-level curiosity instead of an all-consuming desperation.

When both of her friends stay quiet, Natasha says, "Tell me. I can handle it."

"We ran into him on the BeltLine and he told us he saw your

videos." Ifeoma says the words so quickly that they all blend together.

"What? How the heck did he see them?" Natasha asks.

"His mom," the girls say in unison.

"Right. Of course. So, that's it? He saw the videos and that's it?"

Payal starts to say, "Maybe we should—"

"He thought they were really good. Yes, even the one where you said he's boring in bed," Ifeoma says, cutting Payal off. "And then we started catching up with him and, uh, he and that girl broke up."

"You're kidding. Well, that's . . . interesting," Natasha says. The perfect girl? The one who was Anita Auntie approved? "Did he tell you why? What else did y'all talk about?"

Natasha realizes she sounds exactly like Mom when she's on the phone with one of her auntie friends.

Ifeoma takes a deep breath as if to prepare herself for everything she's about to dish out. Natasha scoots her chair closer to the table, feeling more like herself than she has in a long time.

Twenty-Six

Suhani

S o, how are you feeling?" Suhani sits at the edge of Natasha's bed.
"I think I'm better," Natasha says.

"I think you are, too." Suhani smiles.

Natasha's taken the time to brush her hair for the first time in days. Her face looks more relaxed and rested. And she's smiling, really smiling, in a way that reaches her eyes.

That's my sister, Suhani thinks as she's hit with relief and pride. That's the spirited and brazen person she's grown up with.

"What do you think has helped?"

"I dunno if it's just one thing," Natasha says. "I thought it was bullshit when on my first night, the staff kept saying the 'structure' of the ward would help me, but now I think they were onto something. Even though it sounded like torture when I got here, having limitations and a schedule and not being able to use my phone have all been helpful. And everything Alexis said was spot-on about the therapy and medication making things a lot better."

"It usually is a combination of things that are helpful," Suhani says. "But the most important one is your willingness to try any of them at all. You did all this hard work to feel better. I'm so, so proud of you for that."

And I will do everything to make sure you never feel that awful again, she silently promises herself.

"Thanks. It was hard. I think on some level, it'll always be hard." Natasha swings her legs over the side of the bed. "Is it weird that I was a little reluctant to start medication? Even though you and Dad do this for a living? I love therapy, I always have, but for some reason when the team first told me about the Prozac, I wasn't sure if I wanted to do it."

"That's not weird at all. A lot of people feel that way," Suhani says. "It can be scary to take a medication. Were you worried it would affect your creativity?"

Natasha nods. "I thought it would mute me in some way, make it harder for me to do comedy. But hearing Alexis tell me how much it helped her gave me a push."

"That makes sense," Suhani says. "The chances are it'll make you more in control of your emotions and, hopefully, in a better place to create. And remember how Dad and I would always say that if someone's blood pressure or cholesterol was high, they'd get a pill for those? Same thing here. You're taking something to ensure you can be the healthiest you possible."

Even though Suhani's sitting on this uncomfortable bed and staring at her sister in scrubs and nonslip socks, she still can't fully accept that her little sister is a patient, like so many of the patients she's seen and treated over the years. When they're feeling better, Suhani's heard a variety of reactions about how they've felt about the ward.

Many can't wait to leave and say it was a useless experience for them. Some have been traumatized from the confinement. And then there are those few who say it was exactly what they needed. She never thought Natasha would be in that last category, but she's grateful to be wrong.

"So, I do have some news for you," Suhani says. "I spoke to Dr. Chan and she says you're ready to leave tomorrow!"

Natasha's face lights up. "Tomorrow? Really?"

"Really." Suhani hugs her.

You made it, she thinks, wanting to break out into a cheering routine. *You didn't let this break you.*

"So, what do you think is next? You know, after you leave?" Suhani asks.

"I'll keep taking the meds. Stick with the therapy."

But what about your career? Your future? Suhani wants to ask. The truth is, she's always felt a mixture of envy and awe toward Natasha for being able to do what she wants, be free in that way. But she also knows that if Natasha goes back to the life she had before she came here, there's a risk she'll continue to struggle.

But she doesn't want Natasha to think she's pushing her, so she keeps a smile on her face and says, "Sounds like a plan."

Natasha stares at her nonslip socks. She wraps her arms around her legs.

"Do you think there's something innately fucked up about me?" Natasha's voice is soft.

"What? No! Why would you say that?"

"I don't know. It's like for as long as I can remember, it's been hard for me to keep my emotions in control. Be the way other people expect me to be. And there are always these negative thoughts spiraling through my head. Even when I was a kid, I had them."

"That doesn't mean there's something fucked up about you." Suhani grabs Natasha's hand. "You have an illness. And you're getting help for it now. I'm just sorry you've been going through this alone for so long and that I was too blind to help you earlier."

"But what about all of us? Have you ever thought that there's maybe something that runs in our family?" Natasha asks.

"What do you mean? Mentally?" Suhani looks at her and wonders what she's put together.

"Sort of, yeah. We talked about our family histories in group therapy the other day and I started wondering. Nanima"—Natasha says, referring to Mom's mom, who passed away when Suhani was in high school—"always told me that Mom and I have a lot in common, even with our tempers and stuff. After being here, I wonder about Mom. She gets emotional so easily like I do and I remembered those drives she used to go on when we were little, how Dad tried to make them seem like no big deal, but we always knew. And Anuj has told me that his mind has gone to dark places sometimes. He's more relaxed than all of us, obviously, but even he's struggled."

Suhani has been wondering the same thing since she started her residency training. When she sat in lectures that covered everything from personality traits to marital dynamics to birth order, she couldn't help but link certain insights to her own family. She began putting things together that she never had before, like why she and her siblings were parented differently or what traits drew her and Zack to each other.

Natasha smiles. "I mean, I know you don't really get how it feels to hit a point so low that you're totally lost, but, yeah, I do wonder if there's something with our family that makes some of us prone to it."

Suhani bites her bottom lip. Natasha has no idea about the low points she's hit. Nobody does.

"Um, are you okay?" Natasha asks as she scans Suhani's face. "I know it's weird for me to ask you that, considering where I am right now, but still."

Suhani smiles. Now isn't the time to tell Natasha she's so tired of trying to be perfect all the time. What does being the good girl amount to, anyway? It doesn't protect you. It definitely doesn't ensure you'll be happy. Ever since she could remember, every victory gave her a brief, fleeting high. But the goalpost was always moving and she was soon chasing the next one. Perfect GPA, perfect body, perfect manners. She thought it would lead to a sense of security at some point. But all of it only continued to leave her in this limbo between achievement and the persistent, gnawing feeling that she's not good enough.

"I'm totally fine," Suhani says. "And regarding something running in our family, I do see your point."

Natasha peers at her the same way she did before, as if she knows Suhani is keeping something from her. But before she can say anything, Suhani changes the subject and they stick to safe topics for the rest of her visit: a funny joke Anuj made when he stopped by with Dad and Mom last night, how Natasha plans to stay in touch with her roommate, the quirks of the different nurses on the ward, and the excitement of her being out of here in twenty-four hours.

Twenty-Seven

Bina

Natasha is already waiting for Bina by the time she reaches the ward. No matter how often Bina sees her, she can't ever get used to the image of her daughter in these gray scrubs. Her pulse quickens at the thought of Natasha wearing her ratty Georgia State hoodie and sweat pants in a matter of hours. Who ever thought she would miss the disheveled clothing?

"*Beta*, I can't believe you'll be out of here soon." Bina gives her a hug and hands her two yogurt containers, which she still reuses for food storage. The habit started when she and Deepak moved to America and couldn't afford glass containers. The kids would sometimes get annoyed thinking they were opening a tub of yogurt, only to find leftover chole or a ball of dough.

"Mooooom," Natasha says, stretching out the word, pretending to be annoyed but smiling as she takes the dhokla. "You didn't need to bring me food. We're literally going home in an hour."

"And what if you got hungry during that time?" Bina says.

"I would have been fine." Natasha gazes around the room. "I guess this is our last time meeting here. Weird, right?"

"It is," Bina agrees.

She's surprised at how much she's started to enjoy showing up for visiting hours. Somehow, the confining nature of the ward has given her and Natasha the space to just be. This is no longer only a place for people who are mentally ill. It's a place where she's had some sense of understanding with her daughter for the first time in years. The structured environment distilled them down to their essentials, and during these visits, Natasha was both a daughter and a friend. They shared celebrity gossip. They laughed about Deepak's many quirks around the house, from his tendency to fall asleep watching *Shark Tank*; to calling several times, overwhelmed, when he went to the grocery store; to how, even though he'd never admit it out loud, he loved gossiping with them.

"Do you feel that being here helped you, *beta*?" Bina strokes Natasha's tangled curls. She resists the urge to talk about the You-Tube videos.

"I do. I know there's still a long way to go and staying better is going to take daily work," Natasha says. "But when I first got here, I felt like I was trapped, like this mood was a living thing and I was caught in its tight, unyielding grip. Now I can see that I was trapped in some ways but I was also tired. So tired. Tired of pretending I was fine. In a way, I was putting on this constant performance that I was okay enough. And it all caught up to me. But now it doesn't feel that way."

Bina stops herself from saying she knows exactly how Natasha felt and she wants to make sure Natasha never has to pretend she's fine again.

"You really made the most of your time here, *beta*," Bina says.

"It wasn't as terrible as I thought it'd be." Natasha pulls her hair into a ponytail. Bina ignores the urge to fix it for her. Her daughter's hair is a perfect match for her spirit: unruly, stubborn, unique. Hair that Bina spent hours pulling into neat braids until she discovered Natasha went to school and undid them. Hair that made beauticians at the threading salon murmur, *That's some difficult and tough hair*, which made Bina always say, *Yes, she's my tough girl so I expect nothing less.*

"I'm glad it wasn't as bad as you thought." Bina hugs Natasha. "So, Devi Auntie did want me to pass something along to you."

Bina tells Natasha about the internship. (Why don't they call it what it really is: cheap labor?)

Natasha gasps. "Oh my God! *The* late-night show? In LA?!"

"So you're interested?" Bina doesn't mean to sound so weary.

"*Yes.* I really am! I'll call Devi Auntie tonight."

Bina tries to ignore the different feelings building up in her. Happiness at her daughter's excitement. Fear at the thought of her leaving Atlanta. Relief at having her home soon.

"So you really want this, yes?" Bina asks.

"I do." Natasha clasps her hands together. "I really, really do. Thank you, Mom. I never thought you'd be okay with something like this."

Neither did I, Bina thinks.

"I just want you to be happy," she says.

Natasha smiles. "I feel . . . I feel like I've gotten to know a different part of you since I've been here."

"I agree," Bina says. She's about to say the car is parked right outside and that the second Dr. Chan puts in the discharge order, they'll leave that locked door forever. But something pushes Bina into another direction. And she can't ignore it.

"*Beta*, before we go"—Bina takes a deep breath—"there's something I should have told you a long time ago."

Natasha raises her eyebrows. "What?"

"I was in a place like . . . this many years ago."

"What? You were in a psych ward?" Natasha's face is confused as she processes Bina's words. "When?"

"Twice."

"Twice? Seriously?" Natasha's eyes widen.

"The first time was when I was pursuing my acting, in the middle of a rehearsal. I had gotten a really big role, the kind that could have made me a real star." Bina nods. "And then again, right after I gave birth to your sister."

"But . . ." Natasha shakes her head. "I don't . . . that doesn't . . . but you never . . ."

Bina blinks away tears. She pictures the horrified expressions of the other actors, the stern nurse who told her to be quiet, the thin, tall doctor who held the massive needle that was soon injected into her arm.

"I should have told you a long time ago. But Dad and I thought it was better that all of you not know. It was a really hard time for us. I hated everything: the hospital, the doctors, the medications they made me take."

"What happened? Did you try to hurt yourself, too?"

"No." Bina shakes her head and tries to think of the best way to explain that horrific time in her life, the time she's spent so many years trying to forget. "I always had thoughts going through my head that scared me. When I was younger, I pretended all that frantic energy came from another place altogether, like some outside force, as a way to make it seem more manageable. For so many years, I didn't know it had a name: anxiety. But while I was in rehearsal for a movie, a movie where I was opposite a very famous actor, I broke down. I think the doctor thought it was the stress of everything, but your dad and I are still not very sure. All I remember is that everything felt like a blur, and suddenly I got very scared.

I was yelling at people and convinced that there were dark shadows flying all around me. The next thing I knew, I was in an ambulance. They gave me a shot to calm me down. But it was so loud, so intense. The hospital stay was short—thankfully—but it was the scariest few days of my life.

"And then, after I had just given birth to your sister, it happened again. The thoughts, the room spinning out of control. The doctors thought there must have been some reaction with my hormones and the pregnancy. They tried to put me on this medication—your dad agreed with them—but it turned me into a zombie. I was supposed to take it every day and didn't want to breastfeed on it. It was a constant battle, with your dad and me, with the doctors, with my parents, with myself. God, what a hell of a time."

"I don't even know what to say." Natasha rests her head in her hands in a gesture of defeat and sadness.

Bina reaches forward and squeezes Natasha's arm. Natasha keeps her face buried in her palms. Around them, patients are meeting with their family members. For a brief moment, Bina wonders what their conversations are like, how they're all coping with the pain in their lives.

"So I've managed to make my Natasha quiet? Wow, I've accomplished the impossible." Bina laughs in an attempt to make some light of the situation.

But Natasha doesn't laugh back or even crack a smile. "Why didn't you ever tell us? Me?"

Bina considers this. Why didn't she just sit down with the kids and share this with them years ago? It would have all been out in the open and then they could have moved on.

"We thought we were protecting you," she says. "You have to understand, anything having to do with mental illness was so stigmatized in India back then. We think it's bad now, but it was much worse at that time. People who did know about what happened to me made me feel like I was cursed. Some of them even suggested certain prayers or rituals to make me 'cleansed.' And I've always been so scared I could have passed something down to the three of you. I guess Dad and I just wanted to move on from all this, start a new life. I quit acting after the first time. Not that I really had a choice. After everyone I was working with saw my"—she searches for the right word—"episode, I knew there was no way I'd ever be considered for a movie again. And then, after the second one, the psychiatrist said stress was a trigger, and I had to make sure to stick to a routine, not have a life where I'd be prone for this to happen again. Even with how tough all of it was, it's strange to say I'm one of the lucky ones. I was able to return back to myself within a week and I've been more than fine ever since."

Bina remembers the rise of excitement and fear that sprang in her when she and Deepak learned she was pregnant with Natasha, then Anuj. Deepak clutched her shoulder while the ultrasound technician rubbed jelly on her stomach and a hazy gray, black, and white figure appeared on the screen. Bina stuck the ultrasound pictures on her fridge even though she didn't know what exactly she was looking at. In Bombay, it was considered bad luck to show anything related to the baby, but Bina had seen women in soap operas share their ultrasounds and she loved the idea. Years later, when Suhani was in medical school, she taught Bina how to make sense of the pictures.

"I can't imagine how people in India must have reacted," Natasha says. "You and Dad don't even let me tell our extended family there that I'm sad or pissed off. It's like any discussion of emotional health with other people is so off-limits even though Dad's a psychiatrist."

"It is. And that's been a problem there for too long. A problem that we've carried over here. You've been through a more difficult time than I have," Bina says.

"I don't know about that," Natasha says.

"I do." Bina places a firm hand over hers. "Mine came out of nowhere, twice, and, yes, it was very scary. But I'm realizing you've always carried around this weight with you, haven't you?"

Bina repeats her last question in Gujarati, a habit she's had since moving to America. Every time a question holds significant emotional weight, she repeats it in Gujarati.

Natasha stares at the table. With her free hand, she traces the swirly wood patterns. Her nails are chipped with black polish. Bina finds comfort in this, her daughter's nails looking the way they always do, done and undone.

"I guess, yeah." Natasha looks up at Bina. Her eyes are moist. "I'm so sorry you went through that, Mommy."

Mommy. Natasha hasn't called her that in years. Bina feels herself choke on tears.

"It's okay, baby. I'm fine. I just hate that you haven't been . . . for so long. And were dealing with it alone."

Natasha slumps in the stiff wooden chair. "Being here has helped me realize that I've always felt bad about not being happy . . . because you and Dad went through so much worse."

Bina sighs. Just the other day, Mira had brought up that Pooja mentioned something about being depressed. *I had asked her, what do you have to be depressed about?* Mira scoffed. *All of us who had to deal with everything when we were coming to this country, we have the right to be depressed.*

Now Bina wonders how many times she and her friends made those types of comments and what the impact has been over the

years. Instead of encouraging growth or resilience, did it only result in their kids keeping things from them?

Natasha nods. "I felt guilty about being so low when you and
Dad have given us everything. And then I'd hate myself on top of
that, then get frustrated for feeling all these different things. It's
been that way my whole life, this downward spiral that I can fall
into at any second. Dr. Chan helped me realize that my thoughts
have negative patterns. She thinks I need cognitive behavioral therapy to help with my disruptive thoughts."

"I see," Bina says, trying to find the right boundary between being fully supportive and giving her honest opinion, a boundary she's
struggled with when communicating with her daughters throughout their lives. She wants to be the type of mother who can say, *Yes,
do whatever you think is best, I'm here for you.* But she's conflicted. One
part of her is worried that Natasha's focusing on her thoughts too
much may not be helpful, but then another part of her is proud of
her daughter for taking the time to understand herself.

"I still can't believe you've been in a place like this and I had no
idea," Natasha says. "I don't think it's really going to sink in and feel
real. I just can't picture any of it when I try."

"Don't try," Bina says. "What's important is that we focus
on you."

"So, are you going to tell Suhani and Anuj?" Natasha's voice is
crisp.

Bina nods.

"I don't even know how to process this about you." Natasha
gazes into the distance, in the direction of the single large-screen
television that all the patients have to share.

Bina sees the layers of questions behind Natasha's words. She
had the same ones when she made the shift from Ma being her

mother to Ma being a human being, capable of having flaws and making mistakes like anyone else.

"I know, *beta*. It's a lot to take in, especially out of the blue." Bina sits back. There's a chance that Natasha will tell Suhani and Anuj about this the second Bina leaves. Or maybe she won't. Maybe she'll keep this between them.

But for now, Bina won't focus on that. Her daughter wants her to sit here and be supportive. Such a simple wish. And she can ignore her own desires to share her doubts and fears about Natasha's health. She can sit here, in this crowded dining hall, the sound of people in heated conversations around them.

"I'm so sorry, Mom." Natasha's voice wavers. She takes an empty foam cup and starts ripping it into tiny pieces. "I always gave you so much crap. And I'm sorry. It wasn't fair."

"No, no, *beta*." Bina clutches Natasha's small, dry hands in hers. "You didn't know. And it's your job to be a child. My child."

She moves over to Natasha's side of the table and pulls her daughter close to her, never wanting to let go.

Twenty-Eight

Deepak

Deepak slips under the comforter and lies on his side. The gold glow from Bina's bedside light splashes onto his pillow.

He reaches across the bed and touches her long red nightgown. "You did the right thing."

"What are you talking about?" She removes her black-framed reading glasses.

"Telling Natasha. We should have told all the kids years ago."

"You've always said that," Bina says, "but I just never saw the point. And, yes, I am glad I told her today, but now what? Now we are all supposed to go to this family therapy"—she does a back-and-forth waving motion with her hand—"and share our most personal things with a stranger? Have we really done so poorly as parents that we have to put ourselves through that?"

Deepak tucks his hand under his head and stares at the spinning ceiling fan. "I don't understand how you see therapy the way you do when your husband and daughter do it for a living."

But that's not entirely true. In some ways, he does understand. Whether or not she wants to accept it, Bina is still her mother's daughter. Being anything less than perfect to a stranger—even needing a stranger in the first place—just isn't what she was raised to do.

"It's not that I'm against it. Natasha should talk to someone if that would help her." Bina puts her book facedown on her wooden bedside table, next to a sandalwood candle, notebook, and a new issue of *Vogue India*. "I don't understand why we need to be a part of it, that's all. I mean, sharing things with this person that I wouldn't even share with Devi or Anita, it's just humiliating. It sounds like the type of thing that only white people do."

Years ago, Deepak's parents warned him that a woman like Bina was "too bold" and "too complicated," terms he'd later learn were used for women who refused to cave to certain expectations. *She's not from the same world as you*, his mother said the night before he and Bina eloped. Later, after Bina was admitted to the psychiatric hospital, his mother took that as her grand I-told-you-so moment. When Deepak told her not to call him until she was ready to accept his wife, his mother uttered, *You have no idea what you're getting yourself into*.

In a way, she was right. Nobody knows who the person they marry will become. Nobody knows how both of you will be shaped by the things that happen to you. All you have is the faith that this is the person you want to navigate that uncertainty with.

"What's really scaring you?" Deepak squints and waits for Bina to tell him she's not answering that. She hates it when he asks these types of questions right before bed. *Don't talk to me like I'm one of your patients*, she says, half-amused, half-annoyed. But the truth is, he hasn't asked enough questions like this recently. Somewhere along the way, he started taking her for granted. He stopped trying the way he used to.

Bina sinks into her pillow. "I'm scared I've done something to cause Natasha to be this way."

"Of course you haven't. You've been such a caring and loving mother." Deepak scoots over to her and studies her face. The lines of concern on her forehead. Her skin, still as smooth as the day they met, thanks to a combination of genetics and routine turmeric face masks she started during her acting days.

"Then why doesn't it feel that way? Why does it instead seem that I did everything I possibly could, sacrificed as much as I could, and this is still how things ended up for her?"

"Because it's complicated. And it's normal to want an explanation for all of it, but that doesn't mean you have to blame yourself." Deepak refrains from adding that these are perfect points to cover during family therapy. Instead, he pulls Bina closer to his chest. "It's okay." He says it over and over again. "It's going to be okay."

Bina's voice cracks. "You've always been able to get through to her better than I could."

"That's not true. We just have a different relationship," Deepak says.

And even with their bond and his job, he still didn't realize how much she was struggling. He pictures Natasha, then Suhani and Anuj. Whenever he thinks of the kids, he sees them as all their ages at the same time. They're babies with determined fists. They're in middle school clutching brown paper bags. They're signing checks and scrolling through their phones.

"It is true. I used to get so frustrated when she and I would argue all day. Then you'd come home after being gone for twelve hours and she'd run into your arms. I would think, 'Wow, in some ways, the parent who isn't here gets to be the favorite! Isn't that nice?'" Bina sits up, her cheeks flushed. "I was so jealous."

"Jealous? Of me?" Deepak asks.

"Oh yeah! Did you know I realized during one of the Chats Over Chai meetings that I've been jealous of you a lot? You've always been able to do these exciting and meaningful things for people every day. You could be unavailable and uninterrupted.

Even when we went to your doctor parties, people would tell me how all the patients and staff love you. I was so proud and wanted our kids to have the same—big lives with big impact for other people. I just didn't realize that it would take a toll on me at some point. But at some point, I started asking myself, 'What's so wrong with you that you couldn't manage to do anything?' and that voice wouldn't stop."

"Nothing's ever been wrong with you," Deepak says. "And all of us—the kids and I—are who we are because of what you've done for us. And now, with your group, you're doing something bigger than us."

"I don't know." Bina hugs her knees and rocks back and forth. Deepak pictures her in this exact type of pose as a little girl, curled up in bed with a novel. "For so long, I had to try to add things to my life so it felt like I had something that was my own. Do you remember that one time, when I lost it after you asked me to take an acting class when the kids were at school? You were trying to be helpful but it made me even more angry that I always had to be the one to squeeze my passions into small bursts of time, while you had long stretches to think and help and expand. I never had the luxury to just take hours for myself because I had to cut sandwiches or pour detergent into the laundry machine or wrap birthday gifts or hold someone's hand at the pediatrician's office."

Deepak soaks in her words. Once, when the kids were little, she told him she couldn't even use the bathroom alone. Every second, someone needed something from her.

"I never saw it that way," Deepak says. "I'm sorry."

People sometimes assume men don't have strong emotions, but that's not true. Deepak has plenty of them. He has plenty of regrets, too. He saw his wife every single day and still didn't know what she was carrying inside. He didn't say the things he should have said to her. He forgot that appreciation is a vaccine for resentment. Now, as he digs under the layers of Bina's emotional debris, under her irritation and sadness and anger, he uncovers her fear that she as an individual no longer matters.

But he can fix this. He can be there for her in the ways she needs him to be. And he has to find a way to make sure things are better for others, too.

"It's fine," Bina says. "Actually, Chats Over Chai has helped me move past some of this."

An idea materializes in his mind as he processes her words. He lingers on it for a few seconds and makes a quick note in his phone before he forgets.

"I know it has. And it has helped so many others." Deepak puts his phone away and faces Bina. "You really have built something so powerful."

"Eh, I don't know about that," she says.

"I do," Deepak says.

She doesn't go on her drives anymore. Instead, their evenings are spent together. Sometimes they sit side by side as she watches something on Netflix and he reads on his iPad. Other times, they lose themselves in the latest Bollywood film.

"Yes, well, at least if *Samachar in America* shuts us down, I learned some things from it," Bina says.

"We're not going to let that happen." Deepak wraps his arms around her as if to seal the promise.

Twenty-Nine

Natasha

"Families take on personalities of their own. And here our goal is to look at your family as a system, where each member is shaped by the others." Dr. Eze keeps her tone firm and clinical as she continues to give an explanation of family therapy and what they should all expect from their first session.

Sweat pools under Natasha's arms. Even though everything Dr. Eze says is clear, she still can't believe she's sitting here. It takes all her self-control to not bite her nails or, better yet, run out the door.

They're all sitting in a circle. Mom, Dad, and Natasha are on one side of Dr. Eze; Suhani, Anuj, and Zack are on the other. Mom is judging the room's appearance, which, to be fair, is hard not to judge. The wall décor hasn't been changed in at least two decades, from the threatening DON'T DO DRUGS poster to the picture of a man at the top of a mountain that reads PERSISTENCE PAYS OFF. A faded rug with pink and purple flowers covers most of the dusty floor.

Dr. Eze passes around copies of the genogram they helped fill out during the intake appointment. Natasha stares at the pictorial representation of their family's lineage, made up of circles and squares, starting with her grandparents and ending at everyone in the room. She used to see similar-looking charts in high school biology class when they learned about dominant and recessive traits.

"Where do we start?" Natasha asks after Dr. Eze is finished.

"How about with you?" Dr. Eze crosses her legs. She's wearing a leopard-print blouse with a bow, red pencil skirt, and black high-heeled, pointy-toed boots that remind Natasha of Catwoman.

"Well, obviously I've had quite the past few weeks." Natasha flashes a shaky smile that disappears once she makes eye contact with Mom, Dad, Anuj, Suhani, and Zack. They all seem to be in a bit of a daze. Or maybe she's the one who's dazed. Is this really a good idea? What if they all just end up arguing or, worse, being awkward and not saying anything? Natasha wants to tell Dr. Eze that her family never sits around and talks like this. They prefer to communicate the normal way, by bottling up their true feelings until one of them explodes.

"Of course," Dr. Eze says. "How do you feel now that it's been several days since you were discharged from the hospital?"

Natasha shrugs. "Better, I guess. It's still really weird to know I got to a point so low. But I had a lot of time there to think and learn about myself."

Dr. Eze nods and jots something down in a sky-blue notebook. "Is there anything from your experience that you would be open to sharing with us?"

Natasha mentally scans the blur of things that happened during her week on the unit: the conversations with Alexis, medication, group therapy, the visit from her friends, and, of course, everything Mom told her. She hasn't even been able to fully process all of it. Sometimes, when she pictures the stiff bed or the nurse handing her Prozac in a tiny plastic cup or Mom waiting at the wooden lunch table, it still feels like a dream.

"I guess." Natasha draws an imaginary circle on the rug with her foot. "I realized that for most of my life, I never felt like I fit in with my family. Sure, I was popular in school and always had friends, but there was always this part of me that felt like an outcast. One of the reasons I love writing comedy is because it lets me make something out of that feeling, something meaningful. But over the past months, when everything fell apart, I was reminded of how different I am from my family. Certain things seem to affect me more than they do my brother and sister. And I don't want the stuff a girl my age, from my type of family, is supposed to want. I've felt like they'd just be better off without me because all I do is cause problems."

"Has anyone said something along those lines?" Dr. Eze asks.

Mom starts to speak but Dr. Eze gently says, "Let's hear Natasha out."

Dad puts his hand on Mom's arm and whispers, "Remember we talked about this."

Even though Mom nods, Natasha can tell she's practically about to burst from having to keep so many things to herself.

"No, none of them has ever said they'd be better off without me," Natasha says. "It's just the way I've always felt. On the psych unit, I realized I've been living a double life, in a way. Pretending to be fine on the outside—especially to them—but hating myself on the inside. I guess I got used to it. I even pretended to be premed my first two years of college! It got everyone off my back for a little while, reassured them that I was doing what they thought was acceptable."

"So you lied to make things easier?" Dr. Eze doesn't ask the question with judgment but more with curiosity.

"Yeah, I mean, I've gotten used to lying, in a way. I know that sounds bad but it's become default for me to keep parts of myself in hiding. I assumed I'd always lie to my family . . . forever. Because if I didn't, I'd be out."

"It's understandable to feel hurt if you think that the people you love don't appreciate you for who you are. And holding on to all that and lying had to be really tiring," Dr. Eze says.

"It was. It is. So exhausting," Natasha says.

"Anyone have thoughts on what Natasha's shared?" Dr. Eze asks.

"I'm so sorry you've felt not good enough and accepted. That's not fair and you shouldn't have had to go through that," Suhani says. "And I know this might not be what you expect, but we get it. We really do. Anuj and I have felt that way at times, too."

"I don't think you can compare the way I've been judged to the way you guys have," Natasha says to her sister. "You had people who believed in you, revered you. All the aunties, teachers, and relatives told me how pretty and perfect you were and then how sweet and sensitive Anuj was. I knew what they were thinking underneath all that: Natasha's the misfit."

"I don't think anybody thought that," Anuj says.

"Oh, please. Some people straight up told me. You think desi adults keep their opinions to themselves?" Natasha challenges. Her brother can be so naïve. "Y'all just don't understand. You guys get the compliments. I get the criticism."

"Now, Natasha," Dr. Eze holds up her hands. "Going off how you just said they don't understand, I'm wondering if anyone in your family feels similarly, that maybe you don't always under-stand them. Would anyone like to add to that?"

"I would," Suhani offers. "Natasha, it's hard to hear you say that you're the only one who's misunderstood. I've always felt like nobody else here gets what it's like to have this constant pressure to set a perfect example, be everything all the time. It's exhausting. So exhausting."

At first, Suhani's face softens. But then she straightens her shoulders and smooths out the folds in her emerald-green dress. It's as if a neuron in her brain fired off and commanded her to go back to being poised Suhani. "My point is, we're all dealing with something. And you've inspired me to be more open and honest. Bold."

"Bold? I've inspired you to be bold?" Natasha asks, thinking back to what her friends said.

"Of course you have," Suhani says. "Every time I've been worried about something at work or doubted myself, I've asked myself, 'What would Natasha do?'"

"I didn't know that," Natasha whispers.

Even though she's always wondered how many hours Suhani has spent studying and planning and caring, she never thought she played a part in any of it. During Suhani's intern year, she once called Dad and said she couldn't stop worrying about her patients even on her days off. Dad seemed surprised, but Natasha wasn't at all. Her sister was always fueled by an endless supply of self-doubt, never convinced anything she did was enough.

"And I'm sorry you've always dealt with so much pressure," Natasha adds. "You're right. I don't know what that's like."

"I never even get a chance to speak up with you two always talking," Anuj says. "I have no choice but to be the quiet one because you both always have so much going on!"

"I can see that. And I'm sorry for that, too," Natasha says as she thinks back to all the times Anuj has been more like a spectator to their conversations. She assumed he didn't want to say anything, not that he felt he couldn't.

Natasha hasn't apologized this many times in a single week, let alone a single conversation. Why didn't she ever put herself in her siblings' shoes? Why did she always assume she was the only one struggling?

"It's fine." Anuj shrugs. "I'm just telling you because Suhani's right. Why do you think I went to Cornell? I could have gone to Tech or Emory, but there's a reason I wanted, needed, to get away."

"I understand," Natasha says, realizing how much power there is in the simplest words. *I understand. I hear you. I'm sorry.* She thinks back to all the times she's played around with the idea of moving far away, growing new roots in a place that's just her own.

"You never told us that, Anuj," Dad says as he and Mom glance at each other.

"You didn't give me a chance!" Anuj throws his hands in the air. "All of you think that because I don't say much, because I don't ever raise any hell, that I'm fine. Well, I'm not. I deal with stuff, too. And maybe I've always felt like I had to be a certain way for you all to accept me."

"What way is that?" Suhani asks, seeming just as surprised as their parents to hear this.

"Calm. Chill. The one who goes with the flow," Anuj says. "And, yeah, I can roll with the punches more than y'all can, but that doesn't mean things don't bother me."

"Your family is listening." Dr. Eze taps her pen against her notepad. "Is there anything you'd like to say to them?"

Anuj doesn't even pause to think before he says, "Stop treating me like a baby. Stop telling me to be a doctor. Stop talking over me. Just stop. Please."

Mom and Dad glance at each other. Suhani sighs and says, "We really didn't know."

"I know you didn't," Anuj says.

"Oh, this is all my fault." Mom clasps her hands together as if she's praying for forgiveness.

Everyone is in awe that Mom's been able to stay quiet until now. Natasha sees Dad sigh with relief.

"What do you mean by that?" Dr. Eze asks. Natasha's impressed by how Dr. Eze can receive all her family's emotional statements with the perfect mixture of curiosity and compassion. The past weeks have given her a newfound appreciation for mental health providers. She wonders how many times Suhani and Dad have done this for other people.

"I'm the reason my kids have felt pressure and doubt and the need to keep quiet about what's going on with them. I came to this country so scared, with such a chip on my shoulder because I had to let go of my big career. I had to prove to my parents I made the right choice. Then we settled here and I still keep trying to prove to everyone that I'm doing everything right, that I'm a good wife and mom."

"You are those things," Natasha says. She hears murmurs of agreement from her siblings.

Mom shakes her head. "Am I really if this is how my children feel?"

"Well, Bina, I think it may be worth hearing from them." Dr. Eze gives Mom a thoughtful nod. "They all did just learn about a pretty big part of your past."

"Yes, they did," Bina says.

The night Natasha came home from the hospital, Mom and Dad sat with Natasha, Suhani, Zack, and Anuj at the formal dining table and told them about what happened to Mom in India, the real reason she left acting. Everyone gave Mom a hug, but only Zack and

Anuj asked her for more details. Suhani stayed quiet. Even now, she's staring at the floor, her fists clenched.

Dr. Eze notices it, too. "Suhani, can you share what you're thinking?"

"To be honest, I don't know," Suhani says. "During my first year of residency, I learned about how when a woman's stressed during pregnancy and after birth, that stress can potentially be passed down to her baby in different ways. I wondered if something happened with my mom that made me always so on edge. And now I guess I understand why she pushed me so hard my entire life, but—" Her voice catches. "I just wish I knew because I often felt so alone, so under pressure, so scared to let her and my dad down."

"I'm so sorry about that, *beta*," Mom says. "I really am."

"You don't have to apologize." Suhani's voice is soft. "I understand why you kept it to yourself. I just wish I knew, that we all did. I think we all would have been more honest with ourselves if you were more honest with us."

Natasha can tell those words sting Mom because her face crumples up as if she's about to cry.

"I didn't do the right thing by keeping it from you." Tears well in Mom's eyes. "Your dad told me to but I was too stubborn."

"It's okay, Mom. I know you were protecting us in your own way. And now I know you're even stronger than I thought," Suhani says.

Natasha realizes that it's possible for her to wish her family was different and at the same time know that they're all doing the best they can with what they have.

"Bina, I want to go back to the point you made earlier about proving something to everyone." Dr. Eze clasps her hands on her knees. "You had to prove yourself to your parents and that makes a lot of sense. Families often have patterns, especially when it comes to communication. The way our parents spoke to us influences how we speak to our own children."

"I never really thought of that until now, but I do see it." Mom's voice wavers. She squeezes her eyes shut, as though she's staring directly into the sun. "My mom and I argued a lot. She always thought I was a difficult child. And she warned me that I'd understand one day when I had kids. She was so right."

Mom faces Dad, who is already staring at her, on the brink of tears. Natasha didn't realize until now how fortunate she is to have a father who so freely embraces his emotions, even if that wasn't what he was brought up to do.

Mom sighs. "And then after I met Deepak, I was this rising actress, choosing a man for love. I was so determined to live differently than she did, with her concerns about money and appearances and status. But I ended up being more like her than ever. I'm sorry, Natasha, for passing that to you."

"It's okay, Mommy."

Mommy. Natasha's voice breaks as the word escapes her mouth. A fat tear dribbles down her cheek. Mom gets up and walks to her.

A ripple of sadness passes through Natasha as she presses her face against Mom's soft shoulder.

Usually, Natasha has fixed images of Mom that come to mind whenever she thinks of her. Mom, adding cumin to a pan of simmering vegetables. Mom, sitting at the edge of Natasha's bed, her voice strained as she tells Natasha to not make the same mistakes she did. Mom, yelling when she found out Natasha was drinking alcohol in high school. Mom, demanding Natasha think of how bad she will look as a mother if she doesn't straighten up.

And then there are others. Mom, telling Anita Auntie on the

phone that Natasha is vibrant and funny, the light of their family. Mom, stretching out on the recliner next to Natasha, watching a comedy special with her, and really understanding the talent and work it took for the comedian to create that. Mom, a tight smile on her face that doesn't quite reach her eyes as she serves chai and snacks to guests who don't bother to ask her how she's doing, who she hopes to become.

But now Natasha sees that in the back-and-forth web of criticism and companionship that she and Mom have always been caught in, she never thought to consider the life Mom left behind, the parts of herself she gave up along the way. Mom didn't strike her as a woman who ran away from anything.

"It must have been so difficult." Dr. Eze gazes at Mom. "Leaving your family, your career, your country."

"It was. I don't know what I would have done without Deepak and then the kids." Tears pool in Mom's eyes. Before she goes back to her chair, she reaches for a tissue from the box on the table behind her.

Dr. Eze looks at the genogram she gave them a copy of at the beginning of the appointment. "You and Deepak went through things that were traumatic, many of which forced you to suppress your emotions just to get through. Many children of immigrants inherit that trauma in various forms. Some of them want lives that look nothing like their parents' as a way to protect themselves."

Natasha is grateful that their therapist gets it. One of her parents' fears about coming to family therapy was that their provider wouldn't understand the cultural context of their situation. Even Dr. Jenkins used to tell Natasha to stop talking to her family if they were bothering her so much. Natasha didn't know how to explain that it just didn't work that way in desi families. Like so many things, Alexis was spot-on about this.

"I think I tried to protect myself that way," Suhani says. "I saw my mom being resentful and just doing things for others for years. She pushed me to make sure I'd be successful, never dependent on anyone. And I thought if I went out with a guy as different from my dad as possible, I'd make sure to have as different of a marriage from my parents as possible. But at the same time, I chose my ex because he checked off all those approval boxes: doctor, Indian, et cetera. So even though I thought I was following my own path, I was really still giving in to these expectations. And then that person didn't make me happy, at all."

She glances at Zack, who has been quiet this entire appointment, and wants to tell him how much she appreciates his being here. His wavy brown hair is grown out more than usual and splays out in every direction. If it wasn't for his coral button-down shirt and dark jeans, he would look like he'd just woken up.

Suhani reaches for his hand. "When I met Zack, I think I didn't feel like I deserved to be happy. I got scared. And I turned to the only thing that's ever helped me avoid thinking: work. I've used work and accomplishments as an armor. I'd gotten way too good at keeping my guard up, holding everything inside, and it's cost me a lot."

Natasha feels something in her shift. It takes her several seconds to process that it's the image she's always had of her sister. Her beautiful, intelligent, accomplished sister has been carrying around pain for years.

"Zack?" Dr. Eze motions to him. "Thoughts?"

He's leaning forward, his elbows propped on his slim thighs. It's hard to tell whether he's upset or just processing everything Suhani is saying.

"I've always known that about you," he tells Suhani. "It often seemed like nothing was going to convince you that you deserved to be happy and successful."

Suhani holds her face in her delicate hands. Her engagement ring winks when it catches the light. "I never felt like I deserved anything I got and I was convinced that at any second, it could all be taken away. I remember I used to even get mad when Mom would ask what you were eating when I worked late. I took it as her expecting me to be some traditional Indian wife, like she was for my dad, when really, she was just being caring."

Anuj exchanges an uneasy glance with Natasha. Maybe all three of them inherited the seeds of their parents' regrets, but they bloomed in each of them differently.

"I think you absorbing yourself in work and shutting down at home was really hard for me because it reminded me of my dad." Zack's knuckles are white as he grips his hair. "He used the hospital and alcohol to cope with his issues. And my mom and sisters would yell but I'd just go into my room and turn up the music. Withdraw."

"So, you felt some of those scary feelings from childhood coming back?" Dr. Eze asks.

Zack nods.

"It's okay." Dr. Eze's voice is gentle. "Sometimes marriage can do that, especially at the beginning. It can bring back memories from our own parents' marriage and then we can replay out those dynamics from our childhoods because they helped us survive in the past."

Zack slumps forward. Natasha's never seen him like this, sad to the point of hopelessness. She wants to hug her brother-in-law and tell him everything will be okay, the way he's done for her so many times. But she knows that even though they're all here together, this is something he and Suhani need to navigate.

"I'm sorry." Suhani reaches out to grip his arm. "That's awful. I never should have put you in a position where you could feel that kind of pain. I should have talked to you about how I was feeling instead of closing myself off more."

"I should have talked to you more, too," Zack says.

"We all should have talked to each other more," Dad says, his voice soft. Gray stubble dots his chin.

"What do you mean?" Dr. Eze asks.

"I've done things to try and protect my family. And sometimes that's meant staying quiet. But there's no good that's come from that. I should have known that after spending years telling my patients to be open and honest." Dad adjusts his chair so it's facing Mom. Natasha fidgets with the strings on her hoodie.

"I wanted to be a poet. A full-time poet." Dad smiles at the thought. "The reason I even met your mom is because I was outside that theater that night for a poetry reading and her play was after that."

"What? You're serious?" Anuj says. "When I told you I loved poetry, you acted like you had no interest in it."

"I know," Dad says. "I buried that part of me years ago. I did what I had to in order to support your mom and, later, all of us. But when I was growing up and my parents would sell vegetables from sunrise to sunset, I always dreamed of writing poems, reading them to audiences. My parents and brother told me I was crazy. Maybe that's why I've always been easier on Natasha. I understand how it feels for your goals to not make sense, to you, to the people who love you."

Natasha can't speak because her thoughts are in a tight knot. Everyone's looking at Dad with an intense focus, as if they can also feel the emotional tectonic plates of their family shifting while he's speaking. Natasha clenches her fists as she pictures a younger version of him hunched over a notebook and pouring out his most intimate thoughts onto a blank page. Picturing her parents when they were younger, long before she and her siblings existed, always overwhelms her. They had full lives. They had dreams and conversations and fears she never knew about.

"In India, nobody asked us how we were doing emotionally," Dad says. "We just had to keep going and doing what had to be done. If someone was struggling, they were told to pray extra or do some religious ritual. My family never accepted that I wanted to become a psychiatrist, so maybe, somewhere inside, I got caught up with proving something to them, too, and I lost sight of what I believed in the first place. But you kids are showing us another way."

Dr. Eze clears her throat. "You're all breaking the patterns of the generations before you by being here."

"You've showed us a lot, too, Dad," Natasha says.

"We just wanted you all to be happy." Dad's eyes are red.

Within seconds, Mom and Dad envelop Natasha in a tight hug. Hot tears stream down her face. Nothing compares to the safety and warmth that comes from her parents' embrace.

"I know." Natasha says it over and over again. "I know."

Thirty

Suhani

Roshan started changing months into our relationship. But it was so subtle at first that I thought I was overreacting whenever he did things."

Suhani rips off a piece of garlic bread from the warm loaf and dips it into marinara sauce. The impending conversation and her long day has her craving comfort food.

"What kind of things?" Zack folds his hands together and stares at her with intense focus.

Suhani's pulse throbs in her head. Where does she start in telling Zack about what happened? For a second, she wonders if her hesitation means she isn't ready. But then she pictures Zack during family therapy, the crestfallen look on his face when he talked about his dad. Keeping things to themselves is what got them to this point.

They're sitting across from each other at their tiny round dining table, the only one they could find that fit in the space between their kitchen and living room. Suhani's initial idea was for them to go to Nuevo Laredo tonight and talk everything out over jalapeño margaritas and enchiladas. But she's relieved they opted for the quiet of the apartment. Their apartment. She heated up spaghetti and thawed garlic bread from Trader Joe's, a meal that would make both of their mothers shake their heads with vehement disapproval. Three candles flicker in the middle of the table.

"It's okay, honey. You can tell me anything." Zack squeezes her hand. "Everything."

Her breathing slows down. Suhani is reminded of how, from their very first conversation, Zack instilled a sense of safety in her. She could be herself with this man—her true, flawed self. Somewhere along the way, she lost sight of that. Instead of telling him everything years ago, she tucked her past inside herself and hoped it would shrink with time. But pain was a seed and burying it only helped it grow.

"Things were fine with Roshan. Great, even. And then all of a sudden, we had this terrible fight that I thought happened because we were both stressed with finals," Suhani says. "He started yelling at me, like, really yelling. I was in shock because he had never spoken like that before, no matter how heated our arguments got. He apologized after and begged me to forgive him, said he was really worried about his evaluations from his clinical rotations. And then for a while, we were fine again. It was like it never happened. He went back to being his sweet and caring self, the person I thought I knew."

When things were good with Roshan, they were really good. Suhani had dated a few guys by then—all of them sweet and caring—but none of them sent her on an emotional high like Roshan did.

"But then weeks later, he yelled again," she says. "And again. I didn't realize then that he escalated each time. He started using curse words and eventually progressed to a lot of name-calling."

Suhani's hands shake as Roshan's words ring in her ears. "I

know how irrational this is going to sound, but I was able to pretend that all that behavior came from another person altogether, the wounded Roshan, not really the guy I was dating."

"It's not irrational at all. You compartmentalized," Zack says. "You put those feelings and that part of him away."

The tension in Suhani's chest starts to unravel as she soaks in her husband's words. She didn't realize how badly she needed to hear that: the way she felt was valid.

"Did it stay that way?" Zack's voice is soft. "Normal, then explosive, then normal again?"

That's the exact language Zack once used when he told Suhani how his dad was: normal, then explosive. He, Barbara, and his sisters walked on eggshells whenever his dad came home from work, not knowing which version of him they'd get. One Dr. Kaplan took them out for ice cream, made corny jokes, and was devoted to his patients. The other Dr. Kaplan threw glasses that shattered on the tiled kitchen floor, screamed until his face was beet red, and left the house for hours, reeking of vodka when he returned.

Suhani sees now that things are a lot clearer when someone only offers you their worst parts. When things are clearly terrible, you leave. When things are great, you stay. When your relationship becomes a pendulum between terrible and great, you sway with it, infused with enough hope to see which way it'll go.

"It stayed that way for a little while." Suhani takes a sip of her Cabernet. "But then it eventually got to a point where it was explosive more often than it wasn't. So many things could set Roshan off: if I missed his calls, wore a skirt he thought was too short, or was hugging a guy friend too much. Sometimes he'd admit to being paranoid or jealous and then say it was because his mom left his dad. When he tied it to his childhood trauma, that made me feel awful. I told myself that I could love him out of it, fix that pain for him. I thought I was in so deep already and that we had already made it through so much, so I could continue to tough it out for the both of us. A twisted part of me took it as some sort of badge of honor."

"Were you ever able to call him out about the way he was behaving?" Zack asks.

"Multiple times." Suhani's mind jumps back to the times she confronted Roshan in his dark, cramped apartment. "He'd tell me that no relationship was perfect, that we had so much between us that was worth fighting for, and then he'd always turn it back around to how I never wanted a relationship like my parents' where one person had to give up their career, so this is a part of what comes with a more 'equal' one."

"He used your parents' marriage to justify what he did?" Zack's face is full of disbelief. "That is so manipulative. What an asshole."

"I know," Suhani agrees. "And I believed him. His reasoning worked on me."

"I bet it did. He sounds like he was really smart and knew exactly how to get to you."

"He did," Suhani agrees. "I fell for his explanations and promises to be better every single time. I somehow convinced myself that this was a challenge we had to make it through. Isn't that so fucked up?"

That was the most pathetic part to her: she continued to love him. She treated his behavior as though it was some type of illness that just needed the right treatment. On the outside, she wore the mask of a strong, confident woman, the kind who was in a loving relationship and on the way to rising in her career.

"I didn't realize until our family therapy session how big a role timing played in everything. Roshan and I met right when I started feeling a little jaded with medicine, with the power structure and discrimination. I was always so scared that I didn't belong in that world. And then he came in the picture. Suddenly, people at UCLA revered us," Suhani says. "When the aunties back home heard, I knew that this was the type of guy I was supposed to end up with."

"And you didn't tell your family the truth." Zack refills her wine, which makes a hissing sound in her bulbous glass.

"No. I was embarrassed. Can you believe that? I was embarrassed about him behaving that way." Suhani stares at the mint-green place mat. "During residency, I read about how some people try to make their partners feel as low as possible so they aren't abandoned by them."

"He wanted to bring you down so you'd stay," Zack says.

"Subconsciously, yes," Suhani says. A weight collects on her sternum. This is it. This is the last piece of her history she's tried to forget for years. "I found out I was pregnant several weeks before he and I planned to go away for a short vacation. On the last night of our trip, when I was going to tell him the news, we got into yet another fight because he thought our waiter at dinner was hitting on me. It seemed like one of our usual arguments at first. But things escalated and before I knew it, his hands were around my neck. I suddenly realized I was struggling to breathe, that there was this pain and pressure. It felt like I was watching it from outside myself. He even seemed shocked after he loosened his grip. He kept saying he was sorry but I didn't listen. I just got in the car and sped back to my apartment. That week, I went to Planned Parenthood and then my dean's office to take an official leave of absence. I left my work, my patients, a group project I was leading, and curled up in bed for what felt like weeks. I blocked Roshan's number and ignored all his e-mails. Even after I recovered physically, I knew I'd never be the same. I wasn't who I thought I was. I wasn't the perfect example for Natasha or Anuj or the one who would make my parents' sacrifices worth it."

Suhani was always a split self. There's the Suhani everyone sees—accomplished, put together—and there's the Suhani brewing under the surface: broken, racked with doubt.

"Oh, honey." Zack gets out of his chair and pulls Suhani out of hers. In a series of fluid movements, he pulls her onto the floor with him. They stay that way for a few seconds, cheek to cheek, limbs intertwined.

Suhani thinks back to a quote by Michelle Obama: "I understand now that even a happy marriage can be a vexation, that it's a contract best renewed and renewed again, even quietly and privately—even alone." She wonders if Michelle ever kept any secrets from Barack and how they'd navigate a situation like this. She wonders when they discovered that it's possible to peel back the layers of a marriage and find new parts of someone to love.

"I'm so sorry," Zack says as he pushes strands of hair out of Suhani's face.

Suhani tucks her head under his chin. The collar of his navy-blue button-down brushes against her cheek. "No, I'm sorry. I should have told you what happened a long time ago and I definitely should have when Roshan showed up. I was so scared after he threatened to tell people at the hospital how I left med school without any warning. I thought he'd ruin me. So I just kept burying myself in work and avoided facing it. And then I got so overwhelmed with it all, wanting to be the wife you deserved and knowing I was failing, wanting to be a perfect doctor."

As much as Suhani wants to blame everything that went wrong

on Roshan, she knows that it's all much bigger than that. At the core, she never accepted herself. She tried to cure her nagging sense of inadequacy with perfectionism and work and accomplishments. But what she's needed to do this entire time is embrace herself, believe in her inherent self-worth. She needs to show Zack all of who she is. And doing that takes reflection and work, the type of reflection and work she's been avoiding until now.

"I'm sorry. I'm so, so sorry." Her words diffuse into the air and become one with her surroundings. She doesn't cry or even move, but something inside her stirs. It's as though the pain she's been storing in her body is slowly seeping out.

"It's okay, sweetie," Zack says. "It's okay."

"I love you," Suhani says. "I love you so much."

"I love you so much, too," Zack whispers. "Do you remember when I first told you about my dad and you said that if something happens to me, it also happens to you?"

She does remember that. Why did she lose sight of that foundational part of them?

"It goes both ways." Zack strokes her hair. "If something happens to you, it also happens to me."

Suhani nods, once again wishing she had let herself be vulnerable with the person she trusts more than anyone. Sometimes, she has to go against her instinct to handle everything herself. One of the most difficult discoveries she's made is that she needs her independence as much as she needs to be taken care of.

Their potential future unspools in front of her. She and Zack coming home to each other every night, drinking wine, and discussing their days. Zack, stretched out on a lounge chair in Santorini, the sparkling blue water reflecting in his sunglasses. Suhani, giving him NyQuil and ginger tea when he's sick. Zack, surprising her by speaking in Gujarati to the aunties. Suhani, learning how to make perfect matzoh balls. A blur of meals and massages, colors and smells.

She still doesn't know if that future includes a child. But for the first time in years, she feels the freedom to figure it out based on what she wants for their future, not because of something holding her back in her past.

"Being with you is the first decision I ever made because it felt right, not because it looked good or because I thought it was what I was supposed to do. You're my first risk," Suhani says.

"I know. It was pretty obvious when I first met your parents that they thought you'd be with an Indian doctor, like you did." Zack smiles. "I may not be able to save lives, but I can put things into a pretty good-looking Excel spreadsheet, okay?"

"Oooh, organization. You know how much I love that."

"I do." Zack's lips twist into a smile. "Organization and psychiatry terms are my go-tos to put you in a good mood."

"Is that so?" Suhani asks.

"Yep. Let's see." Zack holds up his hand as though he's counting on his fingers. "Self-sabotage, DSM, cognitive behavioral therapy . . . is any of this working?"

"Ha. You're ridiculous." Suhani laughs as she sinks into her husband.

She traces the curve of his jaw and neck. Zack pulls her closer, tasting like red wine when he presses his lips against hers. Their kisses are tender at first, and then a hunger overcomes them both. There's no space for words anymore. There's only her tongue moving against his.

Suhani inhales his natural citrusy scent as she reaches forward and grips his hair. Zack's strong, gentle hands tug at her silk blouse and pull it over her head. Suhani fumbles with the buttons on his shirt and stays wrapped around him as he carries her to their bed. Zack moans when she nibbles his earlobe.

On their cool duvet cover, she's both anchored and free, passive and powerful. Zack explores her body as if they're naked together for the first time. Suhani pushes him closer to her, struck with the awareness that it's possible to feel protected and exposed at the same time.

He grips her ankles and then pushes her legs back as he lowers himself into her.

"I love you so much," Suhani says as her nails dig into his back. She needs his weight on her, the thump of his heart on her chest.

"I love you, too." Zack's breath is warm on her ear. He moves inside her and she's never felt safer in her life.

Thirty-One

Bina

Samachar in America
September 2019 Issue

Community-Voiced Op-Ed
Bina Joshi

I'm sure plenty of people reading this have already heard of me or, rather, heard of some version of me. I'm going to clear all that up with the only thing that makes sense—the truth.

For the past two months, I've been conducting group meetings with women every week to discuss a variety of topics. Our name: Chats Over Chai. The group started as a fun social idea and slowly became a need. My dear friend Devi reminded me of kitty parties, routine get-togethers women had in Bombay. I envisioned doing something similar, where a group of my friends and I would meet at one of our homes, bring food, and just talk.

But I soon realized it was easy for us to discuss our children, the next recipe we were going to try, expectations from our in-laws, problems we may be having with our husbands, things like that. And while I am so grateful for those conversations, I also worried that we were losing a potential opportunity to explore issues in a way that was more honest and impactful.

Both my husband and eldest daughter are psychiatrists. For years, I've been hearing them talk about the power of people coming together in groups to share their stories. They both gave me textbooks on group therapy and a list of online classes where I learned about the value of being a facilitator. I applied some of these concepts to the Chats Over Chai meetings and was surprised to see that the structure allowed us to focus, learn, and connect.

There are so many things—big, difficult things—that members of our community are going through and not sharing. Whether it's mental illness, burnout, or shame, there is a lot we have been keeping to ourselves. There's a danger to that over time, putting on a perfect appearance and not really owning the challenges we all experience.

It's hard to sit there in front of others and just open up. Nobody has ever asked us before to do that, put ourselves out there, ask us how we are feeling about things. So many of us have felt as though our job as women is to serve others, not really think about ourselves. But after that initial discomfort, the conversations took off. Now we always run out of time. Our wait list and sign-up process are to ensure that groups stay limited to fifteen participants.

I've been asked several times about what the group has covered. We've discussed invisible labor, toxic masculinity, what happens to marriages after retirement, depression, abuse, the list goes on and on.

Anyone can suggest topics. We prefer to talk about things that might be coming up in the general media and also have relevance to our lives. Our hope is to continue adding more structure to the group with time.

We were an all–South Asian group at first, but recently we have opened it up to everyone. We really aren't all as different as we like to think we are. Sometimes we put up barriers in the form of labels and language. But whether we are immigrants or not, whether English is our first language or not, there are so many things we all share. Part of the beauty of this country is how it can bring people together.

I'll be honest. When I first heard about the criticisms against me, they hurt. But I welcome them now. Because anyone trying to do something different will get criticized. People will talk anyway, so I might as well do what I think is right.

For every single person who has felt that what I'm doing is "unnatural," I'd like to share a reminder with you: women have been creating their own support systems since the beginning of time.

And men could also benefit from their own forms of emotional support. I'm so proud to share here that my husband, Deepak Joshi, will be starting a Chats Over Chai group for men in Atlanta. He says I inspired him but really, he also helped me build this from the beginning.

I don't know what the future holds. All I know is that I want to focus on making the most of Chats Over Chai. We have ongoing discussions on our Instagram page and are proud that our following grows daily. One thing I've learned for sure is to never doubt a group of women who know how to use social media. We can do anything!

"Wow, Bina. Just wow," Mira says after they've all reread Bina's op-ed. "I don't even know what to say."

"Really?" Bina smiles. "Because you've said a lot."

Murmurs of agreement come from the other ten women at today's meeting. They decided to take advantage of the crisp September weather and meet at Piedmont Park. Mira and Mona each brought a friend who was interested in the group, while the other participants reached out to Bina on the new Chats Over Chai Instagram page. An assortment of woven picnic baskets, wine, sparkling-water cans, cheese, crackers, and sliced watermelon is in front of them.

"That's because the second I finished reading this, I really wanted to whistle. And not some dinky, useless whistle like that Nilay Bhai always does as he looks all proud of himself. I want to teach that man a whistle lesson sometime so he can learn our wedding whistle," Mira says, referring to the shrill, high-pitched sound she and Bina make during toasts and dance performances at weddings. They always elicit a series of stares, followed by a flurry of cheers. And Bina has definitely seen Nilay Bhai look startled by them.

"By all means, let's not hold back here!" Bina puts her index finger and thumb in a circle, sticks them in her mouth, and blows. The sound startles some of the women, while others join.

"Can you teach me how to do that?" Namita, who showed up for the first time today, asks Mira. Bina didn't even know Namita talked, let alone was the type of person who wanted to learn how to whistle. Namita has that quiet smile-and-nod thing that Bina usually associates with people who do a lot of meditation.

"Sure!" Mira says, and points to Bina. "Gloria Steinem over here and I will gladly teach you our ways."

"Gloria Steinem! I'll take it!" Bina declares.

Ironically, Gloria Steinem was a frequent source of arguments between Bina and Ma. Ma's views on Gloria Steinem seemed to shift depending on who was in the room. When it was just her and Bina, she'd laud Gloria's protests. When it was her with friends, she'd lament that Gloria was breaking traditions they'd all worked so hard to uphold.

Bina thinks back to how Dr. Eze said family wounds can be passed down through generations, taking on different forms. Maybe Ma was also confused about where she stood, about what the line was between who she was and who she wanted to be.

Maybe Anita struggled with the same. Anita would have been perfect for Ma in many ways. Bina wonders if that's what drew her to Anita in the first place, a compelling cocktail of familiarity and history. The main reason their breakup was so difficult was because of its shock value. A friend isn't supposed to leave.

She turns to the text message that came to her phone last night.

ANITA: Can we meet sometime?

Bina responded right away. Of course.

She's not sure what to expect when they're face-to-face. Things between them may not be the same ever again. But for now, all she can do is take it one day at a time.

"Well, Gloria Steinem is a fitting nickname for you, seeing as you will be making a public speech soon."

Bina got the e-mail two weeks ago from TEDx asking her to speak about the power of women's support groups.

"I still can't believe that's happening," Bina says. She'll be on a stage. A real stage. It won't be in the way she always envisioned, but that doesn't make it any less satisfying. She spent so many years tied to one picture of fulfillment that until now, she didn't allow it to take any other shapes.

And Natasha's helping her with her speech. Who would have thought that Bina's middle child would be guiding her on how to captivate an audience? Then again, Natasha's taught their whole family how to be more vulnerable. And maybe that's the only way to truly get a sense of belonging with yourself and others.

"Believe it! After all that crap, this is what you're doing," Mona yells. "Screw Bipin!"

"Yes! Screw him!" Nita, Mona's neighbor who recently joined the group, echoes Mona and adds a fist punch into the air.

"Screw Bipin? Really?" a soft voice behind Bina asks.

Bina turns around and is looking directly into her friend's round eyes. "Kavita. Oh my God! What are you doing here? We've been so worried about you."

"We have!" Mira exclaims.

"I got an apartment down the street." Kavita's manicured hand motions toward Peachtree Street.

"You're living alone in Midtown?" Bina asks. "Really?"

"Really!" Kavita nods. "See? Your Devi isn't the only one."

"Oh, she'd love to know that," Bina says.

"She already does. I've been talking to her over the past couple of weeks to figure this out," Kavita says.

"How did this work out for you? Are you okay?" Bina hugs her. Kavita's smiling when she pulls away. Her eyes have a brightness to them, as if she just woke up from a good nap. "You look okay. No, more than okay. You look amazing! Let me see you!"

"Let us all see you!" Mira exclaims as she and all the other women cluster around Kavita.

Kavita does a slow, sheepish twirl as they all take note of her look. Emerald-green dress with a flared skirt. Sleek bob cut. Gold studs in her ears.

Bina and Mira exchange a glance that means *This calls for another whistle.* They blow a series of whistles for the next several seconds.

"Don't hold back on us," Mona commands. "How did you do it? What did Bipin Bhai say?"

"I just told him the truth, the way I should have years ago." Kavita taps her brown heels into the grass. "Sonam helped me a lot. I kept telling myself I was staying because of the children. But my children were aware of everything. And they were miserable because of it! My own daughter doesn't want to get married because of what she's seen between Bipin and me. I woke up one day and asked, 'What are you still doing here, Kavita?' I thought Bipin would put up more of a fight, but in some way, I don't even know if he was that surprised. We had been sleeping in separate beds for so long, living separate lives, really.

"But I'd be lying if I said it's all been easy. I forgot how many things I'd become dependent on, whether it's how he pays the bills or even just the security of knowing he was in the house. Now I notice every little creak; I get bored; I get scared."

"I'm sure it is hard, very hard, in so many different ways," Bina says. "It was very brave of you to do that. It would have been easy— and understandable—if you stayed."

"I know. I felt so guilty about leaving. I was worried about what everyone would think. I know that's why it took me so long. I thought I'd let everyone down, including me. And when Sonam told me she's proud of me . . ." Kavita's voice breaks. "I never thought I'd hear her say that. I almost let guilt stop me from doing what I needed to do for her."

"The guilt. It's always the guilt." Bina blinks back tears, in awe of her friend's honesty, of all women, who hold so much inside for the sake of others. Women change their shapes physically to give life and then change their shapes emotionally every day to sustain it.

"It really is," Mona says in Gujarati. "And even when we try to let it go, it's still there."

Guilt is sturdy in that way, always leaving a residue, even if you manage to sweep it away.

"Actually, what if instead of discussing menopause, we made guilt today's topic?" Bina asks.

"I think that would be great," Kavita says. "Can I start?"

"Of course!" Bina says.

They all assemble back into their circle and stay there for the rest of the afternoon.

Thirty-Two

Natasha

"Next at the Laughing Skull Lounge open mic, we're going to hear from Natasha Joshi!"

Natasha gives her curls one last fluff. Just seeing the dimly lit stage from the side curtains makes her insides squirm as though she ate something undercooked.

A thought from her last therapy session with Dr. Chan materializes: This feeling will often be there. Natasha's mind jumps back to the notes she wrote down after the session:

- This mixture of nerves and novelty means she's about to do something she cares about.
- It's not about the presence of the feeling; it's about how she reacts to it.
- She can let it pass through her, not paralyze her.

She wipes her sweaty palms on her ripped jeans and fiddles with the large gold button on her black blazer. Earlier, Suhani suggested she throw a blazer over her white T-shirt to look a little more polished. Suhani was right. The addition of the jacket does help Natasha feel put together, like someone who has important things to say.

Her Keds are soft against the wooden floor as she goes to the microphone. The buzz of conversation and clink of glasses become softer. Thank God for the two-drink minimum and her extra-strength deodorant.

The thick red curtains are parted to leave room for a microphone under a spotlight. A giant skull with red eyes hangs as a backdrop. Natasha walks toward the microphone. Shit, there are a lot of people here. A lot of quiet people. The smell of beer and burgers makes her stomach grumble.

"I wish we didn't come for the open mic night. The real comedian nights here are so much better," Natasha hears someone say. Another person agrees.

Ignore them, she tells herself. She tries to ignore the trembling in her hands, the beads of sweat collecting across her forehead.

But then another thought comes to mind. Maybe instead of ignoring the comments, she can use them.

"Hi." She smiles. "So, I know some of you are disappointed that this isn't one of those 'Best of Atlanta' nights . . . but you can get the fuck over it, okay?"

A ripple of laughter. Yes!

"I mean, do you people know how hard it is to be up here when you hate yourself?" Her grip is white-knuckled on the microphone. "And for anyone in here who has never hated themselves . . . first of all, you're lying, and second, if you want to know what it feels like, you should try going to therapy with your family."

"Woot! Woot!" Ifeoma and Payal cheer in the back corner.

They showed up, she thinks as relief settles over her. *My girls always show up.*

Their voices and outlines—Ifeoma's curly hair and Payal's pulled back in a tight bun—make Natasha's breathing slow down.

When they told Natasha they'd never miss one of her performances and asked why she hadn't invited them before, she didn't know what to say. That was one of the tricky parts of depression. It made her isolate when she needed the most support.

"Yep, those are my friends," Natasha says. "Where the fuck would we be without those who take us for who we are, am I right?"

Some people clap, but otherwise, silence lingers over the crowd. But she can't let it scare her. She won't.

"So, I've been struggling lately." Natasha breathes into the microphone. "Like, really struggling. As in, I hit rock bottom and needed some serious professional help. And because I'm brown, I didn't just get diagnosed with run-of-the-mill anxiety, okay? I wasn't going to be an underachieving psychiatric case, thank you very much. I had some performance anxiety—when I'm here talking to you people—and major depressive disorder and intrusive negative thoughts and a little too much drinking. . . ."

Natasha can laugh because the diagnoses gave her something she didn't expect: freedom. The freedom to know herself. The freedom to accept herself.

Someone yells, *"You get me!"*

Another voice emerges from the back corner: *"Yes!"*

Natasha points to the crowd and says, "I'm so glad I'm not alone."

And then, from a place that feels like it's outside herself, she says, "Who else understands what I'm saying?"

There's a loud *Wooo* sound that Natasha usually associates with scenes in sitcoms where two people kiss. A woman says, "I feel you, girl!"

Cheers of agreement fill the room. Natasha grips the microphone, feeling connected to something greater. She focuses on the woman for a second who is nodding as if to say, *Keep talking*. She wonders how many people walk around every day carrying pain that nobody else can see.

"Shout-out to everyone out there holding a lot on the inside," Natasha says, taking an unplanned departure from her routine as she thinks of something she wrote in her Moleskine notebook yesterday: *Wounds don't heal in hiding.*

"Thank you!" someone says, then another *"Yes!"* and then a round of soft applause.

Because of the adrenaline, it takes her a second to process what just happened. She really said something that made another person feel understood? She took her pain—her fragile, fresh pain—and created something out of it? The realization fills her with a spark. There is no better rush than this. Feeling terrified and raw when she's doing her comedy is a sign that she's doing it right.

"You know what?" Natasha taps her sneakers on the microphone stand. "Surprisingly, some really good stuff came from my experience. I learned how to be more honest with myself and with other people. The other day, I was walking down Spring Street, and a random man told me to smile. Yup, a random older man just came up to me and told me what to do with my face. I bet the women here tonight know what I'm talking about."

There's a flurry of "YESes" and claps.

"Ah, y'all get it!" Natasha says. "So before, when I used to get unsolicited advice, I'd snap back. But when this man spoke to me, I stopped and said, 'So funny you would say that, because my psychiatrist and I are still trying to figure out the best Prozac dose to make me want to smile all day.' The guy was so taken aback. I'm telling you, just pure shock on his face. So then I said, 'Oh, I'm sorry. Is that too personal and intrusive for you? I thought you gave a shit since you came up to me out of nowhere.'"

Yes! People are laughing!

"So, look, I am still trying to figure out the best Prozac dose, but I got an old white man to shut the fuck up. Win, right?" Natasha asks.

She hears a *"Total win!"* and a *"Screw that guy!"* Someone whistles. Wait, that high-pitched loud sound can only come from . . .

Mom! Mom is whistling!

"Oh, my mom. My sweet, sweet mom," Natasha says. "She raised me to be politer than this. To be fair, my sister is this polite. She's the dream for every Indian auntie . . . except, well, she didn't marry an Indian guy. Then again, she married a Jewish one, which is a total win for desi parents. I mean, my brother-in-law is susceptible to guilt trips, a mama's boy, and can sit through really long religious ceremonies, and aren't those all an Indian family's dream?"

Someone says, *"HIND-JEW,"* which compels Zack to stand up, cup his mouth with his large hands, and yell, *"HIND-JEW IN THE HOUSE!"*

"Look, everyone has their place." Natasha walks up and down the stage. "My sister and brother-in-law are the successful and beautiful ones. My brother is the chill and peace-loving one. And I'm the one aunties come up to and ask, 'You're still not married yet?' or even better, I get a cheek pinch and a comforting, 'Don't worry—someday your life will have meaning, too.' I think the aunties and my therapist might agree on some things. In some ways, an auntie is like a therapist, telling you unflattering stuff about yourself. It's just that I pay my therapist while an auntie gives her opinions unsolicited."

Natasha smirks as she remembers Mira Auntie telling her not to worry because "even Pooja has a job that doesn't make any sense."

"My family really keeps me in check, you know?" Natasha follows up her question with a few impressions of Mom and Dad getting mad at her for her bad grades. "I'd get in even more trouble when I'd ask my parents why they moved to America if they weren't going to hold me to white-parent standards."

She continues her routine, shaky in some places, stronger in others. She still has a lot of work to do in figuring out her voice. But she's okay with that.

When she's done, she gives a gracious smile reminiscent of an actress humbly accepting a Golden Globe Award. "I'd like to thank Prozac for bringing me here tonight." Natasha places a palm over her heart in an exaggerated show of gratitude. "And of course, my family, who has put up with way too much of my shit."

Her family and friends rush to the stage the second she puts the microphone back.

Vanessa, Suhani's friend from work, is extending a glass of Prosecco toward Natasha. Suhani always said Vanessa and Natasha reminded her of each other, with their unapologetic defiance of authority.

"Cheers to you, you star!" Vanessa says. She mouths something to a hot Fabio-looking dude in the audience. "My date's getting a little needy, sorry."

"Cheers!" Suhani yells, seeming about a thousand times more chill right now than she's been in the past year.

"You were amazing!" Anuj says.

"Really?" Natasha feels much more self-conscious than she even did onstage.

Anuj smiles. "Really!"

Dad hands her a bouquet of dahlias. "Come, let's take a family picture. You get in the middle."

"Dad, this isn't my high school graduation," Natasha says as she takes the flowers.

All the other comedians (okay, all the other people in the room) give her a confused look, apparently wondering why this is happening. But Natasha relishes every second of it.

"We are proud of you, *beta*." Natasha smells sandalwood when Mom hugs her.

"You are?" Natasha's in a bit of disbelief at hearing her family express this to her.

She used to worry about sharing her most unfiltered self with her family. She didn't expect that doing so would help them be more honest with themselves, too.

"Yes." Mom nods. "You know, some of it was a little inapp—"

"You can just stop at being proud!" Natasha says. "Thank you!"

They all laugh at Mom not even being able to help herself.

"So you'll be doing more of this in California?" Dad asks as he looks at a man next to them with head-to-toe tattoos and a stud pierced through his nose.

"Yep, this is what I'm going to do after my internship is done every day," Natasha says as she studies the subtle confusion on Dad's face.

It's okay if nobody fully understands or approves of what she's doing. What matters is that they care enough to try. Plus, not being figured out gives her a bit of an edge, one that satisfies her eternal rebellious urge.

"Hmm." Dad nods as if he's listening to some complicated psychiatric patient case. "That sounds like quite an adventure, *beta*. But we know you'll do well. You've always been able to handle anything that came your way."

Ever since Dad started his own Chats Over Chai group with the uncles, he's become much more communicative. He recently told Natasha that men were often encouraged to keep their emotions to themselves and that led to so many different types of problems. He then mentioned that Bipin Uncle was likely never taught how to express himself in different ways. Natasha makes a mental note to discuss this with her siblings later.

"You are a badass," Suhani says. "I know that's also the title of your favorite self-help book, but it's true."

A few minutes ago, Suhani posted a picture of Natasha on her Instagram page with the caption, *My sister is so brave. She inspires through her art and makes all of us around her feel a little braver, too.*

"Oh, being here with everyone is just so . . . It's too . . ." Natasha's voice cracks. "Nice."

Tears start to collect in the corners of her eyes. She's not sure if it's the residual high from her performance or the awareness that she's leaving Atlanta soon, but she's been on the verge of tears all day. Not just sad tears, but also tears of release and restoration. When she was working on tonight's routine, she sifted through her family therapy notes. There, on Suhani and Zack's wooden living room floor, she cried for the woman her mother couldn't become and the woman her sister felt pressure to become. She cried for the dreams her father deferred and the words her brother doesn't say.

She doesn't say any of that now or dwell on it further. One of the things the medication has helped her with is coping with her emotions. Now, when they wash over her, she can manage them. She used to hope that one goal or person or event would cure her. But she knows now that only she can heal herself.

"But I'm not brave," she tells Suhani as she pulls up the post. "You all are."

Brave is leaving a country with a partner you don't know well and coming to another one that isn't sure it wants to quite accept you. Brave is working your ass off, day after day, to take care of

people. Brave is keeping a sense of calm even when everyone
around you is falling apart.

Just as they're getting ready to leave, Natasha feels someone's
hand on her shoulder. She turns around. At first, she thinks she
must be in a daze. But then she takes another look at the buzzed
hair, the sky-blue button-down shirt, and the navy sweater.

"Karan?"

Karan gives her a lopsided grin. Natasha used to see that grin
every day, and now it takes her several seconds just to process it. If
this was a Hindi serial, the camera angles would start spinning and
some ominous music would be playing.

"What are you doing here?" Natasha turns to her family and
best friends, who all look just as surprised to see him. They walk
over to the other side of the bar after giving Karan a quick hi.

"I'm actually here with some work friends." Karan motions to a
table full of guys sharing a pitcher of beer and a platter of fries.

"Nice." Natasha tries not to stare at him or think about how
surreal this moment is. If things had gone according to plan, she
and this guy standing in front of her would be planning their wedding. An entire life flashes in front of her. They would have had an
epic big, fat Indian wedding, the kind uncles and aunties would
rave about for months. Mom and Anita Auntie would have made
sure of that. Natasha pictures herself with Karan at Bhojanic trying
paneer for a food tasting or going for a premarital couples massage
or looking up resorts on a white, grand beach for their honeymoon.
A twinge of sadness passes through her chest. It would have been
a decent life, an easy one. Maybe even a good one. But it wouldn't
have been honest or fair to either of them.

"So, you were good up there," Karan says. "Funny."

"Thanks . . ." It takes everything out of her to not hug him. As much as he's her ex-boyfriend-almost-ex-fiancé, he's also the person she's known since they were in preschool. He was her favorite *Mario Kart* rival, the first person she drove when she got her license.

"I always knew how funny you were," Karan says.

"Did your mom always know, too?" Damn it, why did she have to bring up Anita Auntie? Her mouth always moves quicker than her brain.

She quickly adds, "Sorry, was that too soon?"

Karan snickers. "I think it'll always be too soon."

"I really am so sorry for everything," Natasha says. "I can see now how difficult it must have been to be with me, through all my shit. You deserved better than all that. Than me."

Karan shakes his head. "I assumed a lot. I thought I was doing you—us—a favor by proposing, but instead, I was focused on what I thought I needed to do."

Natasha's not sure how to respond. There's so much she can say. That they both got too caught up in what they thought they were supposed to do instead of what was really right for them. That she's not sure if their parents' friendship will ever heal because of how long she let things between her and Karan drag out. That she hopes he's happy.

But none of it seems right.

Karan flashes her an awkward smile, the same one he had after their first kiss.

"I guess I should get back to my table," he says.

"Of course." Natasha nods. "It was good to see you. Really."

"You, too," Karan says. "I'm proud of you."

"Thank you," Natasha says, knowing he means it.

Within minutes, Natasha is back with her family, who have ordered a round of beers. She rehashes her entire conversation with

Karan. It's clear from Mom's perked face that she has a lot of opinions, but to everyone's surprise, she keeps them to herself. Forget the comedy routine. This was the biggest win of the night!

But really, she's lighter around everyone because she's more herself. Maybe she needed to hit rock bottom to learn who she really is. She sees now that self-respect can only be born after failure and insight mesh together.

And her family is different, too. By visiting their pasts, they were able to pave different futures together. She used to fantasize about what it would be like to have simple ties to her family tree instead of the twisted branches that are in theirs. But she knows now that she wouldn't want them to be any other way. They still aren't always in perfect harmony with one another, but maybe that isn't the point. Maybe being whole and authentic with the people you love is the real victory.

"Come here." Zack pulls them all into a circle. "Ah, I love being a part of this colorful group."

"Colorful?" Suhani asks. "That's a really nice way to put it, honey. I think you mean absurd, out of control, emotional . . ."

"Yeah, okay, those, too," Zack agrees before he kisses Suhani's cheek. "And I wouldn't want it any other way."

"Shall we head back? It's pretty late." Anuj glances at his Apple watch.

"Let's go!" Natasha smiles.

For the first time in a long time, she can't wait to go home.

Acknowledgments

My rockstar agent, Jessica Watterson, is every writer's dream. Thank you for the guidance, feedback, and friendship during such a turbulent year. I am so lucky to be able to work with you and learn from you.

Kristine Swartz, you knew the book I was trying to write and how to get this manuscript there. Thank you for your patience and insight. I am so grateful for your editorial skills, direction, and talents. I can't wait until we can have coffee together in person.

Fareeda Bullert, thank you for being an amazing marketing director and giving me such incredible opportunities. I am so lucky to know you.

Danielle Keir, thank you for getting *WBIW* to places I never could have imagined. I'm so grateful to work with you and be able to celebrate the joys of motherhood with you.

Thank you to Diana Franco for making the post-debut months such a pleasure. Megha Jain, thank you for making the book look so refined and elegant. Thank you to Eileen Chetti for making this story consistent and making sure I didn't have a summer lasting ten months.

To everyone at Berkley, thank you for making your authors feel valued and supported. I am so grateful to be a part of your team. I can't wait until we see each other again.

This book wouldn't have been possible without the love and support of my family. For all of 2020, I lived with my grandparents, parents, siblings, husband, and son. The ages in our house ranged from one to ninety-five. Dad, your work ethic and patience have always inspired me. Thank you for always encouraging us to advocate for others and give back. Your sensitivity gives us safety and your compassion gives us strength. Mom, thank you for being the rock of our house. I'm still not sure how you've taken care of four generations of people for so long. You've given us all a love of art and human nature and for those, we will always be grateful. Maansi, you are the changemaker of our family. Thank you for teaching all of us how to be fearless, unapologetic, and bold. If Natasha could have a friend like you, she'd be the luckiest woman alive. Akshay, you inspire us with your wisdom and wit. It's been an honor to see you as such a caring uncle and I will always be so grateful for how you add peace to our family.

Samir, everything in our lives changed in ways we could have never imagined. You somehow found a way to make an adventure out of new parenthood during a pandemic. Thank you for believing in me when I struggled to believe in myself. Thank you for advocating for me when I struggled to advocate for myself. You read this story before I knew what it would turn into and embraced it as your own. Thank you for being the best partner I could ask for through every draft, character edit, late-night feed, diaper change, and more. I create because of you.

Sahil, you are our everything. Thank you for teaching me how to count the wins whenever they come, relish the present, and embrace uncertainty. We love your endless curiosity for life and can't wait to take you into the world more in 2021 and beyond.

I wrote this book while I navigated new motherhood. Thank you to the mothers in my support network, who kept me going during the tender and tough moments. To my friends, your texts, phone calls, and messages were my lifelines during an isolative time. Jaimini Dave Maniar, thank you for reading the first pages, reassuring me that there was something worthwhile here, and being there for me during every moment of self-doubt. Bansari Modi Shah, thank you for checking in and providing support at all hours.

Sara DiVello, thank you for making my debut year so memorable. I am so lucky to be able to call you a friend. Laura Dave, our chats helped me in so many different ways. You are a true gem and I can't thank you enough for everything. Roshani Chokshi, I don't even know where to start in thanking you for your support during an uncertain debut year. I am so proud of you and grateful for you. Emily Giffin, thank you for all your support from the very beginning and making my debut year special. You will always be one of our favorites.

Thank you to the readers who invited me to your book clubs and brought *Well-Behaved Indian Women* into your lives. A warm thank-you to librarians and booksellers for giving *WBIW* a home during such a chaotic year. I am beyond grateful to the bookstagram community and book bloggers for all their hard work and passion for stories. We are all better because of it. Thank you to my 2020 Debuts, 2020 Debuts POC, and Twitter 2020 group for the invaluable community and inspiration.

I am constantly inspired by the mental health advocacy I've seen over the past years. To everyone who has had tough conversations with those they love, thank you for your bravery, for breaking patterns in yourself, your families, and your communities. I wrote this book during the most challenging time of my life and am grateful for all the readers who brought it into their worlds. To anyone who has ever struggled to feel understood, I hope this story can provide comfort and a reminder that you're not alone.

Mental Health Resources

The National Suicide Prevention Lifeline is a national network of local crisis centers that provides free and confidential emotional support to people in suicidal crisis or emotional distress twenty-four hours a day, seven days a week. If you need help, call 1-800-273-TALK (8255).

NAMI, the National Alliance on Mental Illness, is the nation's largest grassroots mental health organization dedicated to building better lives for the millions of Americans affected by mental illness. For more information, please visit www.nami.org.

What a
Happy Family

Saumya Dave

Discussion Questions

1. What are your thoughts on the title of this book? Do you believe the Joshis are a happy family by the end of the novel?

2. Mental health is a prominent theme in *What a Happy Family*. How is each character impacted by it throughout the story? Why is there so much stigma surrounding mental health? Do you believe this is changing?

3. The book states that "Suhani got a hopeful, struggling mother, which fueled her ambition. Natasha got a strict and scared mother, which instigated her rebellion. Anuj got a softer, more secure mother, which gave him comfort." Do you think this is true? Can the same parents be completely different with different children?

4. Bina left her career as an actress, while Natasha is working to build hers in stand-up comedy. How did both women's relationships with creativity change throughout the novel?

5. Suhani struggles with impostor syndrome despite how much she's accomplished. What contributes to this? How do you feel

about her journey at work? Have you ever navigated this in your own life?

6. This book examines how family members shape one another. Were there any dynamics or interactions that you identified with?

7. Bina takes pride in her strong female friendships. At one point, she reflects on the differences between her bonds with Anita and Devi. How did these women impact her choices and goals? Do you ever see the three of them spending time together?

8. Natasha has always worried that something is inherently wrong with her. What factors do you think made her feel this way? How big of a role did her family play in how she viewed herself?

9. Despite wanting to create their own paths, both Bina and Deepak learn that they internalized their parents' beliefs. How were their kids impacted by this? Do you think it's possible to change longstanding patterns of thinking and behavior?

10. Suhani's shame pushes her to keep secrets from Zack. How do you feel about their marriage after she tells him everything? What do you think their future together holds?

11. It's five years after the novel's ending. How is the Joshi family doing?

Saumya Dave is a psychiatrist and mental health advocate. Her essays, articles, and poetry have been featured in the *New York Times*, ABC News, Refinery29, and other publications. She is the co-founder of thisisforHER, a nonprofit at the nexus of art and women's mental health, and an adjunct professor at Mount Sinai, where she teaches a Narrative Medicine class. She recently completed her psychiatry residency at Mount Sinai Beth Israel, where she was a chief resident and an inductee into the Alpha Omega Alpha Honor Medical Society (AΩA). She currently resides in New York City with her husband and son.

CONNECT ONLINE

SaumyaDave.com
🐦 SaumyaJDave
📷 SaumyaJDave